NEW WORLD . . . NEW ROME

Preacher stood inside the tree line looking out at the city of New Rome. He couldn't believe his eyes.

Large shiny white buildings covered the slopes and tops of four of the seven hills. Construction was going at a feverish pace. Horsemen in scarlet cloaks and shiny helmets cantered about through the confusion. Formations of soldiers raised clouds of dust as they drilled with precision. Preacher blinked in surprise.

"Danged if they don't look just like them old-timey Romans. But that can't be. T'weren't ever any Romans got to the New World. Now I ain't had no sippin' whiskey or awerden'y, so I must be seein' what I'm seein'.

"Danged if there ain't Romans in the High Mountains!"

BOOK YOUR PLACE ON OUR WEBSITE AND MAKE THE READING CONNECTION!

We've created a customized website just for our very special readers, where you can get the inside scoop on everything that's going on with Zebra, Pinnacle and Kensington books.

When you come online, you'll have the exciting opportunity to:

- View covers of upcoming books

- Read sample chapters

- Learn about our future publishing schedule (listed by publication month *and author*)

- Find out when your favorite authors will be visiting a city near you

- Search for and order backlist books from our online catalog

- Check out author bios and background information

- Send e-mail to your favorite authors

- Meet the Kensington staff online

- Join us in weekly chats with authors, readers and other guests

- Get writing guidelines

- AND MUCH MORE!

**Visit our website at
http://www.zebrabooks.com**

WILLIAM W. JOHNSTONE

PREACHER AND THE MOUNTAIN CAESAR

Zebra Books
Kensington Publishing Corp.

http://www.zebrabooks.com

Chapter 1

There's a limit to everything, by dang it, the mountain man known as Preacher fumed to himself. At least that's how he saw it. Birds twittered musically overhead; a fat, white-tailed deer bounded across the meadow in this lush, deep basin. Water burbled, clear and pure, in the narrow stream that cut diagonally through the upper end of the valley and left by way of the entrance gorge to the south. Only marginally on the east side of the continental divide, water courses often did not follow the rule of the land. Tangy pine scented the clear, crisp air, while small puff-ball clouds floated by overhead.

So, why in tarnation would a body come along and spoil a perfectly relaxful fall? Yet, here they were, five of the most vile, stomach-churning, unwashed, buzzard pukes Preacher had ever laid eyes upon. Worse, they looked to be fixin' to ruin his peaceful layin' up for winter by settling down in the selfsame valley he had staked out for its high mountain walls to the north, east, and west. Preacher found himself jealous of sharing the sure, swift stream that ran through the middle, and the ample tall, slender fir trees which abounded on the slopes, from which he could make a stout little cabin and enjoy a source of plentiful wood for heat and cooking. No, it wouldn't do, not at all. That argued around to, Preacher decided to drop down and invite these hog-dirty, walking, talking, slop jars to depart.

Preacher meandered down to where the scruffy frontier trash had put up a disreputable lean-to, and hashed together a pine bough lodge which would not shed water or keep out the cold. Stupid flatlanders, no doubt, he reasoned as he neared. Preacher halted a goodly distance from the men, who had to be bone-stupid to not have noted his approach, and hollered up at the camp.

"Hello, the camp!"

"Howdie, mister. C'mon in an' fetch up a cup of coffee."

"Thank'e. I'll come in right enough." Preacher came to within three long paces of the rude camp, then screwed a ground anchor and tied his horse to it.

Preacher entered camp, his posture one of complete dominance. This was his valley, by damn. One of the unshaven quintet studied their visitor with open curiosity. Only a tad bit over what passed for average height in these days, the man had an air of power about him. From his broad shoulders and thick chest to his narrow waist, he radiated strength. The man Preacher viewed as an intruder raised a hand in greeting. "Rest yourself, stranger. There's coffee over yon."

"I'll not be stayin' for coffee, thank you all the same. M'name's Preacher." He noted how their eyes widened at this news. "I come to offer you an invitation."

"That's mighty nice. What's the invite for?"

"I'm askin' you fellers to pack up your gear and be outta my valley before sundown." His gray eyes, they noted, were cold and hard.

Surprised looks went between the five men. Lomax and Phelps grew angry at once. Windy Creek produced a snarl that came off more a sneer, while Rush and Thumper separated from the others slightly, to get an advantage.

Preacher noted all of that and accepted the fact that his invitation could be a bit more difficult to deliver than he had anticipated. They showed other obvious signs of how unkindly they took his words.

"Lomax, Windy," barked the only one who had spoken so far. "Looks to me we have to learn this boy some manners."

"You got that right, Phelps," Rusk growled from nearly behind Preacher.

From a similar position to Preacher's left rear, Thumper uttered the wheezing gasp that served him for laughter. "This is gonna be easy, Rusk. All we gotta do is jump on him and hol' him down while Phelps and Lomax work him over a bit."

A low chuckle came from the one Preacher identified as Windy. "Then we take him off with us like we was told. He—he—heee." The sound of his laughter came out even worse than that of Thumper. Preacher raised his big hands, palms up and open. He took a deep breath and sighed out as he spoke.

"Well, hell, fellers, if you're set on joinin' the dance, I suppose I have to accommodate."

While they took time to digest the meaning of Preacher's fancy words, he exploded into instant, furious action. He whipped out with one big hand and popped Lomax along the jaw. The contact sounded like a rifle shot. Preacher kept his momentum and spun to snap a hard right fist into the bony chest of Windy Creek. The skinny border rat grunted, and his eyes crossed momentarily.

Preacher followed up with a left to Windy's unguarded cheek. Blood sprayed at the contact. A right cross produced a screeching sound from Windy's mouth that set Preacher's teeth on edge. The spry, if momentarily befuddled, human began to spit out teeth as he danced backward. Rusk and Thumper grabbed Preacher from behind the next instant. Preacher raised a heel into Thumper's crotch and got a satisfying squeal of pain in return. Then the punches began to smack into Preacher's middle and face.

Phelps and Lomax closed in, working with the efficiency of steam engines. Lomax, an ugly brute of short stature, pistoned his arms forward and back, pounding Preacher in the belly with hard-knuckled regularity. Phelps, tall and skinny, worked over his crime partner's head, driving cutting, jarring lefts and rights to the planes of Preacher's face. Blood began to flow from a cut high on one cheekbone. A ringing filled Preacher's head as Phelps lopped him one in an ear. Pain exploded in his left eye, and the tissue began to swell immediately. He'd have a good mouse out of that one, Preacher reckoned.

He chose to ignore the efforts of Lomax. The short, pudgy hard case furiously drove his fists into slabs of work-hardened muscle to no effect, save to sap his own energy. Lomax tagged Preacher on the point of his chin, and stars blazed behind the mountain man's eyes. Preacher sucked in a deep breath and shifted position.

"Well, hell," he drawled, "that's about enough of this."

Preacher stomped a high instep on a foot that belonged to Rusk, yanked himself free and boxed the ears of Lomax. Howling, the squat piece of human debris clapped hands to both ears and spun away from Preacher, to receive a solid kick in the rear as further reward. Eyes widening, Phelps took a step backward and tripped over a snub piece of granite protruding from the grassy turf. He caught a solid punch under the heart that knocked the air from his lungs and momentarily froze his diaphragm. He hit the ground seeing stars and listening to the birdies sing.

Ignoring that pair, Preacher turned his attention toward the remaining three. Rusk, Thumper and Windy Creek stared in confused disbelief. No one man had ever stood up to them like this. Not even just two alone. They had not been told something about this Preacher, the trio immediately suspected. Most of all how goddamned mean he could be. Rusk, Thumper and Windy Creek exchanged worried glances. Windy was known as a champion free-for-all wrestler. It seemed his responsibility to take care of Preacher. The expressions of the other two said as much.

Windy shrugged his shoulders until they hunched to protect his neck, snuffled, and shifted his feet on the ground. When his partners in crime feinted to distract Preacher, he jumped forward, spread his arms and sought to clasp the wiry mountain man in a ferocious bear hug. Only Preacher was not there.

"Huh?" Windy grunted, then let out a howl as pain exploded in the side of his head.

How had Preacher gotten over there without him seeing it? Windy turned to face the threat, ready now, he believed. No time for finesse, he reckoned. He'd just plow right in and throw his man with one massive twist of his shoulders. Or would he get clobbered in the head again?

Much to his surprise, Windy got a good hold on Preacher. He put the point of his shoulder in deep against Preacher's ribs and set his powerful, tree-stump legs. Arms locked at the wrist, he heaved and felt the sudden give as Preacher left the ground. Elation filled Windy as he slammed his opponent down hard on the ground.

Preacher grunted, shook his head and let his mind absorb the pain that radiated from his ribs. It took him only a moment to realize that his assailant lacked the polish and skill of a true grappler. The ancient Greek art of wrestling was better understood by the Cheyenne and the Sioux than by most white men. That gave Preacher a decided advantage as he saw it. He had learned his wrestling from the Cheyenne. While Windy scrabbled to find new purchase, Preacher drew his legs up in front of him.

When his knees reached the middle of his chest, he had Windy humped up like a bison bull mounting a heifer. The illusion lasted only a second, as Preacher put all his effort into violently thrusting his legs outward. A moment's resistance, then Windy went flying.

Preacher bounded to his feet in time to meet Rusk and Thumper. Rusk caught the brunt of Preacher's fury. Hard fists pounded his chest and gut until Rusk dropped his guard; then Preacher went to work on the youthful, if dirty, face of the junior thug. Rusk's grunts and groans changed to yips of pain. Preacher spread the nose all over Rusk's face a second before Thumper grabbed him.

Thumper had only begun to pull Preacher around when he got hit low and painfully an inch above his wide trouser belt. The power in Preacher's punch lifted Thumper off the ground. He did not even have time to wonder where the blow had come from before Preacher sent him into a hazy twilight land. The big, thick-legged mountain man spun around to see what opposition remained.

In that instant, he discovered that the fight had turned serious. Off to one side, Windy Creek held a .70 caliber horse pistol. To Preacher's front, Lomax stood hunched over, breathing hard, and he had a knife out, held low, the edge up in a ripping position. From behind Preacher, coughing and retching, Rusk pulled a short, ground-down sword. That made the day look a little darker, Preacher reasoned.

"We . . . gonna . . . fix ya . . . for this, ya . . . bastid. You boys," a panting Phelps grunted, "throw down on him. We'll . . . hold him . . . while Lomax . . . carves out his liver." Then he, too, drew a big .70 caliber horse pistol.

Faced with this opposition, Preacher did a quick reappraisal. Confronting the .70 caliber muzzles, and wickedly sharp edges, he found their attitude decidedly hostile. Cranky enough, he reckoned, that he'd best do something about it. He twisted his face into a semblance of amiability and raised a distracting left hand.

"Well, heck, fellers, why'in't you tell me this was supposed to be a gunfight?" With that he dropped his other hand to the smooth walnut butt-grips of one of his marvelous .44 Walker Colt six-shooters and whipped it out with a suddenness that left the others still thinking on what they should do next.

With cold precision, he blasted two of the wooly-eared men into the arms of their Maker. His first two slugs punched into Phelps' chest. He rocked back and sat abruptly on his skinny butt. Preacher ducked and spun, to send two more rounds into the surprised face of Windy Creek. Belatedly, Windy's .70 caliber horse pistol discharged into the ground with a solid thud. Preacher ignored it to turn and menace the remaining simpleton trash.

Rusk and Thumper fired as one. A fat ball moaned past Preacher's ear, low to the shoulder enough that he could feel its wind. He gave the shooter, Thumper, a .44 slug in the hollow of his throat. It dumped the thug backward to land in a heap beside the dying Phelps. Rusk's eyes went wide. He had fired his only barrel and had no time to reload. He gained precious seconds, in which to go for a second pistol in his belt, when Lomax charged with a bellow, his knife at the ready.

"Some of us just never get the word," Preacher said with tired sadness as he shot Lomax squarely in the chest. "A feller never takes only a knife to a gunfight," he explained to the dying man at his feet. Then Rusk fired again.

His bullet cut a thin line along the outside of Preacher's left shoulder. With an empty six-gun in his hand, Preacher dived and rolled for cover behind a fallen tree trunk while he drew the second magnificent .44 Walker Colt, which he had taken off the outlaw named Hashknife a couple of years earlier, and answered Rusk with fatal authority.

Rusk dropped his suddenly heavy pistol and staggered backward. Preacher took the precaution of cocking the Colt again. Then he looked around himself. None of the enemy moved, except the gut-shot Rusk, who moaned and curled up on himself, his legs trembling feebly. Preacher crossed to him. He knelt beside the dirty-faced low-life and spoke with urgency in his voice.

"What brought all that on?"

"Come to get . . . you . . . Preacher," Rusk panted.

"Why? What got into your heads to do a fool thing like that?"

"We . . ." The dying man's voice took on a cold, haunting note as he gasped out his last words. *"We was sent."* For a short while convulsions wracked the body; then Rusk went stiff, his death rattle sounded and he relaxed into the hands of the Grim Reaper.

Preacher rose slowly, his mind awhirl with puzzlement. " *'We was sent,'* " he repeated. "Now who in tarnation would have a mad-on at me big enough to send five worthless trash bags like that to even a score?" He let the question hang in the warm, late-August air while he went about rounding up the tools needed for grave digging.

No stranger to the process of burial for his fellow man, Preacher much preferred that the task be left to others. For his own part, when he ever gave it thought, Preacher much preferred a Cheyenne or Sioux burial platform when it came time to give up the ghost. Let them deck him out in his finest, lay him on a bed of sweet pine boughs, on a platform made of lodgepole pine saplings and rawhide strips, exposed before God and man alike, to let the elements do their best with him.

Preacher had neither wife nor, as far as he knew, living child to mourn him, or to quarrel over any possessions he might leave behind—although he wasn't real certain about the children bit. That's what Preacher hated most about the white man's way of caring for the dead. If a feller had anything to amount to a hill of beans, and had so-called loved ones left behind, getting possession of that hill of beans always made enemies of those who professed to most love the departed. Instead of supporting each other in their mutual loss, they quarreled like greedy children to divide even the clothes the poor feller left behind.

Preacher stopped in his task of digging holes for the hard cases he had fought. Why couldn't they do like the Injuns, and gather to lend support to one another? And in the process, leave a feller in peace? Let him take his most prized belongings with him to *Nah'ah Tishna*—the Happy Hunting Ground? Preacher sighed, wiped a trickle of sweat from his brow and returned to the chore he had given himself.

They came upon him shortly before twilight. An old man, his gray hair hanging to his shoulders, unkempt and stiff from being a long time unwashed. He was brewing coffee at his small camp in a mountain valley when the skinny pair of urchins drifted silently out of the woods and stood staring gauntly at the cook fire. It took a moment for the old man to notice their presence. When he did, he gave a start and grasped at the left side of his chest.

"Land o' Goshen, youngins. You gave me a real start. Don't you know better than to slip up on a camp like that?" His eyes narrowed with suspicion and unacknowledged alarm. There could be others out there, lurking, to attack when he became distracted.

"We—we got lost," stammered the skinny, yellow-haired boy with the biggest, cornflower blue eyes old Hatch had ever seen.

"Where you from?"

"We—uh—we don't know, 'cause we don't know where we are now," the boy answered evasively.

"Now that ain't any sort of answer. Where abouts is your home?"

Together they looked at the ground. "Other side of the high mountains. We got took off by some bad folks."

Hatch doubted that. Even so, he pressed for something by which to identify them. "You got names put on you?"

"Yes—yes, we do. I'm Terry, an' this is my sister, Vickie."

Hatch canted his head to one side and made a smile. "Vickie—Victoria, eh? Like the English Queen, huh?"

"I—I suppose so, sir," her sweet, young voice responded.

"What's your end handle?" Hatch demanded.

"We—uh—do you mean our last name?" Terry asked.

Hatch studied them closer then. Both were barefoot and in threadbare clothes that were hardly more than rags. They had missed a good many a meal; bones stuck out everywhere. Their eyes were a bit too bright, feverish mayhap. The boy had a ferret quality to him, his face narrow, hollow-cheeked, eyes too close together and somewhat buck-toothed. He wouldn't look a person directly in the eye, either.

The girl, Victoria, if that was her name, had a precious quality about her. For all her grime and stringy yellow hair, she could smile enough to charm the demons outta perdition. Her figure, although still undeveloped and boyish, held a certain promise. She stood before him now, toes turned in and touching, the hem of her skirt swaying around her knees as she twisted and turned, hands behind her back. Her attitude convinced Hatch.

"There's some extra grub. Welcome to it. But first, you gotta go to the crick and clean up a mite."

"Oh, thank you, sir," Vickie chirped. They started off to the creek hand-in-hand.

"Hold on there," Hatch called after them. "You can't go in there nekid together. One at a time."

"At home we never have . . . ," Terry blurted, then paused, an expression of nervous wariness flickering across his face. "I mean—er—we never had to do it that way when we had a home."

"Well, you're gettin' too old to jump in bare together. Just do as I say."

They took their turns, looking unhappy about it, then returned to the warmth beside the fire. Hatch handed them plates piled high with stew and fresh, flakey biscuits.

"Go on. Eat hearty. You could use a little meat on those bones."

Eloy Hatch glowed with an unusual contentment when he rolled up in his blankets that night. It made him feel good to do something kind for others. Especially youngsters cut off from hearth and home. Tomorrow he'd see about trimming the lad's hair. Maybe scare up a button or two so's to cover more of their bodies. He might even take them along with him to the trading post. Ol' Rube would know, if anyone did, where to find them a home.

He drifted off to sleep with these good thoughts. They held him in such deep slumber, until near midnight, that Eloy Hatch never felt a thing when Terry slid the slender knife blade between Eloy's ribs and pierced his heart. When Hatch's death throes ceased, Terry and Vickie quickly stripped the corpse and campsite of all valuables, took the prospector's horses and stole off into the night. Half a mile from the scene of their latest murder and robbery, they paused to embrace. Vickie shivered with the excitement of their bloody handiwork, and her skin was cold to the touch.

Terry quickly warmed her in the shelter of his strong arms. Their eyes got lost in one another's, and they sighed heavily. "But he was *nice*, Terry."

"If we hadn't done it, we'd get a powerful beatin' when we got home, Vic, you know that."

A sigh. "Yes, you're right, Terry." She raised on tiptoe and kissed him on one cheek. It would be all right now, she knew; it would be like always.

Chapter 2

Face hidden entirely behind the slouch brim of a disreputable, soft, old felt hat, the man moved with exaggerated caution between the lodgepole pines on the northern slope. To his left, another buckskin-clad figure paused, brown eyes searching the terrain from under skunk-skin cap, long-barreled Hawkin rifle at the ready, until his partner halted behind a large fir tree. Then he went into motion, downhill, for a short distance. He pulled up sharply behind the protruding bulb of a gigantic granite boulder.

The first man advanced again. The loose coat he wore opened in the slight breeze to reveal a barrel chest and narrow waist, which put a lie to the salt-and-pepper hair that protruded from under the dirty old hat. With practiced ease, they continued to leap-frog to the valley floor. They glanced back up the steep slope. Each tried to figure out how to get the other to offer to make the long climb back to get their horses and pack animals. A voice spoke to them from the cover of the treeline.

"One-Eye, Bart, you boys coulda saved yourselves a passel of extra walking if you'd just rid straight in."

One-Eye Avery Tookes cocked his head to one side. "Preacher? B'God's bones, it is you, ain't it?"

"Alive an' in one piece," Preacher allowed. "An' I saved

you the trouble of bringin' those mangy critters down here."

That set well with both visitors. They let out satisfied bellows when Preacher came into the open leading their livestock. Then the one Preacher called Bart pursed his thick lips and appraised his old friend with soft, brown eyes.

"We been lookin' for you," Bart Weller advised. He cut his eyes to the fresh mounds of earth and stones close by. The turning of his head caused the tail of his disreputable cap to sway as though alive. "Looks sorta like trouble found you first."

Preacher sighed heavily and rubbed his hands together. "That it did, an' puzzlesome at that. But the tellin' will go better over a pot of coffee an' a bit o' rye." He led the way to his partially constructed cabin and added fuel to the fire in an Indian-style beehive oven-stove combination. He told his old friends about the five men and their actions in the valley. While he talked, the water in the pot came to a boil. Preacher added coffee and an egg shell. One-Eye noted that the shell had considerable size to it and was of a bluish tint. Preacher spotted his curiosity.

"Duck eggs. When I first come into this hole, I found some ducks that liked it rightly enough that they made it a year-round home. Every couple of days, I'd nick an egg from each of the six nests. Et the eggs, saved the shells for coffee. Nothin' settles grounds quite so good. Now, as I was tellin' ya," Preacher launched back into his account of the scruffy intruders.

While he talked, he paid close attention to his visitors. He had known Bart Weller longer. Why, from way back at the Rendezvous in '27, he thought. Didn't seem now his hair had a strand more gray in it than the day they met. A quiet feller, he had already partnered up with One-Eye Avery Tookes before the Rendezvous. Been together ever since. One-Eye Avery was a legend all to himself.

Of an age with Preacher and, like that venerable mountain man, one of the last of the breed, he had not sacrificed an eye to obtain his High Lonesome moniker. Indeed, he still had the clear, light blue orbs with which he had been born. The first white man who had attacked a then much younger Avery Tookes in a drunken rage had been bent on snuffing out the life of the adventurous, youthful trapper. Avery had defended himself admirably, until the huge brute got him in a bear hug. Not eager to kill the man, Avery had resorted to his only other line of offense. He had gouged out the man's eye with a long, thick thumb nail. Howling, the lout had given up, and Avery answered the questions as to why he had not finished the job with the remark that he reckoned one eye was enough. His new-found friend, Preacher, had promptly dubbed him Ol' One-Eye.

That had been years ago, yet both men had maintained their health and strength. Seen from behind, it would be difficult to identify one man from the other. From the front, One-Eye's big, bulbous red nose was a sure giveaway. Tookes had invited Preacher to spend the season trapping with him and his partner. Preacher knew Bart Weller to be a man with plenty sand, and more knowledege about beaver than any human should possess. He had readily agreed, and they had spent the next three seasons together. Like it so often happened, they'd drifted apart at one Rendezvous, only to make infrequent contact over the years. Now, here they were in his valley. He decided to ask them why.

Bart studied on that for a while, then made reply. "Well, we come across several collections of similar trash. Most been headin' northwest, into Wyoming country."

"Wonder what this batch meant by being sent?" One-Eye asked.

"That sort of has me in a hassle, too," Preacher admitted. "Just who an' why would someone send such unclean riffraff into the High Lonesome?"

Bart swept the skunk-skin cap off his head and ran fingers through his thick mane of hair. "Lord knows the place is too crowded as it is." He paused, thought a moment. "You did say these unsavory lads had been sent to get you, right?"

"Right as rain, Bart. I'm flattered someone thought it necessary to send five fellers, but I'm damned if I can put a name to who it might be. Why don't you two light a spell, get rested. Maybe in a day or two we can figger out what this is all about."

One-Eye patted his belly. "Suits. You bein' such a good cook an' all. An' we got some other tall tales to tell. Just for an instance, Bart an' me done heard of some place in the far off supposed to have a bunch of shiny white buildings. A right colorful sight, I'd say."

Preacher shot him a frown. "You got it all wrong, One-Eye. White is the *absence* of all color." That set them all to guffawing, and Preacher set out the Monongahela.

Three mangy, wooly-eared drifters crested a rise in the Ferris Mountains of Wyoming. They had barely raised their heads to the horizon when they halted abruptly, thunderstruck by what they saw. The one in the center mopped at his thick, gaping lips and smacked his mouth closed noisily. He shook his head in an attempt to clear his vision. The seven hills, with their buildings in various stages of construction, remained.

"All them purty buildin's," the sallow-faced lout on his left said in an awed tone.

"What you reckon they's here for, Hank?"

Henry Claypool, the one in the middle, wiped at his mouth again and stared across the wide, deep basin. "Don't rightly know, Jase. There's one thing I do know. They don't rightly belong here."

"But we was *told* . . . ," the shallow-faced Jason Grantling bleated.

"I know what we was told, idjit. I didn't expect nothin' like this, though. But, yep, this is the place all right, the one we was told to find."

"Who ever saw a place like this?" the flatland trash on Hank's right asked.

"Ain't got a clue, have you, Turnip Head? I'd say we done took a step back in time."

Turnip Head, whose real name was Alvin Wooks, and Jason Grantling stared at Hank Claypool as though he had lost his mind.

"H-how you come to mean that?" The slightly dumber Alvin Wooks asked.

Impatient, Hank gigged his horse forward. "I say we ride down and find out for ourselves."

Negotiating the inner slope of the basin proved easier than had the ascent. The smell of rich, fresh grass made their mounts frisky, their tails up and flying in the stout breeze that blew from the far-off structures. It brought with it the tangy scent of raw pine boards. At the foot of the incline, Hank and his companions were forced to rein in abruptly once more.

This time, a group of burly, hard-faced men confronted them. They all carried long poles that looked like spears and had funny round, knobby leather hats fastened on their heads by thick straps with cheek pieces that had been shaped like large leaves.

"Oh-oh, what kind of clothes is them?" Jason asked in a worried whisper.

Silas Tucker peered nearsightedly at the trembling pair before him. Tobacco juice stained his full, pouting lips and discolored the scraggly beard that surrounded the ugly hole of his mouth. He cut his shoe-button black eyes from one child to the other, despising their pale complexions, fair hair and cornflower blue eyes. Didn't look like any git of his at all—at all. His gaze went over their shoulders to where Faith stood in the doorway of the tumble-down cabin he and his women had labored to erect three summers past.

He'd managed sure enough to stamp every one of the brats he'd given her. How'd that peaked Purity manage to override his dark, hill people's blood? Course what with Faith bein' his younger sister, the blood held true, didn't it? Then there was these two. Cotton tops, with their mother's coloring and eyes. But, she was sure a good romp in bed. Li'l Faith hadn't had that much energy since she had given birth to their oldest at thirteen. That was when Pop had run him and Faith off, clean out of the Appalchia country.

"Cousins is fine and good, but yer sisters are jist for practicin' yer plowin', not plantin' a crop," the old man had bellowed when he shooed the shame-faced pair off the rocky hillside that constituted their farm. Well, hell, this place wasn't any better. Biggest crop each year was rocks. Now he had to make sure these ghost-pale git of his an' Purity didn' leave anything behind at the old man's camp-site that could be traced to him. His expression grew stony, and he pinned the boy with those obsidian orbs.

"Tell it again, Terry. You sure this pilgrim ain't gonna go to Trout Crick Pass an' yap to the law?"

"Ye—yes, sir. I done slid that pig-sticker in betwixt his ribs like you showed me."

"D'ya thrash it around like I said?" Silas asked from the depths of his shrewdness.

Silas knew himself to be a dimwit, due to the inbreeding in his family, or at least that was what that circuit-ridin' doctor had said about the whole passel of Tuckers in them hills back to home. But he also knew he was as shrewd as the next feller. More so than a lot. Now he watched with a growing dread as the boy blanched even whiter with guilty knowledge.

"I—ah—I—er . . . forgot."

Rough and horny from hard work, the right hand of

Silas Tucker lightninged out and popped loudly off the downy cheek of the frightened cherub in front of him. Tears sprang to Terry's eyes.

"Dangit, boy! How's we's supposed to stay safe if you keep forgetting the most important part?"

Long hours, days, even weeks alone in the wilderness had given Terry a new sense of self-worth, of independence. It prompted him to an unwise decision at this point. "Maybe . . . maybe if you'd come along and do some of the dirty work for a change, we'd be a whole lot safer."

Silas Tucker had the boy's trousers down and the child bent over his knee in one swift move. His belt hissed out of its loops, and he used it expertly to flail at Terry's exposed bare bottom. Bravely, the lad resisted the impulse to scream out his pain and humiliation. Not so, his sister. Vickie shrieked, stamped her small feet on the hard ground, and pounded ineffectual little fists on the back of Silas Tucker.

"Stop it! Stop it! You're hurting him," she wailed.

"That's what I damn well intend to do, Missy. An' if you don't shut up, you'll git yours next." He did stop, after seven strokes that left angry red welts on the pale flesh of Terry's posterior. "All right. Here's how it's gonna be. You'll both go to bed without any supper for the next week. Bread and water twicest a day is all you see otherwise. The next time you go out, you make sure you stick those fellers good an' proper. Wouldn't do for word to go around that Silas Tucker's brood is doin' sloppy robberies. Now, go. Get out of my sight. An' you best yank up them britches before you give your sister bad ideas," Silas added with a lewd wink.

Hurt and shamed, Terry did as he had been bade. He and Vickie knew all about what Silas had so nastily hinted at. They knew it went on among their half brothers and sisters. For them it had never held an appeal. Each loved the other and had had to look out for one another for as long as they remembered. They didn't have time for that sort of foolishness. Besides, the Good Book said it was evil. Oh, they had read the Bible all right, only in secret.

None of the rest of the Tuckers could string three letters together to make a word, let alone read. And Silas—Poppa—hotly cursed the Bible and preachers in general all the time. He claimed that man had been put on the earth to take his pleasures where he wished, and that book-learnin' an' reeligon got in the way of that something fierce. Only went to show, Silas didn't know everything about anything. Terry had wiped away the last of his tears by the time they got to the cabin. Their momma, Purity, stopped them and asked what had happened and what Silas had decided.

"We got punished for not makin' sure of that last pilgrim we robbed. Sila—Poppa says we get no supper for a week, an' we have bread and water only for our other meals," Terry reluctantly revealed.

Inwardly, he was thinking; *If only there was some way we could leave here and not come back. If we could just be free forever.* Terry had no way to know that his sister shared her version of the same desire, or that the opportunity to escape lay just beyond the next couple of ranges.

One-Eye Tookes and Bart Weller bent over the large cast-iron skillet, biscuit halves in hand, to mop up the last of the pan drippings left from the fresh venison steaks Preacher had fried for their breakfast. The tender meat had gone well with cornmeal mush and fried potatoes and onions. Avery Tookes glanced up from his efforts and eyed the surroundings.

"Mighty larupin', Preacher. Course it woulda been better iffin we had some aiggs. Why don't you get you some chickens and keep a store of aiggs?"

For a brief moment, Preacher eyed One-Eye, uncertain if he was funnin' or not. "I ain't no farmer, One-Eye. Ain't made to chase after some old Dominickers or Rhode Island Reds. Let nature provide, I alus say."

Orneriness twinkled in the pale blue orbs of One-Eye Tookes. "Couldn't be that you're too lazy to tend to some measly chickens, could it?"

Preacher popped upright, spluttered, cussed and slammed his hat on the ground. "Lazy, is it? Who cooked that breakfast to feed your worthless hide and bottomless belly?"

One-Eye patted the slight mound at his middle and produced a fond smile. "And right good it was, Preacher. I'm obliged I didn't have to wrassel you for it, like I hear some visitors got to do."

Steam escaped from Preacher. "That ain't true. Not a word of it. I've never begrudged a man a bite to eat, iffin he be friendly." He drew up suddenly. "Saay, who was it told you I made a body fight for his meal?"

Tookes looked him straight in the eyes. "Bloody Hand Kreuger, that's who."

"That Kraut is a liar, plain and simple. An' I'd say it to his face if he was present to hear it. There's a bit of—ah—bad blood betwixt us. Has been for a few years now. I ride my trails, an' he rides his. We both like it that way."

One-Eye wouldn't let it go. "Might be he knows something about these strange doin's in the High Lonesome. Story is he's been up north the last couple of years. That bein' where all this riffraff is headed, he could be the key to what's goin' on."

Preacher made a face. "I'd as soon kiss a wolverine as be beholdin' to Karl Kreuger by askin' him about it."

Both guests came to their boots and ankled it over to their already loaded packhorses. They adjusted the cinch straps while speculating further on the meaning behind the recent intrusions. Tookes summed it up for the three of them.

"You ask me, it's gonna mean trouble. Too many of

those light-in-the-saddle types driftin' up outta Texas ain't good for man nor beast. They all think they're good with a gun and proddy as Billy-be-damned. If we run across Bloody Hand, you don't mind if we ask him what he knows, do ya, Preacher?"

"Nope. Go right ahead. You ask me, though, I say we'll learn what is going on soon enough anyhow."

Bart Weller, the worrier of the partners, agreed, then added, "We should hope we don't learn of it to our regret."

Arms tightly around each other, Terry and Vickie clung close together. Each could feel the warmth of the other through their thin nightshirts. There was nothing arousing about it, only comforting. They were too bony; Terry knew that for certain. Far too little to eat. He and Vickie were always treated like outcasts. As though they did not belong to the family. When he had been littler, they had both cried about that. Now he was too old for things like that.

He had to find a way for them to get something more out of life than stealing and lying and sneaking around. He refused to think about the killing. He hugged his sister tightly and whispered in her ear. "Are you awake?"

"Yep. So are you," Vickie observed with the logic of a ten-year-old.

"I hate it here," Terry muttered softly.

"So do I," Vickie agreed.

Terry gathered courage. "Sometimes I think the thing we best do is to run away for real."

Vickie stiffened, her eyes suddenly bright in the starlight that seeped through the tiny window in their loft room. "Do you mean it, Terry? Really mean it?"

"Y-yes, I do. D-do you want to?"

"We . . . could try. When? Oh, when, Terry?"

Terry gave that considerable thought. "Why not the

next time Poppa sends us out? We could go and just keep going."

"To where?"

"Somewhere. Anywhere. We could find something."

Vickie had become quite agitated. Her slender form trembled against that of her brother. "Let's do it. *Please,* let's do it."

After a long moment, Terry answered in a hollow whisper. "All right, we will."

Chance decided it in the end. Philadelphia Braddock had been of several minds as to where to go for the approaching winter. He had a standing invite from two old friends who had a tidy cabin on the Snake River. They put out a good table, what with smoked salmon, plenty of elk and venison, a root cellar full of camus bulbs, wild onions, yucca root, some grown turnips and other eatables. Yet, they also kept a pouch of juniper berries to flavor the raw, white liquor they distilled each summer for the following cold time.

When they drank that awful stuff, they got snake-pissin' mean. Philadelphia could not count the number of times he had been caught up in one of their brawls. The two of them spent most of each winter covered with lumps and bruises. And Lord help the outsider who strayed within range of their fists. Naw, he concluded. He'd best avoid that situation.

He also had a standing welcome with the Crow to visit them in Montana Territory. They had always been friendly to the whites exploring in their land. He even knew he would have a nice, tractable bed warmer to occupy his lodge. Might, too, only Philadelphia reckoned as how he had more than his share of half-Crow youngsters runnin' around the High Plains already. No need to build another.

That left him with the long journey to Bent's Fort. In this

late year of Eighteen and Forty-eight, the place was but a pale shadow of its past glory. Only two factors remained, neither of them related to the Bent brothers. There'd be whiskey. Good, clean whiskey, aged in barrels and filtered through charcoal. But a winter there would cost him an arm and a leg. The soft, deerskin pouch around his neck still hung with respectable weight, but the gold would be soon gone at Bent's. Better pass that up for another day.

Which brought him to his final choice. He could head southeast and check out the Ferris Mountains in Wyoming. If that didn't suit, and the weather held, he could go on south to Trout Creek Pass. There, he had heard, some of the good old boys had taken to hanging out over the cold months. He could jaw a little, play cards and checkers, and have a warm bunk to roll up in at night. No pliable Crow girl, nor any hard floosie, for that matter, but a comfort to a man getting on in his years.

By jing! That's just what he would do. Check out the rumors about a man willing to pay out real gold for fighting men in the Ferris Range, then, if it didn't pan out, go on to Colorado country and the High Lonesome. He might even run into his old sometimes partner, Preacher. What with the fur trade all but moribund, Preacher and some of the old boys had taken to hanging a mite closer to civilized living. Might be he could benefit by that, too.

Philadelphia Braddock clucked to his packhorse and yanked on the rope around its neck. Long ride to Trout Creek, but only a day or two now to this outfit in the Ferris Mountains. He'd give them a look-see, that's what he'd do.

Chapter 3

Three days later, in a wide valley, set off by seven low hills, Philadelphia Braddock stumbled upon a sight he could not believe. Alabaster buildings shined from the crests of several of the seven hills that clustered in the upland vale. It became obvious to Philadelphia that some serious construction work was going on along the slopes of the three as yet vacant hills. Flat, layered plain trees had replaced the usual aspen, and tall, slender pines of a blue-gray color Philadelphia had never seen before lined a wide, white, cobblestone roadway that led from the south end of the basin to tall gates in what looked like a plastered stone wall that surrounded a portion of the four occupied hills. From his angle, Philadelphia could not tell if the rampart ran all the way around. This was one whing-ding of a puzzler.

He had never heard of any settlement sprouting up in the Ferris Mountains. Certainly nothing like this. Why, it was a regular city. "I'll be blessed," he said aloud to his horse.

The animal replied with a snort and shake of its massive head. A spray of slobber put diamonds in the air. A peremptory stomp of a hoof drew Philadelphia's attention to a knot of men who broke off from the workers, one of them pointing his direction. Too far off to see detail, the former trapper decided to wait them out. When they drew nearer, he noted that the men wore bright red capotes. No, he corrected himself, longer than the ubiquitous mountain man garb, more like cloaks. A horseman joined them.

"Odd-looking fellers," Braddock advised his mount, while he patted the visibly nervous beast with one hand to calm it.

When they came even closer, he saw that they wore overskirts of leather strips studded with brass knobs. Below that, they wore short skirts. For a giddy moment, Philadelphia wondered if they might be sissy-boys. On their heads they had brown, leather-covered pots of some sort. Odder still, he marked, they carried lances and shields, like Injuns. He changed his examination of the approaching men to the one on horseback.

Wasn't he a sight! He had an even longer capote, scarlet in color, with shiny brass coverings on his legs, chest and helmet—for that's what it was, bright red roach of horsehair and all. The polished cheek pieces were shaped something like oak leaves. Then Philadelphia made out another feller, who jogged along behind the horse. He held some sort of long pole with a big metal banner on top. On closer examination, Braddock saw that it was an eagle, with spread wings, head turned in profile, and something written under it.

Now, old Philadelphia wasn't too strong on reading, but he could make out his letters as good as any man. These read: *S.P.Q.R.*

Within seconds, the rider reined up right close to Philadelphia, rudely crowding his space. He pulled a short, leaf-bladed sword and pointed it somewhere above Braddock's head. "Hold, there, barbarian!" the man bellowed with all the officiousness of a government man in a swallow-tail coat. "What business have you in Nova Roma?"

From habit, Philadelphia made the plains sign for coming in peace as he spoke. "I was only lookin' for a place to hole up for winter. An' I ain't no barbarian."

Glowering, the challenger proved arrogant enough to not need to consult anyone about his opinion. *"This* is not the place. Unless you bear a scroll of safe passage, you are trespassing on the territory of Nova Roma."

Philadelphia's forehead furrowed. "I ain't got no paper on me."

His interrogator motioned two men forward with his sword as he spoke. "Then you are under arrest. You will be put to work with the rest of the slaves, to build our magnificent city."

Philadelphia Braddock did not like that one bit. His eyes narrowed. "Is that so? How long do you reckon I'll be doin' that?"

"Until you prove your worth to be a citizen of Nova Roma."

"That long, huh?" Philadelphia followed his first instinct.

His reins given a turn around the saddle horn, Braddock moved swiftly, hands closing around the handstocks of a brace of .64 caliber Chambers horse pistols. He yanked them free before any of the startled soldiers could react. The muzzles centered on the two closest to him, and he blazed away.

Loud, flat reports shattered the bird-twittering silence, and twin smoke clouds obscured everything for a moment. His actions served his purpose, Philadelphia observed as the greasy gray mass whipped away on a light breeze. The two who were to arrest him lay on the ground, writhing, shot X-wise through their right shoulders. The footmen had scattered, and the snarling leader had been put to flight.

"Appears to me you need a lesson in manners, fellers," Braddock told them.

Satisfied with the results, Philadelphia reholstered the

discharged pistols and slid his Hawken rifle free of its scabbard. With a final, careful appraisal of his would-be foe, he turned the head of his mount to the south and started off, away from this inhospitable place. By then, one of the footmen had recovered himself enough to spring up on his sandals and cock his arm, the hand holding his *pilum* behind his right ear. He let fly the spear with deadly accuracy.

Sharp pain radiated through Braddock's right shoulder as the smooth point penetrated flesh and bone and pinned his shoulder blade to his ribs. Stunned by the sudden, enormous pain, Philadelphia nevertheless managed to swivel at the hips and bring up his Hawken. Leveled on his assailant's chest, Braddock cocked and triggered the weapon. The big, fat .56 caliber conical bullet smashed through the soldier's sternum and ripped a big hole in his aorta.

His sandals left the ground, and he crashed backward head-over-heels to sprawl in the dirt. His valiant heart rapidly pumped the life from his body. Philadelphia Braddock did not wait to check his results, though. He put boot heels to the heaving flanks of his mount and sprinted for the distant pass that opened on the white cobblestone roadway.

With each thud of a hoof, new agony shot through Philadelphia's body. The lance flopped wildly up and down, caught in his muscular back. He did not stop, though, until safely beyond the crest of the ridge. Then he scabbarded his Hawken and painfully wrenched the *pilum* from the wound it had made. His last thought was, *What the hell did I stumble into?* Only then did he allow himself to pass out.

Preacher began his morning with the usual grumping about, slurping coffee too hot and strong to bear by normal persons, and a lot of scratching. He interspersed these activities with a lick of a brown wooden pencil lead and careful application of it to a scrap of precious paper.

He preferred the new-fangled gypsum plaster for chinking logs in his cabin walls. Clay mud did all right, he allowed, but often came with an unwelcome harvest of bugs. He also needed some nails to hold door and window frames together and to build furniture for his digs. When he saw the size of his list, he decided to call it a day around the work in progress and head off for Trout Creek Pass and the trading post.

He could also pick up flour, corn meal, beans, sugar and more coffee beans. With the meat he had already killed, dressed out and smoked, he figured to be set for the long, cold months just around the corner. But he would also have to get a bag of salt. He had not as yet built a corral, so he had to chase down his hobbled mount, the big-chested roan, Cougar, and the sorrel gelding packhorse. That accomplished, he carefully stored all his supplies safely out of the way of raccoons, bears, and wolves alike, and departed. He didn't even cast a casual glance over the graves of those who had so recently come to kill him.

Slowly, the late-summer, pale blue sky frosted over with a thin skein of high cirrus clouds. At first, Preacher paid it no mind. The weather often did this in late August. An hour later, the leaden overcast had blotted out the sun and brought a single worry furrow to Preacher's brow. What the heck? It was too early to snow, he felt certain of that.

Fat, black bellies slid low over the highest peaks an hour and a half later, the temperature had dropped twenty degrees, and Preacher began to worry about how close winter really was with this harbinger of a late-August snowstorm. Odd, he considered. Even a tenderfoot counted on snow not beginning in the High Lonesome before September.

Had his mental calendar slipped a cog? No, not likely.

Shoot, the big, gray Canadian honkers had not yet put in their annual appearance far below and beyond the eastern slopes of the Shining Mountains. What a joy they were to observe from on high, their heavily populated vee formations winging their way south for the winter. With the same regularity they used to hail the approach of the cold, each spring they were also the first heralds of warm weather returning. Yet, it seemed that this time nature had even outsmarted them.

Tiny flakes, invisible to the eye, began to land on Preacher's face and the backs of his hands. Cold and wet, they did not remain for long. Their bigger brothers and sisters would be along soon enough for that, Preacher reasoned. He began to take closer note of his surroundings. One of these northers could blow up in a matter of minutes, and a man caught in the open would soon be buzzard meat. Temperatures could, and often did, drop forty degrees in less than ten minutes.

Given that this late in August the high for the day hovered around forty-eight to fifty, that could have fatal results. Memory played its map pages in his mind. A ways farther south, he knew, there was an old cabin, part of a failed mining attempt. Beyond that, in a rocky gorge, another small cabin fronted a natural cave. Preacher had often wanted to poke around in there, only to have circumstances get in the way. He would put his trust in his own instincts and see how far he got.

For, no matter what he hoped for, he knew danged well it was going to snow. "Best eat some ground, Cougar," he advised his trustworthy mount.

The invisible flakes changed to freezing rain half a mile along the trail toward Trout Creek Pass. Preacher broke out a sheepskin jacket and bundled up, the collar pulled high. His breath came in frosty plumes. Cougar snorted regular clouds of white. No question, this one would be a heller.

*   *   *

Fat, wet flakes drifted downward, twirled by the flukey breeze that sent them skyward again, or into spirals that danced vertically across the ground. Little pinpricks of cold where they lighted on the exposed skin of Preacher, they grew steadily in number. Before he could account the time, Preacher observed that the horizon ahead of him had been curtained off by a swirling wall of gray-white.

In a place where visibility usually stretched on forever, unless impeded by a mountain peak, Preacher could not see even half a mile off. And, dang it, he'd been caught out away from any of the shelters he knew of. Better than two miles to the cave, about three-quarters of a mile to the mine. He took time to wrap a bandana around his head, tied it under the chin, to protect his ears, plopped his hat on his head again and turned up his collar.

"Cougar," he advised his roan horse, "we're deep in the buffalo chips if we don't find shelter. Just keep a-movin', boy."

Over the next half hour, the snow storm turned into a regular, full-blown blizzard. Preacher remained silent through the ordeal, forced to bat his eyelashes rapidly to blink away the clinging flakes that settled after icily caressing his face. Only the largest tree trunks stood out as black slashes in the thick, wild gyration of white. So dense was the downfall that he almost missed the cabin over the mineshaft when he at last came to it.

Preacher saw the reason for that soon enough. Over the years, the abandoned place had sagged to a ruin that more resembled a raw outcrop of rock than a man-made structure. No relief from the storm here, right enough, Preacher regretfully realized. He must push on for the cave, and hope that last year's thunderstorms and resulting fires had not destroyed the cabin there.

Numbness had crept into Preacher's fingers and toes a

quarter hour later when he stopped to pull a thick pair of wool socks over his feet and return them to the suddenly chilled boots. *Fool,* he chided himself. He should have thought to bring along gloves. Or those rabbit-fur mittens, a leftover from the previous winter.

His world had become a wall of white now. To rely on dead reckoning to navigate from one place to another was to lead oneself astray, Preacher reminded himself. And to stay where he was invited a slow death by freezing. He had heard most of his life that it was peaceful, going that way. Then he snorted with derision. Who in hell had ever come back to tell about how easy it was?

Just keep Mount Elbert on my right shoulder, Preacher repeated over and over in a sort of chant. For all its size, the mountain loomed a dark gray, rather than the usual green-shrouded black. In fits and starts it disappeared entirely in the whirl of dancing snow. Preacher rode on, the comforting tug of the lead rope to his packhorse against his left thigh. In that blind world, all sense of time abandoned him.

Whenever he opened his heavy coat to check his timepiece, the resultant small movement of the hands jolted him. The numbness began again in his feet. *Frostbite!* The terribly real possibility of it ate at his vitals. His ears alternately burned and tingled with awful cold. They would be affected first. Preacher ground his teeth and urged Cougar onward. At last his fat old Hambleton registered the passage of an hour. His goal had to be near. Each breath of man and beast brought forth clouds of white. The wind increased steadily.

Preacher found himself leaning into it and realized with a start that he must have somehow circled, for the wind had been at his back from the beginning of the storm. How long had he ridden away from the safety of the cave? Accustomed over long years in the High Lonesome to suppressing desperation, he fought back the welling of panic from deep in his gut. Turn around, find Mount Elbert, and carry on.

It sounded so easy. Something a man could do in a fraction of a minute. But not in this raging blizzard. Preacher reversed himself easily enough. Then, try as he might, he could not find the nearby peak. Lowering clouds scudded through the snow now and blanked out everything. All he could think of was to keep going.

Another half hour crawled by, and Preacher began to note a lessening in the density of the snowfall. To his right the dark gray mass of Elbert swam out of the maelstrom. Reoriented once more, Preacher struck off a couple of points to the west of due south. At least by his reckoning, that's what he did. Within a hundred heartbeats, a darker, regular shape showed itself intermittently through the gyrating clots of flakes. Preacher's eyes stung and burned, and he blinked away more snow that assailed his face. Was that it?

Had he made it to his objective? A dark smear resolved into a straight, black line. A few labored paces farther, another smooth slash joined the other at a steep angle. A roofline, by God! Reserves of strength sent a warm flush through the cold-enervated body of Preacher. He could not contain the anxiety of his tormented flesh. He leaned forward in the saddle and peered intently.

Yes! There she stood. The tiny cabin perched on a shelf above the floor of the gorge. He had found his refuge. Straining his eyes, Preacher picked out the start of the ledge that led to the eroded cutback and the so welcome sight of the tiny cabin. He kneed Cougar toward it, hardly feeling the touch of his legs against the ribs of the horse. They made five small paces forward; then Cougar floundered in a snowbank.

With a frightened whinny, the animal sank to its neck in a hidden wash that paralleled the hillside. Preacher nearly pitched out of the saddle. He held on though and bent forward to scoop away enough of the powder to free Cougar's shoulders. Next he worked a space that would allow him to apply a touch of spur. Cougar responded with a burst of nervous energy that sent a plume of snow above his rider's head. The roan's rear haunches bunched, and he plowed forward in a succession of sheets of white.

Gradually Cougar gained a purchase and surged onto the narrow ledge. Squealing in confused fright, the packhorse followed. In what seemed no time at all to Preacher, he reined up in front of the low, crudely made hut. Painfully he dismounted. First, he eased an icy .44 Colt Walker from the holster and tried the small people door. He found it unlatched and it opened easily.

The whole front of the cabin swung outward, Preacher recalled, to give access to horses. He pulled the wooden pegs that held structure together and eased the facing wall out enough to allow his animals to enter. Out of the direct wind, it felt a lot warmer. He used a lucifer to light a torch, and took note of signs of recent occupancy.

Dry wood had been stacked by a stone stove, which showed a residue of burned-out coals. The cobwebs had been cleared above a double bunk on one wall, and over the single one opposite. He led his animals farther back, where he found evidence of more ancient residents. Petroglyphs carved and painted into the walls of the cave spoke of visits by early man, hunt stories, and some sort of ritual. They made the hairs at the nape of Preacher's neck rise.

After he had secured Cougar and the packhorse, unsaddled them and rubbed them down, he returned to the cabin portion. He quickly kindled a fire, retrieved his cook gear from one of the parfleches on the pack frame and set to boiling coffee, made from snow scooped up outside. Real warmth flooded the secure little shelter.

When the first cup of strong, black brew had become a thing of the past, Preacher shred thin strips from a dry-cured venison ham into a skillet and brought out a scrupulously clean bandana, into which he had tied half a dozen biscuits. He chose two and set them to warm on the rock beside the gridiron over the stove. A little grease from a crock, some dried hominy from a bag put to soak in a small dutch oven, and Preacher considered himself to be in hog heaven.

He poured another cup of coffee and settled back to enjoy it. Exhausted from his fight to resist the cold and battle the storm, Preacher's head began to droop. His chin all but touched his chest when he jerked upright suddenly. What was that he had heard?

He thought chirping birds had disturbed his sleep. Yet, the storm still raged outside, and night was fast coming on. Birds did not twitter in such conditions. There. He heard it again. Preacher came to his boots and edged closer to the front of the cabin.

A more careful listen and the chirpings resolved into human voices. *Small* human voices. Little kidlet voices. Preacher reached up to wipe the astonishment off his face. What in Billy-be-damned would brat-kids be doing wandering around in such a blizzard?

Taking a covered, kerosene lantern from his pack rig, Preacher lighted it and bundled up before stepping out into the storm. He found it greatly reduced. The wind down and the snow light streaks in the twilight gloom. The voices came from below him. He could make out the words now.

"Help! Someone help us!"

"We're gonna freeze out here, I just know it."

"Oh, please, help. Hello! Someone, anyone, help us!"

Preacher investigated the ledge and found it still passable. He raised his lantern on high and called to the youngsters below. "Hello. Stay where you are. I'll come to you."

"Oh, thank you. Thankyou, thankyou, thankyou," a squeaky voice babbled.

Within five minutes, Preacher had descended and located the children. They shivered and shook, and hugged him, fighting back tears. They stiffened, though, when Preacher asked their identity.

"I-I'm Terrance," the slightly built boy replied in a gulp.

"I'm Victoria."

Preacher forced a scolding frown. "What are a couple of babies like you doing out here in this storm?"

Terrance shoved out a thin lip in a pink pout. "I'm not a baby. I'm twelve."

"Well, looo-di-doo. What about you, girlie?"

"I'm ten. Terrance is my brother. We're cold, mister."

"You can call me Preacher. C'mon, I've a warm place up yonder, and some victuals if you're hungry."

Terrance's eyes widened, and he put a hand to his stomach. "Are we? We're starved."

Preacher led them back, moving as swiftly as he could in the drifted snow. He had taken note in the lantern light of their pale skin and blue-tinged lips. Both children shivered so violently they appeared to be caught in some sort of seizure. Once secure inside the cabin, he poured them cups of coffee and urged them to drink. Their coats were threadbare, hardly more than rags. Terrance had strips of cloth wrapped around his feet instead of boots or shoes.

Recalling a pair of moccasins in his kit, Preacher rose and turned to both shaking youngsters. "Now, you strip outten them clothes, down to your long johns, and get close to the fire."

Victoria flushed a deep red. "We ain't got no long johns, not any kind of underclothes."

"Well, then, wrap up in blankets and skin outta your clothes. They need to be warmed and dried. For you, boy, I got a pair of moccasins. They's a tad mite too small for me, an' I figger you'll be able to swim in 'em. But, they're rabbit-fur-lined and a lot warmer than those rags."

Terrance lowered long, blond lashes over wide, pale blue eyes. "I'd be obliged, mister."

"Call me Preacher. Ev'ry one else does."

Terrance snapped his head upward at that. For all his furtive, rodentlike manner, he stared wide-eyed now at Preacher. "Gosh. You're famous."

It became Preacher's turn to blush. "Some fool folks try to make it that way. But, I was alus just tryin' to do my job as I saw fit. Let me git them moccasins, an' then I'll rustle you up some grub."

He turned away to do as he had promised. The fire's warmth, the food, and hot coffee did their job. The children became more animated. When Preacher considered them past the point of desperation, and relaxed enough to answer sensibly, he opened a little inquiry into their background.

"I know you said you were Terrance and Victoria. Only, what's your last name?"

Terrance gave him that now-familiar ferret stare. "Are you a real preacher? A Bible-thumper?"

"Nope. I reckon I'm about as far away from that sort as a man can get. Though I do consider myself on good speakin' terms with the Almighty."

"What's your name, then?" Terrance challenged.

Preacher hesitated a moment. "Arthur's m'given name."

"What's your family name?" the boy persisted.

The mountain man puzzled over that a while. "Well, by dang, if I don't think I've plumb forgot it. Folks have called me Preacher for so long, it's sort of stuck."

Terrance brightened. "Then, I reckon that's the case with us. We don't know what our family name is . . . or even if we've got one." He gave Preacher a "so there" look.

"I'll buy that. Now, tell me, how come you were out in that tempest?"

"That what?" Victoria asked, puzzlement on her wide, clear face.

"How'd you come to be out in that blizzard?"

Terrance took up the answers. "We've been wandering around for days—weeks now. Those we were travelin' with got lost in the woods. They stumbled around, and the food got real short," the boy continued, his expression one of far-off construction. "When they runned clean out, they abandoned us. Just dropped us off in a canyon one day."

Preacher scowled. That didn't ring true. "Who were these folks?"

Terrance scrunched his high, smooth brow. "Some real mean fellers. They—they stole us from our home far, far away."

This had begun to sound to Preacher like one of those melodramas in one of the Penny Dreadfuls. "An' I suppose they made you do all sorts of awful things?"

"Ye—yes, sir," Terrance acknowledged.

Preacher's flinty eyes bore into the boy. "Like what?"

Terrance flinched. "No—nothin' below the belt. Me an' Vickie wouldn't allow that."

"If they were that mean, what choice would you have?" Preacher taunted, not the least interested in pursuing the salacious topic he had introduced. He merely wanted a means of verifying the boy's truthfulness.

"They—they really weren't that mean until they got lost and ran short on food. One time they made us rob a cabin that the folks were away from. Another, they offered to sell us to some Injuns." Preacher noted that Terrance would not look him directly in the eye. The boy's own pale blue orbs shifted nervously as he related his tales of horror.

After half an hour of what Preacher considered the largest collection of fibs he had heard in a long time, during which Terrance continued to stuff himself with venison ham, the lad's eyelids began to droop. Preacher took advantage of that to hustle them off to bed.

"Time to turn in, I'd say. Snow'll be down enough by midday we can head out. You'd best roll up an' get some sleep."

Yawning, they agreed. Preacher saw them settled in, then curled up in his blankets, a thick buffalo robe over top. After the day's ordeal, sleep came quickly and went deep. Well into the night, when everyone should have been sound asleep, Preacher heard some creaking from the twin bunks across the room. He breathed deeply and turned his head that way in time to see two small, naked forms rush swiftly toward him. It quickly became obvious they intended to subdue and rob him. The larger of the pair competently held a long, thin-bladed knife.

Chapter 4

Although loath to harm children, Preacher had to fight for his life. For all her frail build and small size, Vickie turned out to be a wildcat. Scratching and biting were her game. She raked Preacher's left cheek with bitten nails, hardly long enough to break the skin. She bit him in the shoulder when he attempted to throw her off him. Screaming a blue string of obscenities Preacher doubted she knew the meaning of, she kicked him in the ribs with a bare toe.

For all her ferocity, Terry proved the greater danger. The knife he wielded flicked through the air an inch from Preacher's eyes, then whipped downward, a hairsbreadth from the skin over his ribs.

"Dammit!" Preacher roared. "What's got into you? Leave be. I ain't gonna hurt you."

"We want it all, everything you've got," Terry shrieked.

Preacher grabbed his wrist behind the hilt of the knife and bent the arm away with ease. Vickie kicked Preacher in the groin. Hot pain exploded through Preacher's body. He gave a terrier shake to Terry and flung the boy across the cabin. The kid cried out when he struck the rickety table and sent it crashing to the floor. He quickly followed while Preacher came to his feet.

Small pebbles bit into the bare soles, and Preacher was thankful that he wore moccasins most of the summer and spend time barefoot. Vickie came at him again. She bit him on the belly, just above the drawstring top of his long john bottoms.

"Ouch! Don't do that, dammit," he barked.

Preacher's thumb and forefinger found the nerves at the hinge of Vickie's jaw and pressed firmly. Her mouth flew open, and he yanked her off her feet. She instantly began to kick. Sighing away the last fragment of any regret, Preacher began to administer to her a solid, tooth-rattling shaking.

It reduced the slender girl to hysterical tears in a matter of seconds. He gave her a single, hard swat on her bare bottom and hurled her onto the upper bunk across the room. "Now, you stay there, hear?" he growled.

Preacher turned in time to see Terry lunge at him. He sidestepped and smacked the youngster alongside the head. Stunned, Terry lost his grip on the knife. Preacher yanked Terry high in the air and shook him until sobs nearly choked the boy. With them both relatively calmed, Preacher lighted his lantern and sat them, draped in blankets, at the table.

"Someone goin' to tell me what that was all about?"

Terry and Vickie exchanged silent glances. Preacher leaned close to their faces.

"You'd best one of you open up. I don't abide sneak-thieves. Nor those who abuse a body's hospitality. Turns out you're guilty of both. I promise it will go easier if you do. You—" he nodded to Terry—"you said I was famous. Then you must know that if I am who I said I was, an' you crossed me, I would squeeze the life out of both of you and never blink an eye. I could skin you alive, an' not feel a pang." He loomed over Vickie. "I could eat your liver."

Vickie turned deathly pale, and her lips trembled. "Oh, no—no. *Please!*"

"Then you'd best be tellin' me what's true and what's not."

Terry mopped at the single tear that ran down his downy, soft cheek. "We—we were abandoned by our parents more'n a year ago. They hated us, said we were even more violence prone and bloodthirsty than they themselves. There weren't no other mean fellers. We been out here ever since. We've lived since by takin' things from unsuspecting travelers we come upon who were dumb enough to take us in."

"Like me." Preacher prodded, his mad not entirely quenched.

"No, not like you," Terry hastened to correct. "You're different all together. Not like them at all. I—I kinda like you, an' I'm sorry we tried to rob you."

"If I hadn't whupped you, would you be sayin' that?"

Terry looked at Preacher in naked horror, and his face dissolved. "You—you're right. We're both awful, ugly kids." He buried his face in his hands and sobbed wretchedly, no longer a would-be killer, only a small boy alone and frightened.

Uncertain as to what to do, Preacher decided to hog-tie them for the rest of the night and take them along with him to Trout Creek Pass. Surely someone at the trading post would be able and willing to take them under charge.

Pacing the polished granite floor caused the purple stripe on the hem of the tall man's toga to ripple like a following sea. Through the window, beyond his broad shoulders, the western peaks of the Ferris Range gave off a rose glow from the rising sun opposite them. The newborn orb struck highlights from the rings that adorned six of his eight fingers and the gold and silver ornaments on his bare forearms. Anger gave his long, narrow face a scarlet hue that clashed with his sandy blond hair. He reached the limit of the large, airy room and turned back. Before he spoke he drove a fist into an open palm.

"Five men have failed to return and no one says anything about it? Why was I not told of this at once?" he demanded of the other man in the atrium.

"The centurion of the guard did not consider it an important event, First Citizen."

The sandy-haired man shook his head sadly as he examined the other. He saw a burly man, with wide-set legs, thick and muscular, protected by shiny brass greaves. A barrel chest, encased in the brass cuirass of a Roman officer, rode above a trim waist and was topped by a full neck and large, broad-faced head. The horsehair-crested helmet tucked under one huge arm seemed a part of him. His white and red kilt was skirted by brass-studded leather strips. On his feet, the plain, brown leather marching sandals. Taken together these factors made him every inch the mighty general of the Legions of Nova Roma that he was. Yet, he allowed laxness and mistakes to weaken those powerful forces.

Any newly made corporal would have known to see that such vital information be relayed upward. The First Citizen sighed before he spoke. "Gaius Septimus, I chose you as my constant companion and commander of my legions because you are awfully good at what you do. The years you spent with the barbarian army before leaving their ranks for—ah—a freer life are invaluable to Nova Roma. You must maintain the proper attitude among your subordinates. Is that not possible?"

Gaius Septimus Glaubiae, whose real name was Yancy Taggart, responded with such vehemence that it shook the pleats of his kilt and rippled his long, scarlet cloak. "Not when all I have to work with is border trash and frontier riffraff, Marcus Quintus." They had been speaking in the classical Latin as taught at Harvard and other schools in the East. Gaius/Yancy changed to English for the benefit of the three men standing behind him now as he went on. "Speaking of which, I have brought the new men along this morning to introduce them to you. Then there is some rather bad news to relate."

Marcus Quintus raised a hand imperiously. "Spare me that for now. Bring these newcomers forward."

Gaius gestured to the trio standing a respectful three paces behind the general. They came forward and made a halfhearted effort at the proper salute; clinched right fist brought upward to strike the left breast. Gaius winced. Then he took on the formalities.

"First Citizen, let me introduce our newest recruits for the legions. This is Claypool, Grantling, and Wooks. Men, the First Citizen of Nova Roma, Marcus Quintus Americus."

They saluted again, and Marcus Quintus smiled at them, rather like a shark contemplating an unguarded baby dolphin. "You could not have come at a better time. You will be given proper Roman names once you have proven yourselves in the ranks and learn Latin. Until then, your barbarian names will have to do. Gauls, aren't you? The names sound like it. Never mind," he hurried on. "I am entrusting to you an important mission, outside the realm of Nova Roma. Recently, five of your fellows were sent out to capture a notorious individual who might be a threat to Nova Roma. I have learned only this morning that they have failed to return, with or without their captive, the legendary mountain man, Preacher. It is his destiny to fight gloriously in the coliseum," Marcus Quintus continued their briefing.

While he rambled on, Gaius Septimus let his thoughts roam over what he knew of the man who called himself Marcus Quintus Americus and had the audacity to take the title First Citizen. Glaubiae/Taggart considered Quintus to be more than a few flapjacks shy of a stack. Born Alexander Reardon, into the fantastically wealthy Reardon family of Burnt Tree Plantation, Duke of York County, Virginia. He'd had the best education affordable. Only, somewhere around the end of his primary school, Yancy Taggart recalled, Alexander began to fixate on Ancient Rome. As little Alexander grew, so did his mental disorder.

By the time he was graduated from Harvard, he was, as the rough-and-tumble mountain men would put it, *nutty as Hector's pet coon*. When his father died in a riding accident, Alexander inherited. Alex quickly converted everything into gold and set out to establish his dream, **Nova Roma**, the New Rome. Yancy saw Alexander as some sort of combination of Caesar Augustus and Caligula. For, oh, yes, Alexander had a vicious, sadistic streak. And his sexual appetite would have shocked even the emperor Tibirius.

In addition to a number of slaves he had brought from the old plantation, Marcus Quintus had enslaved many Indians, and the hapless victims of raids on cabins or wagon trains. These he had put in charge of Able Wade, now named Justinius Bulbus, master of games and owner of the new Rome's gladiator school. Over the years, Quintus had constructed a replica of the Circus Maximus and the Coliseum of Trajen. And he had revived the practice of throwing Christians to the lions. In this case, cougars, Septimus corrected himself.

The physical appearance of Quintus lent to his persona as a Roman emperor. Although tall and broad shouldered, Quintus was built close-coupled, with a bit of a pot belly, and balding pate, fringed with yellow-brown hair. In a toga, with his gold-strapped sandals and golden circlet of laurel leaves, he looked every inch the emperor. Gaius Glaubiae reflected bitterly that he had deserted from the United States Army for something far better than this madman. Yet, he never sought to put it all aside. He yielded far greater power, and enjoyed far more comfort and luxury now, than even the product of his wildest dreams. He jerked slightly to free his mind as he realized that Marcus Quintus had been addressing him.

"Yes?" he asked coolly.

"I want you to see that these men have everything they will need for a long journey in the wilderness and send them on their way."

"Right away, of course." Septimus gestured for the three scruffy drifters to leave the room. "Now, I have something else. I regret to say it is also the doing of Centurion Lepidus."

"Go on," came Quintus' icy invitation.

Quickly, Septimus outlined the situation in which two legionnaires had been wounded and a third killed, and how the mountain man who had done it had managed to escape. He concluded lamely with the familiar remark: "The centurion saw nothing in that threatening enough to report it until this morning. It happened two days ago."

Rage boiled in the face of Quintus. "He is *Legionnaire* Lepidus as of now. I'd have him in the arena if he weren't a citizen. By Jupiter, this is outrageous. I want you to put out cavalry patrols at once to find the trespasser. He must not be allowed to carry his story to the outside world.

"It is far too early, as you must know, for New Rome to begin a war of conquest among the Celts and Germanic tribes. They, and the barbarian Gauls, must remain in ignorance for a while longer. There are still more of them than there are of us," he cautioned. Then a twinkle came to his eyes. "Although I have a way to make each of our legionnaires the match of any ten of the savages. It will be revealed at the auspicious time."

"And when will that be, Quintus?"

A crafty look stole over the face of the First Citizen. "Mars will make it known to me."

Mars! My God, he has gone totally mad. Septimus shook such thoughts from himself and made to answer. "It shall be as you will, First Citizen. I will not fail you. And Lepidus shall be dealt with. *Ave Caesar!*"

Once Septimus departed, Quintus left his audience chamber and passed down a narrow, dimly lighted corridor into the bowels of the palace. Two turns and down an incline, he came to what appeared a solid, wooden plank wall. Behind a hanging tapestry, his hand found a lever and pulled it away from its recessed niche.

A hidden panel swung outward, and Quintus swept the tapestry aside and entered. Flint and steel provided the spark to ignite a pine-resin torch. The flames danced through the room, banished shadows and revealed a soft, metallic glow from the long racks of carefully maintained weapons.

Several makes of the finest, most modern rifles lined the walls. It always calmed Quintus, gave him renewed confidence, to view his magnificent arsenal. Now he crossed to a rack of Winchester .45-70-500 Express Rifles and caressed the butt-stock of one while he purred aloud his sense of impending triumph.

"Soon now, my beauties. Very soon now, I will call in all of this border trash my good Septimus has recruited and enlisted in the ranks of our legions. Their testing will be done before long. When my legions are welded into ranks, they will be trained and honed into a fine-edged fighting machine. Then we will march to the north against the red savages, acquiring new colonies for Nova Roma." He paused to stroll over to where a rank of six twelve-pound Napoleons rested on their high-wheeled carriages. He patted the muzzle of one affectionately.

"That will test the mettle of my men for the time when they will conquer the true, Gallic enemy to the east. We shall claim every scrap of land from Canada to Mexico and east to the Mississippi. Oh, how mighty shall be the name of Rome!"

Preacher spent an uneasy night. It just weren't natural, but them two brat-kids insisted on sleepin' all huddled together like peas in a pod. Swore they didn't do anything naughty, only that they couldn't sleep any other way. Weren't right at their age. Though from his observations, they seemed a good mite younger actin' than their ages would account for. Boys of twelve were usually on the edge of being *serious*.

This Terrance, or Terry as his sister called him, seemed no more grown up than an eight-year-old. It worried Preacher. Was they both touched in the head a little? Could be, what with all their talk of violence, robbin' an' killin'. Huh! What was he doin' wastin' his time frettin' over the lives of a couple of woods waifs? It didn't sit right. He had set out for Trout Creek Pass to jaw with others about strangers comin' into the High Lonesome. Couldn't take time to stew over a couple of candidates for an institution for wayward children. Take what they had done just this afternoon.

It wasn't warm enough for a man to take a decent bath, what with this late snowfall and the coming of fall. Yet, when they had stopped for their nooning, those two scamps had flung off their clothes and jumped into the creek buck naked. For a swim! Not a hurried bath, mind, just to play. Enough to drive a man to the crazy house. Preacher had yanked them out, one-by-one, and wiped them dry with an old flannel shirt. Gave them a good talking to, he thought. At least until he heard their giggles behind his back. *What was a body to do?*

Hunkered down in the brush, Philadelphia Braddock hid on the edge of a stand of golden aspen and watched the strange men from the valley search for him. He was good, one of the best, and he knew it. Braddock had left a confusing trail that should keep these amateurs meandering through the Big Empty country for a good long time. And they would never catch a glimpse of him.

A good thing, too. His shoulder hurt like the fires of hell.

In a fight he would have to rely on pistols. He remembered the spear cast that had wounded him. It had been from a distance that made a pistol shot an iffy matter. It made him shiver to think about it. Ah! There they went. Hounding off on another false scent. Must be light-headed from all this blood loss. And maybe infection, though he didn't want to think of that. Thing was, those fellers all seemed to be in some sort of uniform.

And they acted like soldiers. But whose? He'd never seen the likes in all his born days. Not live ones, anyhow. He had to get back to Bent's Fort and tell someone what he had stumbled onto.

Through the haze of fatigue and weakness, Philadelphia Braddock recalled that Trout Creek Pass lay a lot closer. That would have to do, he decided. He couldn't hold out much longer than that. Quietly he eased back into the aspens, their brittle yellow leaves giving off a dry bone rattle as they quaked in the slight breeze.

With a maze of zigzags over the next hour, Philadelphia Braddock left the last of the thoroughly confused soldiers far behind. When he lined out on the trail south out of Wyoming Territory, headed for Trout Creek Pass, he had time to reflect on the men he had seen. *Funny,* he mused, *they looked like them fellers I seen in paintings of the Crucifixion of Christ.*

He held that thought until he made night camp and refreshed himself on broiled rabbit. He could sure use some bison. Man feeds himself regular on bison heals right fast.

Chapter 5

Thin ribbons of white smoke rose above the saddle that separated Preacher and his young charges from the trading post in Trout Creek Pass. Preacher had never been so weary of a self-imposed duty as this one. Had this pair been grown up, their bones would be picked clean by buzzards and coyotes by now. Being as how they were children, he felt obliged to spare them and bring them to folks who would see to their proper upbringing.

Although, he had to admit, it might be too late. It was written in the Bible that a child must be made straight in his ways by the age of seven or he was lost to righteousness. It was a hard thing to think of little nippers of eight, nine, ten or eleven roasting forever in hell because they had not been brought up right the first seven years of their lives. That was deeper theology than Preacher had delved into for a long while. He shook the images from his mind and plodded on. Terry and Vickie sat astride the pack saddle frame on a not-too-willing horse.

"When we gonna get there?" Terry asked.

"Yeah. We've never beened there before," Vickie chirped.

"You've never *been* there," Preacher corrected the girl. She made a face. "That's what I said."

Preacher calculated the angle of the sun. "We'll be there

by mid-afternoon. Those are the noonin' cook fires, an' ol' Kevin Murphy's smoke house you see beyond the rise. He makes the bestest smoked hams. An' his bacon will melt in your mouth."

"Ugh!" Terry blurted. "I wouldn't like that. I like to *chew* mine. Is it spoilt or something?"

"Just a figger of speech. Means that his bacon is delicious. Now, you two quit pullin' my leg. I've got a sudden, bodacious thirst a-buildin', an' I figger to tend to it soon as I get you all settled in."

"Where are we gonna stay?" Vickie demanded.

"I been over all that before. You'll go to whoever will take you in."

Fear showed in both their faces. "You won't split us up, will you?" Terry asked nervously.

It was the first time Preacher had seen such emotions displayed by either, except for when he'd broken up their attack on his person. "I'll try not. No tellin'."

"We won't go to different folks." Terry grew stubborn.

"If you send us, we'll run away." Vickie cut her eyes to her brother for confirmation. He nodded solemnly.

Preacher lost hold of it for a moment. "Dang, can't you blessit tadpoles ever make things easy for a feller? I can't guarantee anythin' because I don't know what situation we're gonna come into. Put a rein on them jaws until we get there."

Terry and Vickie resumed a sullen, sulking silence. Terry's pink underlip protruded in a pout. Preacher snorted in disgust.

Preacher reached the trading post at a quarter past two that afternoon. "Tall" Johnson, as opposed to his cousin and partner, "Shorty" Johnson, greeted Preacher from the roofed-over porch of the saloon half of the frontier general store.

"Preacher, you old dog. I heard that you were holed up for the winter." His eyes widened when he took in the children. "You a fambly man now, Preach?"

"Not for any longer than I can help it, Tall," Preacher grumbled. "You wouldn't happen to be in the mood to play father, would you?"

Tall Johnson wheezed out his laughter. "Shorty would never hear of it. He sees kids as somethin' like warts. A feller needs to cut them off his hide as soon as possible. Besides brats needs wimmin. An' we ain't got no wimmin. Decent ones, that is. Just a couple of Utes."

Preacher faked a disapproving glower. "*Utes* is ugly, Tall."

"Not this pair. Now, you just take that back, Preacher, or you buy the first drink."

Preacher's eyes sparkled with mischief. "I'll not take it back, an' I'll be proud to buy you the first drink. Soon's I get shut of these youngins."

Tall Johnson made his point markedly clear. "A feller could die of thirst before that happened."

Preacher chuckled. "Chew a pebble, Tall."

He dismounted and helped the children down. He took them with him into the trading post side of the large, stout log building, which had been built like the corner tower of a fort, the windows narrow, with thick shutters into which firing loops had been cut.

Ruben Duffey, the bartender, greeted him warmly. "Hoo-raw, if it ain't Preacher. What you got there?" he asked. "Sure, it's a couple of partners you left out in the rain to shrink?"

"Nope. They's kid-chillins right enough."

"Seems I might know them, don't I? Lemme get a closer look?" Duffey studied Terry and Vickie a moment, and his full lips turned down in distaste. "I was right, Preacher. Ye've got yourself a pair of genuine juve-nile criminals on your hands, don't ye know? Sure an' it's a better thing if ye bring them with me. I've got the right place for them. Come along then, won't ye?"

Preacher led the youngsters in Ruben's path, out through the back hallway, past a storeroom. Outside, the smiling Irishman directed them to a small storage building with a low door and no windows. He opened up and made a grand gesture with a sweeping arm to usher them inside.

"Faith now, an' we'll just lock those heathen devil's spawn in here for a while. Could be we might get enough men together later on to decide their fate, don't ye know?"

"They are that bad, Ruben?"

"Aye, every bit of it an' more, I'm sayin'."

They walked back inside, and were joined by Tall Johnson. Ruben poured whiskey for the three of them; then he told Preacher the real story behind Terrance and Victoria. His tale, in his lilting Irish brogue, took the listening men back three years.

"There was this family, there was. Name of Tucker. Sure an' they was dressed like rag-a-muffins. Don't ye know, I, like most folks, saw somethin' strange about them right off, we did. A whole passel of kids they had, an' nerry a whole brain among 'em, there wasn't. There was something even more strange about them, wouldn't ye know? This Tucker and his mizus looked enough alike to be brother and sister. Sure an' they could be, for all I know. They squatted around the post for a few days; then they hauled out to a canyon some thirty miles northeast of here.

"That's when things started happenin'." Ruben leaned close and spoke in a confidential manner. "Sure an' things started disappearin'. A man would lose his shovel, or a pig, or maybe a couple pair of long johns a-dryin' on a bush. Then a prospector turned up dead. One day, ol' Looney Ashton come in for a nip of the dew. He swore an' be damned that two nights before, out around his digs, he saw that two-headed pair sneakin' off with a brace of mules that belonged to Hiram Bittner. It was the full moon an' he saw them right clear."

"Stranger things have happened," Preacher said dryly.

"No stranger than this tale gets. Ya see, the two little nippers were stark naked."

Silence held for a moment. Then a cherry-cheeked Preacher added verification to Ruben's story. "They do like to get out of their clothes a lot. I found that out on the way here."

Ruben raised both hands. "So there it is, isn't it?" He took note of the empty pewter mugs and poured more whiskey. "Whose payin' for these?"

Preacher and Tall turned to each other. "Preacher." "Tall."

"Ah, saints preserve us, I'll buy, 'cause it's good to see you again, Preacher, it is."

Ruben dropped coins into the wooden till under the bar and went on to tell how the little depredations, and an occasional killing, went on right up to the present. He concluded with a suggestion. "So, if ye'll tell me what dastardly act you caught this pair performing, maybe it is we can drag the whole family in and dispatch them."

Silence lengthened while Preacher thought over all he had heard. Try as he might, he could not visualize these two as so profoundly evil as Ruben painted them. He had brought the children here to find them a good home, with stepparents who would raise them properlike. He could not turn his back on that promise in good conscience.

"I dunno, Ruben. I'm thinkin' they can be shown the error of their ways and, given a good home, turn out all right."

"Don'cha tell me ye've turned soft-hearted, Preacher, don't ye?"

"Ruben, if you weren't such a little-bitty feller, an' all fraillike, I'd break you in half for sayin' that. I'm the same man I've always been. It's only that I've got to know them over the past two, nearly three days. They can be sweet-tempered enough and obey right smartly, if a firm hand is applied."

"To their bottoms, I presume, I do." Ruben poured another drink. For all of Preacher's disparagement, Ruben stood six-two in his stocking feet and had the body of a double beer barrel.

"I have yet to do that. Though when they come at me to rob me, I shook 'em until their teeth rattled. That seemed to get their attention."

"I wonder why?" Tall Johnson spoke for the first time. "You were serious, then, when you asked me about bein' a poppa?"

"Not really. I know how you and Shorty live. Not a place for kids. No offense intended."

"None taken. There's a feller over a couple of valleys, runs horses. I hear he's been wantin' to take in a couple of yonkers to help work on the place. If that's any help."

"He have a woman to wife?"

"Sure does. And three kids of his own."

"Sounds fine. I might look into it, failing I find any closer."

A sudden shout and curse in French from the cook at the hostelry brought the old drinking friends out of their cups and onto their boots. Preacher, wise in the ways of his captives, reached the back door first. He got there in time to see the cook on his rump, legs splayed and upraised, a pot of as-yet unheated potato soup soaking him from floppy stocking cap to the toes of his moccasins. Beyond him was the open door to the store shed—and the rapidly disappearing backs of Terry and Vickie.

"You had the right of it, Ruben. They's nothin' but trouble," he shouted as he set off afoot in swift pursuit.

Being no stranger to running—Preacher had engaged in

many a foot race against Arapaho and Shoshoni braves—
the rugged mountain man soon managed to close ground
on his quarry. Terry lost more precious space with fre-
quent, worried glances over his shoulder. With longer,
stronger legs and more endurance, Preacher far out-classed
the youngsters. Then providence gave the children a
much-needed break in the form of several habitués of the
trading post.

"Hoo-haa! Lookie there. Ain't that ol' Preacher playin'
the nursemaid?"

"Shore be. Don't he look cute a-high-steppin' it like
that?"

"Shut them yaps, Ty Beecham, an' you, Hoss Furgison.
Them kids is my responsibility."

"Strike me dead. Preacher's done become plumb
domesticated." Tyrone Beecham rubbed salt in Preacher's
wounded pride. "Nextest thing we know, he'll take to wea-
rin' an apron and skirts."

That did it. Preacher slammed to a stop and whirled to
confront his detractors. No man, unless he was a tad light
in the upstairs, ever suggested that a denizen of the High
Lonesome might have sissy inclinations. To question a
fellow's manhood most often called for a shooting.
Preacher did not want to kill these old friends, and sometimes partners, but Beecham had stepped over the bounds.
The least that would satisfy now was a good knuckle drub-
bing.

And Preacher was just the man to deliver it. He stepped
in without a word and popped Beecham flush in the
mouth. Surprise registered in the dark, nearly black eyes of
Tyrone Beecham as he rocked back on his boot heels. He
swung a wild, looping left at Preacher's head, which, much
to Beecham's regret, missed.

Because Preacher did not. He followed his lip-mashing
punch with a right-left-right combination to Beecham's
exposed rib cage. Each blow brought an accompanying

grunt, expelled on the rapidly depleting air in Beecham's lungs. Droplets of red foam flew from Beecham's mangled mouth. His head wobbled with each blow. Right about then, his friend, Hoss Furgison, decided to join in.

He came at Preacher from the mountain man's blind side. Raw knuckles rapped against Preacher's skull, behind his left ear. Sound and sparkles erupted inside, and Preacher stumbled before he delivered a final right directly over Beecham's heart. Then he spun, his left arm already in motion, and drove his back fist into Hoss Furgison's nose.

Blood spurted, although nothing had been broken. Preacher continued his punishment with a right uppercut that clopped Furgison's surprised jaw closed. Furgison stomped on Preacher's right instep. Preacher gritted his teeth and ignored the pain. He still didn't want to hurt these two badly, only drive home the lesson that there was still a lot of spit and vinegar in this old coon. Everyone witnessing their battle had seen two-on-one plenty of times, sometimes even four or five. Most had seen Preacher handle those odds with ease. It didn't take long for the betting to begin.

"I got a cartwheel says Preacher pounds them both onto their boots," Tall Johnson declared.

An old-timer next to him elbowed Tall in the ribs. "I got me a nugget that assays as one and a quarter ounce pure says those younger fellers will plain bust his bum for him."

Thirty-five dollars, Tall thought. A reg'lar fortune. Temptation, and his confidence in Preacher, overcame his usual prudence and his near-empty purse. "You're on, old man."

Preacher made to dodge between his opponents, then stopped abruptly and reached out to snag the fronts of their shirts. He thrust himself backward on powerful legs and slammed his arms together at the same time. A coonskin cap went flying from the top of Ty Beecham's head as the two noggins clocked together. It was time for them to see stars and hear birds sing.

Preacher did not let up. He shook both combatants like small children and then threw them away. Ty Beecham bounced off the ground and started to get back on his boots. Preacher reached him in two swift strides and towered over the fallen man.

"Don't."

All at once, Beecham saw the wisdom in this and remained down. Not so Hoss Furgison. He came at Preacher with a yodeling growl. Preacher mimicked it and danced around like an Injun, flapping a hand over his mouth in time with the sound that came out. Somehow that further enraged Furgison, who abandoned all semblance of a plan, blinded by the taunts.

He walked into a short, hard right to the chest, which he had left unprotected in order to grapple for a bear hug. Unkindness followed unkindness for Hoss. Preacher stepped in and pistoned his arms into soft belly, until Hoss hung over the arms that punished him. Preacher disengaged his arms and stepped away. Hoss fell to his knees.

"You'd do yourself a favor if you stayed there, Hoss. I wasn't fixin' to do any real harm. Push it, an' by dang, I surely will."

"You win, Preacher. You win," Hoss panted.

Tall Johnson looked to the old man. Grudgingly, the gray-beard dug under his grimy buckskin shirt and pulled out a small pouch. From it he took a large gold nugget, crusted in quartz. Tall reckoned it to be worth what the old feller said.

"You got enough in yer pocketbook to have paid, had yer man lost?" the ancient demanded with ill grace.

Tall puckered his lips and threw the sore loser a wry look. "Well, now, we'll never know, will we?"

"Don't get another hidey-ho goin', Tall," Preacher admonished. "I still have to go after those brats."

"So you do," Tall answered cheerily. "And I wish you the joy of it."

"Dang it, Tall, if my knuckles weren't so sore, I'd knock some of the dust off 'em on that ugly puss of yours." So saying, Preacher stomped off for the front of the trading post and his trusty Cougar.

Preacher reined in and dismounted. The troublesome pair had found a stretch of slab rock which made it impossible to track them. Instead of crossing directly over, Preacher skirted around the edge counter-clockwise, leading Cougar. He had gone only a quarter of the way when he found traces. Something about them bothered him.

Then he saw it clearly. These prints had been made by moccasins, right enough, and Terry had been wearing the pair Preacher had given him. But these were of a different pattern than those the boy had. These marks had been put down by an Arapaho. Preacher continued his search, and found no sign of where the children had left the wide stretch of exposed granite. Had the Indians taken the boy and girl?

One way to find out. He set out to follow the trace left by the Arapahos. An hour later, he encountered their evening camp. Among them he soon found old friends. Bold Pony was an age with Preacher, and in fact they had spent several summers as boys in their late teens together. Now the Arapaho settled Preacher down to a ritual sharing of meat and salt.

Bold Pony had held his age well, Preacher noted. He still made a strapping figure, his limbs smooth and corded with muscle. He wore the hair pipe chest plate of a war chief and proudly reintroduced Preacher to his wife and three children. His boy was eleven, with a shy, shoe-button-eyed little girl of eight next, followed by a small boy, a toddler of three.

"Makes a feller know how many summers have gone by," Preacher confided. "Last I saw of you, that biggest of yours was still peekin' at me from behind his momma's skirts."

"You have weathered the seasons well, old friend," Bold Pony complimented.

"Yep. Well . . . beauty is as beauty does." Preacher's observation didn't mean a damned thing, but Bold Pony nodded sagely, arms crossed over his chest.

"What brings you into the hunting place of the Arapaho?" Bold Pony got right to the point as he pushed aside his empty stew bowl.

Preacher described in detail his encounter with Terry and Victoria, described them and recounted how they had managed to bowl over Frenchie Pirot and make an escape from the trading post. Bold Pony nodded several times during the explanation, then sat in silence as he lighted his pipe.

After the required puffs sent to the four corners of the world, and the two to the Sky Father and Earth Mother, Bold Pony drew one more for pleasure and passed it to Preacher. "We know of these children," he said with a scowl.

Preacher repeated the ritual gesture and sucked in a powerful lungful of pungent smoke. "Do you now? Any idea where they might be right now?"

Bold Pony accepted the pipe back, puffed and spoke. "I may know that. My son and his friends,"—he nodded to the other lodges in the small encampment—"range far on their boyish hunts. It is possible they saw these young white people not long ago. It is possible that they are with their no-account family in a canyon not far off. One that is hidden from the unskilled eye."

"Is it also possible," Preacher asked after another drag on the pipe, "that you can give me directions on how to find that canyon?"

A hint of smile lighted the face of Bold Pony. "It is possible, old friend. I could tell you simply to follow your nose. They are dirty, an unwashed lot. You can smell them from far off. Or I could tell you to follow your ears. There are many children there, and they seem to squabble all the while—very noisy. Or I could tell you to journey half a day to the east until you come to a big tree blasted by the Thunder Bird. There you would find a small stream that comes from a narrow opening to the north. Follow that and you will find them."

"I am grateful, old friend."

"It is good. Now we must eat more or my woman will be unhappy."

"I'd rather to be off right away. But—" he looked up at the stout, round-faced, beaming woman and waggled one hand in acceptance—"I reckon another bowl of that stew wouldn't do no harm. Half a day will put me there a mite after the middle of the night. I can hardly wait," he said to himself with sarcasm.

Chapter 6

Eight men, dressed in the traditional diaperlike loin cloths and heavy, spike-studded sandals, marched out of a stone archway after the clarion had sounded and the portcullis had been raised. Four of them looked entirely unwilling. They had every reason to be, considering that they were captives from an ill-fated wagon train, not professionals as were their opponents. When the eight reached the lavish, curtained box, they halted and raised their weapons to salute the *imperator* in the sanctioned words.

"Ave Caesar! Morituri te salutamus!"

And, right here on the sands of the Coliseum of Nova Roma, they really were about to die. At least the four pilgrims, who possessed a woeful unfamiliarity with the odd weapons they had been given. One had a small, round, Thracian shield and short sword. The second had the spike-knuckled *caestus* of a *pugilist*—a fistfighter. The third had a net and trident of a *retiarius*. The fourth bore a pair of long daggers, with small shields strapped just below each elbow, in the style of the Midianite horsemen. The professionals bore the appropriate opposing arms. They looked expectantly beyond their soon-to-be victims of the *imperator*.

Marcus Quintus Americus rose eagerly and gave the signal to begin with his gold-capped, ivory wand. At once, the gladiators ended their salute, each squared off against his primary opponent, and the fight commenced. Shouts of encouragement and derision rose from the stone benches filled with spectators. Many of these people, the "citizens" of New Rome, had been here for years. Not a few had formerly been the inmates of prisons and asylums for the insane. Whatever their origins, they had acquired a taste for this bloodiest of sports. That pleased Quintus, who resumed his seat on the low-back, X-shaped chair beside his wife, Titiana Pulcra, the former Flossie Horton of Perth Amboy, New Jersey.

"Rather a good lot, this time, eh?" Quintus asked the striking blonde beside him.

Pulcra/Flossie tossed her diadem of golden curls and answered in a lazy drawl. "Come, Quintus, you know the games bore me. They are so gruesome."

From her far side, the small voice of Quintus Faustus Americus, her son, piped up. "But that's what makes them so exciting, Mother."

Pulcra gazed on him coolly. "I was addressing your father, Faustus. Really, Quintus, for a boy of ten years, he has truly atrocious manners."

"Eleven, my dear," Quintus responded. "He'll be eleven on the nones of September."

"Which makes it all the worse. He needs a proper teacher. There's geography, history, so many things, including manners, he should be taught."

"Eleven is a good enough time to begin formal education," Quintus countered. "A boy needs to be free to indulge his adventurous spirit until then, doesn't he, son?" he added fondly as he reached across his wife to tousle the youngster's yellow curls.

Quintus Faustus Americus had his mother's coloring, her gray eyes and pug nose as well. A thin, wiry boy, he had inherited his father's sadistic traits. He enjoyed tormenting small animals and treated all other children as inferiors.

Gen. Gaius Septimus Glaubiae summed up the lad best, as being mean-spirited, filled with a deep-seated evil.

"Yes, Father. Oh, look!" Faustus blurted, pointing to a small, nail-bitten finger at a fallen man on the sand. "He's gone down already. I *told* you he was too old and frail. You owe me ten dinarii."

"Done, my boy. Right after the games end," Quintus responded laughing.

Out in the arena, the oldest immigrant lay in a pool of blood, his life slowly ebbing, while the professional gladiator who had downed him with a simple, straight sword thrust with his *gladius* stood over him. He looked up at the box. Quintus gave him the sign to dispatch the unfortunate.

A short, sharp scream came from the old fellow when the *gladius* pierced his heart. To the left of the unfeeling gladiator, a sturdy young farmer, who had been bound for Oregon, smashed a surprising blow to the face of his opponent with the *caestus*. Blood flew in profusion. A chorus of boos came from the audience.

"I say, rather good!" Quintus cheered on the amateur. "Smack him another one."

Before the brave farmer could respond, his opponent's length of chain with the spiked ball at the end lashed out and struck him solidly in the chest. Yanked off his feet by the effort to extract the spike point from the deep wound, the farmer fell face-first to the sand. His opponent closed in and stood above his victim while he swung the wicked instrument around over his head. The farmer rolled over, eyes wide with fright, and lashed out with his blade-encrusted fist. The tines dug into the partly protected calf muscle of the professional gladiator, who leaped back with a howl.

"He's going to die anyway, isn't he, Father?" The small hand of Faustus tugged at the edge of his father's toga.

"Yes, of course, they all are."

Gray eyes alight and dancing, Faustus clapped his hands. "Oh, good."

Two attendants rushed from the gladiator entrance portal to help the wounded professional off the sand. Another, armed like a Nubian, complete with zebra-print shield and long spear, took his place. He quickly finished off the second of the four pilgrims. With the farmer dead, that left only two. Faustus grew more excited with each feint and thrust of the four men before him. He stuffed his mouth with popped corn, a feat made difficult by the broad, wet smile that exposed small, white, even teeth, like those of a wolverine. A great shout came from the crowd as one surviving immigrant stumbled over the body of the first slain and went to one knee.

"Oh, splendid!" Faustus squeaked as the gladiator in Thracian armor swiftly closed on the off-balance amateur.

With cold deliberation, the Thracian swung his curved sword and cleanly decapitated the downed outsider. Faustus bounced up and down on his cushioned chair, his breathing roughened, as little gasps escaped his lips. His eyes grew glassy. He moaned softly as the headless corpse toppled sideways to flop on the sand. To his right, his mother gave him alarmed glances.

"Hasn't it been quite a good day at the games, my dear?" Quintus remarked idly to Pulcra.

"Yes, I suppose it has. Apparently Faustus thinks so."

Faustus licked his lips repeatedly now and groped for more popped corn while he fixed his lead-colored eyes on the death throes of the last captive. A low, soft moan escaped as the hapless man breathed his last.

Quintus spoke in low, confidential tones to his wife. "I only hope the men I sent will be successful. And, that they get back in time for the birthday games for Faustus. We will have the spectacle of spectacles when that living legend, Preacher, is on the sand. What a crowning event that would be for the boy's birthday!"

* * *

Preacher had other things on his mind at the time. Slipping unseen through the woods in late afternoon, he spied out the Tucker compound shortly before sundown. To grace it with the name of compound, Preacher reasoned, had to be a gross exaggeration. It consisted of a low, slovenly cabin, the second story of which seemed to have been added as an afterthought. A rickety corral stood to one side, partly shaded by a huge old juniper. The mound and recessed doorway of a root cellar occupied space on the opposite side. Preacher spotted right off a dozen brats.

They stair-stepped from a toddler of maybe two to a gangly youth of perhaps fifteen. The younger ones went about blissfully naked. The older ones were every bit as ill-clothed as had been Terry and Vickie. While Preacher observed, he began to note that all of them appeared to have some physical or mental defect. All except Terry and Vickie, who showed up in the last glimmer of twilight.

Perhaps they had a different poppa, Preacher speculated. Or another momma? A moment later, the situation became clearer when three adults showed themselves in the tree-shaded, bare, pounded ground in front of the cabin. The man and one woman looked enough alike to be twins, both with black hair and eyes, like most of the children. Preacher recalled the speculation on the part of Ruben Duffey.

That seemed to make more sense when he studied the other woman, whom he saw to be fair, with long, blond hair and pale blue eyes. To Preacher's consternation and as an assault on his sense of propriety, the man was openly affectionate to both women. He hugged them and bussed them heartily on their cheeks, held hands with the dark one while she gathered in the children.

Like most youngsters, the black-haired tribe frisked about some, holding out for only a few minutes more before surrendering to the indoors. The dusky woman cupped hands around her mouth and loosed a raucous bellow.

"All right, that's enough. Inside this minute or no supper for anyone."

They scampered for the house with alacrity. All except Terry and Vickie, who doddled along as though reluctant to face a meal in that house. Terry continuously scuffed a big toe against the firm ground. Preacher continued to watch until the adult trio disappeared inside. Disgusted by this *manage a trois*, and apparently an incestuous one at that, he settled back to lay plans of how he would deal with them. Some of the alternatives he came up with seemed distinctly grim.

Deacon Phineas Abercrombie and Sister Amelia Witherspoon stood stock still, thoroughly astounded. The men who surrounded their three-wagon train, which comprised their "Mobile Church in the Wildwood," looked exactly like soldiers of Ancient Rome. Yet, how could that be? Here, in Wyoming Territory, in the Year of our Lord 1848? One of them came forward into the flickering bonfire-lighted clearing from the surrounding woods.

He bore a large Imperial Eagle on a long, wooden rod, the laurel leaf wreath, which, like the eagle, appeared to be of pure gold, below it encircling the famous emblem of Rome—**S.P.Q.R.**, *Senatus, Populusque, Romanus*—Deacon Abercrombie recalled from his Latin studies. *The Senate and the Roman People*. What madness could this be?

One, obviously their leader, stepped forward, haughty, fierce-eyed, every inch the domineering Roman centurion in his crested helmet, cuirass, kilt and greaves. "What are you barbarians doing in the realm of Nova Roma?"

New Rome? the stunned deacon echoed in thought. That

accounted for it, then, his dizzied mind supplied. Still unsettled by this apparition, he spoke in a near babble.

"Why, we are not barbarians. We are Christian missionaries. We have come to spread the word of God to the heathen lands, to do the work of the Lord."

Cutting his eyes to a subordinate, the centurion commented, "Good Christians, eh? We'll get to see the lions again, eh, Sergeant?" His smile was decidedly unpleasant, Abercrombie thought.

His *contubernalis* produced a wicked smirk. "That'll be just jolly. I hope they save this fat windbag for last," he went on, with a nod to Abercrombie.

Astonished that he had no difficulty in understanding their Latin, Deacon Abercrombie flushed with crimson outrage at the depiction of himself. He was about to launch into an indignant protest when the centurion's next words stoppered his mouth.

"All right, round them up and get them in chains. First I want to ask a couple of questions." He turned to Abercrombie and spoke in perfect English, albeit heavy-laden with Southern accent. "We're looking for a man. He's been wounded, and probably traveling slow. Have any of y'all seen such a person?"

While Deacon Abercrombie struggled to frame a reply that included a protest, a startled yelp from his right silenced him. "Take your hands off me," Sister Amelia snapped. "I'll not abide any man to touch me, let alone a rude stranger."

A hard-faced legionnaire barked back at her. "Shut up, lady. The *contubernalis* says we put you in chains, that's what we're going to do."

"Why, the very idea! The nerve. How dare you treat us like this?"

"Sister, please," Abercrombie interrupted in an attempt to defuse the situation.

The soldier acted as though he had not heard a word.

"Because we've got the weapons, Sister. Now, cooperate or suffer for it."

Quickly the twenty men and sixteen women were rounded up and thrust into chains. Few voiced protest. Several women began to pray aloud or to sing hymns. The crude legionnaires laughed among themselves and made nasty comments. Soon, the job had been completed. The centurion had as yet to get an answer to his first question. He bore in on Deacon Abercrombie.

"You seem to be in charge of all this. I want an answer, or it will go hard on y'all."

Abercrombie tried to compose himself. "What was the question?"

"Have you seen a wounded mountain man?"

"No."

"That's all? Just no?"

Deacon Abercrombie sighed in frustration. "No, none of us has seen such a person."

Eyes narrowed, the centurion put his face right in that of Abercrombie. "You sure y'all ain't hidin' somethin'? Not bein' entirely truthful?"

"Sir, I am a churchman. I do not lie."

The centurion pointed contemptuously at the Bible tucked under the deacon's left arm. "You ask me, that's all you do, is lie. Pack of nonsense between those leather covers. I'll ask one more question, then all of you back in your wagons or on horses. Have you, by chance, encountered a scruffy man goes by the name of Preacher?"

Several of the cowed missionaries shook their heads in the negative. Abercrombie drew himself up and glared defiance at his interrogator. "Of that, I am absolutely certain. Had we encountered anyone with so outlandish a pretension in this wilderness, we would have remembered."

"Am I to take that to mean no?" the centurion asked with a sneer.

"Precisely. It is possible that this wounded man you are looking for saw us first and hid himself. So it may be that we have passed by on his way, without knowing so. As to this Preacher you are speaking of, there's been no such person."

"So, if you are going to stick to that, you might as well load up. Maybe the curia's torturers can loosen some tongues."

"Where are you taking us? I demand to know," Abercrombie unwisely blustered.

"To New Rome, of course. Y'all are in our country without permission. The First Citizen will likely call you all Gallic spies. Whatever he decides, it's the coliseum for the lot of you."

At the news of this, wailings and lamentations rose among the faithful.

By ten o'clock that night, Preacher had it figured out. He waited until midnight, then glided out of his place of concealment. Bent low, walking in moccasins for quiet, he crossed the clearing to the tumble-down cabin. A stench of neglected, spilled food and unwashed bodies leaped out to assault him. His nose wrinkled. The shambles of an outhouse behind the log structure gave evidence of being a total stranger to quick lime.

He had been up wind of the wretched hovel, Preacher recalled as he closed on the rickety front porch. He made not a sound as he crossed the warped, weathered gray boards to the front door. There Preacher paused while he reached for the latch string. Strangely, considering where the cabin was located, it hung outside and welcoming.

Preacher eased it upward and winced at the slight scraping sound the bar made as it raised. When it came free, Preacher waited tensely, one hand on the butt of a Walker Colt. After half a hundred heartbeats, with no alarm shouted from inside, he eased the door inward. Another mistake in wild country. The hinges should provide added resistance against anyone trying to break in. Sucking in a breath, Preacher edged around the open portal.

He made not the slightest sound as he entered the smelly structure. He eased the door shut behind himself. A long wait to allow his eyes to adjust to the dimness within. Slowly, objects began to define themselves; a counter along one wall, with crude cupboards above, a cast-iron stove, tilted rakishly because of a broken leg, a hearth and fireplace mantle, a large, leather-strung bed beyond a gauzey curtain. Satisfied, Preacher ghosted past the slumbering adults lying together in a tangle of naked arms and legs.

Carefully, he tested the rungs of a ladder that gave access to the loft where, he surmised, the children slept. He gingerly put weight on the first and thrust upward. No squeal betrayed him. Preacher took a second and a third step. Surprising for the slip-shod construction in general, the ladder still did not give off a single betraying squeak. In due time, Preacher brought his head above the level of the elevated flooring.

Here and there in the starlit darkness he made out the huddled forms of sleeping children. Beyond their relaxed bodies, he found Terry and Vickie, asleep together as usual, fully clothed, their arms around each other. With that accomplished, he went back down to take care of the adults.

What a ruckus that caused! Perhaps Preacher had not chosen the wisest way of extracting brother and sister from the family bosom. What he picked to do was stand in the middle of the cabin floor, by a large table, and bellow his intentions to the parents.

"All right, folks. I want you to stay tight in that bed. Don't even twitch an eyeball. I've come to take those towheaded youngins outta here to someplace decent."

In the next instant, the women erupted in a hissing,

spitting, nail-clawing cat-fight mode. Bare as the day her mother birthed her, the blond one hurled herself at Preacher with fingers arched into wicked talons. He deflected her with his raised left forearm, but not before she raked his cheek with sharp nails.

"You bastid, keep yer filthy paws off my babies!" she howled.

"They as much mine as yorn, Purity. T'same man fathered them as mine," the other wailed, closing in on Preacher's right.

Preacher back-peddled and shoved the black-haired vixen away, toward the bed. Silas Tucker had not moved a hair. He sat in the middle of his harem bed with a bemused expression on his ugly face. He laughed at the startled look on Preacher's face.

"You done kicked a hornet's nest, mister," he declared through his mirth.

Preacher shook his head, determined not to be bested by a pair of fillies. "More'n likely *they* did."

They rushed him again and Preacher had to duck. A sizzling kick hurtled toward his groin. A hot rod of pain thrust into the outside of one thigh. This could prove more than he bargained for, the mountain man reckoned. Shouts from the loft joined in the pandemonium. Blond curls flying, the mother of Terry and Vickie charged in while Preacher held off the other woman.

Her fists pounded ineffectually off the broad, firm back of Preacher while she cursed and spat at him. He felt the wetness of her saliva on his neck, and it rankled some.

"Enough of that," he bellowed as he backhanded her in the upper chest.

She went tail over tea kettle across the table. Preacher had time to gather only a short breath before the dark one bounced in the air and came at him with fists flying. He ducked, blocked what he could and took a stinger on the already black eye. It smarted more than he would admit.

All of a sudden, the other woman had him around the ankles.

She held on for dear life. It deprived Preacher of any means of avoiding the wrath of the one throwing fists and feet at him. It began to look worse with every passing second. Then Silas Tucker roused himself enough to get into the fray. He came at Preacher low and mean, a long, wicked-bladed knife held in one hand.

Chapter 7

Preacher swatted the blonde aside and cleared a space for a swift kick. His moccasin toe bit into the meaty portion of Silas Tucker's right forearm. The knife went flying. Preacher quickly hurled the furious black-haired gal full into Tucker's chest.

Tucker went flying with a yowl, which quickly turned to a bellow of pain when his bare rump made contact with the still-hot stove. He came off it mouthing a string of curses, and his hand groped blindly for a weapon. He found the short, hooked, cast-iron stove poker and launched himself at Preacher. Evidently the blond woman had learned her lesson. She hung back and satisfied her outrage by hurling metal cups, plates and other cookery items at the dodging figure of Preacher.

A white-speckled, blue granite cup clipped him as it zinged past Preacher's ear. He jumped to the opposite side, to have his moccasin caught up in the tangle of legs and arms of the dark hoyden. Abruptly, he went down in a heap. Black curls swirled over his face as his wily opponent scrambled on top of him. She immediately began to pummel him with her fists.

"Git back, woman," Silas Tucker bellowed. He came at Preacher with the poker.

Faith Tucker rolled off Preacher in the wrong direction

and at the wrong time. The descending poker caught her on the exposed point of her left shoulder. Her shriek of pain ended with a curse; then she added for emphasis, "Idjit, you done broke it."

Stunned, Silas looked upon his injured sister and dropped the metal rod as though it had been heated in the fire. Preacher used the brief interlude to spring to his feet. A large stew pot filled the entire range of his vision. He ducked and received only a slight graze across the top of his head. That bought valuable seconds for Silas Tucker.

He bolted to the corner of the cabin, by the fireplace. There his hands closed around the smooth, use-polished, hickory handle of a double-bit axe. He hefted it once, grinned stupidly and advanced on Preacher's back, the deadly tool held high, ready to split the mountain man's skull. He learned how stupid he had been a moment later.

A shout—he thought it could have come from Terry— warned Preacher. He spun, took in the menace, now only four feet from him, and drew in one swift, sure motion. The hammer came back on his .44 Walker Colt and then dropped on the primer of a brass cartridge. Fire flashed in the cabin in time with the comforting buck of the six-gun in Preacher's hand. Smoke billowed, but not before Preacher saw the axe fly from Tucker's hands, and a spray of blood from the back of the man's shoulder showered both of his women.

They went berserk. Howling and screaming, they rushed to their wounded male, like females in a pride of lions. They completely ignored Preacher, who turned and headed for the loft. Pandemonium reigned above. Suddenly awakened, the children shrieked, screamed and wailed in confusion and fear. When he loomed up through the opening in the loft floor, Preacher rightly read a warning of fight in some of the older youngsters. Two of them came at him before he gained purchase on the flooring.

Preacher cuffed one of them aside and climbed off the

ladder. He lightly felt a stinging blow to his side and yanked a naked, spluttering boy of ten or so off his feet. Preacher gave a disapproving cluck of tongue against teeth as he tossed the lad into three more who advanced on him.

"Enough!" he roared. The command had its effect.

Some of the smaller children clapped hands over their mouths and went round-eyed. Yet another brat challenged him. Growing amused, Preacher batted at the ineffectual blows in the manner of a man swatting mosquitos. His diversion lasted only a moment, until the sturdy boy of about thirteen snapped a kick at Preacher's groin. It connected before he could block, though without striking any vital targets. Preacher popped the youngster high on the cheek in reply and sat him down on his bare butt. The rest drew back in fear.

Preacher advanced toward the dormer alcove where Terry and Vickie had withdrawn. "C'mon, I'm takin' you outta this hell-hole," he commanded.

Accustomed to mistrusting all adults, Terry responded with defiance. "What if we don't want to go?"

Preacher cocked his head to one side. His expression clearly declared that he would not take a lot of that. "Do I have to hog-tie you, like before, an' drag you outten here? It can be easy or hard, your choice, either way we gotta move fast. 'Cause them she-cats down there are like to recover from their weepin' an' wailin' over their head he-coon and come after me with a vengeance."

"One of them is our momma," Terry continued his challenge.

A flint edge turned Preacher's eyes, and sarcasm his words. "You got any idee which one?"

Terry had not expected that tack. "Why-why, the yeller-haired one, of course."

"If you expect to see her go unharmed, then you'd best move fast. There's knives and forks and things down there that can do a feller real harm. I don't intend to stand around an' let her poke any of them into me."

His head of steam deserted Terry, and his frail chest deflated under the raggedy shirt. "We'll go."

"Yes, Preacher, we'll go with you anytime," Vickie added, her cobalt eyes dancing in starlight.

"Now, that's more like it. 'Sides, you'll be better off where I'll be takin' you, better by far than livin' with this sordid riffraff."

Terry produced a pout. "She's still our maw."

Enough had come and gone for Preacher long ago. His face clouded, and his words rang in hollow command. "Git down them stairs. Grab what belongin's is yours, especially any coats."

"Coats? You flang the only ones we had in the fire," Terry protested.

Nonplused, Preacher could only shrug. "Rags. They was mostly rags," he defended his action. "Now, scoot!"

Oblivious to the deep chill, the youngsters scampered barefoot down the ladder. Preacher followed. The thirteen-year-old, still smarting from the punch Preacher had laid on him, shouted after. "Paw's gonna wrang your necks oncest he catchen up to y'all."

Preacher turned his iron gaze over one shoulder. "You tell him to come on, as I reckon it'll be me does the wringin'."

On the ground floor of the cabin, the women still whooped and hollered over the wounded Silas Tucker. Silently, Preacher wished them the joy of it, then led the way to his horses.

"I don't *want* to sit still!" Terry Tucker sassed Preacher from atop the packsaddle at midmorning the next day. "It hurts my behind, ridin' like this."

"You spook that pack-critter an' I'll show you a hurt behind," Preacher warned.

Terry tried his repertoire of cutes. "Why can't I ride with you?" he asked coyly.

"Cougar ain't used to carryin' double," Preacher grumbled.

"He can *learn*."

"Not now, he cain't, Terry. Not no-how," Preacher insisted.

Right then, Cougar's ears twitched. The packhorse whuffled. Preacher reined in sharply and listened. His ears, then his nose caught the message. Injuns! Friendly, without a doubt. Else they would not have let the three whites ride in so close. Preacher nodded, raised his right arm and signed the symbol for peace. Then he waited.

Always perceptive, Terry spoke in a mere whisper. "What's wrong?"

Preacher's lips barely moved. "Cain't you smell it? They's Injuns out there."

Terry's eyes went wide and round. "They gonna scalp us?"

"I don't think so."

Fear and insecurity shivered through the boy's skinny frame. "You don't *think* so?"

"Take it easy, boy. No sense in gettin' them riled . . . if they ain't already."

Preacher signed again. This time a familiar figure walked his spotted pony out onto the trail. Preacher raised in the saddle and signed "friend."

"Ho! Ghost Walker, we meet again."

"Ho! Bold Pony, it is a good meeting."

"The hunting is plenty. We stay to fill our travois." He looked pointedly at the two towheads on the packhorse. "You found them, I see."

Preacher thought over the ordeal of last night, and the

trials of this morning. The kids had taken to being bratty, as usual, right after breakfast. "Yep. More's the pity."

"You would tell me about it?" Amusement twinkled in the eyes of the Arapaho war chief as he rode in closer. He examined Preacher's face. "The parents were not so pleased with parting with their dear ones?"

Preacher grunted. "Sometimes your eyes are too keen, Bold Pony."

He went on to relate the visit to the Tucker house. The more colorful his description grew of the brief fight in the cabin, the more Bold Pony laughed and held his sides. Although unaware of why, the amusement of Bold Pony had an effect on the children. Before long, Terry and Vickie broke into fits of giggles with each revelation Preacher made. It put him in a scowlly mood.

Preacher rounded on them to growl. "That's enough of that." He turned back in appeal to Bold Pony. "You see what I mean? These two have been a pain in the behind from the git-go." Then he told of their morning's fractiousness.

Bold Pony studied on the predicament in which Preacher found himself. At last he answered cautiously, albeit with a hint of laughter in his words. "If my people did not believe that spanking a child is wrong, I'd suggest that you do just that."

Preacher soberly considered his friend's words. "Well," he announced at last, a gleam in his eyes, "these warts ain't exactly Arapaho. So, mayhap a willow switch would be just the thing."

Bold Pony nodded sagely. "I will leave you to your important work. May the sun always rise for you, Preacher."

"May the wind always be at your back, Bold Pony."

Without a backward glance, Bold Pony turned his mount and rode off silently. Preacher turned his attention to the youngsters, who had grown deathly pale. He dusted his hands together and kneed Cougar in the direction of a creek bed, where a long, narrow stand of weeping willows beckoned.

Terry read Preacher's intent in a flickering and blurted his appeal, thick with tears. "Oh, no, you ain't gonna do that. Please. You ain't gonna whup us?"

"You broke my only fire trestle, burnt the cornbread, dang near ran off the packhorse, an' shamed me by jibberin' like a pack o' monkeys in front of Bold Pony. Suppose you tell me just why I shouldn't?"

"'C-'cause Paw always whups up on us somethin' fierce."

Determined now, Preacher ignored the boy. At the creek bank, he dismounted and tied off both horses. Then he selected and cut a suitable willow switch. Stripped of its leaves, it made a satisfactory whirr as he flexed it through the air. Face somber, Preacher walked over to the children.

"You first, Missy," he directed to Vickie.

Reluctantly, she came down from the packsaddle. Her eyes flooded as Preacher knelt and bent her over his knee. He upended the hem of her skirt and exposed a bare bottom. Swiftly, without any show of anger, he delivered four sound whacks. Vickie bit her lip to keep from crying out, but her whimpers tore at Preacher's heart.

Dimly, from memories best left buried, he dredged up images of the few times he'd been thrashed as a boy. Once begun, though, he could not stop in midstream, so's to speak. He set her on her feet and went for Terry.

"Don't touch me," Terry wailed. "I'll git'cha. I'll git'cha in your sleep," he threatened to no avail.

Preacher had him in the strong grip of one hand and hauled the slight lad off the packsaddle. Willow switch between third and little fingers of the other hand, he quickly had the boy's britches down and his wriggling torso over an upraised knee. For only a moment did Preacher hesitate, then six fast, expertly delivered smacks left red spots, but raised not a welt. Returned to his upright position, instead of pulling up his trousers, the silently sobbing boy yanked on his shirt to expose his chest and back.

Angry, fresh red lines, knotted here and there with spots of infection, showed over the welter of earlier scars Preacher had seen in the cave. "See? You're no better than he is, Preacher." Then Terry broke into a gushing flow of tears. Vickie joined him.

Seeing the terrible punishment meted out by the animal who called himself the boy's father and hearing their pitiful sobs tugged at Preacher's heart. Impulsively, he reached out and hugged them to him. He held them tightly while their blubbering subsided.

"Nah—nah, that's all right, yonkers. You ain't hurt that bad this time. An' a feller's got to learn that he does wrong, he's gonna git punishment, swift and sure. It's what distinguishes us from the animals." Preacher stopped and jerked his head back, a surprised expression on his face. "Listen to me; speakin' words with more syllables than my tongue can tickle over. Next thing you know, I'll be takin' to Bible-thumpin'."

Out of their anguish came laughter. Preacher continued to press his case. "Understand, I want things to go right for you. I promised I'd find a home for the both of you, with someone who will love and care for the both of you. An' I'm gonna do it."

Sniffling, Terry and Vickie dried their eyes and padded barefoot back toward the packhorse. Vickie spoke first. "I promise not to give you a hard time anymore, Preacher. Really I won't."

"Me—me, too, Preacher," Terry croaked hoarsely. "It's hard. After so many years of bein' bad, it's—it's a *habit.*"

Preacher answered gruffly, his own throat constricted by a lump of memory. "See that you tend to your p's and q's an' we'll git along just fine."

He restored them to their perch atop the pack animal

and mounted up. Preacher led the way out, much relieved, the children considerably subdued.

Preacher crouched by the hat-sized fire he had built in a protecting ring of stones. He looked up from the skillet of fatback and beans, savoring the aroma that rose. He had found some wild onions, added dried chili peppers, salt and a dab of sugar from his supplies, and water from the creek that flowed soundlessly a hundred yards away.

Only a fool, or a greenhorn flatlander, camped right up beside a noisy mountain creek that burbled and gurgled over rocks and made musical swirls as it rounded sandbars and bends. A whole party of scalp-hungry Blackfeet could sneak up on such a foolish person. Preacher had learned that before his voice changed. It had saved his hair on numerous occasions. He paused in his cooking duties.

"Terry, go fetch that foldin' bucket full of water for the horses."

"Why didn't we just camp by the crick?" Terry offered in a revival of his earlier attitude.

There you go, Preacher thought to himself. Flatlanders an' fools. He drew a breath, ready to deliver a blistering rejoinder, then mellowed. "Because it's foolish, even dangerous, to camp where the sound of water fills your ears and you can't hear anyone sneak up on you. Didn't I explain all that to you before?"

To Preacher's surprise, Terry flushed a rich scarlet. One big toe massaged the top of the other. He cut his eyes to the ground right in front of them. "I—reckon you did. I—I . . . forgot."

"Well an' good. You owned up to it, an' that's what counts."

Unaccustomed to praise for any reason, Terry glowed, his eyes alight and dancing, his cheeks pink for a far different reason. Preacher gave him scant time to rest on his laurels.

"Git on, now. Gonna be dark before long."

After her brother scurried off on his errand, Vickie came to Preacher. With all the natural wiles of a woman, she draped one forearm on his shoulder and bent toward him with an expression of earnest absorption. "When will we be at the trading post, Preacher?"

"Some time in the mornin', provided you two carry your end. We git up, eat, clean up, an' git. All before the horizon turns gray."

Vickie made a little girl face. "Why do we have to wake up so early? I like to sleep until the sun is up far enough to shine in the loft an' I can smell breakfast a-cookin'."

"There's no loft here, an' we be in a hurry," Preacher answered shortly.

"What's the hurry for?" Vickie asked in sincere ignorance.

Preacher studied her a moment. "You don't think your poppa an' them herri-dans of his'n is gonna kick back and say, 'Ol' Preacher done stole our prize pupils. Ho-hum.' "

Vickie's eyes went wide. "You mean . . . they's a-comin' after us?"

"Count on it. Sure's there's stink on a skunk."

Twenty minutes passed, with Terry not yet back from the creek, when Preacher's prediction proved true.

His teeth gritted against the constant pain in his shoulder, Silas Tucker had held steadfast to his determination to exact revenge upon the crazy man who had broken into their cabin and stolen his best earners. Why, then two could steal the gold from a man's teeth without him knowin' it. And the boy, even though Silas had no intention of letting him know it, was turning into a right capable killer.

With those two bringin' in the goods, Silas would soon

have his women dressed in silks and himself in a woolen suit. Reg'lar nabobs they'd be. Then, along comes this mountain wild man and spoils it all. Silas' brow furrowed, and he flushed with mounting anger as he looked down into the small valley where Preacher and the children had made camp. They'd soon see, Silas decided. He turned to Faith and spoke in a whisper.

"Be sure not to hit them brats. I know you're a good shot, m'love. Allus was. That's why I want you to stay back up here and give cover fire, y'hear?"

"I know, Silas, I know. It's that Purity cain't shoot for beans."

Silas gave her a broad wink. "That's why she's comin' with me. I c'n sorta keep an eye on her." He paused and gave consideration to something that had been gnawing on him since Terry and Vickie had been stolen. "You know, I been thinkin' maybe I should git a couple more brats offen her. They's whip-smart, her git."

Faith hid the jealousy that nearly gagged her. "What's wrong with me?"

"We gotta face facts, woman. Those youngins of ourn ain't travelin' with full packs. Somethin's sommat wrong with them."

"They're kin an' kin to our kin," Faith defended stubbornly.

Silas ground his teeth. "So be it, woman. Now you just get ready."

Preacher had poured himself a final cup of coffee when a bullet cracked sharply over his head. He lunged to the side and rolled to where he had rested his Hawken against the trunk of a grizzled old pine. The finely made weapon came into his hands with fluid ease. He turned back to the direction from which the shot had come.

His eyes took in a flash, bright enough in the twilight to

be readily seen, and a puff of gray-white powder smoke. He sighted in the Hawken. The hammer had not struck the percussion cap when a fat lead ball smacked into the tree, two inches above his head, and Preacher flinched in a natural reaction. Bits of wood and bark stung as they cut the back of his neck. That caused his round to go wild. A hell of a shot, whoever it might be, Preacher considered.

"You youngins stay low. Hug the ground."

"It's Silas, come to git us," Terry announced, his voice quavering with his fear of the man.

Preacher mulled that over. "May be, but if so, he's gonna leave his bones here for the varmits."

"No," Vickie wailed. "No, he's gonna kill us all."

More shots came from closer in. Preacher dived for another position. But not before one ball cut a hot path across the top of his left shoulder. He came up in a kneeling position and took aim at a hint of movement among the aspens along the trail. The reloaded Hawkin bucked and spat a .56 caliber ball into the tree line.

A grunt and muffled curse rewarded Preacher's effort. He put the rifle aside and drew one of the pair of new-minted .44 Walker Colts. Another shot came from uphill and forced Preacher into a nest of rocks at the edge of the camp. Vickie yelped, and Terry uttered words that should never be in the mouth of a twelve-year-old. Preacher fired into the aspens and moved again.

Emboldened by Preacher's apparent retreat, Silas Tucker came into view. A red, wet stain glistened in the waning light of the sunset. He had taken Preacher's ball in the meaty flesh of his right side. Enough fat there, Preacher reckoned, to make certain nothing vital had been hit. Still, even a cornered rat had a lot of fight left in him. Silas peered short-sightedly around the clearing and located Terry, hunkered down on the grassy turf. Sudden rage at the boy's defiance blotted out his earlier evaluation of the youngster's worth. He raised a single-barrel pistol and took aim on the boy's slim back.

A hot slug from the .44 Colt in Preacher's hand shattered the radius of Tucker's right forearm a split-second later. Impact caused his .60 caliber pistol to discharge skyward. Instinctively, he dived for a hiding place. Preacher started after him when another shot cracked from the aspens.

This could be a little harder than he had expected, the mountain man admitted to himself. He sure hated to kill a woman, but who else could Tucker have with him?

Chapter 8

In rapid succession, three bullets sought a chunk of meat from Preacher's hide. He banged off two fast slugs at the hidden shooter and again moved to better cover. A fallen log seemed to offer the best advantage.

He had barely settled into position and begun to lament the lack of his rifle when a scurry of movement in the open caught his attention. On hands and knees, Terry scampered toward Preacher, Hawken, powder horn, ball pouch, and cap stick slung over his slender back.

"Git back, you little varmint!" Preacher shouted at him. Terry kept coming. "You need these," he countered.

Well, damned if I don't, Preacher acknowledged to himself.

Terry reached the fallen tree in under five seconds. He paused as a ball smacked into the bark inches above his towhead. Then he adroitly flew over the rough surface of the trunk. At once, Preacher snatched the rifle from the boy, taking time only to pat the lad on his head in gratitude. A moment later Silas Tucker made his move.

"Git out there, woman," he bellowed as he charged, a pistol in each hand.

First one, then the other barked, lead cracked overhead and Terry scrunched lower behind the tree. The ramrod still in the barrel of the Hawkin, Preacher set it aside and answered the two-person charge with his .44 Walker Colt.

A freak change of direction on the part of Silas Tucker caused Preacher to blow the heel off the degenerate's right boot.

Preacher exchanged six-guns as Tucker and the woman bore down on him. Biting his lip, Preacher sighted in on the center of the woman's chest. She fired at him, missed by a long ways, and Preacher saw her golden hair streaming from under a bonnet. The mother of Terry and Vickie! Imperceptibly, Preacher changed the aiming point of his Walker Colt and triggered a round.

Hot lead tore a shallow crease along Purity Tucker's rib cage. She stumbled and sprawled headlong in the dirt. "Momma!" Vickie screamed.

Silas Tucker did not even miss a stride. Hobbling, he came on, determined to end it right there and then. Preacher was glad to oblige him. His .44 Colt bucked once, then again. Silas Tucker jolted to a stop, turned partly away from Preacher and looked down in amazement at the twin holes, which formed a figure eight in the center of his chest. He made a feeble attempt to raise his weapon again, then crumpled bonelessly into a heap on the ground, while his lifeblood pumped into his chest through a shattered aorta.

Made haunting by distance and the echo effect of the basin, a curse descended upon the living in the clearing. "You baaastarrrd!" A shot followed.

Calmly, Preacher completed the loading drill for his Hawkin and hefted it to his shoulder. "You up above. You can give it up now. No harm be done to you if you do."

He waited for a reply. It gave Faith Tucker time to reload. A shower of bark slashed down on Preacher and Terry. Preacher grunted his reluctance away and took aim. He fired with cool precision. A weak wail that wound down to breathless silence answered his shot.

"D'ya git her?" Terry asked hopefully.

Preacher sighed heavily. "I reckon so, though I sure am

sorry to have had to do that. Killin' a woman's not somethin' a man lives with easily."

"She treated us as mean as Silas did." To Preacher, Terry's justification lacked conviction enough to vindicate what had been done. "What about our momma?" the boy asked.

Recalling the grazing wound he had given the woman, Preacher came to his boots. He swung a leg over the downed tree and cleared it with ease. Terry quickly followed. Rapid steps brought them to the side of the fallen woman. Preacher knelt and felt her wrist for a pulse. He found one, strong enough, if a bit rapid. She moaned, turned her head, and opened one eye.

"My babies?" she asked first off, surprising Preacher. "Are they all right?"

"Sure are, ma'am," Preacher assured her. "Terry's right here beside me."

"Silas would have killed them. Sure enough that black-haired bitch sister of his would have."

Preacher broke the news with the usual mountain man's lack of delicacy. "She won't be doin' no killin' anymore."

"She's dead?"

A straight face hid Preacher's feelings. "Yep. She was tryin' to take my head off with that rifle."

"She is—er—was a good shot."

"Shootin' downhill throws a body off some. Now, there's somethin' I need ask of you. In fact, I damn well insist you do it. Once I get you patched up, I want you to go back for the rest of the children and lead them to the trading post at Trout Creek Pass. If you have any love for your own two, you had best do as I say, and mend your ways. You're gonna have to do that, and give them the care and love they deserve."

"They have done some terrible things," Purity offered in faint hope of sloughing off her responsibilities.

"I know that. But they's youngins an' were forced into

the life they led. You're not and nuther am I. We got rules to live by, and for you to teach this pair. Let me get on about fixin' you up."

"What if I just leave here an' keep on goin'?" Purity sought yet for a way out.

Preacher cut his hard, gray gaze to her eyes. He remained silent long enough to cause Purity to flinch. "Well, consider this. If you have any idea of duckin' out, with or without those other youngsters, keep in mind that I will hunt you down and drag you in to the tradin' post, where they'll be obliged to put a rope around your neck."

Purity Tucker swallowed hard and nodded her understanding. With her children gathered around, Purity sat still while Preacher cleaned up the shallow gouge in her side, packed it with a poltice of sulphur, moss and lichens, and bandaged it. Then he lighted the fire and set out the makings for coffee.

"Come morning, you set out north; we're headed south." Purity started to raise her voice in protest. Preacher showed her the palm of one hand to silence her. "Nuf said. Now, do I have to tie you to a tree?"

Purity shook her head and settled down to sip coffee in silence. An hour later everyone lay down for a restless sleep.

Dawn seemed to come extra early. After one of Preacher's substantial breakfasts, Purity sent Terry to recover the horses used by her and the dead pair. Preacher admonished the boy to gather all of the weapons. When Terry returned, Preacher tightened the cinch on one animal and helped Purity to mount. Without even a goodbye to her children, she rode away to the north.

Terry turned imploring blue eyes on Preacher. "Think she will really come back?"

Preacher shrugged and snorted. "I wouldn't bet more'n a nickel on it."

With that he assisted the boy and his sister into the

saddles of the newly acquired mounts, and the three rode off toward Trout Creek Pass.

Philadelphia Braddock looked up from the moccasin he was repairing on the front porch of the trading post at Trout Creek Pass. He worked with a bison bone awl and a curved, fish rib bone needle. He sewed the sinew thread in precise, neat stitches. He was putting on thick, smoke-cured, bull hide "traveling" soles. The soft, distant sound of approaching horses had attracted his attention. Philadelphia squinted his bright green eyes. The brown flecks in them danced in the tears this produced. He peered over the top of the hexagonal half-glasses perched on the bulb of his nose.

From the cut of him, that big feller in the lead could be Preacher, he reckoned. Philadelphia ignored a small twinge in his shoulder wound, which was mending nicely under the care of an unlicensed doctor, who had journeyed west, turned to trapping and later to hard drink. To his credit, the pill-roller abstained religiously whenever he had a patient who needed the best of his professional skills. Yep, he saw more clearly now. Couldn't be anyone else.

Philadelphia shook his long, auburn hair in eagerness, which made his over-large ears, with their long, floppy lobes, flutter like wings. He snorted his impatience as it seemed to take forever for Preacher and the smaller folk with him to descend the high grade to the northern saddle out of the pass. Did his eyes play tricks, or did those folk ride some ways behind Preacher?

No, he realized a minute later as Preacher drew near enough to make out his face. They was kid-folk. Preacher with a pair of brats? And whose, at that? Be they his? Philadelphia literally danced with urgency, yet he knew he would learn the answers soon enough. Preacher swung clear of the main trail and entered through the gateway of the palisade that surrounded the trading post compound. Already, his keen vision had identified Philadelphia, and he waved enthusiastically to his old friend.

"Whoo-weee! Preacher, as I live an' breathe," Philadelphia exploded, unable to contain himself.

When Preacher reined in and dismounted to tie off his big-chested roan stallion, Philadelphia rushed forward with a wild war whoop. Preacher spun and met him at midway. Both had their arms extended and charged into a chest-banging embrace that raised a cloud of brown around them. At once they started a toe-stomping fandango that raised more dust. The longer they went on, the more violent their greeting became. Concern began to crease the high, smooth forehead of Terry Tucker. At last he could contain himself no longer.

"Hey! Hey, mister, go easy," he shouted at Philadelphia. "He's been wounded."

"Hell, that's never slowed Preacher none, boy. Mind yer business an' we'll mind ourn."

All of the improved deportment he had learned in Preacher's company deserted Terry. He looped the reins around the saddle horn and jumped off the back of the horse acquired from the Tuckers. "That done it!" his squeaky voice declared. "Damn you, old man, I'm gonna kick you right in the balls!"

Terry charged forward, only to be plucked off his feet by Preacher, who grabbed the boy by the tail of his shirt and the waist of his trousers. Terry squirmed and made ineffectual thrashing with his legs and arms. "Lemme go! Lemme go. I'll fix 'em, Preacher."

Their hugging welcome ended by Terry's intervention, Philadelphia Braddock stepped back and turned those startling green eyes on the lad. He cocked his head to one side. "Whose your bodyguard, Preacher?"

"He's not a bodyguard," Preacher growled. "He's a bother."

Philadelphia gave Preacher a fish eye. "Since when you be travelin' with children?"

"Ain't the first, won't be the last time, nuther," Preacher rumbled.

For some reason, Preacher felt loath to go into all the lurid details behind Terry and Vickie. Philadelphia would find out soon enough, and no call to embarrass the youngsters. He clapped Philadelphia on the shoulder and changed the subject.

"I got a powerful thirst, Philadelphia. Be you buyin'?"

"I be. Best get these babies some milk." He made a face at the prospect. "An' a sugar stick to suck on; then we can settle down to some serious depletin' o' Duffey's supply of Monongahela."

Preacher lowered Terry to the ground and looked hard into the boy's eyes. "You gonna behave yourselves? Not gonna pull a stunt like last time?"

Terry shrugged skinny shoulders. "We ain't got nowheres to go."

"That mean you'll stay?" Philadelphia cocked an eyebrow at Preacher's manner of speech.

"Yes."

"Yes, what?"

"Yes, sir."

"Fine. Now, go help Vickie down an' scoot inside. Ask Duffey for something to eat. C'mon, Philadelphia. Let's go wet our throats. By the by, I see you look a mite peaked. Been off your feed a little?"

"Not perzactly. It's a long story. One best told over a flagon of rye."

Once settled at a crude table in one corner of the saloon side of the trading post, Philadelphia related his tale of the strange city and the stranger men, how they dressed and acted and that they spoke in a funny, foreign tongue. When he had finished, they drank in silence for several long minutes while Preacher wondered on it. At last he made up his mind.

Slapping a big palm on the damp wooden tabletop, Preacher spoke plain and clear while he looked Philadelphia straight in the eye, his own orbs hot with invitation. "I reckon I needs to see these people. I want to learn all I can about them."

"Suits. I got my curiosities aroused, too."

"There's more. That city you told me about. Seems I've heard of it somewhere before. Something is nigglin' in the back of my brain pan, says I've seen such a place, or read about it. Buildings is all white, right?"

"Seen 'em with my own eyes," Philadelphia assured him.

"Hummm." Preacher drained his pewter flagon and hoisted it to signal for another round. Ruben Duffey complied with a will. When he departed, Preacher went on. "Thing that really rubs me where I cain't itch is all these folks, an' all those buildin's bein' out here in the first place, an' me not knowin' a thing about it."

Philadelphia tried to hide his own eagerness. "Well, I cain't say I blame you a bit for that."

"Tell you what, Philadelphia. When that shoulder wound you got from them downright unfriendly fellers heals, I'd be mightly beholden if you were to lead me to this strange city growin' in the wilderness."

For an instant, relief flashed in those brown-flecked, green eyes. "You got yourself a deal, Preacher, that you surely do."

Chariot wheels rattled noisily over the smooth, nicely set cobbles of the wide Via Iulius, which led to the foot of the Pontis Martius—the Hill of Mars—and the gladiator school of Justinius Bulbus that nestled in its shadow. Swelled with pride, young Quintus Faustus Americus held the reins as he stood beside his father. Although usually the task for slaves, driving the chariot had made the day into a golden one for the patrician boy. His bony chest swelled even more when he slowed the horses at the proper time and received a fond pat on the head from his father.

He halted the animals in good order and stopped the vehicle without incident, due to the hand brake, an improvement over the original design. Bulbus stood in the gateway to welcome them. Born Able Wade, Justinius Bulbus looked the ideal director of a school for gladiators. His thick, burly body, low brow, jutting jaw and hairy ears made a clear statement of his past as a brawler and a thug.

Cunning and ruthlessness lighted his pale blue eyes, rather than intelligence. When recruited out of the dockside slums of Boston by Marcus Quintus, Able Wade had been more than enthused by the proposition made to him. He had babbled on and on about various weapons and fighting styles of the ancient gladiators. It became clear to Quintus that Wade had likewise shared the benefits of a classical education. Only the lack of a keen intelligence, and his father's sudden loss of a vast fortune, such as that of the Reardon's of Virginia, had ended that schooling abruptly and left Able in the lowest strata of society. Quintus could not have cared less. So long as the newly named Justinius Bulbus could run a school to teach men exotic ways to slay their fellows, he would be amply rewarded. Quintus now returned the greeting salute of the master of games and dismounted from the chariot.

"You are just in time, First Citizen." Bulbus had had little difficulty becoming fluent in Latin, recalling snippets of it from his years in the finest schools. "We are about to begin the morning session. Come, join me in my box."

"With pleasure, good Justinius. You know my son, Quintus Faustus?"

"Of course—of course. A bright lad." Bulbus peered

closely at his guest. "He certainly takes avid interest in the games."

"That he does. The games to honor his birthday are coming soon. I am sure you have prepared a magnificent program?"

"Oh, yes. You see, we have this new contingent of Christians. I'm sure the boy will fair pop a—ah—button at the spectacle I have planned."

Faustus brightened even more; his face writhed in expectation. "Christians, Father? How wonderful." He clapped his hands in emphasis.

Bulbus directed his important guests to the small, private box that overlooked the practice arena. Exactly one-third the size of the coliseum, it afforded space for only two pairs to fight at once, or for rehearsal of half of one of the "historicals" or farces at one time. The rest of the participants in the latter two presentations looked on from behind bars set into one wall of the arena. They studied the movements of their counterparts, then changed places and did the routine themselves. Final rehearsals would naturally be held in the coliseum. Bulbus made sweeping gestures to cushioned chairs in the front row, and father and son seated themselves.

Bulbus raised an arm. "All right, let it begin."

"Will Sparticus fight first?" Faustus asked the master of games.

Offended by this slighting of his star gladiator, Bulbus answered sharply. "Certainly not. Sparticus is my grand finale. Lesser-knowns are for opening the show. Today, and this will be a preview of your birthday games, young man," he confided, "Baccus Circus will open. He has taken to training well and shows real aptitude."

"He's a magnificent specimen." Quintus brought the subject back to Sparticus, who had appeared while Bulbus spoke to the boy, and was working out in a side cage that could be seen beyond the wall of the arena. He nodded to the huge black man.

"Our legionnares found him wandering on the high plain east of here. No one in Nova Roma knows his real name. He's a runaway slave, of course. And, frankly, I don't care to know his identity. He is the best gladiator in Nova Roma, as I am sure you know. But, a slave is a slave, so Bulbus owns him. Sparticus likes his work.

"He's never been intractable or rebellious. That must also be true from before he came here." Quintus paused. "If you examine him closely, you'll find there's not a whip mark on him."

Bulbus was not to be put off a lecture on his favorite subject. "Timing is everything with the games. It is like the theater." He would have said more, but the shriek of wrought-iron hinges interrupted as the Porta Quadrila opened and two gladiators stalked out.

Big and burly, the first blinked at the sudden, bright sunlight. Thick muscles rippled in his shoulders and arms. He bore a spiked club and a small shield. His opponent, Baccus Circus, carried a round "target" shield and a twin-bladed dagger. Of nearly sword length, it made a formidable weapon. They paced across the sand and saluted Bulbus and his distinguished guests.

"Begin," Bulbus commanded in a bored tone.

That this would not be a fight to the death soon became obvious. The middle-range fighter squared off with Baccus Circus, and they began a series of set-piece drills. They consisted of four or five varied attacks, at the end of which, they engaged shields and weapons and rotated a quarter way around the arena. Both men soon glistened with sweat. Their smoothly shaven bodies sparkled in the sunlight. The speed of their drill increased with each engagement. Quintus, bored by so routine a performance, looked to his son.

Faustus stared intently at the battling men, jaw slack, lips parted, eyes glazed with excitement. His breath came harshly from a dry throat. Slowly, the pink tip of his tongue slid out and licked his lips. It was not, Quintus noted, a quenching gesture, rather one of unhealthy arousal for a boy so young. He quickly cut his eyes back to the contestants.

Their contest ended in the third quarter, when Baccus caught one of the spikes in the head of his opponent's club between the two blades of his weapon and disarmed the man. Quickly, Baccus stepped in and laid the flat of his dual knives against the throat of the other.

"Well done!" Bulbus shouted over his applause. "You are doing magnificently for a beginner, Baccus Circus." He turned to Faustus. "Now it is time to see some real blood flow, eh, lad?"

Faustus brightened. "Yes! Oh, yes . . . please."

Bulbus made a full arm gesture and called to his staff. "Bring in Sparticus. And . . . one of those teamsters from the freight wagons, I think."

Baccus Circus winced when he heard that. He hated the name given him. To himself, he would always remain Buck Sears. He hated what he had been forced to do. Most of all, he hated it when a fellow teamster captured in the high plains or the mountains was slaughtered needlessly to slake the appetites of some crazy fool who believed he lived in ancient Rome.

Buck had been brought here six months ago, after his train of freight wagons had been ambushed by men in the weirdest outfits Buck had ever seen. When he heard them speaking a foreign language, Buck at first thought the country had been invaded by the Mexicans. Only two years past the big war with Mexico, it seemed likely to him. Put into chains and forced to walk with the other survivors and captives, his first sight of New Rome stunned Buck.

This could not be. He didn't have a lot of book-learning,

only six years of grammar school. Yet, he had a haunting suspicion that he should recognize the sprawl of shining white buildings and the seven hills they occupied. Rage almost earned him the lash when the captives had been led to the market, stripped, and sold like those unfortunate slaves in the South. He and half a dozen others had been purchased by a man whose function he did not then know.

Then he had been taken to the gladiator school. No stranger to fighting, the idea did not bother Buck, until he discovered that the contests were to the death. For all his moral objections, eventually he became resigned to it. At first, their training had been in English, with some Latin words worked in as they grew familiar. Now he spoke Latin with all the ease of those born in Nova Roma. Buck glanced up as they neared the portal and passed through with the first sensation of regret he had known in a long time. Against his better judgment, he quelled his reflections and remained at the iron lattice to watch the slaughter of his brother teamster.

Sparticus gazed coolly at the sorry specimen standing beside him. This wouldn't take long. The best Sparticus could recall, this one had not been at the school more than a month. What could he have learned in that time? Oh, well, the white boss say, "You do dis," you sho'nuf do it. He say, "Do dat." You do that. He shrugged it off and raised his arm.

"Ave Maestro! Morituri te salutamus."

"Give us a good show, Sparticus," Bulbus told the big black gladiator.

Now, that would be a hard one. Sparticus lowered his arm and prepared to step into position. Frightened to desperation, the shivering teamster did not stand on formalities. He struck swiftly and without warning. Only by the barest of margins did Sparticus elude death.

"Bis dat qui cito dat!" the spoiled little boy jeered down at Sparticus.

He gives twice who gives quickly, Sparticus thought angrily. That was supposed to apply to charity—snotty little brat. He made a quick lunge. His opponent dodged clumsily. Sparticus pressed in on him.

With wild slashes, the hapless teamster defended himself. Metal shrieked off metal, a spark flew. Then another. The clash of blades became a constant toll of chimes. In a surprisingly short time, the teamster's wrists began to weaken. Sparticus played with him like a cat with a mouse. Small cuts began to appear and stream blood from the chest, arms, and belly of the amateur. Eventually the big black man grew bored with his sport. Swiftly, with a confusingly intricate movement, Sparticus struck again.

The short, Etruscan sword went flying. For all his furious action, the teamster went pale. Sparticus loomed over him. Tasting defeat, his opponent lowered his shield and let his chin droop to his chest. Sparticus looked up at the box.

Before Bulbus could signify the fate of the teamster, Quintus interposed a request. "Since it is close to his eleventh birthday, and he will be *imperator* at the games in his honor, I'd like to make a present to Faustus at this time."

"Go ahead, Your Illustriousness."

"Faustus, you may have the honor of deciding the fate of this wretch."

Faustus gaped. "Thank you, Father." Then young Faustus leaned even farther over the arena and thrust out his arm, the fist closed, thumb extended. With an exalted expression of ecstasy, he made a quick, jerking movement and turned the thumb down.

Chapter 9

By the third day after their return to Trout Creek Pass, Preacher had to admit he had all he could handle to keep up with Terry and Vickie. Much of it centered around behavior *they* considered entirely ordinary, yet that which most of society frowned upon, or saw as outright immoral. If ever he was to find a family to take in the youngsters—he had long since given up on the return of their mother—Preacher felt obligated to instruct them in manners and other socially acceptable conduct. To that end, he established an open-air classroom in a stand of fragrant pines.

Squirrels chittered and birds sang from above while the children sat on the low stumps of trees harvested to build the trading post. It was going the same way it had during the past morning and afternoon sessions. Terry and Vickie sat politely, still and attentive, their cherubic faces upturned to Preacher. One-by-one, Preacher dealt with their moral short-comings, as he and his culture saw them. They listened, he felt sure of that. Then, in the most innocent of words, they dismissed entirely every manner of conduct that differed with the way they wanted to do things. This afternoon's session had finally gotten around to their sleeping habits.

"Now, over the past days, I've been tellin' you a lot about how decent people do things. Also about the sorta stuff the good folk would never do. Some of it, I'm sure you understood. What sticks in my craw is how you manage to make it sound out of the ordinary and your way to be better. To tell you straight out, that cain't be with what I want to talk about this afternoon. There comes a time— ah—when youngins reach a certain age—that decent folk just don't countenance them sleepin' together, if they be of opposite sorts."

"What do you mean?" Vickie asked, all sweetness and light.

"Take the two of you. Terry is twelve, you ten, Vickie. Decent boys and girls of those ages don't sleep together nekid, especially if they's brother and sister. They don't even sleep together in nightshirts. Or even like you sometimes on the trail, in all your clothes."

"Why not?" Terry prodded.

Preacher's face clouded. "We been over this before. You both told me you knew about animals an' stuff. How they get their young. An' that sort of thing went on a lot among that brood of kids with your folks. Well, if you an' Vickie continue to sleep like you do, other folks are gonna think it goes on betwixt you."

"But we *don't!*" they protested in chorus.

"I know that. But decent folks are gonna *think* you do."

Terry took on an expression of sullen defiance and challenge. "If they think those kinda thoughts, seems to me they cain't be too decent themselves."

Preacher's cheeks turned pink. "Now, there you go, boy. Deep in my heart I know I'm right, especial for brother an' sister. Yet, danged if I don't have to agree with you. Only dirty minds could dwell on those sort of notions."

Terry and Vickie gave him a "so there you are" expression. Preacher cut his eyes from one to the other, stomped the ground and turned away. Images of Indian children, all curled up together in furry buffalo robes, marched through his head. Over his shoulder he announced to them. "All right. Dang-blast it, all right. School's out for today. At this rate, I'll never make you fit to live among proper folk," he grumbled to himself as he walked off.

Preacher did not get off the hook that easily. Early the next morning, over a plate of fried fatback, beans and cornbread, he found his good mood spoiled by Anse Yoder, the factor of the trading post. A strapping, amiable Dane under most circumstances, Yoder had his visage screwed up into the best expression of disapproval and anger that his broad, pink face under a tousled mop of straight, blond hair could produce.

"Py collie, Preacher, those little hellions of yours have gone too far. Hoot Soames got howlin' drunk last night. When he passed out, I put him to bed in the common room. Those devil's spawn snuck in there, and they dribbled molasses all over Hoot's face. Then they cut his pillow. He woke up this mornin' thinking he had been tarred and feathered."

Preacher's first response was to let go an uproarious belly laugh. He restrained himself and considered the situation over another cup of coffee. From what he had dragged out of Terry and Vickie, the children saw their former criminal activity as high adventure. It had taken some powerful talking for him to convince them to find another outlet for their charged spirits. He hadn't expected them to turn to stinging jokes on the customers at the trading post. He would definitely have to do something about it. That decided, Preacher prepared to relax, when Anse dropped the other boot.

"Just the other day it was Olin Kincade near to killing himself trying to get out of the chicksale. Ya see, what those *schnorrers* of yours did was to rig some rattlesnake rattles under the bench in there, right by the opening. They had dem so that they made a purty real sound when a string got pulled. So, what happens? Olin went in to answer a call of nature. Those brats waited until he got settled all well an' good, then let go. Olin came up off that seat with a roar and nearly tore himself apart tryin' to get out. He forgot he had slid the latch bolt closed when he went in."

"Now, that's nothin' that ain't been done before," Preacher defended, all the while making a powerful attempt to hold in his laughter.

"*Aver*, that's grown men playing a gag on one of their fellows. No, sir, I tell you, Preacher, I tell you true. You have to find a home for them and damned fast at that."

Grumbling to himself, Preacher finished his breakfast and looked up from his place. "All right, Anse, I'll do just that." With that he left to find Terry and Vickie.

"Nope. Sorry, but I heard about them two already. What I want is for them to be as far away from me and mine as anyone can get."

Preacher found the story the same wherever he went. Not a single household wanted anything to do with Terry and Vickie Tucker. After one silver-tongued effort to beguile a thick-set timber cutter, and father of four, the man rounded on him, double-bit axe in hands made hard by work.

"No, sir. I'd as leave have the devil hisself move in. Why that pair would pollute my youngins faster than a man can say go. Those Tuckers was nothin' but trash. Plain ol' hill trash from the west part o' Virginny. They just natural have the morals of an alley cat and the urges of a three-peckered billy goat. It's those mountains they growed up in, I think. Even the Injuns called them big medicine. The Cherokees, before they was removed from Carolina and Georgia, wouldn't set up a camp there. Only went for religion things. Whatever it is, it's done twisted those white folk that live there. Say what you might, Preacher. I just ain't gonna have them here."

After they rode off, Preacher's keen hearing hadn't any difficulty picking out the faint sound of sniffling. The children had dropped back slightly, so he turned to see what caused it. Tears filled the eyes of Terry and Vickie. Caught in an embarrassing moment, Terry took a quick swipe at his nose with the back of one hand.

"There ain't anyone wants us, is there, Preacher?" Vickie asked, her voice shaky with weeping.

Preacher roughly cleared his throat. "We ain't seen *every-one* yet."

"Don't matter," Terry fretted. "No one's gonna take us in."

Eyes squinted, Preacher challenged the boy's conviction. "I wouldn't be takin' any wagers on that, Terry." He sighed and looked back at the roof peak of the cabin they had just left. "Maybe we ain't gone far enough."

"But, you already said we'd come ten miles from the tradin' post."

Exasperated, Preacher snapped. "Right enough. Only maybe that ain't far enough, considerin' the reputation you Tuckers has hangin' on you." Then he softened his harsh words. "We'll look some other places."

After four more refusals over the next three days, Preacher had about talked himself into accepting Terry's cynical version of their predicament. He had even agreed with his doubting side that given another turn-down, he would return to Trout Creek Pass and keep the kidlets with him, at least until he had time to journey to Bent's Fort and hopefully hand them off to some unsuspecting pilgrims a-westering.

What an awful thing to do to both sides, he thought charitably a few minutes later. He had crested a low saddle and saw beyond a tidily build, inviting-looking cabin of two stories, complete with isinglass windows that sparkled in the afternoon sun. Thin streams of smoke rose from two well-constructed chimneys at opposite wings of the building, one of them of real brick. A lodgepole rail fence surrounded it, and defined a generous kitchen garden to one side of the front. A corral of the same material featured high sides, and a sided lean-to for sheltering stock from summer's heat and spring's rain.

A half barn abutted it, no doubt the remaining portion dug into the hillside. Then, on another small knoll, a huge, gnarled old oak shading the plot, he noted three small, fresh mounds of dirt behind a split-rail fence that guarded the final resting place of those who had departed. Preacher confounded the youngsters by removing his battered, floppy old hat and holding it over his heart as he rode past. At a hundred yards, he halted and hailed the house.

"Hello, the cabin!"

"Howdy, yourself," came the answer from the doorway to the barn, where a man appeared, a pitchfork in one hand.

"We be just the three of us. These youngins an' me are friendly, oncest you get to know us."

Their host squinted, then nodded. "I know you, right enough. Know *of* you anyway. You're Preacher, right?"

Terry groaned. "We might as well ride on," he said under his breath.

It didn't escape Preacher. "Now, hold on there, boy. Let him tell us that." To the stranger, he answered, "That I am."

"Ride on in, then. My wife's bound to have coffee on the stove. An' there's buttermilk or tea for these two," he added.

"My goodness, *tea*, as I live and breathe," Preacher said from the corner of his mouth. It brought a giggle from the children. "Mighty obliged, mister."

Down at the cozy, large cabin, Preacher learned that they were Cecil and Dorothy Hawkins. Two rug-crawlers clung to Dorothy's skirts and peeked shyly at the mountain man, their eyes widening when they saw Terry and Vickie. Tears sprang into Dorothy's eyes as she studied the tow-headed youngsters.

"Are they . . . yours?" she asked in a low, grief-roughened voice.

"No, ma'am. They're not. You might say they is orphans. At least for sure on their pappy's side."

Cecil interrupted in an effort to spare his wife more sorrow. "You can tell us about it over some plum duff and coffee, Preacher."

"Obliged, Mr. Hawkins."

"Call me Cecil."

They entered the house, the children showing the nervous excitement common to the good smells they picked up. This Mrs. Hawkins must be the best cook in the whole world. Seated at a large, round oak table in the center of the main room of the cabin, Preacher felt himself relaxing—this was a house full of love. This was also a house that had experienced a recent tragedy. He longed to ask about it directly. Good manners prevented him from doing so.

"What brings you this way, Preacher?" Cecil asked as though their earlier conversation had not occurred.

Preacher took a big bite of the plum duff that had been set before him. "Well, like I said, Cecil, I'm lookin' for a home for these tadpoles." His hosts lowered their eyes. Preacher made a note of that. *Strike,* he thought in a cliche that had originated long ago in some army's surgical tent, *while the iron is hot.* "Did I say anything wrong?"

A long silence followed. At last, his eyes brimming with unshed tears, Cecil Hawkins answered him. "No, Preacher. Likely you said something right for the first time in a long time."

Always sensitive to the emotions of others, Preacher spoke softly. "How's that, Cecil?"

"We—we just lost our three oldest youngsters, Preacher. It was—was a fever that sort of sprang up all of a sudden. There ain't any doctors anywhere around here, not for a thousand miles. We didn't know what to do. We doped them with goose grease and sulphur, put cold cloths on their heads and chests. Nothin' did any good. It . . . took a long time. We buried the last only three days ago."

Sadness drew down the corners of Preacher's mouth. "I'm powerful sorry to hear that. The Almighty gives and He taketh away. It don't matter no-how what we wish things to be; the final outcome is in the hands of our Maker. I don't imagine, in your grief, you'd be willing to take on responsibility for two wild colts?"

Cecil and Dorothy cut their eyes, one to the other. A long, silent message seemed to pass between them. Cecil drew a long breath. "You say they are orphans?"

"Same as. I kilt their pappy, an' their momma has gone and deserted them."

"Are they well-behaved?" Dorothy asked.

Preacher took a deep breath, then let the words out in a rush. "They could be, if you've a strong hand and a powerful will of your own."

Another silent conference occupied the Hawkins. Cecil scooted back his chair and came to his boots. "You'll excuse us for a moment?"

"Certainly. Take your time."

Preacher drummed his fingers on the table while the pair left the cabin. Their muted voices came from outside. He could make nothing of what they said. At last, they returned. Expectation lighted Dorothy's face. Cecil cleared his throat, his hands doing nervous things with one another.

"We—ah—we talked it over, Preacher. Losin' those babies almost destroyed Dorothy. Our oldest was about an age with this boy. You're Terry, right?" Terry nodded, his face blank. "We know that—that you could never completely fill the place in our hearts that Tommy held, but would you . . . will you try?" He turned to Preacher again. "We want them to come live with us. We need their help and we believe they can help us. Our other two are so young, and Dorothy says she is—in a family way again. With a new baby, she'll need someone to help with the chores. So, if it's all right with you, Preacher, and you children? We'd like to make you a part of our family."

Beaming, Preacher came to his boots. "Them is splendid words, Mr. Cecil Hawkins. I'm mighty happy for all of you. What do you say, Terry, Vickie?"

"Yes," Terry blurted. "I—I guess."

"Your two children are so cute, Mrs. Hawkins," Vickie made her thoughts known. "I'd love to help you with them, if I may."

"Of course, my dear." She opened her arms, and Vickie rushed into her embrace.

Preacher cleared his throat, finding it quite restricted. "Well, then, that's all settled. You two might as well stay here. Philadelphia an' I are headin' to the northwest to look into what is going on in the Ferris Range. I'll drop off your things on the way by."

"Oh, thank you, Preacher," Vickie squealed, rushing to hug him and turn up her face for a kiss.

"Thankyou, thankyou, thankyou, Preacher," Terry squeaked. Then he pushed out his lower lip in a pout. "But I really would like to go along and see those strange men."

"Another time, boy. Not now. Well, I'd best be gettin' on my way. Thank you folks for bein' such good Christian souls." He cut his eyes to the ceiling. "I'm sure the Almighty will give you a fittin' reward." If he was aware of the irony, he didn't show it.

Filled with deep-rooted satisfaction, Preacher rode away some ten minutes later. Terry ran down the lane to catch up and leap up on Preacher's leg. The mountain man caught the boy, which freed Terry's arms to give Preacher a big hug.

"I'll never forget you, Preacher. Goodbye." The boy turned his head away to hide the rush of tears.

Preacher released the lad and brushed a knuckle at the corner of one eye. "Goodbye to you, Terry. Remember what I taught you about the things decent people expect of children."

And then he rode away.

Preacher counted the days on his fingers. He had been off on his quest for a week and a half by the time he raised the chimneys and rooftops of the trading post. He gigged Cougar into a fast trot. When he drew near, he recognized the stout figure of Philadelphia Braddock on the front porch. Philadelphia spotted him at the same time and bounded down the steps, his body visibly charged with energy. They met fifty yards from the double cabin that formed the trading post.

It instantly became obvious to Preacher that Philadelphia had made great strides in his healing. His face held its usual ruddy color, and he bounced around like a young puppy. His eyes twinkled with mischief as he questioned Preacher.

"I see you're alone. What happened, Preacher? Them two runned off again?"

"No. I found them a home. Let's go get the trail dust out of my throat and I'll tell one and all at the same time."

Inside the saloon, Preacher downed one pewter flagon of rye, signaled for another and waited for it to arrive. All the usual hangers-on crowded into the room. Their faces revealed how anxious they were for a good tale. Preacher soon obliged them.

"Yep, my quest ended in success," he declared the obvious. He went on to detail the search for a home, told of the Hawkins family and the evident pleasure Terry and Vickie had shown at being taken in by them. He concluded with an observation.

"Strange enough, they did not appear too happy about partin' with me. For all I drubbed their heads and switched their bottoms."

Ruben Duffey answered with sober sincerity. "Not so strange, Preacher, I'm thinkin'."

Preacher blushed. "What's done is done. Tomorrow Philadelphia an' me are off to the Ferris Range. I aim to get me a good look at these strange soldiers, or whatever they are."

"Need some company, Preacher?" a couple of the regulars shouted.

Preacher pursed his lips and gave it a moment's thought. "That's mighty nice of you, Clem. You, too, John. This first time, though, I reckon the less of us they see, the better. But stick around. Might be we'll want some help later on," he added prophetically.

Buck Sears sat on a stone bench in the dressing room of the public baths of New Rome. Gathered around were five of the new "gladiators." One man wore a hard, belligerent expression. He ground a fist into one palm when Buck told them that the penalty for refusing to fight or attempted escape was death in the arena. No matter how many a fellow fought and bested, he would die there on the sand.

"I don't wanna go back to those cells they keep us in. Filthy, smelly, with rats and other critters runnin' around at night. I'm willin' to risk death to get out of here."

"Good. That's one of you."

"What are you getting at, Buck?" the pugnacious one demanded.

Buck studied him a long moment, until all five leaned

toward him in anticipation. "I've found a way out of here. I need me some good men, ones with enough fire and fight in them to make an escape."

"But you just said yourself that the penalty for attempted escape is death," one pilgrim with a receding chin and pop-eyes protested.

Buck stared him down. "That's only *if you get caught.* I don't intend to. From what I hear, the trouble is in those big ol' black dogs this so-called Bulbus keeps. We try to break out of the school, they give the alarm, and any who doesn't get eat up are condemned to the arena."

"How'er you gonna get around that?"

Buck studied the mousey little fellow. "I'm tellin' that only to those willin' to go with me."

Pop-eyes averted, the captive gladiator turned away. "Well, I—I don't know. At least, we're still alive."

Anger flared in Buck's chest. "For how long? Sooner or later, we're all gonna be pitted against Sparticus. When that time comes, you'd better be ready to meet your Maker."

The angry one looked at his timid companion with contempt. "Count me in. I don't aim to be dog meat, an' I sure know I'm no match for Sparticus."

Buck cut his eyes to the others, hope shining in his face. "How about the rest of you?"

Slowly they turned away, shame-faced, and muttered feeble excuses. Disappointed, Buck stomped out through an archway to wait for the guards to escort them back to the gladiator school on the Field of Mars. A moment later, his only recruit joined him. He extended a hand.

"M'name's Fletcher. Jim Fletcher. When do you reckon on doing this?"

Buck gave him a relieved look. "Soon, friend Jim. Soon's we have enough to make it work."

* * *

Later that night, when the inmates of the school slumbered in deep exhaustion, the skinny pilgrim with the receding chin quietly left the small cell he occupied, released by a discreet guard. Blinking in the bright light of oil lamps, he was brought into the presence of Justinius Bulbus. Bulbus studied him over fat, greasy fingers.

"You have some information for me?" he asked, licking meat juices off the tips.

Voice shaking, the informant replied softly, "Yes, I have."

Bulbus gestured to a tray piled high with steaming meat. "Have some roasted boar. It's really quite delicious. Besides, you need the meat to build you up."

In spite of the obvious intent behind the invitation, the betrayer indulged himself greedily while he informed Bulbus of what he had overheard at the baths. Bulbus listened carefully and considered the problem a while before making answer.

"You have been most helpful. Circus is a splendid gladiator. It would be a shame to lose him. Perhaps . . ." Bulbus paused, thinking. "Yes, perhaps a flogging, administered by Sparticus, would serve as an object lesson to all concerned." He turned to his chief trainer, who lounged on a couch at right angles to Bulbus.

"See to it, will you? Say ten lashes. No lead tips on the flail, either. I don't want him marked up." Bulbus sighed heavily. "Ah, such a magnificent specimen. When his time comes, I want him to shine. See that it is done tomorrow morning, right after breakfast."

Chapter 10

Philadelphia Braddock halted and turned in the saddle to look directly at Preacher. He gestured to a notch in the ridge ahead. "By jing if it ain't been a week's time since we left Trout Crick. Over yonder is that strange city I told you about."

Preacher thought on it, as he had been doing over the past seven days. "I reckon if they have people out scoutin', we'd best hole up somewhere until dark, then move in close."

"Good idee, Preacher. But, first, don't you want to size it up in daylight?"

"Of course. If we stay inside the tree line, we can reach the back slope of the ridge unseen. We can pick a spot from there."

It went as Preacher expected. Near the saddle that provided a pass through to the basin, his keen ears picked out the brassy notes of several bugles, yet they saw no sign of soldiers beyond the gap. On the opposite side, he found an entirely different, and amazing, situation.

Philadelphia had been right. Large, shiny white buildings covered the slopes and tops of four of the seven hills now. Construction, even at this distance, could be seen to go on at a feverish pace. Horsemen in scarlet cloaks and shiny helmets cantered around through the organized confusion. On the Campus Martius formations of soldiers raised clouds of dust as they drilled with precision. Preacher studied the scene for a long while, then grunted his satisfaction.

"Over there." He pointed to a thick stand of slender pines, as yet not fallen to the hunger of the axemen. "We can ease our way over there and be within range to look over that place by spyglass."

Philadelphia licked his lips. "Now, that shines. If I'd a had my smarts about me, I coulda done the same thing." For a moment he looked crestfallen. "Only m'spyglass is broke."

Preacher gave him a smile. "No time like the here an' now, I allus say."

Silently, and with the great skill of the mountain men, they worked their way to Preacher's suggested vantage point. They left their horses muzzled with feed bags to silence them, and crept through the undergrowth which crowded the stand of lodgepole pines. Preacher settled in, his Hawkin rifle across his lap, and extracted a long, thick, bullhide tube from his possibles bag. From that, he slid a brass telescope.

He fitted the eyepiece in place and peered at the scene below. Men dressed in only sandals and diaperlike loincloths sweated in the warm afternoon sun. Many, Preacher noted, had scars from a heavily applied lash on their backs. Overseeing them were men in tunics and rough leather aprons. Here and there stood uniformed soldiers. Preacher blinked, and pursed his lips.

"Danged if they don't look just like them old-timey Romans. But, that cain't be. T'weren't any romans got to the New World."

"That's what I thought," Philadelphia whispered back. "Then I reckoned my wound had got infected and I was seein' things. But, by gol, if you see 'em too, then they must be real."

"Only too real. We can't learn too much about them from here. We'll wait until night, then go down among them buildings and see what they're up to."

That suited Philadelphia fine. He settled back for a comfortable afternoon snooze. Preacher continued to study the oddly dressed men. He saw what he believed to be a chariot, pulled by a pair of sparkling white horses. Some big shot no doubt. Twenty men in uniform marched down a wide avenue toward the largest hill. They all carried long, slender spears. An hour shy of sundown, a shrill note sounded, as though from a reed flute, and the men quit working. They lined up and had chains fastened on their arms and legs. Then the men in tradesmen's aprons marched them away, out of Preacher's sight. Slaves, Preacher thought with disgust.

Preacher did not hold with slavery. Far from a frothing-mouthed abolitionist, he still did not think it right for one man to own another, like a horse, or pig, or cow. Quite a few Indians had slaves, mainly captive women or children from other tribes. Most times, once they had learned the ways of those who captured them, the children were adopted to fill the place of a child that had died, or the women married men affluent enough to afford two or more wives. Somehow, that didn't seem to Preacher to be so harsh a system. What was going on here, though, rankled.

"May an' have to do something about that," he whispered to himself.

Time edged toward sunset. Preacher stretched out the kinks in arms and legs and munched a strip of jerky. An hour after dark, he awakened Philadelphia. He bent close and spoke lower than the serenade of cicadas.

"Eat yourself a bit o' somethin' an' we'll move out in another half hour."

"I'll admit I ain't looking forward to this too much, though it does have my curiosity aroused."

"Not a big problem. Certain sure they ain't got senses

half as sharp as an Injun. We've sure snuck into enough Cheyenne and Blackfoot camps to know how it's done."

"Even so," Philadelphia warned, "we could die here."

Silent as ghosts, Preacher and Philadelphia crept through the streets of New Rome. Every block brought new marvels. In moccasins, with rifles at the ready, pistols loaded, primed and waiting in their wide belts, they accosted marble statues; tall, alabaster columns of the same material supported high porticoes over stately porches. Philadelphia pointed a finger in amazement when they came upon a large, bronze brazier flaming with the eternal fire before the Temple of Vesta.

"Lookie there," Philadelphia whispered in awe. "I'll betcha someone is paid to keep that goin' all the time."

"More likely a slave," Preacher amended in a sour note, his mind on the shackling of the workmen at quitting time. "Cost less that way."

"Any way you look at it, somebody has to tend it. That must be some sort of church."

"More likely a pagan temple, if this is what we think it is."

"Better an' better." Philadelphia rubbed his hands in anticipation. "That's where they hold them orgies, huh?" He pronounced it or-*ghees*.

Preacher and his friend had no time to contemplate that vision. They rounded a corner in the forum and came face-to-face with the night watch. Armed with cudgels, flaming torches held above their heads, the city guard reacted instantly. With a shout of alarm, they dashed at the two surprised mountain men.

"Looks like folks know we're here," Philadelphia declared flatly as he flung away one of the watchmen.

Preacher saved the talking for later. Two burly sentries closed on him, their cudgels swung with competence.

When they raised them to strike, Preacher ducked low and stepped in under the weapons. Quickly he popped one with a right, the other with a left, under the chin. They rocked back on their heels. The chubbier of the two sat down abruptly, eyes wide with wonder. Preacher turned to finish the other one, when a cudgel caught him in the side.

He grunted out the pain and shock, then delivered a butt-stroke from the half-moon brass butt plate of his Hawkin that broke teeth and cracked the jawbone of his attacker. The clatter of fast-approaching sandals on the cobbles sounded like hail on a broad-leafed plant. A swift check of the immediate area told Preacher that between them they had accounted for four of the six. With a little luck, they still might make it.

Good fortune deserted the mountain men. A dozen more of the night watch rounded into the *Via Sacra* and pounded down on the Temple of Vesta. Preacher caught a blow from a closed fist in the side of his head that made lights flash and bells ring. A short sword flashed in the hand of one watchman, and Preacher forgot all about his determination not to use firearms.

The Hawkin barked. Burning powder sparked in the wake of flame that erupted from the muzzle. Smoke rose in front of Preacher while his opponent twisted his mouth into an ugly gash, stumbled backward and clutched at his ravaged shoulder. Then the other guards arrived, and the great square of the forum became a welter of struggling human shapes. Many of the blows delivered by the sentries fell upon their fellows. Enough found their intended target to bring an end to the battle.

A ringing, thudding pain exploded in Preacher's head, and the Hawkin slipped from numbed fingers. Shooting stars cut through the darkness that gathered in his head. He tried to turn, to put his back to that of Philadelphia, though he knew it to be already too late. Philadelphia had sunk to his knees, hands around his head to protect it, while the heavy blows of cudgels rained on his bent back. The next smash with the thick-ended nightstick made the darkness complete for Preacher.

Early the next morning, Preacher and Philadelphia awakened in a small, damp, slimy cell. The odor of human vomit hung heavily in the dank, still air. Preacher's head throbbed, and he located four separate goose-egg-sized lumps on it. The sour taste in his mouth told him who had vomited. Beside him, Philadelphia groaned.

"Where are we?"

Preacher answered glumly. "In the lockup. Damn, my head hurts."

"So's mine. Ah! Aaaah—aaah, my back, too. They tried to turn my kidneys into mush. I'll be piddlin' blood for a month."

"Be glad it ain't runnin' out your ears."

Philadelphia quickly forgot his own misery. "You hurt that bad, Preacher?"

"No. But no thanks to those fellers."

Footsteps tramped loudly in the corridor outside. A jingle of keys came to Preacher's ears. They sounded sharp and tinny through the buzzing in his head. A key turned noisily in the lock, and a low, narrow door banged open.

"Come out, you two," a voice commanded in clear English.

"Where are we going?" Philadelphia wanted to know.

"You've got a hearing before the First Citizen."

Preacher scowled. "I don't like the sound of that. If I recollect, I've heard that before. It escapes me what it means."

Outside the cell, each man was given a bowl of water and a crudely woven towel with which to freshen up. Then the indifferent turnkey passed over a lump of coarse bread and a clay flagon of sour wine. "Eat up, eat up," he snapped. "We don't have all day."

Preacher shot him a flinty gaze. "Maybe you don't."

Three uniformed soldiers joined the procession at ground level. In short minutes they found themselves once more in the open area of the forum. At this early hour few citizens filled the walkways and steps of the temples. They were directed to a building next to the Senate. Above the columns, inscribed on the portico of the capitol, was the single word, *"Curia."*

Preacher saw it and shrugged. "Looks like we get our day in court."

Inside, they were rudely shoved through a curtained archway into a brightly lighted room, a hole in the domed roof to allow smoke out and sunlight in. Before them, three men sat on a marble dais. The one in the middle had a wide purple band around the hem of a toga. The ones flanking him had two thin lines on theirs.

"Who brings charges against these men?" the burly man in the center demanded.

"The tribune of the watch, Your Excellency."

"What are those charges?"

A tall young man, his head swathed in bandages, stepped forward from a stool to one side. Preacher recognized him as one of those he had smacked with his rifle butt. "I, Didius Octavius Publianus, tribune of the *vigilii,* charge these criminals with trespassing in the domain of Nova Roma, of being enemies of the State, and spies for the Gauls."

Gauls? Preacher thought. How silly could someone get? He could not let that one lay. "Why, Your Worship, this whole thing is crazy. Downright redic'lous in fact. What Gauls? There ain't any Gauls anymore, an' this sure as hell ain't Ancient Rome."

Quintus raised a restraining hand. "Ah, but it is, my talkative spy. It is Nova Roma, New Rome. Let me introduce myself. I am Marcus Quintus Americus, First Citizen of Rome. These are my fellow judges, Pubilus Gra—"

Before he could complete the introductions, Preacher exploded. "By damn, I remember now. First Citizen means dictator."

Quintus displayed a surprised, impressed expression. "Why, that's quite correct, my good fellow. Duly elected to that honored position by the Senate. You seem quite learned for such a rough and rude specimen of the frontier."

"Just because I've spent most of my days out here, don't mean I didn't get any learnin'. I studied history, includin' ancient Rome, at the University of the Shinin' Mountains."

"How odd. I've never heard of it."

Preacher eyed Quintus suspiciously. "Small wonder. From that accent, I'd say you got your book-learnin' way back east somewhere. Maybe Princeton? Or Harvard?"

Quintus widened his eyes at this astuteness. An amused twinkle lighted the gray orbs. "You amaze me. That's quite remarkable. Harvard it was. Class of Thirty-six. I would really like to take some time to talk with you about this university of yours." He sighed. "But, the duties of office, and your crimes, make that impossible. Tribune, are you ready to put on your case?"

"Yes, Your Excellency." Quickly the tribune outlined the encounter in the forum the previous night. His version markedly differed from Preacher's recollection. He made note to dispute them when his turn came. The opportunity came too quickly for him to marshal his arguments.

"Is there anything possible you can say in your defense?" Quintus leaned forward to ask condescendingly.

"Only that it ain't so. Not the way he tells it. We was just takin' a little stroll through your fine city, seein' the sights, so's to speak. We come around this corner and these fellers jumped us right off. We had no idea who they might be, so we had to fight back. I will admit he was right about how many we downed before it was over. Musta been a baker's dozen or more." He gingerly touched his head. "An' I must say they got in their licks, too. Well, no real harm done, an' no hard feelin's I say. Now, to that bein' an enemy of the State," Preacher went on.

"We ain't enemies of no state. Not at all. An' we come here on our own. We don't spy for anyone. At least not anymore, nohow. There was a couple of times we done some scoutin' for the Dragoons. I suppose some as would call that spyin'." Preacher put his hands behind his back and began to pace. "Like I said, there ain't any Gauls anymore, so that charge is out the window, too. Taken all in all, we'll just say we're sorry about bustin' up your watchmen here, and bid you a peaceable farewell."

"I think not!" The voice of Marcus Quintus cracked like a rifle shot. "My fellow judges and I will confer and render our verdict. Jailer, take them away."

Preacher and Philadelphia found themselves in a small, windowless room with a sobbing young girl. Curiosity prompted Preacher to ask her what had brought her here and caused her distress.

"I—I'm to be branded as a runaway," she wailed, her English rusty. "But I didn't really run off. I was caught by a terrible thunderstorm and had to stay over the night at the farm of Decius Trantor. It wasn't my fault. But the watch caught me before I could reach home and explain to my master."

"Why, that's hardly fair," Preacher commiserated. "What brought you here in the first place?"

"We—my family—were on our way with some others to the Northwest. Our wagons were attacked. I was—I was— they had their way with me, and then I was sold into slavery."

"Why, them black-hearted devils. How long you been here?"

"It seems forever. At least two years. I remember my last free birthday was my fourteenth. We had a party right on the trail. There was music from a violin and a squeeze box." She put her head in her hands and began to sob wretchedly.

Preacher cut his eyes to Philadelphia. "When we get out of this fuss, we're gonna have to do somethin' about that."

"Yep," Philadelphia agreed readily. "*If* we get out."

Shortly before the noon meal, the guards came for Preacher and Philadelphia. Hustled into the trial room of the curia, they again faced Marcus Quintus and his fellow judges. Quintus looked at them sternly.

"It is the considered decision of this court that you are guilty as charged. You are to be scourged, then sold into slavery for life. Give your names to the clerk."

Preacher gave Philadelphia a quick wink first. "M'name's Arthur. I don't rightly know what my last handle happened to be. I been out here since a boy not yet in my teens."

Eyes suddenly aglow with interest, Quintus leaned down toward Preacher. "That's most interesting. Come now, do you also happen to answer to the name Preacher?"

Preacher hated deliberate lies. He swallowed his objection to untruthfulness and answered with a straight face. "I heard of him, of course. Why is it you ask?"

"I'm . . . most interested in this wildman Preacher. I've sent men after him, to have him fight in our arena, but none have returned."

"With good reason, too," Philadelphia answered sharply. "Preacher's the wildest, wooliest, ringtail he-coon in the High Lonesome. 'Less you send about a dozen or more, you'll never see hide nor hair of Preacher, other than he wants you to."

Anger tightened the skin around the eyes of Quintus so

that they became flinty points. "You'll learn manners as a slave, or you'll be dead at a young age. Tribune, have the guards take these men off to be scourged." Quintus paused and sighed. "It is too bad you are not Preacher. What a glorious fight we would witness on the sand. See they are whipped quite soundly, but do not mark them. And notify Justinius Bulbus of these splendid fighting men we will have on the sale block."

Chapter 11

"Everything is turned topsy-turvy in this dang city," Preacher lamented as their escort conducted them to the small square off the forum, where a raised platform filled the center.

A crowd of men pressed close to the edges, faces turned up, eyes fixed on the shapely young woman standing there beside a burly fellow with a coiled whip over one shoulder. He held a long reed pointer in one hand, and gestured grandly as he called off what he clearly saw as selling points.

"She's broad-hipped and will deliver with ease. Notice those smooth, straight shoulders, gentlemen. She can carry heavy burdens. All in all, a treasure for a bargain price. Now what am I bid?"

"Six," a voice called from the throng.

"What? Only six *sestercii?*"

"No. Six *denarii,*" came the answer, followed by laughter.

"Surely you jest? Why, I would gladly pay ten talents for her myself."

"Then you buy her," the heckler taunted.

A more serious buyer bid himself in. "I bid four talents."

Brightening, the auctioneer located his bidder. "Now, that's more like it. I have four, who'll give me five? Five-gimme-five—five-five—yes! Now six." His chant rolled on until he had worked the sale price to eleven talents. A lot of gold for a young woman.

Her new owner claimed his prize and took her to the cashier's table to pay his fee. The auctioneer motioned for the next sale lot. A muscular, bullet-headed assistant shoved forward two small boys. Their red hair, freckled faces, and dark brown eyes marked them as brothers.

"Lot number seven. Two house servants. They are brothers, aged nine and eleven. They were taken from a wagon train one month ago, and have mastered enough Latin to show they are quick learners. They will make ideal body servants for sons of gentlemen. Now, I'm going to open the bidding at ten sestercii, take your choice."

"They been cut?" a suspicious buyer demanded.

"No, sir. I'll guarantee that."

Not satisfied, the skeptical one pressed on. "A good look's the best guarantee I know of."

Sighing, the auctioneer tucked his pointer under one arm and reached for the white loincloths the boys wore as their only item of clothing. He gave hard yanks, which exposed them to all eyes, and humiliated the lads to their cores. Blushing all over, they stood with heads hung, tears running down their cheeks. "As I said, they have not been gelded."

"Why, that egg-suckin' dog," Preacher growled. "I'll fix him good when I get up there."

Philadelphia nodded to the javelin-wielding guards at the side of the platform. "More likely those bully boys would pin you with their pig stickers while that feller used his whip on you, Preacher."

Not one to waste breath on "if only," Preacher sighed heavily and accepted the inevitable. "It sure ain't the High Lonesome anymore. This sort of thing is downright shameful."

"Then maybe we oughta be thinkin' about takin' our leave," Philadelphia muttered silently.

"Now your talkin', Philadelphia. We'll both work on that, keep our eyes open. First chance, we be gone."

"Count on it."

Their turn came sooner than either mountain man had expected. Not surprisingly, a burly man with a face mean enough to stop the charge of a bull bison purchased them. "You'll make fine additions to my gladiator school," he told them as armed and armored men hustled Preacher and Philadelphia away.

Hoisting a gold-rimmed cup, Marcus Quintus called across the expanse of table to his principal guest, Gaius Septimus. "The two barbarians who were captured night before last will make excellent additions to the birthday games for Quintus Faustus, will they not?"

Septimus curled his lower lip in a deprecating sneer. "That sort of man is entirely too independent to make a good slave, let alone a gladiator. Do you not agree, Justinius?"

Bulbus, the third guest, glanced up from his intense study of a lovely young dancing woman. "Quite to the contrary, Septimus. They are quick and strong, and used to fighting for their lives. Once their spirit is—ah—molded to my liking, they become marvelous in the arena. Some are absolutely fearless."

"Yes, like Preacher, who I fear is still on the loose," Quintus snapped.

"Will I get to watch your new slaves die?" Faustus, at the fourth table, asked.

The two senators who had been invited hid their reaction to the boy's rudeness behind pudgy hands. Bulbus glanced idly at the youngster, who had been included at this all-male dinner party by his doting father. There was something . . . not at all right about the child, Bulbus thought not for the first time. His reaction to the games was—odd. Were he a couple of years older, Bulbus considered, it might be ascribed to the erotic fires of puberty. For all his suspicions, he answered cordially enough. After all, the youth was the son and heir of the First Citizen.

"No, young Faustus. They show much too much promise to be dispatched so soon. Unless, of course, someone lands an unfortunate blow."

"Why is that?" Faustus asked, genuinely interested.

"Keeping a crippled gladiator is like having a pet elephant. The cost of feeding him is ruinous." Bulbus laughed at his own joke. "But, you are quite right, Marcus Quintus, these last two specimens are in superb condition. I will intensify their training so that they can appear at your son's birthday games."

Flattered by this, Quintus ignored the admonition of Bulbus about sparing them for future games. "Wonderful. It will surely be marvelous. They will die magnificently," he burbled on, his eyes fixed on some unseen distance.

In a numbing cadence, the bored voice of the drill master barked out the commands. "Strike left . . . strike right . . . strike left . . . strike right."

Another chanted to his victim of the moment, "Shield up! Parry! Strike target! Parry, dammit!

"Duck! Duck, you idiot!" quickly followed as the heavy wooden ball on the opposite arm of the practice frame swung around and clobbered the hapless former immigrant. His dreams of the Northwest had long been abandoned in the rigors of the gladiator school. He looked up pitifully as Preacher and another gladiator stomped by, trading sword blows with weighted wooden weapons. The metronomic throb of the drum beat used to mark movements accelerated to a rapid roll and ceased.

At once, the student gladiators ceased and headed for the large fountain in the center of the training yard. Dripping with sweat, they plunged bare torsos in to the waist. Preacher found himself a place beside Philadelphia.

"To carry off that escape we talked about," he observed to Braddock, "we must first get out of this dang-blasted gladiator school. An' I don't allow as how I've figgered out a way to do that as yet, what with them big dogs."

"We'd best find it soon. We've been here the better part of a week now. I've got bruises where I didn't know a man could get them."

Standing to Philadelphia's right, Buck Sears listened on in interest. Here was a pair who sounded like they still had some grit left. A quick check over his shoulder showed Buck that the trainers were occupied elsewhere. He decided to take a chance.

"Don't worry about that. I have it all figured out. And, believe me, it's the only way you can get out of the school." He paused to check on their overseers. "If you promise to take me along, I'll show you how."

Philadelphia gave him a gimlet eye. "Got it all figured out, huh?"

"Yep." A smug smile brightened by sudden relief bloomed on the face of the teamster. "I'll tell you all about it at the baths after tomorrow's training session."

"Mighty decent of you, Buck," Preacher said agreeably. "We'll be obliged for the help. An', sure, you can go along."

"That's a relief. I can't stand it in here much longer."

Preacher nodded and smiled back. "None of us can, son. Not a one."

Due to his lifestyle, Arthur proved to be a magnificent standout at gladiator training. In early afternoon the next day, a bemused Justinius Bulbus stood in his private box watching the ripple of muscles in the arms and shoulders of the big mountain man. He could not believe his good fortune. Bulbus had his doubts that the legendary barbarian, Preacher, who so preoccupied the thoughts of Marcus Quintus, could be much better.

Whatever the case, the master of games intended to match this one against Preacher when, or if, the famous denizen of the mountains was captured. Bulbus' shaggy eyebrows rose as he watched the big one batter down another of his trained gladiators. He raised an arm to halt the man scheduled to next face the powerful barbarian.

"Crassis, you take him," he instructed one of the trainers.

With a big grin born of overconfidence, the heavily muscled Crassis came forward, his small shield strapped to his forearm held up to protect his chest, blunt sword poised. Bounding like a panther, Preacher surged out to meet him. He struck the wooden shield with such force it split down the middle and broke the forearm behind it.

An expression of surprise flashed on the face of Crassis, quickly replaced by a grimace of pain. Preacher swung again and caught Crassis against the side of his head with the flat of the blade. Rubber-legged, Crassis stumbled away to drape himself over the lattice of iron strips that formed the training ring. A ragged cheer went up from among the captive would-be gladiators. Preacher looked around for another opponent.

Bulbus quickly provided one. A bigger trainer, one who taught the net and trident, came forward. "Julian, bag him with your net and teach this upstart a lesson," Marcus Quintus called from the cushioned chair upon which he sat, beside his wife, Titiana Pulcra.

They had arrived unannounced and put the school into a tizzy, not the least Bulbus, who wanted always to put on the best of shows for his benefactor and patron. He had hastily devised this test of strength for the enormously powerful mountain man. It now seemed to have turned out ill-advised. Even his trainers could not best the agile, resilient man. Bulbus cut his eyes anxiously from husband to wife.

At least Pulcra appeared to be enjoying the exhibition. She squirmed in her seat with each excellent blow by the mountain man. Now, while Bulbus covertly studied her, she crossed her legs and began to swing one nicely turned ankle. A sure sign a woman had a naughty itch to soothe, Bulbus thought lasciviously.

"I'll have you down to size in no time," Julian taunted. "Then I'll prick your hide to give you a good lesson."

Julian feinted to the right, dodged back to the left, spun a full circle on his heel to gain momentum, then whipped out his weighted net. Preacher ducked, picked up the edge of the fan-shaped snare and did a wrist roll that collapsed it into a long, folded filament. This he quickly climbed, mock sword in his teeth. When he reached the forearm of Julian, he let go with one hand and closed his fist around the hilt.

A swift swat to the temple and Julian went down, a stone dropped into a fathomless pool. And with hardly more than a ripple. Preacher came to his moccasined feet and turned toward the box. A steady flow of sweat blurred his vision and stung his eyes. It kept him from clearly seeing the occupants, though he rightly guessed one to be Bulbus and another Quintus.

Exasperated, Bulbus clapped his palms together. "I'll have an end to this at once! Two of you, have a go at him at the same time."

A pair from the training staff came forth. One wore a *caestus,* its usually sharp bronze talons blunted with India gum. The other bore a curved Persian sword. Preacher greeted them with a nasty grin.

Above him, Pulcra veritably writhed in her chair, her leg swinging ever faster, small beads of perspiration breaking out on her upper lip. Fascinated by this enthralling demonstration by the mountain barbarian, Marcus had eyes only for what went on in the arena.

Preacher went for the swordsman first, after a glance at the blurred figures in the box. He came in low, leading with his sword. The tactic thoroughly distracted his opponent, who raised his weapon to parry the blade with enough force to knock it from Preacher's hand and do a quick reverse that would have, had his own been sharp, disemboweled the hapless antagonist who so insulted their abilities. Only it did not work that way.

At the last second, Preacher let the tip of his sword drop, so that the edge of the other one slipped across the flat without making contact. Startled, the trainer stumbled off balance while Preacher drove straight in. He rammed the point of his weapon into the helpless man's gut. It drove the air from his lungs in a gush.

Preacher wasted no time on finishing him, rather spun to confront his second threat. The armored fist lashed out at him and forced the mountain man to duck. Even with the sticky gum on the four triangular blades, they could inflict a terrible injury. Preacher avoided the *caestus* and hacked at the trainer's belly. Far quicker than the man with the sword, the trainer dodged the blow and tried to backhand Preacher in the head.

In a flash, Preacher went down at his knees and extended one leg. With a powerful push-off from one hand, he spun on his heel and swept the feet from under his opponent. A startled yelp came from twisted lips as the burly brawler left the ground and painfully landed on his rear. Preacher jumped to his moccasin soles and towered over the dazed man. He reversed his hold on the practice sword and rapped the trainer soundly at the base of his skull.

Preacher stepped back and let him fall. Then he placed one foot on the unconscious man's chest. Slowly he raised his eyes to the box.

"Blast and damn! Enough. You are through for the day, Arthur," Bulbus bellowed angrily. "You have won more than you have lost, so you get early baths, along with the other winners. Now, get out of here."

Beside him, Titiana Pulcra reached over and touched her husband's arm. "I'm going to leave now. The sun is too hot, and glaring. It has given me a headache."

"Very well, my dear. There is snow-chilled wine waiting us at home."

She smiled sweetly. "I know I'll enjoy it."

Someone else had watched Preacher's performance—albeit with far less cupidity than Titiana Pulcra. Sister Amelia Witherspoon saved her feelings of desire for an image of Preacher as deliverer. When they had arrived in this horrid New Rome, they had been condemned to die in the arena, thrown to the lions.

Now, Sister Amelia was quite familiar with the heroic stories of Christian martyrdom in the days of the mad Nero. Yet, deep in her heart, she knew that she was not ready to be fed upon by beasts for the sake of her faith if it could be reasonably avoided. She saw no conflict between her retreat from the martyr's role and the depth of her belief. Amelia had a healthy respect for life. And she wanted to escape from this horrid place like all get-out.

From the first time she saw this magnificent specimen of male prowess, Amelia just *knew* he was the answer to her prayers. Arthur would save them. Like her captors, Sister Amelia did not know that this brave, strong man was the legendary Preacher. She knew him only by the name those hated Romans called him. Now she felt all trembly at the sight of how swiftly and surely he had handled those men. How could she make her plight, and that of her brothers and sisters of the Mobile Church in the Wildwood, known to him? She hurried off to make her thoughts known to Sister Charity and to seek her advice.

Thick steam rose from the surface of the large pool in the *calderium* room of the *thermae publicus* of New Rome. Preacher gratefully sank his bruised hide and aching muscles into the hot depths. During his six days in the gladiator school, while he learned the ways of the strange new weapons, he had taken his share of punishment. He would ache for a while yet, he felt certain.

Taking a bath in the raw, in the presence of other men, had never bothered Preacher. He vaguely recalled weekly Saturday excursions from his early homelife in a single, large, wooden tub, and older brothers squirming around in it together with him. The first time he discovered that women, and children of both sexes, readily joined the men of New Rome in their baths, he had been quite disconcerted. Now he handled it with greater ease. He took care, though, to look the other way as best he could. He also made an effort to banish the blood-racing thoughts certain of the ladies engendered in his mind. All of which left him unprepared when a loud splash announced the presence of a shapely young woman who made a shallow dive into the hot pool.

She swam around him in circles, as graceful and as wriggly as an eel. At last, she let her legs descend and stood before him, the water up to her shoulders. Her long, blond hair hung wetly down her back. She smiled and touched a small, slender finger to his chest.

"You're that exciting new gladiator at the school of Bulbus," she stated coyly in English.

Tension added bluntness to Preacher's words. "Not by any choice of my own."

Teasingly, she moved her hand to his shoulder and draped it across the top. "You should be grateful. If you fight well, win a lot of battles, you could gain your freedom. You could even receive the *rudis.*"

"What's that?"

She puckered her mouth. "You really don't know. It's the wooden sword that is the symbol of your retirement from the arena. A free man, a citizen, and one who no longer has to fight. It's something to work for."

A sudden suspicion bloomed in Preacher's mind. "Are you allowed to talk to slaves?"

"I'm allowed to speak to anyone I chose. I'm Pu— Pricilia," she responded with no small heat. "Let's scrub down. I'll scrape you and you can scrape me. Then we can move on to the *tepidium.*"

Preacher found himself less reluctant than he had been when she had first appeared. After all, it had been a long time since any woman, especially one so young and attractive as this one, had shown interest in the rugged mountain man. It might be fun, he decided, shedding another inhibition, to partake. After all, she wouldn't bite. He screwed up a smile.

"If that's what you want, it's fine as frog's hair with me."

"How quaint," she said through a titter.

After a thorough cleansing, the pair swam across the wide pool and climbed out. In the next room, the *tepidium,* they entered the luke-warm water eagerly. It made their skin tingle. Preacher had grown painfully aware of their nakedness while scraping her silken skin with a *stigilis,* the curved, bronze, knifelike implement used in the manner of a washcloth.

Now they frolicked like youngsters. Exactly like . . . Terry and Vickie, he thought suddenly. Soon the bright pinkness left their skin, and the water began to feel less refreshing. Pricilia tapped Preacher on the chest, her head canted to one side atop her long, graceful neck.

"Race you to the *frigidium.*"

"You're on!" said Preacher through a shout of laughter.

Now, that would be more like it, Preacher thought. Cold water being something he was most familiar with, he expected that a dip in it would calm the odd stirrings that teased his body. He crossed the pool with powerful strokes. Out and onto the warm tile floor. Through the curtained doorway.

Preacher beat her by half a length to plunge into the icy water that flowed directly into the pool from the stream outside. They splashed and swam for several minutes, until goose bumps appeared on Pricilia's shoulders and arms. She edged to the shallow end and drew herself out of the water to her waist on the marble-tiled steps. She threw her arms wide in a gesture of invitation.

"Come warm me, Arthur. I'm frozen."

After all his efforts to resist, Preacher found himself beguiled into dumb obedience. He crossed the frigid water in five long strokes and entered her embrace. After he had twined his strong arms around her, she drew his lips to hers.

In no time, they caused the icy liquid of the *frigidium* to reach a near-boil with the energy of their amorous romp.

Chapter 12

Fully sated, Preacher lay on a bench, covered by a towel, when Pricilia made her departure. Entering as she left, Buck Sears and Philadelphia Braddock got a good look at her. One glance at their companion and they knew what must have gone on.

"You loon-witted he-goat!" Buck Sears blurted in shocked surprise. "You tryin' to get yourself killed before we can escape?"

Preacher sat upright, the sappy expression wiped from his face. "No? Why? What did I do that could cause that?"

Flabbergasted by Preacher's response, Buck worked his mouth for several moments before he could get any sound to come. "Don't you know who that was?"

Preacher blinked, suddenly suspicious of his recent amour. "Not for sure. She said her name was Pricilia. She was quite . . . friendly."

"I'll just bet she was. That happens to be Titiana Pulcra, the wife of Marcus Quintus Americus." He struck his forehead with the palm of one hand. "I wondered why those guards were not letting anyone enter the baths. If the Praetorian guard learns that we got by their watch at the door and saw—anything at all, they'll kill us along with you."

Preacher could not believe what he heard. Fooling

around with another man's wife was definitely not a part of his code. Anger blended with self-disgust as he questioned Buck further. "Are you sure? D'you mean she's the dictator's woman—his wife?"

"I am only too sorry to say that I am sure," Buck lamented.

"Dang-bust it, I've been tricked. She done lied to me." His face turned dark red. "Me dossin' another man's wife. I'll never live it down. Though I don't reckon I should waste time tryin' to explain it to him. Only one thing for it now. We gotta go ahead with our plan to escape. Suppose you tell us how you got in mind for us to do that, Buck?"

Buck shrugged, then produced a smug smile. "It's plain as could be. In fact, it's right under your noses."

"What'er you gettin' at?" Philadelphia growled. He, too, felt his friend's chagrin.

"We all agreed we could not escape from the school. So that leaves having to be outside the school to make a break. And the only time we are outside is to get to the coliseum to fight or here to the baths."

"They told us we go to the arena by tunnel."

"That's right, Preacher, they said that," Philadelphia agreed.

"Then it has to be here. What about the guards."

Buck gave slow answer, his expression one of awe and bemusement. "You . . . are . . . *the* Preacher?"

"That I am, Buck. But there's no time to talk about that. How do we get out? What about the guards?"

Buck produced a sunny smile. "They are a sufficiently lazy lot. They're convinced there is only one way in and out of this place. I found out better, before I was sold to be a gladiator for hittin' my so-called master."

Preacher exploded with curiosity. "Go on—go on, tell us."

"I worked here at the baths. Part of my job was to clean out anything that got caught in the water system. The water comes in big tunnellike things. There is a way to get to them from behind a wall of the cold room. All we have to do is get to there, then walk and swim our way to freedom. Because, all the water that comes in has to go out."

"That shines. I like it. Don't stand there, show us the way."

"You mean right now, today?" Buck seemed uneasy.

"Do you want to wait around until that Marcus feller finds out I rode his filly?"

Buck grimaced at that graphic depiction. "All right. Come with me."

Preacher stopped him with a hand on one arm. "One thing, though. I don't figger to leave without my brace of Walker Colts."

Buck dismissed him. "We'll deal with that when the time comes. First thing is to get away from here and out of the far end of the entrance tunnel."

Preacher squared his shoulders and reached for his clothes. "I'm game. Let's go."

At first progress came easily. Ledges had been cut into the tunnel walls, a good two feet above the water that flowed with regularity into the *frigidium* pool, and beyond into those of the heated tanks. After some thirty paces, Preacher estimated that they had reached a place somewhere out near the middle of the forum. Only the single long, covered opening presented itself to them.

Preacher, Philadelphia, and Buck followed it beyond what must have been the southern edge of the forum. The walls grew wet and slick. Thick hanks of roots hung down above their heads. From his spyglass reconnoiter, Preacher recalled a garden, with bushes and hedges trimmed into the shapes of animals. That had to be what they passed under now.

Their pathway became narrower and closer to the water. The latter swirled by in oily blackness, its surface alone illuminated by the torch in Buck's hand. He had taken the lead, naturally enough, since it had been he who discovered this way out of Nova Roma. Preacher came next in line, with Philadelphia bringing up the rear. Little light reached the big-eared mountain man, and he stumbled occasionally, with a muffled curse for each time.

Philadelphia had about run out of cuss words, when an even worse situation came to them. Buck halted his companions and gestured ahead with the torch. "We walk in the water from here. At about what I guesstimate to be a hunnard yards from the inlet, we have to swim for it."

"So nice, this route of yours," Preacher told him acidly.

Buck removed his slave's tunic and wrapped it atop his head, then stepped off into chest-deep water as he spoke. "Be glad there is any trail out of here, Preacher. These New Romans are damned thorough in everything they do."

One by one they followed him. Chill water swirled around them. Buck reasoned aloud that once out, so long as they moved through the city with an air of going about their usual business, their slave costumes would not be a danger to them. They could even get to within a hundred paces outside the walls.

"Then we cut and run," he added grimly.

Preacher eyed him sternly. "Now, that's why I want my Colt re-volvers an' Cougar. I can run a damn sight faster on a horse."

Buck lectured him in how to accomplish that. "There are storerooms in the house of the master of games for all that sort of captured things. Also a stable. Since it is built into the outside wall of the school, on the Via Martius, we should have no trouble getting there. It's the getting away that bothers me."

Preacher gave him a grunt and a knowing nod. "You let me an' my Walker Colts handle that."

Shaking his head in wonder, Buck spoke with awe. "You actually have a pair of those Texas guns?"

"Sure enough. An' a dang good Hawkin. I left my fancy Frenchie rifle at Trout Creek Pass." He nodded to Braddock. "Philadelphia's got him four of the nicest two-shooter pistols a feller could ever want. Sixty caliber they be. Ain't no spear-chucker can stand up again' our firepower for long."

"And I'll have my pick of what's in there, too," Buck added with a note of anticipation.

He led off once again and soon discovered that this late into summer, the water level had fallen enough that they did not have to swim at any point along the tunnel. Soon, a soft, gray glow emerged in the distance, around a bend. When Buck reached the turn, he paused a moment.

"Dang, I was afraid that might be," he spat.

"What's that?" Philadelphia asked.

"I worked the tunnels. All we ever dragged out was small bits of wood, a dead rat or two, some other animals caught in the water. Stood to reason they had a way of keeping bigger things out of the water course. See up ahead? There are bars across the opening to the river itself."

"Then we're stuck here?" Philadelphia demanded.

"Not necessarily," Preacher advised. "First let's get a look at them bars."

To Preacher's delight, they found them old, rusted and neglected. The current was stronger here and threatened to sweep them off their feet. Preacher gauged the weakest appearing ones and took hold. He dug his feet into the sandy silt on the floor of the tunnel and heaved with all his might.

A bit of rust flaked off, nothing more. "You two, get in place to the sides. Each take a-holt of one of these and pull when I do," he instructed.

This time a faint groan could be heard above the rush of the water. The muscles in Preacher's bare shoulders bunched as he exerted even greater effort. Philadelphia braced himself and heaved again. Opposite him, Buck planted his feet against a smooth rock and strained against the resistance of the worn iron bars.

At first, nothing happened. Then a mighty shriek came from the grommets into which the rods had been fitted. Small chunks of stone and mortar rained down on the heads of the escapees, and the first bar popped free. Philadelphia flopped backward in the water.

"Consarn it," he yelped.

Preacher eased it into the hands of his friend and turned to put his full force on the iron rod in Buck's grasp. Together, they tore it loose with seeming ease. A gathering of driftwood floated through the opening in a lazy spin. Preacher studied the situation.

"Another one."

Facetious, Philadelphia added, "Make it two more an' we can drive a wagon through there."

"All right," Preacher agreed readily. "Two it is. Your side seems weaker. We'll take those next in line."

"Awh, Preacher, one'll do," Philadelphia retracted his attempt at sarcasm.

Fate turned a jaundiced eye on the fleeing men. The next barrier held stubbornly in place, refusing to pop out of its header or footing. Buck and Philadelphia lined up on one side, Preacher on the other. He anchored himself on the neighboring bar and surged with his legs. In the back of his mind, as in those of the others, he held the thought that the alarm could be given at any moment of their being missing.

It added the necessary extra erg of energy. With a grinding, cracking sound, the upright came free. They let it fall where it would. Quickly they waded through and up on the sloping bank of the river. Panting, Philadelphia wiped himself partly dry and put on his tunic. Preacher and Buck followed suit.

"I wish I had a wax tablet," Buck announced. At the look of curiosity from Preacher, he explained. "Anyone with a tablet of some kind is accepted as being at something official, and he's ignored. At least, that's the way I've seen it around here, and before in big cities, like St. Louie."

Preacher grinned and clapped him on one shoulder. "By jing, if you ain't got the right of it, Buck. Maybe we can— ah—borrow one somewhere on the way. Now, show us the way back to the school and that storehouse you talked about."

Buck cut directly across the burgeoning city of New Rome. He walked with the stride and head-up posture of an important slave. Preacher and Philadelphia followed suit. Few cast them a glance. At a market stall, Preacher paused. While Philadelphia distracted the owner with talk about onions and turnips, Preacher filched a wax tablet from a ledge inside the display of vegetables. They quickly caught up with Buck, and Preacher handed it to him.

"There you go," Preacher told him jokingly. "Now you can be as important as you've a mind to."

Amazement glowed on Buck's face. "Where'd this . . . ?"

"No, don't ask."

"Thank you, Preacher, but stay close from now on."

On the far side of the forum, well away from the *Via Iulius,* the street took on a twisty course around the base of the Hill of Mars. Buck slowed and gestured the others close for a quick word.

"If the alarm has been given, we'd best try to make for the outside."

"And if it hasn't?" Preacher prompted.

"Then we get what we need and head for the high country."

* * *

Shut away in her private wing of the nearly completed palace, Titiana Pulcra lay sprawled on her downy bed. Her heart still fluttered from the intensity of her magnificent encounter with Arthur. Her body glowed. She hadn't had felt *this* good in a long time. What advantage was the life of the rich and powerful if one's appetites could not be fully indulged at will? That thought brought her mind to the disturbing topic of her son's recent conduct.

She supposed all small boys took pleasure from tormenting insects and small animals. Her own brothers, in another life, another world, had often gleefully tormented cats. That violent aspect of the conduct of Quintus Faustus did not unsettle her, although being on the cusp of eleven seemed awfully old for such behavior. No, it was something else.

Since that time three weeks past, she had paid careful attention to his conduct at the games. Reflection on the hour just past made all too vivid images of how he had responded to the nearly naked bodies and violent deaths of those who lost on the sand. In her memory, his gasps and quiet moans had sounded utterly too much like her own strident ones in the strong arms of Arthur. She stifled a thrill of horror. Surely Faustus could not be so—so *twisted*. She forced a change of subject.

Would she enjoy Arthur's presence soon again? Could she possibly risk it? Her husband was entirely too dense to ever suspect her. This wasn't the first time that a handsome gladiator slave had aroused her beyond caution. Pulcra was practical-minded enough to realize it would not be the last. Silently she offered a petition to the gods that Arthur prove a really good gladiator and last a long, long time. An anxious, if servile, scratching at the doorpost diverted her.

"What is it?" she demanded.

A clearly agitated slave entered, his forehead and upper lip bedewed with oily fear sweat. He advanced awkwardly. "A message for your husband, my lady."

"He is occupied elsewhere."

"May I ask where?"

"You may not. He is not to be disturbed." At least not until she had bathed. "You may give it to me."

"It's a matter of state, my lady."

Temper, mingled with sudden guilt, flared. "Dammit, must you be so obstinate? Give me the message."

Trembling now in fear of the arena, the slave stutteringly complied. "Three of the slave gladiators are missing, my lady."

Alarm stabbed at Pulcra. "Really? Their names?"

"Philadelphias, Baccus, and the champion of the day, Arturus."

Oh, God, Pulcra thought in pain. *I am alone. Utterly alone.* Duty demanded she rally herself. She girded her frazzled nerves. "Have the games master organize a search. I assume he has already conducted a roll call?"

"Yes, m'lady."

"Good. He's not the lack-wit I suspected him of being. Tell Bulbus to have the city searched first, top to bottom. Then the surrounding fields. They are not to be allowed to get away. More lives than theirs depend upon it."

She cast a quick glance into a mirror, evaluated her posture reclined on her bed. Her pride swelled as she saw the steel she had in her when she needed it.

Chapter 13

Ahead lay the entrance to the home of Justinius Bulbus. Two professional gladiators stood outside in light armor, with *pilum* at the ready. Behind them, along the Via Iulius, Preacher, Philadelphia, and Buck heard the sounds of a search being organized. That told them they had been found out. They had to move fast. Preacher came up with a rudimentary plan.

"Wait here. I'll go up and get the attention of those two."

"How do you figger to do that?" Philadelphia inquired.

"By telling them what they expect to hear." With that he set off.

Preacher approached the two sentries with a blank, slave expression plastered on his face. "I have a message for your master," he announced.

"He is out."

"Where is he?"

"In the city. You need know nothing more."

"Yes, I do. Look, I have it right here. Do either of you read?" Preacher bent low, groping in a fold of his tunic.

Automatically the two guards leaned with him. When Preacher had them where he wanted them, he balled both fists and slammed them hard at that sensitive point under the jaw. Both men went down in a clash and clatter of bronze. Philadelphia and Buck came on the run.

"Quick, put on their gear and take their places."

Preacher went in like a wraith. He slid silently past the steward's office and followed Buck's directions down a long hall to a tall, thick, double door. An iron ring served as an opener. Preacher yanked on it, and it swung on well-oiled hinges. He went through and pulled the door to behind him. He found himself in a roofless courtyard. From one side he heard stable noises, and his nose identified it at the same time. Hugging the slim concealment afforded by the balcony overhang, he skirted the wall that enclosed the yard from the house. A two-piece door yielded easily.

Inside, he located Cougar and Philadelphia's mount, and the pack animal. He picked one for Buck, saddled all, and led them from the stalls. Outside, he took the animals at an angle across a tiled area where a fountain splashed musically. He ground reined them while he opened the portal that should lead to a treasure trove of belongings and weapons.

Buck's description proved to be right on the money. Preacher quickly found his .44 Walker Colts and Hawkin rifle. Philadelphia's weapons came next. Dressed in buckskins again, Preacher fastened his wide, leather belt around his trim waist. He stuffed his knife and war hawk behind it, adjusted their position and added two .60 caliber pistols, then covered it all with his slave tunic.

Padding softly along the line of firearms, he selected a serviceable rifle and four pistols for Buck. Then he set about loading all. He doubled up on powder horns, boxes of percussion caps and conical bullets. He added sacks of parched corn, a big bag of jerky, another of coffee beans, flour, and a final of corn meal. Salt and sugar concluded his shopping list.

Outside again, he packed away all his booty and started for what had to be the gateway that led outside. Its latch gave with a mild squeak; then the hinges squealed with noticeable protest. Preacher winced. At once, a wizened

little clerk appeared through the doorway to the steward's office, a scroll clutched in one hand. His eyes widened and showed a lot of white when he saw the man in slave's clothing with four horses.

"What are you doing here?" he demanded in Latin. Preacher looked blank, and the clerk gestured toward the horses, changing to English. "What are you doing here with those animals?"

"Oh, I come to get them for the—ah—master of games," Preacher bent the truth slightly.

Emboldened by his freeman status and accustomed to having slaves cringe before him, the bean counter took two steps forward. "Not with all those weapons. You're— you're trying to escape, that's what you are doing."

Preacher gave him an expression of genuine regret. "Now you had to go and say too much for your own good, didn't you?"

Lightning fast, Preacher closed the remaining distance between them. His arm shot out, and he grabbed the surprised clerk by the throat. He throttled the frail little man into unconsciousness, then turned to leave.

"Not so fast," came a more authoritative voice behind the broad back of Preacher.

Preacher turned to find a man in the by-now familiar uniform of a centurion. He had his sword half drawn and advanced with a menacing tread. Preacher reached under his tunic and drew his Green River knife, with a blade almost as large as that of the *gladius* in the hand of the centurion.

"Well, shucks," Preacher said through gritted teeth.

No doubt the Roman soldier had been well trained. He completed his draw and held the leaf-bladed short sword competently as he brushed past the sparkling fountain in the middle of the courtyard. His only weakness came from the fact he had rarely fought against another armed man, particularly one so well versed in the various means of killing his fellow creature.

With a soft, grunted challenge, the centurion launched his attack. Preacher parried the thrust easily enough and slid the keen edge of his Green River along the muscular forearm of the soldier. It laid open the back of his hand and the meaty portion at the elbow. The young officer cursed and jumped back. Preacher just jumped back. They squared off to face one another.

"You still have time to look the other way, Sonny," Preacher suggested.

"It's my duty to protect the home of my employer," he rejected Preacher's offer.

A little job on the side, eh? Preacher thought. They circled while Preacher evaluated what he knew of this man so far. At last he worked out something. "You cain't have been borned here, your English is too good. When were you captured?"

Strange emotions surged across the broad face of the centurion. "About—about six years ago. At least I think so. What is it to you?"

Preacher favored him with a comradely smile. "Then you ain't one of them Roman lunatics. Think of your past, man. Think of getting back there?"

Loyalties warred on the face of the wanderer, who'd had his life turned upside down some six years ago. He had once had a wife and three children. Where were they now? Yet, he had won recognition and been rewarded by his captors, many of whom became his friends, or he now commanded. What was life supposed to be for him? Maybe he should ask *which* life? Past and present swirled in his mind, merged, and forged out his decision. With a shout, he launched himself at Preacher.

"Wrong choice, friend," Preacher told him sadly.

Nimbly, Preacher stepped outside the arc of the *gladius* in the centurion's hand. The tip of his own knife found the gap between the breast and back plates of the officer's cuirass, the wide, sharp-edged metal quickly followed. Preacher wrenched sideways, twisted the blade, and freed it. Slack-legged, his opponent gasped out his final sigh and fell dead. Off to his left, Preacher heard the hurried scurry of sandaled feet. More trouble from that direction.

He turned to see a quickly retreating back. Time to hurry. He cleaned his knife and replaced it, then went to the horses. Swiftly he led them out of the compound and toward the front door to the residence of Bulbus. His two friends saw him coming and instantly abandoned their pretense of being guards. Philadelphia Braddock swung into his saddle with practiced ease. Grinning, he patted the stock of his favorite rifle.

"I see you found old Betsy. Now, we'd best take our leave of this palce."

Jokingly, Preacher made himself appear in a casual mood. "What's your hurry, Philadelphia?"

Braddock frowned. "One of the servants of that Bublus feller come squawlin' out the door, didn't look left nor right, just runned off down the street like ol' Nick hisself was after him. I reckoned you had a part in that, an' also that our escape is no longer a secret."

Laughing, Preacher patted Cougar on the neck. "Right you are. We'd best go while we still have a chance."

Buck nodded and started them along the *Via Iulius*.

It was utterly reprehensible, Deacon Phineas Abercrombie thought to himself for what must be the hundredth time. It was so degrading, so demoralizing, to be herded together like this in a single, large cell. Not a hope of a moment's privacy. Men and women, whole families thrust cheek and jowl against one another. And that foul-smelling trench at the narrow end of the holding pen as their only place to relieve themselves. With not a curtain or blanket to conceal the most private of personal acts.

Voiding themselves right out in the open, like animals! Unspeakable. He could find no other word for it. He had complained at every opportunity. Only to be laughed at and told to turn his back if he did not wish to observe. It smelled so foul in here, so fetid, and dank. It had come to the point where he could no longer eat. Even if he tried, it came back up. Would they ever see the light of day again, or the light of freedom?

Somehow he doubted they would experience either. Sighing, he turned to hear the appeal of young Mrs. Yardley. "Deacon, my boy, Johnny, he's got himself a case of the runs. Real bad. Says his belly aches somethin' fierce, and it is sore to the touch."

Deacon Abercrombie followed the woman to where a small boy of eight lay on filthy straw near the center of the herd of missionaries. The child whimpered when Abercrombie knelt beside him and lifted up his tattered shirt. At least no unusual swelling, the untrained man diagnosed. That could bode even worse if cholera got loose among them. Well, he would have to tell the Yardley woman something.

"I'm afraid you are right, Sister Yardley. See that he gets all the fluids you can find for him. Keep him covered, and all we can do beyond that is pray."

For a moment, anger flared hot and red in the eyes of Mrs. Yardley. "We've *been* praying, Deacon. All of us, day and night. As yet, it appears the Lord has not seen fit to hear us."

Abercrombie's eyes widened. He raised an admonitory, pudgy hand. "Careful, Sister, lest you stray into blasphemy. I will tell the others, and we will join in group prayer for your boy."

Chastened, Mrs. Yardley lowered her chin and spoke

meekly. "Thank you, Deacon. Thank everyone for me. I'll try to find Johnny some water."

Pursuit began at the edge of the Forum of Augustus. Shouts came from the *vigilii* posted there, and they set off on foot after the mounted fugitives, leather straps slapping their scarlet kilts. People along the way, most in the grubby garb of "common citizens," pointed accusing fingers to direct the watchmen.

At least one thing served as an advantage to the fleeing men. All of those forced to accept life in New Rome had long ago learned that the clatter of horses hooves in the city streets signaled to get out of the way. As in its historical counterpart, Marcus Quintus had found it necessary to erect vertical stone plinths across the avenues to slow the speed of young rakes in their chariots. That forced the horsemen to zig and zag, yet kept them well ahead of the policemen. Slowly, they even gained some. Then the main body of searchers joined the chase.

They came at right angles to the *vigilii*, effectively forcing Preacher and his companions to swerve onto another street that did not lead directly to a gate that gave access to the outside. Several of the newcomers rode horseback, and they pushed on ahead of the yelling men behind them. The gap began to narrow. That's when Preacher noted some of the details of the construction that went on all around.

A block ahead, a tall engineer's scaffold had been erected. It consisted of a beam that pivoted from a central point. Equipped with a counterweight, it allowed large blocks of stone to be lifted by ropes and lowered into place by means of pulleys. The mechanism was operated by a horizontal capstan, manned by sweating slaves. At present, Preacher noted, a huge, rectangular slab of marble hung suspended over the street. More slaves pulled frantically on ropes to swing the walking beam. Without hesitation,

Preacher rode in among those around the capstan, their pursuers almost at the heels of his horse. Their mounts filled the center of the street.

Preacher pulled his war hawk from his belt and gave it a mighty swing. It severed the thick cable to the capstan with a single blow. The braided hemp parted with a musical twang. The pulleys responded instantly. With a loud shriek, they payed out the loose rope and allowed the three-ton marble slab to descend in a rush on top of the mounted searchers.

Preacher could not resist a backward glance. The carnage was terrible. Only one horseman had escaped the bloody pudding which had been made of his companions. He sat slumped in his saddle, numbed by shock. Once more, the gap between fugitives and hunters widened. Preacher estimated another three blocks, once back on the Via Ostia, the main route to the gate and freedom.

He led the way around one corner, then a sharp turn to the right on the Via Sacra. With only a block remaining, Preacher discovered that the word had gotten to the soldiers. The legion cavalry had joined the search. They thundered forward to cut off Preacher and his friends along the Via Ostia. Ahead, the sentries labored to swing shut the heavy gates.

Preacher held back in the small plaza formed directly inside the gate to empty a cylinder load from his .44 Walker Colt. It slowed the cavalry considerably. Preacher exchanged his marvelous six-guns and watched as Philadelphia, then Buck streamed through the narrowing gap in the gate. His turn now. He spurred Cougar and bent low over the animal's neck. They hit the opening at a full gallop. Preacher further slowed its progress by blasting one guard into eternity with a .44 ball.

Outside, the trio did not slacken their pace until they had ridden beyond the last cultivated field. Gasping in excitement, Philadelphia slapped one thigh. "We got away. By jing, we done it."

Preacher looked beyond him at the nearly closed gates. "I'd not break my arm pattin' m'self on the back just yet. Them gates is gonna slow the cavalry, but they're comin' after us. You can be certain sure of that."

At the crest of the southern pass, Preacher called another halt. He and his companions looked back. Far back among the plowed fields they observed hurried movement along the roadway. Preacher took out his telescope and extended it. Peering through it, he made out the billowing scarlet cloak and dancing plume of a centurion. Behind him, the mounted troops of New Rome strung out in a ragged formation that more resembled men fleeing for their lives than determined hunters. He nodded, satisfied at the lead they had, created by the confusion at the gate.

"They won't be catchin' up any time soon. Well, boys, what's your pleasure now?"

Philadelphia considered that a moment. "I say we high-tail it to Trout Crick and gather up as many good ol' boys as we can. Then come back here and kick us some crazy Roman butt."

"Sounds good to me," Buck agreed. "But, I ain't a mountain man. Will they accept me goin' along on this?"

Preacher considered him with keen eyes. "If you kin hit what you shoot at, they'll welcome you like a long-lost brother. If you kin do that and not make noise goin' through the woods, they'll give you their sisters."

Buck turned him a straight face. "I know better than to walk on my heels. Spent some time with the Kiowa whilst I was freightin' on the Santa Fe. They taught me to walk on the edge of my foot, and I'm at home in moccasins."

Preacher and Philadelphia nodded solemnly. "You'll do.

Only first, I think we ought to confuse them fellers a little before we leave these parts, don't you?"

Broad grins answered him. They set off, making no effort to conceal their tracks.

The stratagem worked. For only a moment the legion cavalry reined in where the escapees had halted. Then they set off at a rapid trot. Totally lacking in scouting skills, they made no effort to look ahead or to the sides. They stared only a few yards in front of their horses' heads, eyes fixed on the sign of those they sought. It didn't work.

The Roman soldiers soon found themselves in a box canyon. Confused and disoriented, they milled about at the face of the high wall that denied them further progress. Centurion Drago cut his eyes from one to another of his men. He was up for *primus pilus*—first spear, or adjutant to the legate—and dared not fail in this mission. Tradition in the *Legio XIII Varras Triumphae* said that the *primus pilus* was always elevated to command of the legion upon the retirement or death of the legate. He wasn't about to throw that away.

"Find how they slipped out of here without our seeing the trail," he commanded.

Thirty minutes later, a young cavalryman trotted up and saluted. "We have found it, sir. They crossed over the stream and used the trees to screen them."

"Brilliant. A first-week recruit could figure that out. How many are they now?"

"Only two, sir."

On the heels of his remark came a solid, meaty smack, followed by a brief scream and the rolling crack of a rifle shot. Before Drago and his troops could recover, the centurion heard the rapid drum of departing hooves. Right then, Centurion Drago made an uncannily accurate observation to his men.

"Jupiter blast that man. First Citizen Americus may not know it, but I think he had this mountain man, Preacher, in his hands all the time."

Philadelphia looked up as Preacher ghosted in to the grove of aspen where he and Buck waited for the crafty mountain man. A broad grin spread when he saw the new layer of powder grime on Preacher's right hand. Preacher slid from the back of Cougar and dropped the reins. At once, the broad-chested stallion went to munching grass.

"There's one less of them."

"How far behind us are they?" asked the always practical Philadelphia.

"I'd reckon at least half an hour. Most likely more, their horses haven't had any rest, like ourn."

"The bad news is there is only one trail out of here, unless we want to spend our lead climbing one ridge after another. Well, back to the trail."

Preacher led the way. Two miles down the wilderness road they found another meander that circled a steep pinnacle and went beyond, with a side-shoot that ended atop it. They rested up there, eyes fixed on the winding trail through the Ferris Range, while they munched strips of jerky and crunched kernels of parched corn. By the fat turnip watch in a pocket of Preacher's vest, forty minutes went by before the greatly subdued cavalry rode into view. At once they put away their eats and reached for rifles.

Preacher honed in on the third from the last man in the column. Philadelphia took the second, and Buck the rear soldier. They fired almost as one. Swiftly, Preacher and Philadelphia began to reload. Below them, the trio of legionnaires jerked in their saddles and fell sideways off their horses. Shouts of dismay echoed upward to the ears of the shooters. Buck finished reloading last. Once more they took aim.

Three shots rippled along the canyon walls. Cries of alarm raised again, and Drago halted the column. A terrible mistake. It allowed the intrepid mountain men to reload and take three more from the backs of their mounts. Then Preacher was up and leading the way to their horses. Ten down, and they still had a quarter-hour lead.

Preacher led the cavalry of *Legio XIII* into four more blinds and successfully ambushed them, carving great gaps in the ranks. They had only settled down in another spot to pick off more, when the thunder of hooves alerted them to a danger they had not anticipated.

Fully fifty mounted troops, most foot soldiers unaccustomed to horseback, lumbered awkwardly toward their hiding place. Drago rallied his cavalry and charged with determination. No matter how well they fought, regardless of how many they killed, Preacher knew at once that they were doomed.

The Roman troops swarmed over them, took dreadful losses from the rifles, pistols and revolvers of the mountain men. Several received nasty knife wounds, and two had their skulls split by Preacher's tomahawk. At last, though, they prevailed. After suitable punishment for their prowess, the soldiers trussed them up and slung them over their saddles. Preacher, Philadelphia and Buck found themselves on their way back to Nova Roma.

Marcus Quintus Americus looked up sternly from the written report of Justis Claudius Drago. His brows knit, while anger ran rampant across his features. His words formed carefully.

"Our laws are clear on this. Not only have you murdered twenty-seven members of our Thirteenth Legion, but you have escaped. The penalty for escape is death in the arena. My only regret is that you will not have long to regret your deeds and fear your ultimate death. My son's birthday is three days from today. There will be games, of course. You three will be the central attraction."

Chapter 14

Excitement sent an electrical charge through the missionaries of the Mobile Church in the Wildwood. During all of their lengthy captivity they had never heard of anything so hopeful. Blue eyes shining, her long, golden curls a-bounce under the fringe of her modest, white-trimmed, gray bonnet, Sister Amelia Witherspoon hastened to take the latest news to her friend, Sister Carrie Struthers.

"It's a sign from God," Sister Amelia declared confidently. "If someone can escape from this dreadful place, then someone else can as well."

"But you said yourself that they were men," Carrie complained, her freckled face agitated below a wreath of auburn curls. "What can we possibly do, mere women?"

Amelia looked at her friend, blinked and answered sharply. "What can we do? We can put our foot down, that's what. Demand that the *men* in this company make some effort to effect our escape."

"Well, I'm not so sure . . . ," demure Carrie began, long, coppery lashes lowered over dark brown eyes.

Fists on hips, Amelia responded forcefully. *"I am sure!* The least they can do is try to get away from this insane community."

Deacon Phineas Abercrombie bustled over, his considerable girth inflated with righteous indignation. "Here now, what is this all about?" Amelia quickly told him. It did not sit well at all. He peered disapprovingly at her down his long nose. At last he spoke his mind. "I am sure you will agree. If it is God's will that we become martyrs, then so be it. Who are we to question Him?"

Stubborn, Amelia continued to press her point. "What sort of martyrdom is it to be killed by lunatics who believe this wretched place is some rebirth of Ancient Rome?"

Abercrombie dismissed that reasoning. "That is for the Lord to decide, Sister. I am afraid I must forbid you to discuss this topic with any others of our flock. Besides, I hear that the men who escaped have been recaptured. It is really all so futile," he concluded with a bored sigh.

Not one to be easily intimidated, Amelia Witherspoon flounced off to speak with others of their small congregation. In open defiance of the deacon, she urged them to join in making some sort of plan to effect an escape. Watching her from a distance, the deacon grew angry at the impertinent young woman. He made a casual, angled course to the bars at the front of their communal cell. There he made a covert signal to one of the guards.

A few minutes later, with Sister Amelia still urging at least resistance if not actual escape, a centurion arrived outside the iron gate to their prison. "Which one is Deacon Abercrombie?" he demanded.

"I am he," the deacon volunteered.

With a curt gesture, the centurion sent two burly guards into the holding pen, and they roughly dragged Deacon Abercrombie out into the stone corridor. Without another word, the centurion started off with his prisoner in the firm grip of the pair of thugs.

Buck Sears looked across the dining table in the gladiator quarters at his new friends. "We're going to be taken over to the coliseum tomorrow. There are to be rehearsals for the spectacles."

Preacher looked up, lines of concern etched in his forehead. "How do you rehearse being fed to the lions?"

"It's them Bible-thumpers, ain't it?" Philadelphia asked. "You're worried about them."

"There's women and children among them," Preacher made explanation.

"Fools for comin' out here, I say. An' so'd you just a short while ago."

Preacher sighed. "Your right, Philadelphia. On both counts. It's only with them bein' youngins it's all so—so uncivilized bein' a cougar's light lunch."

"No matter. There ain't a thing we can do about it."

"Right again. Only keep your wits about you, and if an opportunity comes to . . . well, just be ready, hear?"

Philadelphia pulled on one large ear lobe. "Oh, yeah. For certain sure. I don't know what sort of weapon they might give me, but I sure would like to wet it in a little Roman blood."

Preacher forced a laugh he did not feel. "That's the spirit. How about you, friend Buck?"

Buck shrugged. He had been giving that question considerable thought since their recapture. "I'd rather be dead than forced to fight every time they have some sort of holiday."

Preacher rubbed dry, callused palms together. "That's settled then. We'll look to give them a show like they've never seen before."

Philadelphia's sour expression belied his enthusiastic words. "Beats daylight outta sittin' around wonderin' which one o' them profess'nals is gonna do us in."

Bejeweled fingers aglitter, Marcus Quintus Americus caressed the gold wine cup he held, then set it aside as the centurion from the gladiator school entered with a portly, pompous-looking man with graying hair and the eyes of a prophet. The first citizen had dined sumptuously on roasted bison backribs, stuffed quail and an enormous fish. Recalling it made Quintus salivate. Then a flicker of annoyance shot across his face. Why could they never get the wine just right? It always tasted more like vinegar than a vintage selection. After a protracted three minutes, he raised his eyes and spoke.

"Yes, what is it?"

"He claims to have information for you, First Citizen."

Quintus studied the prisoner in silence, sipped from his wine goblet and motioned the captive forward. "Bring him forth, then."

Given a not-too-kindly shove, Deacon Abercrombie staggered forward. "I—I've come to you with a plot for an escape."

Quintus threw back his head and laughed loudly. "Did you now? Would it surprise you to learn that they were captured earlier today and returned to Nova Roma?"

Although quaking internally, Deacon Abercrombie stood his ground. "No. Not in the least. I am not referring to those three men. This has to do with some of my own flock. They are talking about overpowering some of your guards and making a break for it. A young woman, Sister Amelia Witherspoon, is behind it."

Quintus narrowed his eyes. "When is this to happen?"

"I . . . am not certain. Though I would imagine it would be when we are taken to the coliseum tomorrow."

Considering this, Quintus jabbed a ring-encrusted finger at Abercrombie. "And why is it that you have come to me?"

Abercrombie drew himself up, an other-worldly light illuminating his face. "I have reached the conclusion that it is our destiny to be martyred. Our Lord wishes to call us home."

Quintus despised these sanctimonious churchmen for their weakness. He could not keep the sarcasm out of his tone of voice. "How very convenient for your Lord that we have such efficient means to accomplish that. However, I am not clear as to why you slunk off to inform me of this. Hummm?"

For the first time, Abercrombie looked embarrassed. "I—I have come to the conclusion that while martyrdom might be a suitable end for many, and sacrifice for our Lord is always desirable, I—I simply feel that I have much more important work to accomplish during my time here. I have years of good works ahead of me. So, all—all I ask is that I be spared. My wife and I, that is."

Quintus feigned surprise. The jeweled rings on his fingers sparkled and sent off spears of brightness as he moved one hand to his chest in mock distress. "What is this? Do you mean to say you want special treatment?"

"Well . . . yes—yes, I suppose you could say that."

"Oh, you'll get special treatment, all right." Quintus produced a wolfish smile. "You will have the privilege of fighting your way to freedom. After all, the *rudis*—the—ah—wooden sword of retirement—is a cherished custom of the games. Think of it, my dear deacon. If you manage to fight and claw your way over the bloody, broken bodies of your fellow Christians, you will be a free man, a citizen of New Rome and able to do whatever you wish."

A low cry of anguish came from deep in Abercrombie's chest. His knees sagged, and the men who held him tightened their grip. Quintus gestured to the centurion.

"Take him back. No, take him right now to the coliseum. Put him in one of the small holding cells alone. It wouldn't do for him to have pangs of remorse and confess all to his followers." As the guards frog-marched a stricken Abercrombie out of the dining chamber, Quintus looked across the room to his son, reclining on a dinner couch.

"By the gods, how I hate such craven villains. They haven't one drop of the sap of manliness."

Those words stung Phineas Abercrombie, although what followed utterly humiliated him. "Will he die in the arena, Father?" young Faustus asked.

"Oh, assuredly. He'll be the last to be chewed by the lions, because he will cower behind his people. And when he dies, it will not be with a roar, but rather a whimper."

Word came by way of the slave grapevine. Preacher, Philadelphia and Buck took the news with grim expressions. Someone among the passel of Bible-thumpers had started stirring them up with escape in mind. The time for this attempt would be the next morning.

"And confound it, there's two things wrong with this. First off, what I hear is it is a fe-male critter who done the stirrin' up *and* the plannin'. Whatever she come up with, you can be sure it won't work. That's for starters. Now, what's it you heard those guards sayin', Buck?"

Buck, the only one of them who spoke Latin, produced an expression of contempt and disgust. "It appears as how one among the gospel group tattled on them to this-here Marcus Quintus."

"You mean to that ol' he-coon of this whole place?" Preacher asked.

"The same. Thing is, what can we do about it? They're due to be thrown to the lions at the games two days from tomorrow."

"Yes," Philadelphia agreed. "That looks like the end for them."

Preacher took over. "Simple. There's little we can do about whatever they have in mind for tomorrow. What we have to concentrate on is to defeat our opponents in the arena, force our way out of there and take these soul-savers along with us."

Philadelphia gave him a blank face. "Oh, you make it all sound so easy, Preacher."

Early the next morning, two small boys splashed and laughed together in the *tepidium* of the palace private baths. Without their clothing, one could not tell that the blond, curly haired lad wore the purple-striped tunic of a patrician, while the black-haired, shoe-button-eyed kid was his body servant. Master and slave had grown up together and formed a deep bond. Young Quintus Faustus confided all his really juicy secrets to little Casca.

Loyal Casca kept his silence about these revelations. In fact, he often shared in the more entertaining of them. Today, their early morning bathing was energized by their awareness of the looming excitement of the birthday games to be held for Faustus on the last day of September. The birthday boy was beside himself. He jumped and surged in the water, splashed his whole arm, flopped like a seal off the slick tile of the edge, and dived between his only friend's legs.

Casca did the same. Then they swam the length of the lukewarm pool and climbed out with their arms around the shoulders of one another. Light danced in Casca's eyes. "Is it for sure, Faustus? Your father is going to let you be *imperator*? All by yourself?"

"Certainly. I will be eleven, you know," he added solemnly.

"Yes. And I will be in two months."

"You're coming to the games with me. I have just decided. You can hand me ices, feed me grapes, we'll sit under the awning and you will have a parasol to shade us both."

"It sounds wonderful."

Faustus put nail-bitten fingers on his servant's shoulder. "It's the least I can do, considering you can't attend the birthday feast as a guest."

Casca produced a brief pout. "Yes. I know. And I understand. I really do."

For a moment Faustus looked like he might cry. "You're a true friend, Casca. You're the best friend any boy could ever have."

"You're my best friend, too, Faustus." His eyes twinkled as he tapped a finger on his friend's wet knee. "Will you—will you sneak me a bowl of your birthday custard?"

"Of course. This time it is a new kind of custard Mother learned about. It is called ice cream."

From an archway of a side entrance, someone cleared his throat in a deeper tone. Marcus Quintus stepped into the damp room, wearing only a towel over one shoulder. "There you are, son. I hoped I would find you here. You may go, Casca."

"See you in the *frigidium*," Casca called over one shoulder to Faustus. After the boy had padded barefoot toward the cold bath, Quintus sat on a bench beside his son.

"How does it feel? It's only two days away now. Are you really ready for it?"

"Yes, sir. I'm so excited. I wish it was this afternoon."

"It will keep. I wanted to urge you to remain stalwart. When you are the honoree master of games, you must retain your poise. Avoid any excessive show of emotion. Listen to Bulbus in regard to giving death to any of the professionals. And, do not flinch at assigning death to those who deserve it. You must show the people that you have the fortitude. Remember one thing. Your performance at the games will show that you either do or do not deserve the title *Princeps Romanus*."

Prince of Rome! How heady it sounded to Faustus. He got a faraway, glassy look in his eyes as he mentally reviewed past kills he had enjoyed in the arena. His nostrils flared and his breathing became harsh as he answered.

"Don't worry, Father. I *like* to see the blood flow."

Early the next morning, the guards roused the professional gladiators first, and they trooped through a wooden door to the tunnel that connected the school with the coliseum. They would have their breakfast there and spend the morning hours braiding up their hair and oiling their muscular bodies. This was done to prevent a handful of hair from being used against them, and to keep lesser fighters from holding on to them in a bear hug. Too much time and money had been spent on them to allow their defeat by an amateur.

Next, the lesser trained gladiators were escorted by guards through the underground passage to identical, dank stone cells in the bowels of the large stadium. Preacher judged that an hour passed before the burly, well-armed warders came for him and his companions. As condemned men, they were kept separate from all other participants.

They had only reached the far end of the tunnel when the condemned missionaries got rousted out of their holding pen and directed into the tunnel. Angry shouts rose as Preacher, Philadelphia and Buck were roughly shoved into a cell. The sounds of a struggle came to their ears after the clang of the closing iron-slat door. It appeared the guards had been prepared for this resistance. The hollow, north wind whistle and fireworks crack of whips followed immediately, along with the cries of pain from those who received the lash. Meaty sounds of cudgels on backs and shoulders told Preacher and his friends of the swift end of the brief resistance. So much for their big escape.

Preacher spoke quietly to his companions. "At least some of them Bible-thumpers have got some sand. Maybe we can make use of that when we get out there."

Philadelphia did not agree. "More likely, they got what little spunk they had whupped out of them. Them laddies wield a mean whip," he added, as he remembered the scourging they had received after their recapture.

"With or without them, we're goin' over those walls and out of this place," Preacher declared hotly. "When they come back from practicin' that thing they're supposed to do before the lions, I intend to talk to a few of 'em."

Preacher had his opportunity shortly before the noon hour. The captives were driven back inside the lower levels of the arena and given a chance to slake their thirst. All of the regular gladiators had been released from their cells to be equipped for the practice fights. Preacher had been decked out in the flanged, peaked helmet, net and trident of a *riatarius*. For a while he strutted around the common room, in imitation of the professionals, until the wary guards grew lax. Then he sidled over to the bars of the cage that held the missionaries.

Quickly he outlined his intention to make an escape and reviewed the plans with several of the younger men. He concluded with a logical suggestion. "The more of us that makes the try, the better chance we have of getting away."

A middle-aged Bible-thumper stepped close. "It sounds like you have given this considerable thought. Only, we cannot be a part of it. We're nonviolent. Surely, the government has learned of this dreadful place. They will put a stop to it."

Preacher studied the man like he would a strange insect that had just crawled out of his shirt sleeve. "No man ever got free by whinin' about it until the government gave him freedom as a handout. Government don't give people freedom, they *take it* from them."

"You don't mean that. Our government—"

"Ain't no different in that respect from any other. That's why I spent most of my life out here."

With a self-righteous sniff, the pilgrim announced, "Our trust is with the Lord."

Preacher cocked his head to one side, a twinkle in his eyes. "Might be you need to look a little further into that Bible you're so fond of quotin'. Seems it's writ in there somewhere that the Lord helps them what helps themselves."

Without another word, Preacher turned on one heel of his fighting sandals and walked away. From a short distance off, Sister Amelia Witherspoon looked after him with a longing that was not the least bit sexual. She had been wondering about the whereabouts of Deacon Abercrombie when he had begun to talk with the men. What he said made her completely forget the deacon. She hungered for a man of courage like this one. Someone who would lead these timid souls to freedom. Sounded to her like this could be the one.

Chapter 15

Two days went by swiftly, Preacher took Buck and Philadelphia aside for a final discussion on their plan to escape from the arena. His words were as grim as they were low.

"We cain't know when or how we'll do this. I figger we hoss one another up the inner wall and make a run through the on-lookers. They won't be armed, and most of 'em will plain panic when we swarm in among them with weapons drippin' blood. That'll keep the guards away."

Overhead the coliseum filled with noise as early spectators filled the rows of stone benches. Concessionaires could be hard hawking their wears. To Preacher it sounded like something they would do back east. A July Fourth celebration or something.

"I think the best thing is to do it right off. Go after that brat kid of Marcus Quintus and use him as a shield," Buck opined.

Preacher slowly shook his head. "No, the guards will be watchin' right close at first, when we're fresh and all. If we can string it out until the gospel-spouters are brought in, we can probably get a half dozen or so to come along. We've all been in enough tussle to know when's the best time. Use your judgment, but keep an eye on me."

The long, valveless trumpets sounded, announcing the entry of the day's master of games. The crowd roared.

Another fanfare, and then the other musicians joined in. Metal creaked and grated as the portcullis raised enough to let out a party of clowns. Preacher watched them with divided attention.

They did somersaults and cartwheels, ran into one another, took pratfalls and rolled in the sand. One, with an animal bladder filled with water, pounded on his companions until the thin skin broke and soaked the victim. The crowd howled in merriment. When the last buffoon scampered back inside the dark interior of the coliseum, the attendants went out to smooth off the killing ground. That accomplished, the trainers came to line up the whole company of gladiators and condemned prisoners.

A moment later, the trumpets sounded again, clear and crisp. The gate rumbled upward, and the lead fighters in the Company of the Dead stepped out onto the sand.

Young Quintus Faustus Americus entered the *imperator's* box with the first fanfare. Dressed in snowy toga, with a broad purple hem stripe, he wore a circlet of gilded laurel leaves, with gold-strapped sandals. Followed by his body servant, Casca, he went directly to the center seat of the front row and raised his right arm. In his hand he held an ivory staff with a gold eagle on the top. He turned from side to side, as he had been instructed, and waved to the cheering crowd.

Some stomped their feet, others cheered and whistled. Led by the paid clique, they chanted his name in a wavelike roar. Eyes sparkling in pleasure, he nevertheless maintained his composure while he seated himself and stared serenely across the sand at the giant portal behind which the gladiators and condemned prisoners waited. Casca popped a grape between the lips of Faustus. His father and mother joined him and took seats at either side. Bulbus came next, followed by a dozen patrician boys who had been invited by Faustus. When the box had filled, Faustus rose and elevated the wand. The trumpets roared again.

"The auguries are good! The gods are pleased. Let the games begin!" he called out in his squeaky boy's voice.

Casca handed Faustus a chilled cup of wine as the portcullis squealed open and out spilled the clowns. Their antics delighted the crowd. Their erratic tumbling absolutely captivated the birthday guests. Faustus laughed until the tears ran and he held his sides. Then he suddenly remembered the seriousness of his position today. He cast an uneasy glance at Casca, who winked at him, then sobered and forced unwilling facial muscles into a placid expression. The *real* fun, he reminded himself, would come later.

When the clowns ended their performance, the trumpets blared again. The portcullis raised the full way, and the Company of the Dead marched forth. In the lead came the ranks of professionals, followed by those in training, and lastly the prisoners. A small smile of expectation flickered on the lips of Faustus. In perfect formation the participants in the games reached the base of the "emperor's" box. They raised their weapons in salute.

"Hail Caesar, we who are about to die salute thee!"

Faustus rose to speak the lines he had prepared. Leaning forward, he addressed them while Casca shaded him with a parasol. "Friends. Thank you for the spectacle you have prepared in honor of my birthday. I am sure that I will enjoy it. Now it is time to begin. Parade yourselves for my other friends to see, then bring on the first pairs."

It having been spoken in Latin, Preacher did not recognize a word. "Lotta jibber-jabber you ask me," he whispered to Philadelphia.

Drums and wind instruments struck up, and the gladiators turned smartly to make a circuit of the arena. Behind them came the "accommodators" to smooth the sand.

Although the air was cool on this last day of September, Preacher had worked up a sweat from the closeness of the coliseum and the heat of the sun by the time they returned to the cool interior of the underground cells.

At once, the clarions summoned the first two fighting pairs. Four professionals stepped out onto the sand. They faced off, one-on-one, saluted one another and set to. A *riatarius* tested his skill against a gladiator dressed as a Samnite. The long, curved blade in the Samnite's hand danced a blue-white arabesque in the air. The trident man looped his net in a hypnotic pattern before the eyes of the swordsman. He prodded with his three-tined spear. Preacher and Philadelphia stood close to the iron lattice of the portcullis and watched intently.

Beyond the fighters, he saw Faustus lean forward raptly, his mouth sagged open, pink tongue flicking in and out. There was a grunt as the Samnite lunged with his sword. A moment later the crowd roared as the retiarius flicked out his net and snared his opponent's blade and right arm. The trident darted toward his exposed, bare belly.

Dancing on tiptoe, the Samnite turned to his right, away from the spear and free of the knotted lines of the net. A mighty shout came from the spectators. Lightning fast, the retiarius came after the retreating gladiator. The Samnite's sword slashed through the air and bit deeply into the wooden shaft of the spear.

"Gotta remember to keep from doin' that," Preacher said to himself.

"What's that?" Philadelphia asked.

"I was talkin' to myself. That feller almost got his spear chopped in half. Careless."

"There's a lot to learn for this kind of fighting," Philadelphia agreed.

On the sand, the net flared outward and fluttered down over the head and shoulders of the Samnite. At once, the retiarius ran around his helpless opponent and secured him in the snare. Then, with a powerful yank, he jerked the swordsman off his feet. He pounced on the supine body and raised his trident for the fatal blow. He hesitated at that point and looked up at the box.

Faustus, lights dancing in his eyes, leaned forward and shot out his arm. At the last moment, his father reached over and touched him lightly on his bare knee. Disappointment painted the boy's face momentarily. Then he turned his thumb upward. The mob shouted its approval.

When their bedlam subsided, a scream came from the lips of a gladiator with a spiked-ball flail. He had taken his eye off his opponent for a split second. That was all it had taken. With blurring speed, the gladiator with a *gladius* made a diagonal slash from the incautious fighter's right nipple to his left hip. Howls of approval and jeers for the wounded man.

"It's Brutus. Stupid Brutus."

"Brutus has never been any good." More insults came from the audience, though Preacher did not understand them.

"Finish him!" a woman's voice shrieked.

Brutus shuddered as he walked more into Preacher's view. Blood streamed down his torso in a shimmering curtain. He brought up his shield to cover his vulnerable body and began to swing his flail back and forth. The sword came at him again. Brutus blocked it with his shield and converted his sideways motion into a circular one. When the heavy, spiked ball reached a position directly behind its handle, he lashed it forward.

It struck with a clang on the small shield of his opponent. With a powerful yank, Brutus jerked the protective disc out of the other gladiator's grasp. At once he tried to free his weapon. That proved his undoing. The opposing gladiator came at him with a blizzard of varied attacks. It ended with a horizontal slash that opened the belly of Brutus an inch above his navel.

Brutus sucked air deeply and dropped the handle of his flail. He sat abruptly. His eyes grew wide, and he worked frantically to stuff his intestines back inside his body.

"That's dumb, Brutus," a critic directly over Preacher shouted.

Preacher looked over at the box along with the victorious gladiator. Panting in his excitement, Faustus wore the mask of a child demon as he eagerly thrust out his arm and turned his extended thumb downward. The swordsman quickly stepped over and struck the head from Brutus' shoulders. The crowd went wild.

Shoulder to shoulder, the three surviving gladiators marched to salute the young boy in whose honor this display of gore was being held. Then they returned to the gate which rose to admit them. The trumpets blared and four more professionals came out. A quartet of confused, frightened men followed.

They saluted the *imperator* from the center of the sand and set to it with speed and energy. This round of combats lasted only a short time and the blood flowed freely. Two of the half-trained fighters died within a minute, dispatched by the down-turned thumb of Quintus Faustus. The survivors strutted back to the holding pens. Another fanfare brought out the clowns.

Only these were not the same frisky children who had performed first. They appeared to be dazed, uncertain of where they were, or what their purpose might be. Handlers quickly goaded them into fighting one another. Some were armed with tubes of sewn skin, filled with sand, others with air-filled bladders. Another group carried straw-stuffed objects that Preacher could only guess at being animal parts. He watched them with a growing frown as they began to flail away at their companions.

Philadelphia approached him and nodded toward the

grotesque performers. "I hear around that those poor folk are captives who have been tormented into states of craziness. They're supposed to whoop it up out there for a while, then comes the really bad part."

"What's that?" Preacher asked him.

"Wait, an' you'll see."

"Sounds grim. Might be you an' Buck can get more cooperation out of those Bible-thumpers. Why don't you go in among them and give them a little backbone?"

"Suits. I'll get Buck." Philadelphia turned away and went to find the teamster. Preacher soon saw them talking earnestly among the missionaries. He looked away, back at the sand, when gales of laughter filled the arena.

"Pears to me that it's them that's watchin' an' laughin' that's got the sick minds," he grumbled to himself.

The sorrowful clowns had milked their antics for all the laughs they could generate. At a signal from the real master of the games, Bulbus, small gates opened around the arena. Out rushed huge, ferocious, starved Mastiff dogs. Screams of terror came from the pitiful, demented clowns as the dogs fell on them. The audience loved it. Preacher made a face of disgust as he looked beyond the slaughter to the small boy in the marble box.

Faustus squirmed in a frenzy of excitement. It made Preacher's stomach churn.

"I tell you, friend, if you don't decide to fight back, you'll get what them poor fellers out there are gettin'. It don't feel nice gettin' ripped apart by a cougar." Preacher told three intently listening young missionaries. "Believe me, I know. I done got mauled by one some years back. If I didn't have a big knife an' a war hawk with me, he'd a-been dinin' on my innards before noon."

One of his audience swallowed hard and made a gagging sound. "If I have something to fight with, I'll fight," he declared shakily. To the angry glare from the son of Deacon Abercrombie, he added, "I have a wife and two children to protect."

"A child has the right to decide for himself," Philbert Abercrombie replied snippily.

Defiance crackled in the words of the young father. "If a child cannot make decisions about property, or his schooling, or anything else, Brother Philbert, I say he cannot properly decide to die for the greater glory of the Lord."

"Careful Brother Fauts, you are close to blasphemy."

Fury born of his protectiveness exploded. "*Damn* your blasphemy! I'll fight, and you would, too, if you had any stones."

Philadelphia left them to further pursuit of that possibility when a burly handler gestured to him with his coiled whip. Buck, too, had been gathered in. Their warders took them to where Preacher stood. Three of the toughest professionals joined them a moment later.

"You will fight in pairs. You condemned men, if you win this match, you will be paired with another gladiator until you are killed. So, fight your best and give the people a good show."

When the last of the demented victims succumbed to the ravening jaws of the Mastiffs, the accommodators cleared the arena. Hawkers moved through the aisles, selling wine, popped corn, slices of melon and other fruit. Others cut shaving-thin slices off roasted joints of meat and built sandwiches. The spectators ate and drank and talked through their laughter as they recalled their favorite kill by the vicious dogs. It all made Preacher want to drive the three tines of his trident into their guts and twist while they shrieked in agony.

With the clean-up completed, the clarions brayed again, and the six fighters stepped out onto the sand. They advanced in two ranks, Preacher, Philadelphia and Buck behind the professionals. At the center, they halted and saluted the boy *imperator*. Faustus rose and addressed them, his voice husky with barely suppressed emotion.

"You three who defied the authority of New Rome will die here today. And I will take great pleasure in watching your blood soak into the sand. So, do not slack. Give us a good fight, so we can thrill in your agony." He pointed his ivory wand at Preacher. "Especially you, my magnificent specimen. I expect great things from you. Now, let the fighting begin."

Trumpets shivered the air. All six fighters squared off. Preacher knew he had to make this quick. He began to circle his opponent, the net held loosely in his left hand. He feinted tentatively with the trident. Suddenly, the gladiator opposite him burst forth with a frenzy of furious blows.

Tall, lean, and muscular, Vindix bore in on Preacher with a smooth network of thrusts and slashes. He smiled grimly as Preacher gave ground. He batted the trident aside and pressed forward with a springy right leg. Blinding hot pain erupted in his thigh as Preacher recovered from the beat and drove two of the three tines of his weapon deeply into the flesh of an exposed thigh.

A fraction of a second later, he hurled the net, ensnaring Vindix. With a stout yank, Preacher hauled the gladiator off his sandals. He drew the small dagger from his belt and knelt beside the fallen fighter.

"I'll make this quick, to spare you pain."

Vindix smiled through his agony. "That's what I intended for you. No need for us to provide entertainment for that sick, twisted child."

Preacher looked up at the boy, to see an expression of fury on the soft features. "You were too fast. That's not fair. Spare him," Faustus' squeaky voice commanded.

Preacher replaced his dagger and offered a hand to Vindix to help him come upright. The crowd cheered.

Vindix was a favorite. Preacher spoke softly to him. "You live to fight another day."

Vindix gave him a grim smile, face contorted with pain. "More's a pity." He limped away, to be replaced by another gladiator. This one bore the spiked mace. He came after Preacher in a rush.

Philadelphia had been matched with a squat, brawny brute who took particular pleasure in maiming his opponents before finally finishing them off. Despite the lingering discomfort of his old wound, Philadelphia Braddock danced lightly away from the *gladius* that darted before his eyes. Sweat began to trickle down from his temples. He concentrated on the eyes of Asperis and the tip of his sword.

So quick Philadelphia almost missed it, Asperis widened his eyes in anticipation of a slash that would sever the mountain man's left arm, leaving him without a shield. With a swift jerk, Philadelphia raised the round metal protector, and the iron blade in his opponent's hand rang loudly against it. Philadelphia swung his right leg forward and pivoted, to smash his armored *caestus* into the point of the left shoulder of Asperis. The triangular blades bit deeply, and blood flowed in a gush when Philadelphia withdrew his *caestus*. He shifted his weight and kicked Asperis in the belly.

Numbed and bleeding profusely from the shoulder, Asperis doubled over, and Philadelphia clubbed him with the armored fist. Unfortunately it left him vulnerable for a moment, during which Asperis drove the tip of his sword into the meaty portion of Philadelphia's side. Fire flashed through the muscles of Philadelphia's torso. Biting his lower lip, he hauled back and rammed the spikes of his *caestus* into the side of Asperis' head. The gladiator went down in a flash.

A low groan came from deep in his chest, and Asperis began to twitch his arms and legs. Philadelphia knew what he had done and wasted no time checking with the pouty-faced brat for the signal to finish Asperis. Behind him, the portcullis clanged again, and another contender entered the arena. Philadelphia turned to see it would be a retiarius.

"More trouble," he grunted.

Buck Sears faced a gladiator done up as a Nubian warrior, complete with zebra-painted shield, towering head-dress and assagai spear. Braided elephant tail hair and feather anklets circled his legs above bare feet. They rippled hypnotically as he bounced and jounced up and down in an advance punctuated by sharp cries from a mouth ringed by a wide smear of black grease paint.

Buck took this all in and lowered the tip of his sword to the sand. He threw back his head and laughed. "Now, ain't you just the silliest damn critter I've ever seen."

The gyrations abruptly ceased. "Huh?"

"I said you look like a fool," Buck called out.

Howling in outrage, the imitation Nubian charged with his spear held over his shoulder in one of the classical positions employed by the Zulu and Masai, whom the ancient Romans lumped together as "Nubians."

Buck lunged out of the way of the advance. He swung the flat of his blade and smashed it into the ribs of his opponent. Laughter rose from the stands. Buck began to enjoy himself. Before the Nubian could turn, Buck booted him in the seat of his pants. He stumbled and lowered his shield. Buck thrust with his sword and cut a line along the gladiator's forehead right below the gaudy headdress. A sheet of blood poured out. The mob loved it.

Even that evil-minded brat had started to giggle and clap his hands, Buck noted. He quickly found out he had paid too much attention to such matters. Solis had recovered himself and came at Buck driven by fury. He battered and hacked at the shield Buck carried. Buck's strength wavered momentarily, and Solis seized the advantage. Setting his feet, he slammed his own shield into Buck's face.

Buck's knees buckled, and he dropped onto the left one. Blackness swam before his eyes. He shook his head in an effort to clear it while he fended off the plunging assagai. With a desperate effort, he brought his *gladius* around and drove it through the fire-hardened zebra-print shield. The tip sliced three inches into sweaty flesh. Solis grunted, gasped and loosed a thin wail. Buck pulled back and regained his feet.

Above him, all around the coliseum the throng went wild. They stomped their feet and pelted the sand with greasy strips of paper that had held sandwiches and popped corn. Some threw cushions they had brought along for comfort on the stone benches of the common bleachers. A gray pallor had washed over the face of Solis. He blinked back fear, sweat and blood and tried to focus on his opponent.

Sucking in large draughts of air, Buck found Solis easily enough. His shield arm sagged; the knob-hilted assagai hung in an unresponsive hand. Pink froth bubbled on his pain-distorted lips. Balefully, Buck advanced on him. Deep inside, he did not want to do this. Then he remembered he was supposed to solicit a decision from the *imperator*.

He turned his head upward. Faustus seemed to be on the edge of ecstasy. He rapidly licked his lips and stared fixedly at the bleeding wound in the chest of Solis. At last he regrasped what was expected of him. Solis was a professional. Faustus spared him.

Two arena helpers escorted him out. Another gladiator took his place. The six men—three sapped and worn from their earlier battles, the other trio fresh—faced the box and saluted.

"Awh, hell, we've gotta go through this all over again," Buck muttered. He squared off with the others, and the attacks came immediately.

Chapter 16

Through the open squares formed by the iron gate to their holding pen, Sister Amelia Witherspoon looked on. At first she viewed the grisly spectacle in horror. Then, as the mountain men and their teamster ally bested one after another professional gladiator, her perusal changed to amorous fascination with Preacher. He had to be the bravest, strongest man ever born.

A shiver of delight ran through her slender body, hidden under the prim, gray dress and wimpollike bonnet. If what he did before her very eyes was not so absolutely terrible, she might suspect that she was becoming enamored of him. Possibly even falling in love. *Stuff and nonsense,* she told herself. Cries of trepidation came from others among the missionaries. One of the young men convinced to put up some resistance by Philadelphia spoke quietly beside Sister Amelia.

"Is any of them going to be around to lead the way to freedom?"

An unusual light sparkled in Amelia's eyes. "I'm sure that one will. Arturus. He has finished off three gladiators so far. Spared the lives of two. He is a true champion."

With an indulgent chuckle, the young man nodded toward Preacher. " 'Arturus' is it? That may be what these crazy folk call him, but the one named Philadelphia told me he is really the mountain man we were questioned about, Preacher."

Amelia's eyes widened. "I knew it! I knew he had to be the best there is. Oh, Preacher, fight for us," she offered up prayerfully.

Out on the sand, it appeared as though Preacher had heard her appeal and responded accordingly. He swung his net, snared another gladiator, and hurtled the hapless fighter toward the deadly tines of the trident. A moment before the barbed spikes entered vulnerable flesh, a high, thin voice barked from above and behind Preacher.

"Hold!" Preacher released his victim. "He has fought well," Faustus continued. "He is free to retire. You will face yet another, more worthy opponent," he told Preacher. "At once."

Looks like the folks in the imperial box have got impatient. Not gonna wait for all of us to finish our fights, Preacher thought to himself as the gate ground open and a huge fellow lumbered out. Taller by a head than Preacher, he was armed with a *caestus* and a twin-bladed dagger. He immediately went for Preacher with a roar.

He swung the *caestus* with practiced ease, and the spectators greeted him by name. "Dicius! Dicius! Dicius!"

Like an elephant attacking a toad, he loomed over Preacher and contemptuously swept aside the net when it hissed toward him. He stepped in and engaged the trident with the dual-bladed knife, gave a mighty twist and yanked it from Preacher's grasp. Preacher tried with the net again and missed as Dicius danced away. Then the muscular gladiator came at Preacher again.

He bounded forward, jinked to his right, tempting another throw of the net. Preacher obliged him. The tar-stiffened, knotted snare fanned out and lofted over the head of Dicius. Before it could descend, Dicius leaped to his left and struck a powerful blow with the *caestus*.

Fortunately for Preacher, the punch landed askew, to glance off the side of Preacher's head. One of the blades cut a ragged line in the hair above one ear. Stunned, Preacher sank to one knee. Dimly he heard the shrill scream as Amelia cried out.

Philadelphia Braddock looked up at the sound of that anguished wail. He saw Dicius poised with his *caestus* raised above his head to deliver a fatal blow. For the moment Philadelphia ignored his own tormentor to grasp his sword in front of the hilt and hurl it like a lance. It flashed in the afternoon sunlight as it sped to the target.

Paralyzed by enormous misery, Dicius emitted a faint moan as the *gladius* pierced his side and sliced through the soft organs in his belly. He rocked from heel to toe for a moment, and the *caestus* dropped without force to land on Preacher's shoulder. Shaking clear of his momentary blackout, Preacher scrambled to retrieve his trident.

He stood over Dicius, who feebly tried to cut the hamstring of Preacher's left leg. With a powerful thrust, Preacher drove the middle tine through his opponents throat. He looked up with a nod and a smile for Philadelphia.

"I reckon they aim to kill us for certain sure. No reason we have to play by their rules," Preacher told his friend as he abandoned his trident. Then he bent, retrieved the *gladius* and tossed it back to Philadelphia.

So astonished by the swift action that he failed to press his attack, the gladiator contesting Philadelphia only then broke his frozen pose. He came on strong, yet the mountain man managed to elude his darting weapon. Philadelphia gave ground slowly, eyes alert for an opening. While he did, Preacher retrieved the spiked mace of an earlier opponent and looked to the portcullis, where his next enemy would appear.

It turned out to be Sparticus. At sight of this, Faustus bounced up and down on his chair, thrilled by the prospects. Preacher did not greet it quite so enthusiastically. He gave a tentative swing of the spiked ball at the end of its chain and advanced on the huge escaped slave. A moment later, Philadelphia got too busy to watch.

With catlike grace, the gladiator advanced on an oblique angle to Philadelphia. He prodded at him with the tip of his *pilum*. The slender spear had been equipped with a soft lead collar at the base of the tip to prevent it from being withdrawn from a wound. Altogether a nasty weapon. Philadelphia gave it due respect. His opponent's advance forced him toward where Buck had just dispatched his latest enemy. Weakened by his recent wounds, Philadelphia could not maintain his balance when he backed into the supine body of the dead gladiator.

His knee buckled and he stumbled. At that critical moment, the professional thrust the javelin toward him. Only at the last possible moment, Philadelphia covered himself with his shield, turned the *pilum,* and regained his balance. He hacked at an exposed knee, and the blades bit into flesh at the bottom of the gladiator's thigh. That let Philadelphia recover completely.

Ignoring the threat of the javelin, he pushed in on his opponent. At that moment, Philadelphia would have given anything for a good tomahawk. The short sword would have to do, he decided. At least until he could equip himself with something better. At first he made good progress, his antagonist hobbled by his wound; then Philadelphia planted his foot in a pool of blood while attempting a thrust to the chest.

His feet went out from under him, and he plopped onto the ground. Hoots and jeers rose from the onlookers. Eyes alight with renewed hope, the gladiator moved in on Philadelphia.

Eager to win Sparticus as an ally, rather than have to kill him, Preacher raised his left hand in a cautionary gesture; the net hung limp in his grasp. "It don't have to end here, Sparticus," he prompted.

"Don't talk that talk to me, white man," Sparticus growled truculently.

Preacher ignored him. "I mean it. You can get out of here, too."

Sparticus would have none of it. He came at Preacher with a huge cudgel, a single, long spike protruding through the side of the thick tip. It swished through the air as Preacher jumped backward. Muscles rippled under the oiled black skin as Sparticus planted another big foot on the sand and advanced again.

Preacher whipped the air with his flail. The spiked ball smashed into the boss of the shield on Sparticus' left arm. It made a resounding, thunder-clap sound. Instead of retreating, Sparticus stepped in. The men found themselves chest to chest. The muscles in Preacher's left arm and shoulder strained to hold the powerful arm that supported the cudgel.

To the on-lookers they appeared to be dancing as they shuffled their feet to find better purchase. Some began to clap rhythmically. Cries of "Fight! Fight!" rang in the tiers. Preacher spoke quiet reason to Sparticus.

"Even though slavery is the law of the land, it don't amount to a hill of bison dung out here. If you join us in winnin' free, an' takin' them helpless missionaries with us, I'll personally guarantee that you can make a new life for yourself in the High Lonesome, an' live a free man."

Sparticus curled his lips in a sneer and snarled his reply while he cuffed Preacher with a backhand blow with the cudgel. "What do I want that for? I'm due to earn the *rudis* soon. That'll make me a wealthy man, an' free. Why should I risk all of that for a passel of white folk who prob'ly owned slaves before they got captured?"

Preacher gave it another try. "They're Bible-thumpers. Mission folk. Their kind don't hold slaves."

"Knowed me a preacher-man down South. He owned hisself three house slaves. I'll be a big man around here after I kill you an' retire."

Unable to obtain dominance above, Preacher used an old Indian trick. He shifted his weight to one leg, shot the other forward and hooked his heel behind the ankle of Sparticus.

With a swift yank forward, he toppled the big black gladiator off his feet. At the last second, Preacher rolled away as Sparticus crashed to the ground. Impact forced grunted words from Sparticus' mouth.

"You're good, I give you that. Who are you, anyhow, Arturus?"

Preacher decided to gamble it all. He turned his flinty gaze straight into the eyes of his opponent. "They call me Preacher."

An expression of respect, flavored with awe, filled the gladiator's face. "Fore Jesus, I didn't know."

They had come to their knees now. The force of their impact with hard-packed sand had knocked the flail from Preacher's hand. He saw the trident only a scant foot from his grasp. Sparticus hefted the club and licked his lips.

"I'll be the richest man around if I finish you," Sparticus declared.

"*IF.* I'd think on that were I you."

Sparticus found that to somehow be funny. He threw back his head to laugh, and Preacher quickly unfurled his net and flung it over the kneeling man. Sparticus flung it off like a mere cobweb. Though not before Preacher could snatch up his trident. Opposite him, Sparticus bounded to the soles of his high-laced sandals. Preacher seemed to react slowly, gathering his net.

With the quickness that made him famous, Sparticus charged. The cudgel led the way. Preacher deflected it with the shaft of his trident and prodded at the chest of his opponent. Sparticus laughed mirthlessly and came on. Forced to give ground, Preacher brought his heel down on the haft of a dropped weapon. Instantly, he stumbled and tottered off to one side.

Sparticus seized the moment. "You gon' die, Preacher-man."

Preacher recovered himself as the deadly club swished past his left ear. The haft of the lethal object slammed painfully into the top of his shoulder. Already directed to its target, the trident cut a ragged gash in the lean side of Sparticus. Dizzied by repeated injury, Preacher missed an opportunity to end it.

Pain made his next cast erratic. The net slid from the oiled skin of his opponent and fluttered to the ground. Goaded by the press of time, Preacher hastily gathered it. A blur of movement told him Sparticus had anticipated the miss. The black man bore down on him and forced another retreat.

Feeling the effects of blood-loss, Preacher stumbled again. Seized by a frenzy, the crowd howled and stomped their feet. Sparticus acted at once on the tiny break given him. Overconfident now, he stepped in for the kill, only to have Preacher let loose the net again, this time tightly furled. Using a technique he had learned from the instructors, he sent it out like a sinuous snake to coil around Sparticus' ankles.

Immediately he recovered his balance. Preacher ran swiftly around the black gladiator and bound his legs together. Then, a hefty yank took Sparticus off his feet. In a staggered rush, Preacher closed with him and held the trident poised to drive two tines into the man's thick neck. Slowly, reluctantly, he looked up at the imperial box.

Quintus Faustus had bounded to his sandals moments earlier. He jumped up and down in agitation, his face white, eyes wild, his small, red mouth twisted grotesquely. His breathing came rapidly, and he showed obvious signs of arousal. He cut his pale blue eyes to Preacher's hot, gray orbs as he stuck out his arm.

Slowly, almost lasciviously, he turned his thumb down.

"Last chance," Preacher told Sparticus.

With considerable regret and hesitancy, Sparticus nodded in the affirmative. Preacher relaxed the position of his weapon. Above him, the shrill voice of Faustus held an edge of hysteria.

"Kill him! Kill him!" he wailed.

Calmly, ignoring the willful child, Preacher reached down and unbound the legs of Sparticus, raised him to his feet and disarmed him. Then he turned to the box.

"He yielded," he said simply.

Face clouded with tantrum warning flags, Faustus shoved out his lower lip in a spiteful, pink pout. "I don't care. It's my games, and my birthday, and I want to see men die."

Preacher replied with calm restraint. "I will not kill a man who yields to me."

White froth formed in the corners of Faustus' mouth. He dropped his wand of authority into the cushion on his chair and made small fists of his slim, long-fingered hands. His sallow face flushed scarlet as he stamped one foot like a girl.

"I want him dead! Now! Now! Now!" he shrieked.

To his surprise, Preacher looked on as Marcus Quintus rose from his chair and spoke into his son's ear. At the first words, the boy went rigid, and he shook with the intensity of his childish fury. The more Quintus spoke, the lower the shoulders of Faustus drooped. At last, his tower of rage was reduced to a pitiful bleat.

"But, Father."

"Do it!" his father hissed loud enough to be heard by the men on the sand.

In a show of bad grace, the boy gave a reluctant nod of agreement. He picked up his wand and raised it above his head. The trumpets blared. By then it had become unnecessary. The spectators perched on the edges of their seats in silent expectation. Faustus pointed to the surviving gladiators one by one.

"Come forward," he intoned.

Preacher, Sparticus, Philadelphia, and Buck did as commanded. They were the only ones. Faustus shook with his barely suppressed outrage, and he stammered as he addressed the four fighting men. He again pointed at each one with the staff of office.

"Since you three are under sentence of death for attempted escape, and you, Sparticus, have made a cowardly surrender and are already a dead man in our eyes, you shall all be thrown in with the Christians and lions. Let the games proceed."

Chapter 17

Preacher faced the frightened missionaries in the large holding pen. Arms folded across his chest—a gesture of strength and determination he had picked up from the Indians, rather than one of weakness—he addressed them in a low, hard voice.

"I am only going to say this once. The only way out of here is to fight. There will be plenty of weapons about the arena. I seen 'em puttin' out swords and some spears. They won't be as good a quality as what the gladiators have, but you can kill with them."

"To kill another man is to damn your soul for eternity," Philbert Abercrombie blustered. "Not a one of us will do that."

Preacher cocked his head to one side and eyed Abercrombie with a cold eye. "I was thinkin' on them mountain lions. They're fixin' to eat you before you have a chance to turn a sword on a man. You'd best be willin' an' able to stop them before you go worryin' about facin' a man."

Raising a stubborn chin, Philbert answered stubbornly. "If it comes to that, we'll be martyred with a hymn on our lips."

"Where's your pappy, Sonny? Best be hidin' behind his skirts. Phaw!" Preacher grunted, then turned to the others, ignoring the pompous Abercrombie. "Your best bet is to

fight back to back, four of you together. Protect your wimmin an' children inside the squares. That way no lion can
come at you unexpected. When the last one is finished off,
that's when we go for the walls. Help one another up an'
over and then we make a dash for it."

Encouraged by Preacher's positive outlook, Sister Amelia Witherspoon came forward. "Do you think we really
have a chance?"

"If you do what me an' my friends say, you have a lot
better chance than followin' this feller here who seems
hell-bent on dyin' for no reason. Seems to me he's a few
straws shy of a haystack. For the rest of you, I reckon you
know what to do when the time comes."

"What if we do kill the lions, only to be faced by men?"

Preacher gave them a nasty smile. "Well, there ain't
many of them left. Or didn't you watch us out there? But,
by damn, if that's the case, you kill them, too. It's the only
way."

Tingling notes sounded the final fanfare.

Out on the sand, the missionaries stood in blinking confusion. Boos and insults greeted Preacher and his fellows.
Ignoring them, the four fighting men quickly armed themselves. Cat calls and jeers rang down on the terror-stricken
Gospel-shouters. Tentatively, Sister Witherspoon began a
hymn.

That brought gales of raucous laughter. More mocking
retorts came from the audience. One blood-thirsty specta-
tor pointed at Amelia. "Hey, that one's good-looking.
Wonder how she'd be in . . ."

"Why aren't they in the buff, like usual?" inquired another.

"Where's that fat one I saw brought in?"

A smaller, low gate swung open, and one of the handlers
gave a mighty shove to the back of Deacon Abercrombie.

He stumbled out onto the sand, bare to the waist. His pale, bleached-looking skin and flabby condition produced a windstorm of scornful sniggers. His wife ran to him, tears bright in her eyes, face a-flame with embarrassment.

"Cover yourself with my shawl."

Shame encrimsoned the deacon's face. "You might not want to be kind to me, my dear. I—I betrayed you all to that monster Quintus. I only wanted freedom for you and I. I fear I may have prevented your one good chance to escape."

She draped the shawl over his shoulders and patted him consolingly. "There is a strange man, one of the gladiators, who says we still have a way to get out of here."

"Where is he?" Abercrombie asked eagerly.

"Over—over there." Agatha Abercrombie pointed to Preacher.

Phineas Abercrombie scowled. "The troublemaker. I'd not put much stock in him my dear."

And then they let out the lions.

At once, Deacon Abercrombie began to edge toward Preacher. The spectators cheered and shouted. They rose and clapped their hands in a wavelike motion around the tiers of seats. At first, the cougars seemed as confused and blinded by light as their intended victims. They padded about without direction, sniffed the air and uttered menacing growls. Tension built while the short-sighted critters sought to locate their prey. Two met head-on and traded swats and snarls. Three of the Mobile Church in the Wildwood's women uttered shrill screams.

One big, anvil-headed beast raised up from sniffing and turned baleful yellow eyes toward the sound. The women screamed all the more. One of the men broke and began to run to the far side of the arena from the deadly animals. At once the golden-orbed puma changed into a study in liquid motion. Flawlessly he streaked through the frightened missionaries, most of whom had remained stock still.

It rapidly closed the ground and launched itself at the back of the running Bible-thumper. Long, curved claws ripped mercilessly into tender flesh and raked along the back of the helpless man. His screams of agony set off a new explosion of yelling, stomping and applauding among the on-lookers. At once, Deacon Abercrombie's flock came to life and scrambled as one to put distance between themselves and the ravenous animals.

Preacher turned with all the fluid ease of the deadly cat and hacked through its spine, above the shoulders, with a single blow from the *gladius* he held. It died at the same time as the missionary it had attacked. Instantly, Preacher turned to face another of the beasts bent upon attacking him.

"Dang it," he roared as he split open the nose of the offending puma, "do like I said!"

With Philadelphia on his right, Buck on the left, and Sparticus behind, the four fought off three more cougars. First two, then six more of the missionaries got the idea from this efficient means of downing the snarling bundles of lightning-fast fury. They quickly armed themselves and formed defensive squares. Only Deacon Abercrombie remained alone and exposed. One big cat soon discovered this. While his wife screamed with terror and the deacon made squawking noises, the cougar pounced.

"Stop! I command you in the name of the Lord," Abercrombie found voice to thunder. Then he was shrieking out his life. The sand soon pooled with red. A woman among the missionaries screamed when a mountain lion dragged her out of one formation.

Only a short distance away, Preacher took two fast steps forward and plunged the leaf-bladed *gladius* to the hilt in the animal's chest. It released the woman, shivered mightily, arched its back, and fell dead as Preacher drew out the sword. Fickle as always the crowd went wild.

Now the spectators cheered the beleaguered missionaries. They had thought to be amused by the pitifully useless antics of the condemned wretches, only to find objects of admiration in the sudden courage displayed by desperate people. Preacher took note of it and spoke to his companions.

"Imagine that. All of a sudden they're on our side. Reckon that'll jerk the jaw of that bloody-minded boy-brat."

Buck answered through a grunt of effort as he split the skull of yet another cougar. "He likes to see blood run, right enough. But I don't think it's that of his prize cats. That one's sick in the head. You can tell by the look in his eyes."

"Best save our breath for fightin'," Preacher advised. "Let's get these folk on the move, form up close together, in two lines. Less target for the cougars that way."

One of the tawny creatures leaped into the air for a high attack. Preacher squatted and split open its belly with his *gladius*. "What good will that do?" Sparticus grumbled as he drove a *pilum* into the chest of a raging puma.

Preacher answered quickly. "We can move around the sand like the hands on a clock. Finish off what's left in no time."

At the shouted urges of the mountain men, the desperate missionaries began to form into two lines, back-to-back. Over his shoulder, Preacher called to those behind him. "Can you walk backwards an' still fight them critters?" When they assured him they could, he issued a loud, if imprecise, command. "Then let's git to it."

The crowd howled in glee as the enraged cougars died one at a time. When only a single pair remained, those on the sand could not hear a word said by anyone beside them. All around them, the last of the big cats could smell the odor of their dead companions. Fangs dripping the foam of their fury, they flung themselves at the wall of human flesh that inexorably forced them to move. A scream emboldened them as an inexperienced missionary went down, his chest and belly clawed open. The cougar that had felled him did not get to savor its victory.

Even before the line had formed, Amelia Witherspoon had taken up a *pilum* and had speared one of the cats. Now she sank the javelin into the side of the blood-slobbering beast that had disemboweled Brother Frazier. The creature screamed like a woman, arched its back and lashed out uselessly with weakened paws. Amelia hung on to the shaft and felt the power of the animal vibrate through her arms. The hind feet left the ground, and she had to let go quickly to keep from being dragged down onto the dying cat.

"Good girl," Preacher said, though no one could hear him over the roar of the mob in the stands. "I knew she had some pluck."

An instant later, he had to defend his life against the last of the beasts. It hurtled at his part of the line with a mighty, bowel-watering roar. Preacher buried his *gladius* in its chest, though not before it had its forelegs wrapped around him and the claws bit agonizingly into his back. Then, half a dozen swords, javelins, and tridents sank into the golden coat to drive the last of life from the animal. Pressure eased in Preacher's back, and he felt the gentle touch of Philadelphia as his friend pried the claws from him.

"It's all done."

"I doubt that, Philadelphia."

Once assured that no more mountain lions lurked to spring upon them, the surviving force turned as one to face the blighted little boy who ran the games. Preacher saw through the haze of pain, and the sting of sweat in his eyes, that Faustus' face had been twisted into a mask of evil. With a sudden-born smile of such sweetness as to melt the hardest heart, the boy made a signal with his imperial baton.

* * *

First came the cleaning crew. They hauled off the carcasses of the dead cougars, spread fresh sand over the pools of blood, then exited. It gave everyone time to catch their breath. It also allowed the timid among the missionaries to exercise their imaginations on what might come next. Preacher, Philadelphia, Buck, and Sparticus considered the same thing, though not colored by fear and trepidation.

"I reckon that little monster is going to throw something else at us," Philadelphia opined. "Why ain't we moving?"

"He'll have to do something. He's got his neck stuck a whole ways out sayin' how we would all die," Preacher agreed. "Whatever it is will maybe give us a better opening." Preacher turned to the black gladiator. "What do you figger, Sparticus. And—ah—it'd be kinda nice to know your real name."

Sparticus flashed a white smile. "It's no better'n the one they hung on me. It's—you won't laugh?—Cornilius."

Preacher fought the quirk of a smile. "Then Sparticus it is."

"Obliged. I expect as hows that li'l bastard will send in the whole rest of the gladiators. They'll finish these weaklings fast. Then it'll be up to us."

"Not if I can come up with something better," Preacher promised.

"It had best be good," Buck put in his bit.

Above them, the trumpets brayed. The portcullis raised to admit the twenty remaining trained gladiators. Their weapons were of the serious type. No gaudy costumes or colorful shields. They carried workmanlike swords, flails, javelins, and two had bows. They advanced, their arms at rest, to salute the box. That's when providence handed Preacher a large portion of good fortune.

"I gotta make this fast. All of you sheep listen up. Whatever we do, you do. And that starts now! Run at them,"

Preacher shouted as he set off at a fast trot toward the unprepared gladiators.

With their weapons aimed more or less at the advancing gladiators, the missionaries followed in the wake of Preacher and his companions. Preacher let out a caterwaul as the unexpected charge closed with the newcomers. It froze them for a vital moment. Preacher smashed one to his knees with the flat of his blade, and shoved through to stab another in the gut. Beside him, the arms of his friends churned in deadly rhythm.

Philadelphia drove a *pilum* into the gut of a burly gladiator who had leaped aside to swing his spiked ball at Preacher. When the tip entered his flesh, he dropped his weapon and doubled over on the shaft of the spear. He clutched it with trembling fingers as he sank to his knees. Philadelphia left the *pilum* in his victim, snatched up the flail and shoved on into the melee of struggling gladiators. The audience lost their minds while the four courageous fighters hacked and slashed their way through the ranks and came out on the other side.

At once, Preacher led the way to the gate, which had not as yet begun to close. He darted under the pointed ends of the portcullis and downed a guard with a sword thrust. Beside him, Buck Sears killed the guard at the windlass that controlled the wooden-framed iron barrier and quickly grabbed hold to secure it.

Behind him came Philadelphia and Sparticus. They made short work of the three astonished handlers who stood gawking at the furious battle. Then they turned back to hold the opening for the missionaries.

Hewing like gleaners in a wheat field, the Mobile Church in the Wildwood members smashed through the ranks of gladiators. They streamed by ones and twos toward the open gateway. Preacher noticed that the handsome young woman with the spear fought with the ferocity of the men. While he registered this, she poked the iron tip of the *pilum* into the eye of a huge man with a long sword. He fell screaming. The iron-slat gate held motionless while they dashed under its pointed ends.

When the last one cleared the barrier, Buck let it go. It crashed down with a resounding roar. Buck quickly slashed the rope that supported it. Led by Preacher and Philadelphia, the missionaries rushed down the stone corridor, into the bowels of the coliseum. Amelia Witherspoon had dropped her *pilum* and clung to Preacher all the way.

"Where are we going?" she panted in question.

Preacher nodded to the tunnel entrance. "To the home of the master of games."

"But, why? Isn't that dangerous?"

"Not so much as *not* doing it. For one thing, I'm not leaving here without my horses and my shootin' gear. I've got me a pair of Walker Colts I've grown right fond of."

"Walkers? I've not heard of that breed before."

"They ain't my horses, Missy, they's shootin' irons."

"Oh! . . . *OH!*" she squeaked.

Preacher chuckled. Then he thought he had better explain it to these featherheads so they'd know. He slowed his pace, halted them midway in the tunnel and spoke in a low, earnest voice that still echoed off the walls.

"Listen up, folks. This ain't over yet. We're goin' to the storehouse at the games master's house. You can get better weapons, an' you'll need them, and horses to make a quick getaway."

"You mean there'll be more fighting?" Agatha Abercrombie asked in a trembling voice.

"Sure's sh—er—skunks stink, ma'am. There's the better part of two legions out there."

"Oh, dear, dear, maybe we should not have done this," she wailed.

"You could have always gotten et up by the lions, like your husband," Preacher told her coldly.

"You cruel, cruel man," she chastised.

"*I'm* cruel? What about that devil's spawn brat who ordered all that? I got no more time for you. Keep movin' folks."

Entering the storeroom at the house of Justinius Bulbus from the gladiator school proved easier than the frontal approach. The two guards at the far end of the tunnel had gone down like one man when Preacher and Sparticus unexpectedly appeared. With them out of the way, Preacher had called upon the great strength of Sparticus to help him breach the iron gate.

It gave with a noisy screech, and the refugee missionaries stumbled through. Being empty, the school had an eerie quality to it. Buck Sears led the way to the passageway that issued into Bulbus' residence. Preacher took the point with long strides past the colorful tile murals that lined the hallway. The subjects being gladiators in various forms of killing and maiming, he paid them scant attention. He signaled for a halt when he reached the far end.

A wooden-barred gate closed off the passage. Preacher gave it a try, and it swung open on well-oiled hinges. He found himself again in the courtyard with its tinkling fountain. This time, the steward happened to be out picking posies for his master's table. He saw Preacher and let out a yelp that could have been heard at the Temple of Vesta, had there not been such an uproar from the coliseum. It did serve to summon three burly sentries.

They soon showed that they did not lack in the courage to engage the gladiators who boiled out of the passageway to the school. For all their willingness to fight, they did not last long. Their leader, an off-duty *contubernalis* from *Legio II*,

Britannicus, took on Preacher—much to his regret as it turned out.

By far not a skilled swordsman, Preacher had nevertheless learned tricks in the gladiator school that were foreign to this stolid soldier. The sergeant lost his sword hand in his first precipitous rush. Preacher nimbly sidestepped him and chopped downward with his *gladius.* The hand, and the weapon it held, appeared to leap from the end of the legionnaire's arm. Desperately he clutched the blood-spouting stump with his other hand while he sucked air in a muted whoosh. With the shield lowered, Preacher got a shot at an exposed neck. A swift cut ended the life of the sergeant. Preacher looked to his left.

Sparticus held one of the guards over his head, straightened out like a man asleep on his back. The startled yelp that came from him broke the illusion of slumber. His scream ended with a loud crack when Sparticus hurled him against the lip of the stone fountain. At once, the huge black gladiator strode across the courtyard to where Buck held half a dozen more sentries at bay in the doorway of the guardroom. Preacher looked the other way to check on Philadelphia Braddock.

To Preacher's right, Philadelphia let go a bear growl and smashed the shoulder of the last guard. Stunned, the man went to one knee, his shield up to protect his head. Laughing, Philadelphia swept the soldier's supporting leg out from under him and crowned him solidly on the top of the head with a heavy cudgel.

"Sparticus, stay there with Buck. We'll bring you weapons, food and a horse."

"Sho'nuf, Preacher." Sparticus grinned and rippled the muscles of his shoulders and arms.

In the arms store, the more aggressive among the young missionaries acted like kids in a vacant candy store. Preacher three times had to caution one or another about taking too many rifles. "Takes too long to reload. Tire your horse, too. Take four or six pistols instead."

He quickly found his favorites and loaded them all. He turned to the suddenly belligerent pilgrims and instructed, "Load up every one you take. We'll be needin' 'em to get out of this place."

That prediction proved only too true the moment they reached the street. Two *contaburniae*—twenty soldiers— trotted their way in formation down the Via Iulius. Shields up, their piliae aligned perfectly, the legionnaires advanced, only their shins and grim faces visible. In his insane state as Marcus Quintus Americus, Alexander Reardon had made only one mistake. He had insisted on accuracy in arms and armor, and the Romans had fought long before gunpowder came into being.

Preacher knocked the sergeant of the first rank off his feet with a .56 ball from his Hawken, then laid the smoking rifle across his lap. He let fly with one of his .44 Walker Colts. In rapid succession, three more soldiers fell. His friends, Preacher noticed, accounted for themselves rather well also.

Philadelphia dumped two in the second rank and went for another pistol. A legionnaire yelped, and blood flew from a scalp wound as the .36 caliber squirrel rifle in the hands of Amelia Witherspoon barked to Preacher's right rear. He decided the time had come to depart this place. Setting spurs to Cougar's flanks, he led the charge on the dismounted men.

Their advance became a rout. Shot through the shield and chest, one soldier staggered to the side to lean on the wall of the gladiator school. He died before the last of the escapees rode out of sight. Panic broke out in the streets. Women screamed and men shouted in angry tones, until they saw the thoroughly armed band that thundered down on them. Then they gave way rapidly.

In seemingly no time, the fugitives reached a gate.

Preacher took aim and shot down the guard who wrestled to draw closed the thick, heavy barrier. Then he shouted good advice.

"C'mon, folks, don't dally. We've lots of miles to put between us and them."

Chapter 18

Confusion and surprise turned to panic when the order to shut the gates was taken too literally by the stadium staff. Spectators swarmed into the aisles, only to find the entrances to the coliseum barred against them. They began to push and shove, then to fight among themselves. In the imperial box, his face a flaming scarlet in childish fury, Quintus Faustus shrieked impotent demands and threats. Robbed of his bloody climax, he lost what tenuous hold he had on his reason.

Marcus Quintus saw the trembling boy with slobber and foam flying from his lips and rose to confront his son. He put a hand on Faustus' shoulder and squeezed gently. Frenetically, Faustus jerked away from his touch. Exasperated and embarrassed beyond endurance, Quintus lost his grip for a moment. He swiftly raised an arm and delivered a solid backhand slap. A red spot appeared on the pallid skin of his cheek, and Faustus bugged his eyes.

"Control yourself," his father snapped.

Faustus sat down abruptly and buried his head in his toga. His thin shoulders shook violently as he bawled like a baby. Marcus Quintus knew at once that he must take command. He raised cupped hands to the sides of his mouth and shouted over the tumult.

"Open the *vomitoriae!* Clear these people out of here." In

stentorian tones, he brayed for his army commanders. "Bring Legate Varras. I want his cavalry after that vermin at once. Bring me Legate Glaubiae! Start a search of the city. Do it now!"

Varras appeared beside Quintus and saluted. "Get out of here, use the private tunnel. Organize your cavalry and get after those people," Quintus screamed at him. Varras saluted again and departed hastily.

Gaius Septimus Glaubiae came next, his face flushed with the effort of climbing the steep steps to the box. Quintus raised his arm casually to return his salute. He leaned slightly forward and screamed in his general's face. "I want the legions organized at once. Outfit them for a long time in the field. They are to search for the escaped prisoners. I want them back. All of them."

"Do you believe they have gotten out of the city?" Glaubiae asked.

Quintus' eyes narrowed. "They will have by the time order can be restored."

Then he began to scream at the panicked crowd. He was still screaming orders when the escaping prisoners swarmed out the southern gate.

Preacher led the fleeing prisoners at a fast pace down the Via Ostia, named for the port to the west of ancient Rome. Why the madman who had created this place had picked that name for the road to the south, Preacher did not know. He doubted that this Marcus Quintus feller knew either. Two miles beyond the corrupt city, he slowed the pace to a quick walk. Elation slowly swept over all but one of the missionaries, he grumblingly noted as they began to chatter among themselves.

"We've lost everything," wailed Agatha Abercrombie. "Our wagons, our portable organ, even the pulpit."

"Be thankful we got out of that place alive," Sister Amelia Witherspoon told her coldly.

That pleased Preacher mightily. That li'l gal had some pluck. She was learning fast. For the first time Preacher looked at her in another way than as a nuisance. Pretty little thing, he mused. Clean her up a little, get some clean clothes on her. . . . He suddenly had to cover his mouth to hide a broad grin and suppress a hearty guffaw that bubbled in his throat as they continued their exchange.

"*Excuse me?* I am unaccustomed to accepting such criticism from anyone. Especially from my inferiors."

Sarcasm dripped from Amelia's words. "Oh, that's quite obvious. Only I don't see myself as your inferior. I didn't see *you* raise a hand to defend yourself, let alone anyone else back there."

Outrage painted Agatha's face. "How dare you!" She looked around herself for some support, only to see a laughing Preacher. His shoulders shook with his mirth. She redirected her anger. "This is all your fault, you heathen barbarian!" she lashed out.

Nodding, Preacher choked back his hilarity. "Yep. It sure is. An' right proud of it, I am. Weren't but five of you folks got harmed. Might be if you'd lent a hand some of them would be with us now. As fer this fine young woman, she carried her share of the load, fought bravely and did for a couple of cougars, two gladiators an' a soldier. On my tally sheet, that puts her head and shoulders your better, ma'am. Danged if it don't." Preacher's eyes widened, and he screwed up his mouth as though to spit out a wad of chaw tobacco. "By damn, there I go speechifyin' like a politician. I'd best put a lid on my word bucket."

He held his peace until the cavalcade crested the saddle notch and halted on the far side. By then he had worked out what needed to be done. He called them together in the shade of a tall old pine that soughed softly in a fresh breeze. "Everybody rest some; drink a little water and eat something." Then Preacher began enlightening them on something that had been bothering him for a long while.

"The way I see it, our best chance lies with splittin' up. That way it thins out them that comes after us. Now, there's somethin' we need to decide on. I declare, that place is the foulest nest of snakes I've ever runned across. Ain't gonna change much, from what I guess. So, this nasty business has to be ended right and proper. To do that, we have to have help." He pointed to Philadelphia and Buck.

"I want you to set off to find any old wooly-eared fellers that's nestin' out there somewhere. Philadelphia, you take the west trails; Buck, you head east. I'll cut down to the southwest, find Bold Pony an' his Arapahos. A couple of those prisoners who died at the hands of Quintus' gladiators were from his band, I learned. That gives him a stake in fixin' this tainted meat. Sparticus, you done good to join us. I want you to stick with these pilgrims. Teach them more about how to fight for when the time comes they need to. Take the big trail south to Trout Creek Pass; it's well marked. We'll all rendezvous there and lay plans."

"Preacher, how do I get any of these mountain men to join us?" Buck asked.

"You tell 'em you're askin' in my name. An' I'll send along a note to that effect. Most of these boys can make out writin' good enough, an' those what can't do know my name an' my Ghost Wolf sign."

"I—I want to stay with you, Preacher," Amelia Witherspoon spoke up.

"Why, the brazenness of that—" Agatha Abercrombie began, to be cut off by a hard look from Preacher.

He shook his head as he spoke to Amelia. "No, it'll be too dangerous."

Undeterred by this logic, she continued to press her issue. "What could be more dangerous than what we just faced?"

To his surprise, Preacher did not have any quick reply

for that. He mulled it over a moment. "I can't answer that, Missy. Danged if you don't argue like one o' them Philadelphia lawyers." He shot a glance at his fellow mountain man. "No offense, old friend. But, the answer is the same, Miss Amelia. Where I'm going, the Injuns mightily favor a long lock of yeller hair on their scalp poles."

"Bu—but you're friends with them; I've heard Philadelphia say so."

Preacher smiled to soften his demeanor. "We're friends when they're in the mood for it. Otherwise, they'd lift my hair, too. This time I've got a reason for them to keep right cordial. It wouldn't do, though, to provoke them before I get out my message."

Preacher turned to the rest of them, the subject closed for his part. "So, we'll all rendezvous at the tradin' post. I'll bring in the Arapaho last to prevent a panic."

Preacher took a narrow trail to the southwest when he departed from the others. Leading his packhorse, he made much better time than Sparticus and the missionaries. He was far out on the Great Divide Basin when sundown caught up with him. He made a hasty cold camp and settled in for the night. He doubted he would see anything of the soldiers from New Rome, yet he did not want a fire to betray his presence. No, he'd not see the legions of New Rome again, not until he wanted to. Far off, in the rolling hills behind him, he heard the musical call of a timber wolf.

"Hang in there, ol' feller. We's a pair, we be," he said softly to his distant brother.

That night, Preacher slept well under a blanket of stars that frosted the night as a harbinger of the coming winter.

Marcus Quintus Americus hurled a gold-rimmed wine cup across the room to splinter on the plinth of a bust of

Augustus Caesar. Thin, red wine washed over it and stained the first Roman emperor purple. Shocked, Legate Varras of the cavalry watched as the liquid pooled on the marble floor.

"Are you totally incompetent? How can you come to me with a report like this?"

Varras answered mildly. "Because it is my duty, and it is the truth. Beyond the territory of New Rome, we found no trace of them. A large body of the fleeing prisoners rode south on the main trail for some while; then their tracks faded out."

He did not know of the drags that Sparticus had rigged on the last horses in the column, which spread out from side to side on the trail and obliterated every trace of their passage. It was an old trick Sparticus had learned on the Underground Railroad. It would not have fooled a Blackfoot, Cheyenne or a Sioux, but it did confound the inexperienced trackers of the cavalry legion. Quintus fumed a long, silent moment, then turned partly away from Varras. His voice dropped from its previous furious bellow.

"How could four barbarians and that lot of pitiful Christians defeat professional gladiators and outwit my well-trained soldiers to make good this escape?"

Varras was smart enough to remain silent. His first sword centurion stood rigidly at his side, helmet tucked under one arm like his commander. He cut his eyes to Varras and grimaced. Quintus collected himself after his rhetorical question.

"Well, they'll not get away with it. I want you to get out there by an hour after sundown. Best possible speed. Catch up to those vermin, kill only those you must, and bring back the rest. Take what supplies you need and don't leave any area unsearched. Now, leave me. I must talk with the commanders of the other legions."

Glaubiae and Bruno entered together. Quintus eyed them coldly, arms folded over the front of his toga. When they both grew uneasy enough, he poured wine around and handed each general a cup.

"Your health, gentlemen. I must compliment you on the thoroughness of your search of our city. Unlike that incompetent ass, Varras, who lost all trace of the fugitives, you did come up with three escaped slaves. That they were not involved with those from the coliseum is not important. Given that those condemned prisoners had already ridden out of the gates, you did the best you could. Now, I have to ask more of you. I am not convinced that we have seen the last of those miscreants. Here is what I want you to do."

He began to pace the floor as he spoke. "I want you to establish watch towers completely around the rim of this basin. Staff them with enough men to be alert around the clock. Also set up heliographs and signal fires. Have horses so a messenger can reach the city well ahead of whoever comes back." His pacing grew faster. "Set your engineers to manufacturing ballistas, catapults and arbalests."

"You are certain they will attack us?" Gaius Septimus asked.

"Of course," Quintus snapped. "I have learned only this morning that there are enough of these barbarian mountain men with savage allies to form a force that will outnumber us. The important thing is not to let the Senate and the people know that. If we are prepared, if we have advance warning, the quality of the legions and the power of some—ah—weapons I have provided will assure our victory."

That caught the interest of both generals. "What weapons are these?"

Quintus answered guardedly. "Some firearms. Also a few cannon that will far out-perform our other artillery." A wicked smile illuminated his face.

Septimus and Bruno caught up his enthusiasm. "How many firearms? What sort of cannon?" Septimus urged.

Thinking on it, Quintus answered evasively. "Enough to tip the scale."

Bruno wasn't buying into it. "And when do we train men to use them?"

Quintus surprised him with his answer. "We start this afternoon. Now, get out of here, get orders published for what is needed, and get to work."

Buck Sears had traveled the trails of Texas, driven teams on the Santa Fe Trail, and most recently, had rented his talents to those seeking to take goods overland to the Northwest Territory. It made him fairly savvy about movement where Indians were a factor, how to repair wagons when the nearest wheelwright or coach shop lay five hundred miles behind. It had not taught him how to find mountain men when sent to round up any who remained in the ranges of the Rocky Mountains. In fact, it was they who found him, more or less.

"You there, stumblin' around in the bush," a voice called out as Buck floundered around in an attempt to find the trail he had been following, which had abruptly disappeared a quarter of an hour earlier. The unknown voice called again.

"If you be friendly, sing out an' let us know who you might be."

"Hello. The name's Sears. Buck Sears. I'm a freight wagon teamster."

A low chuckle answered Buck, then words made soft by amusement. "You're sure an' hell a long ways from any wagon route. C'mon in, set a spell, an' have some coffee."

That completely amazed Buck. "You—uh—you've got a *camp* out here?"

"Shore enough do. Head yourself due north an' you'll run into it."

Buck blundered through the brush, leading his mount,

until he came to a small clearing surrounded by ash and juniper trees. Three men sat around a stone-guarded, hat-sized fire over which a coffeepot steamed. Buck ground reined his horse and came forward.

"Well, here I am. Buck Sears."

The one who had called out to him spoke first. "M'name's Abel Williams, but folks most call me Squinty. This here's Jack Lonesome and that other feller is Three-Finger. Git yourself around some Arbuckles," he invited, with a gesture toward the blue granite pot.

"Obliged," Buck responded.

Settled on a mat of aspen leaves, Buck sipped the strongest coffee he had ever tasted, worried for the lining of his stomach, and exchanged incidentals with the three mountain men for several minutes. Then, when Squinty Williams hinted delicately at what business brought Buck into the mountains, he unveiled his story of New Rome.

They listened in amazement, doubt written plainly on their faces. Buck noted this and concluded his personal story to get to the heart of the situation. "The thing is, six years after I was taken by these lunatics, two of you mountain men were captured; Philadelphia Braddock and Preacher."

"Naw. Couldn't be," Jack Lonesome rebutted. "No amount of fellers runnin' around in skirts could best Preacher."

"All the same, it's true," Buck insisted. "He said I might run into some—ah—resistance. Sent along this note." He dug into his shirt pocket and produced the scrap of paper upon which Preacher had scribbled his appeal.

Squinty took it and peered intently at it. At last he nodded. "That's his name, right enough. An' his Ghost Wolf mark. What's it say, Jack?"

Jack Lonesome took the message and read it aloud. *This is to ad-vise any fellers contacted by Buck Sears that we has us a large problem needs solvin' right fast. Buck will ex-plain it to you an' I ask you to come fast to Trout Creek Pass and lend a hand. Yours for old times, Preacher.*

Squinty cocked his head to one side. "Well, I'll be damned. You got our help, Buck. Tell us about this place again; then we'll make use of the rest of this day gettin' out of here."

Buck related the final days in New Rome and what Preacher and Philadelphia were up to at the moment. All three mountain men thought on it; then Squinty came to his boots. "We know where half a dozen of our friends are fixin' to hang out for the winter. We'll go get them and then head for this rendezvous with Preacher. I ain't never seen me a man in a skirt before, but I reckon we can sure put the fear of God in a bunch of 'em."

On his fourth day away from New Rome, Philadelphia Braddock ambled into a camp in the Medicine Bow range occupied by Blue Nose Herkimer. There he also found Four-Eyes Finney, a wild Irish brawler turned mountain man, Karl "Bloody Hand" Kreuger, Nate Youngblood, and surprisingly to him, Frenchie Dupres. After a few bear hugs, some foot stomping, and a lot of genial cussing, Philadelphia filled them in on what had been happening in the Ferris Range. Bloody Hand Kreuger flat did not believe it.

"*Pferd Scheist!* That's all it is, horse shit. I was through there back a ways, and I never saw anything like that."

"How long ago was that, Karl?" Philadelphia asked, using the German mountain man's given name because he knew Bloody Hand did not like it.

Bloody Hand thought on it a moment. "Ten . . . maybe twelve years ago."

"A lot can happen in that time. An' it surely did. That's about the time this crazy feller, calls himself Marcus Quintus Americus, came out here. Boys, I've been there, saw the buildings, took baths in a fancy buildin', and fought for my life in a place where folks come an' watch ya die for the fun of it. Preacher was there with me, like I said. Now, fellers, what'll it be? Are you goin' to join us in doin' away with this place of corruption or not?"

An old and dear friend of Preacher, Frenchie Dupres rose and dusted off the seat of his trousers. "I am ready, *mon ami*. These people sound to be *tres* evil. If Preacher needs our help, I say we give it to him."

"You can count on me," Nate Youngblood agreed.

"I'm with you, Philadelphia," Blue Nose Herkimer added.

Four-Eyes Finney tugged at a thick forelock of sandy hair. "Sure an' it sounds like a fine donnybrook. Count me in."

Although the Kraut mountain man had a long list of grievances against Preacher, Karl Kreuger sighed heavily and nodded in acceptance. "I'll go. What the hell, Preacher is one of us, and no fancy Roman is gonna put down a mountain man."

Philadelphia could not hide his happy smile. "By jing, that shines. Ya can all head out at first light; it's a ways to Trout Crick Pass. I'm leavin' now to see if I can scare up some other fellers."

Chapter 19

Preacher found Bold Pony and his band settled down in their winter camp in a tidy little valley. He was welcomed with stately courtesy. Then Bold Pony noticed Preacher's injuries. He sent at once for the medicine man.

"I coulda taken care of that for myself," Preacher protested without sincerity. The poltices the shaman put on his cuts and bruises felt cool and soothing. And the Arapaho medicine man could get to the claw marks on his back better than he had been able to.

"Not while you are in my camp, friend," Bold Pony responded. "You will speak of how you received these injuries at the council fire tonight?"

"Yes. I sort of hunted you down for that exact reason. There's some mighty bad people out there that need a lesson taught them."

"We eat first. And drink coffee."

After filling himself with elk stew, Preacher sat back and belched loudly, rubbed his belly to show how much he had enjoyed it, and allowed as how he was ready to talk to the council. They gathered around a modest fire in the center of the village. Bold Pony spoke first, as was his right, then formally introduced the man well known to them. Preacher rose and addressed the council while Bold Pony translated.

He told them of New Rome and what had happened

there. "Until some dozen years ago, only the Crows and the Blackfeet roamed through the Ferris Range," he began. He went on to describe the city that had grown there, of the cruelty of the people who lived in it. When he came to the games, Bold Pony used the Arapaho words for "savage" and "barbarian." That amused Preacher. Although he knew the Arapaho tongue well enough to pass the time of day, Preacher wanted to be sure the whole sordid story of New Rome came across clearly. It appeared to him that Bold Pony was doing that right enough.

Angry mutters rose when he described the Arapaho warriors who had been enslaved and killed, and added, "We sang their death songs after the gladiators finished with them." He concluded his account with the escape and an appeal for help in destroying this menace. Buffalo Whip, an aged and seamed former peace chief, rose to speak against the Arapaho involvement. "We do not know these people. They have done us no harm. Those men you told about are not of this band. It is not for us to avenge them. It is not wise to take the war trail against people who do not have anger toward us." He rambled on awhile, then repeated the admonition to avoid war.

Preacher rose again. "Thing is, they've got anger toward everyone. They call us barbarians, an' you folks, too. A feller who had been there six years told me they plan on fighting everyone out here. An' he tells the truth."

Another older councilman stood to argue against joining in Preacher's fight. A third followed him. Preacher considered that it wasn't going well. Then came the turn of some of the younger men. Yellow Hawk took his place in front of the assembly.

"There are too many white men out here now. Most are like our friend, Preacher. These men have bad hearts. They hurt women and children. I say we fight them."

Badger Tail agreed. Buffalo Whip spoke again. Two more of the fiery, youthful warriors responded, urging a war party to be organized. The debate raged on into the night. The fire burned low, and young boys, apprentice warriors, built it up again. At last, Bold Pony put a hand on Preacher's shoulder.

"You might as well take some sleep, old friend," he advised. "This will take a while."

Preacher nodded and came to his boots. Stifling a yawn, he ankled off to the lodge where he would spend the night.

Birds twittered in the trees outside the Arapaho camp while the eastern sky turned pink. Preacher emerged from a buffalo hide lodge as the velvet dome above magically turned blue overhead. He wore a huge, relaxed smile on his leathery face. He tucked his buckskin hunting shirt into the top of his trousers and paused. He turned back to wave a sappy goodbye to the occupant, one thoughtfully provided by Bold Pony, and received a very feminine giggle in reply.

After his morning needs had been taken care of, he sat down with Bold Pony to a bowl of mush that sported shreds of squirrel meat. They ate contentedly. Then Bold Pony nodded toward the center of camp, where the debaters had already begun to assemble.

"You must have other visits to make, Ghost Wolf. You may as well tend to them now. This will be a long time deciding. Go to the trading post and wait for us. We will be along, if we are coming, within two days.

In New Rome preparations for war went on at a fevered pace. The two bold legions—actually their strength compared more realistically with two understrength platoons—conducted mock battles on the Field of Mars. The Campus Martius swarmed with armed and armored troops, their faces grim and set in concentration. Centurions raised their swords in signal, and the sergeants of the *contaburniae* bellowed the command to lock shields and prepare to form the tortoise. The centurions lowered their weapons rapidly.

"Form . . . up!" the leather-lunged sergeants commanded.

At once, the soldiers in the middle of the squares raised their shields overhead, shielding themselves and the outer two ranks as well. Each *pilum* pointed outward, a hedgehog of defense. A shower of blunted arrows moaned hauntingly to the top of their arcs and descended on the shields. They clattered noisily as the brass-bossed, hardened hides shed them. At another command, the ten squads disengaged their shields and faced the same direction.

"Forward at the quick time," came the order.

At once the soldiers stepped off at a rapid pace, their javelins slanted forward. Twenty paces along the base course, the commands came again. With more assurance the formation evolved into the famous tortoise. Standing in his white chariot, its basket supports set off in gold, Marcus Quintus Americus looked on with satisfaction. His heart thundered with excitement. Elsewhere, those men who had proven to be passable marksmen drilled with the rifles. What a shock that would be when those mountain rabble returned. Gaius Septimus rode up on a white charger. The stallion snorted at the scent of its fellows drawing the chariot. Wet droplets of slobber stained the sleeve of the military tunic worn by Marcus Quintus.

"A couple more run-throughs and my legion will be ready for a cavalry charge."

"Excellent. They are learning faster than I expected, and I'm pleased."

"Here's the bad news. Some of your spies have ferreted out the information that the condemned man, Arturus, was in fact Preacher."

Color flared on Quintus' face. "By all the gods! All that while I had my hands on Preacher and did not know it? How could that have happened?"

Septimus looked embarrassed. "I suspected it when I saw him fight at the school. Yet, I had nothing to prove it."

"Who verified his identity?" Quintus demanded.

"Bulbus for one. He overheard one of the other gladiators call him that."

Quintus scowled. "The fool. He should have reported it. We could have kept him in a cell alone, and fought him differently. None of what happened would have been possible."

"And we wouldn't be running around like chickens with our heads cut off trying to prepare for war," Septimus muttered to himself.

"What was that?"

"Nothing, Quintus. I have to get back to my *primus pilus.*" His need to meet with his first spear—his adjutant—was a convenient excuse to avoid the wrath of Quintus.

Half an hour later, a messenger came from Glaubiae that his troops were ready for the cavalry. He sent the man on to another part of the Field of Mars, where the mounted troops had been practicing. With whoops of glee, they whirled into attack formation and rumbled across the turf toward the defensive squares of the Thirteenth Legion. A shower of javelins hurtled toward them.

Quickly the spear carriers resupplied the hurlers, and the squares bristled like aroused porcupines. By design, the spears landed short, albeit not *too* short. Marcus Quintus was tickled pink. Not a waver. Not a man broke formation. Those Celtic fools called the plains barbarians the finest light cavalry in the world. Let them come up against the tactics of the legions and see what happens to them. The cavalry whirled and made another approach.

Again the rain of javelins broke their charge. Suddenly the tortoises broke apart and the legionnaires counter-attacked, the keen edges of their *gladiae* striking blue-white ribbons from the autumn sun. They descended on the stalled cavalry and began to break into man-to-man duels.

Dust became a blinding curtain, from which only sparks from upraised swords could be seen. Quintus knew that Septimus and his officers would be judging the effectiveness of both forces and was not surprised when a *buccina* sounded to end the battle.

Proud of their ability, Varras, the cavalry *legio*, trotted his men forward to salute the First Citizen. Marcus Quintus was beaming with satisfaction, thrilled with how well this mismatched rabble had welded themselves into a disciplined army. That pleasure ended quickly when he recognized his eleven-year-old son, in full armor, in the front rank of cavalry, face begrimed, sweat trickling from under his helmet. It instantly struck him that the boy had been fighting in among all the others.

Riveted by that thought, he advanced to the next obvious revelation. *He could have been killed!* For all their well-conducted performance, the legionnaires were only partly trained. One could have gotten carried away, gone farther than orders allowed. And Faustus could be lying on the ground, bleeding, or headless. It chilled his blood and brought an imperceptible shudder to his burly frame. Before he could control himself and rethink the situation, he burst out with a bellow.

"Quintus Faustus, get out of there!"

Faustus could not believe what he had heard. "But, Father, I . . ."

Imperiously Quintus pointed to the driver's position in his chariot. "Get off that horse, come over here, and get in this chariot."

"But, Father, Varras said it was all right, that I would be safe."

Blood boiling, Quintus narrowed his eyes. "There is no such thing as 'safe' in a battle. Even in practice, mistakes happen."

Faustus' voice rose to a near whine. "Father, *please!* I'm not a baby anymore."

"Come here now!"

Faustus swung a bare leg over the neck of his mount and hung from the saddle, to drop to the ground. He walked stiff-legged across the space that separated him from the chariot. With each step his face turned from white to a deeper red. His lower lip slid out in a pout until he discovered it; then he sucked it in and bit it with small, even teeth. The first tears slid down his cheeks as he reached one large wheel of the two-person vehicle. The driver stepped to the ground, and Quintus snapped at him.

"Bring that horse and come with me," he commanded. To a thoroughly frightened Varras, he growled, "I'll see you later at the palace, Varras."

He said not a word while he drove straight to the palace. There he started to lecture Faustus, who bolted and ran off sobbing, to cry his heart out. Still disgruntled by how he had handled the situation, Quintus found little sympathy from his wife.

Titiana Pulcra stared unbelievingly at her husband. Small, slim hands on her hips, she stamped one slender, sandaled foot. "How could you, Quintus? To humiliate the boy in front of all those soldiers like that is unconscionable. It could have a terrible effect on my son. It could even make him into a sissy."

Burning with his own demons, Quintus turned deaf ears to his wife's protests. This impending war would be the ruin of him yet. *Goddamn you, Preacher!* he thought furiously.

Vickie reached across the darkened room and lightly touched her brother on the arm. "Terry, Preacher's comin' back," she whispered.

"Who told you that?" Terry asked crossly.

"Nobody. I just . . . *know*."

"You an' your knowin' things," Terry heaped in scorn.

"It's like you sayin' he was in real big danger. A body can't know those sort of things."

Vickie defended herself staunchly. "Well, I can. I sort of . . . feel things. Preacher's been hurt, too. I know that, so there."

"How'd he get hurt, smarty?"

Tears threatened in Vickie's words. "Oh, Terry, I can't tell you that. I don't know how I know these things."

Terry pondered that a moment. "What do you suppose we should do?"

The tears leaked through this time. "Don't ask me. That's for you to figger out."

Pausing a long moment in the dark night, Terry turned that over in his head. "Why don't we go to meet him?"

"We don't know where he's coming from," Vickie objected.

"Yes, we do. He went north from here when he left us our new clothes. We'll just go north."

"Really? Do you think it will work?"

"We won't know unless we try. And we can't tell anyone."

"When do we go?"

"Tomorrow."

Sister Amelia Witherspoon stood in the center of camp. Another two days to reach this trading post. She remembered one they had come upon along the North Platte River. Low-slung buildings, with crude thatch roofs, smelly and dirty inside, hardly more than a poor excuse for a saloon. It reeked of stale beer, spilled whiskey, greasy food and human sweat. She had almost gagged when she entered.

If they had not needed supplies so desperately, she would have prevailed upon the new Deacon Abercrombie to pass this pestilential place by. Thought of their former leader, and how he had died, brought a pang to her heart and a lump to her throat. She swallowed hard, hoping she would not break into tears, because she also recalled that he had betrayed them when the first attempt had been made to escape. And that brought her to Preacher.

Oh, how handsome he had looked when he left them on the trail. She remembered him as a shining knight in buckskin on that day he rode off from them, for all his disreputable appearance. She wondered how he would look when he had washed off all that blood, dirt, grease and powder grime, and had a chance to shave. She would find out when he reached the trading post and rejoined them. She could hardly wait.

A sharp report of a pistol from across the campsite drew her away from her favorite subject. Laughter followed. "Brother Lewis, you're supposed to take that thing out of the holster before you pull the trigger."

A thoroughly shaken, crimson-faced young missionary stood with a group of those who had elected to continue to fight. Smoke ringed his knees, and Amelia saw the splintered leather at the bottom of the holster fastened at his waist. Poor Lewis Biggs, she thought. He had always been so clumsy. Only now he could get seriously injured, or even killed, for it. If only Preacher were here to teach them.

That brought back images of the lean mountain man. His eyes normally held a far-off look, as though he saw things a thousand yards away. She really knew so little about him. Though she had heard plenty of wild stories from Sparticus. Her practical side found little of it credible. Like wrestling with a bear and killing the beast with a knife. Or leading a wagon train of women from Missouri to the Northwest Territory. No one man, no matter how able and clever, could do that alone.

Which got her to wondering how Preacher had resisted the charms of so many unattached ladies. With a shiver of delight she thought how much she would like it if Preacher succumbed to *her* charms. Her missionary zeal abandoned, Amelia imagined those strong arms around her, holding her tight. His full lips pressed to hers. She wondered how her somewhat bony, angular body would be fitted to his hard, muscular frame. Oh, when would they reach the trading post? When would Preacher join them?

Chapter 20

Trout Creek Pass looked mighty good to Preacher when he reached the trading post there three days later. One-Eye Avery Tookes spotted him first and let out a whoop. That brought his partner Bart Weller, Bloody Hand Kreuger, Squinty Williams, Blue Nose Herkimer and Frenchie Dupres. The others were out hunting game for the table. The back slaps, shoulder punches, elbow rib gouges, to say nothing of the general jumping up and down and stomping the ground, went on for a good fifteen minutes.

"We heard you was lookin' for fellers to join a real, ringtailed mixup, Preacher," One-Eye Avery Tookes declared when the welcoming calmed some and the participants had repaired to the inside of the saloon.

"That I am, Ave," Preacher allowed. "Philadelphia an' me got ourselves in one hell of a fix up north in the Ferris Range."

Three of the mountain men rounded up mugs and dispensed whiskey and foaming flagons of beer while the others pressed close around. Frenchie Dupres spoke for them all.

"We learned some of it from Philadelphia, Preacher, but we would like to hear it from you."

Preacher studied on it a moment, downed half a mug of beer to soothe the trail dust from his craw, then launched into the story of New Rome. "Seems there's this feller, 'bout three beaver shy of a lodge, who's took it in his mind that he's the emperor of Rome. Built him a right accurate copy of the ancient town in this big valley in the Ferris Range." He went on to describe the highlights of the stay he and Philadelphia had endured.

Several times, one or another of the mountain men would interrupt with a question. Through it all, only Karl Bloody Hand Kreuger maintained a skeptical expression. When Preacher concluded, he spoke slowly, through a thick German accent.

"Dot don't zound right. Vhy haff vun of us not seen dis place in der twelf years you zay it has been there?"

Preacher gave him the benefit of a one-eyed squint. "How many pelts have you taken in the past dozen years, Bloody Hand?" he asked mildly. "For that matter, how many of us has been in the Ferris Range in the same time?"

Shaken heads answered him. It urged Preacher to push on a little further. "You all know the fur trade is dead as last year's squirrel stew. There ain't a one of us what has made a living entire off of takin' beaver. Shoot, there ain't even enough beaver for us to harvest them like we used to." He paused to pour off the last of the beer. "Monongahela rye, Duffey," he called to the barkeep. Then he turned back to Bloody Hand Kreuger.

"Now, you listen to me, Bloody Hand. I seened all that with my own eyes. So'd Philadelphia and that young 'prentice, Buck Sears. An' that reminds me. If Buck ain't got him a handle hung on him already, I reckon to call him Long Spear."

That brought hoots of laughter. Blue Nose Herkimer asked through his chortles, "Is that for what I think it is, Preacher?"

Preacher pulled a face of mock disappointment in his fellow men. "No. It ain't. It's because he done some fierce fightin' with one of them *pilum* things the Roman soldiers use in their army." He downed a respectable swallow of whiskey, smacked his lips and continued. "Buck ain't near as good as some of us; but he's got sand, and he carries his own weight an' then some. He learns quick. And we need every gun we can get for this fight with the crazy Romans."

"Vhy vould anyone lif dot vay?" Kreuger pressed, disbelief plain in his small pig eyes.

Preacher cocked his head to one side, sipped more rye. "Y'know, that's a question I asked myself a good many times. Don't seem that anyone a-tall, with any brains worth countin', would put up with the loco things this feller calls hisself Marcus Quintus Americus expects of 'em. They dress in these outlandish clothes, all robes and nightshirt-lookin' things, and wear sandals, too, like them brown-robed friars come through the Big Empty back in Thirty-one, weren't it? Why, their soldiers even wear skirts."

That proved too much for Bloody Hand Kreuger. "I told Philadelphia that dis vas horse shit, *und* dot's vhat it iss. *Pferd Scheist!* No zoldiers vear zkirts."

Preacher's dark gray eyes turned to flint. "You callin' me a liar, Bloody Hand?"

Kreuger, who had already decided it was a good time to take Preacher to task, barked a single word. *"Jawohl!"*

Preacher downed the last of his Pennsylvania whiskey and dusted dry palms together. "Well, then, let's get to the dance."

"Outside! Take it outside," a nervous Ruben Duffey shouted from behind the bar.

"More'n glad to oblige, Duffey," Preacher told him amiably.

He started to rise, then shifted his weight and lashed out his booted foot in one swift movement. The dusty sole caught the chair in which Kreuger sat at the center lip of the seat and spilled it over backward. Preacher got on him at once. He grabbed the confused and startled German by the back of his wide belt and scruff of shirt collar and made a speedy little run toward the front door. Kreuger dangled in Preacher's powerful arms, feet clear of the floor.

With appropriate violence, the batwings flew outward when Kreuger's head collided with them. Preacher took quick aim and hurled his human cargo into the street. The Kraut mountain man landed in a puddle of mud and horse droppings at the tie rail. Immediately Kreuger let the world, and Preacher in particular, know his opinion of being so used.

"Verdammen unehrliche Geburt!"

"Oh, now, Bloody Hand, you know better than to call Preacher a damned bastard," Frenchy Dupres observed dryly from the porch of the trading post saloon.

A few chuckles went the rounds; then the fight turned serious. Kreuger came to his boots shedding road apples and urine-made mud. Before he could locate his enemy, Preacher walked up from behind him and gave him a powerful shove that sent Kreuger back into the quagmire.

Hoots of laughter ran among the mountain men. Kreuger's face went so darkly red as to look black. On hands and knees he crawled toward the dry, hard-packed ground. Unwilling to lose an important good shot in so critical a battle as the one he visualized upcoming, Preacher determined to go easy on Kreuger. He knew the cause of some of the bad blood between them, yet had not seen the man in some while and could only guess at what other grievances and faults the German had assigned to him. On the other hand, Kreuger sincerely believed this to be the time to tumble Preacher from his high perch, to show him to be no more than any other man. Through the red haze of his fury, he spotted his foe.

Springing quickly to his boots, Kreuger swung a looping left that connected with the point of Preacher's shoulder. Preacher shed it easily, then whanged a hard fist that mushed Kreuger's mouth. Blood flew in a nimbus that haloed Kreuger's head. The huge, bullet-headed German absorbed the force of Preacher's blow and took a chance kick at the mountain legend's groin.

Preacher saw it coming and danced aside. He whooped and jumped in the air, waggling one open hand under his chin at Bloody Hand. Kreuger stared at Preacher uncomprehendingly. On the way down, Preacher enlightened the Kraut as to the purpose of his childish taunt. His target sufficiently distracted, he swiftly jabbed two of those extended fingers toward the man's eyes.

Kreuger recoiled so violently that he tottered off balance. Preacher's boot toes lightly touched when he launched a one-two combination at the midsection of Karl Kreuger. Dust puffed from the buckskin shirt Kreuger wore as the piston fists connected in a rapid tattoo. Grunting, he rocked on back. He went over his center and plopped to the ground on his rump. Anxious to end this before harming even this uncertain an asset, Preacher swiftly stepped in on Kreuger.

Only too far!

A well-aimed kick from Kreuger landed deeply in Preacher's groin. Sheer agony radiated outward from Preacher's throbbing crotch. When the yawning pit of blackness receded from his mind, Preacher recovered himself in time to clap his open palms against the sides of Kreuger's head. So much for going easy, he thought grimly.

Their fight turned deadly serious. Not that Preacher would willingly go so far as to kill Kreuger, so long as the German mountain man would let him avoid it. Howling in pain, Kreuger dived forward and wrapped his arms around Preacher's legs. Digging in with a shoulder, he drove Preacher off his boots. Preacher landed heavily. Dust rose around him as he tried to suck in air.

Kreuger did not give him the chance to fully recover. He climbed Preacher's legs, grunting and growling as he went.

Savagely, he bit Preacher in the thigh. Then his forward progress got halted abruptly with a sledgehammer fist. Preacher drove it down on his opponent's crown with all the force in him. A shower of colored lights went off in Kreuger's head. Preacher heaved mightily and sent his antagonist flying. Wincing to hold back a cry of agony, Preacher came upright and stepped over to Kreuger.

"Give it up, Bloody Hand. This ain't fittin'. We got us a whole wagon load of trouble out there we need to be facin' together."

"You go to hell, Preacher."

Their fight might have gone on longer had not the long-expected arrival of the missionaries put a quicker end to it. They streamed in through the stockade gate as Kreuger sputtered out his defiance. In the lead, Sparticus halted them abruptly with a raised hand.

"No need mixin' up in that folks. Preacher, he got ever'-thin' in hand."

And indeed it appeared he had. After Kreuger's outburst, Preacher leaned down, took him by the shirtfront and yanked the German forward while he pile drivered a big right to the broad forehead below an unruly shock of wheat straw hair. The birdies sang loudly between Kreuger's ears. Groggily he tried to get his feet under him. Preacher shook him like a rag doll.

Kreuger pawed at Preacher's arm. Preacher punched him again. Kreuger went rigid, and his eyes rolled up in their sockets. He sighed wearily, and his legs twitched a few seconds before he went still and limp.

Amelia Witherspoon looked on in mingled admiration and horror. She reached out a hand now to touch Sparticus lightly on the arm. "That man? He isn't dead, is he?"

"Naw, Missy Sister Amelia. I figger Preacher to be a

more careful man than that. I also reckon he be mighty glad to see you again."

Amelia flushed. A hand flew to her mouth. "Do—do you think so?"

"Pert' near a certain thing," Sparticus answered with confidence as the downed man recovered consciousness.

Kreuger started to roundly curse Preacher, and Amelia covered her ears with her hands. Her eyes went wide when Preacher treated the swearing man like one would a foul-mouthed boy. The sound of Preacher's backhand slap cracked through the chill, high mountain air.

"Lighten up, Bloody Hand, or you'll be sleepin' with a pitchfork in your hands tonight."

"Go diddle yourzelf, you zon of a—" The hand returned with more punishment.

"I'm gonna leave it at this, Kreuger. Someone dump a bucket of water over this sorehead. It'll cool him off." Preacher turned to walk away, only to stop in surprise. "Well, I'll be. You folks been there long?"

"Long enough," Amelia Witherspoon responded snappishly, only to stop and blush in confusion as she realized how in conflict were her spinsterish words of criticism and the emotions in her heart.

Preacher cut his eyes to a spot on the ground somewhere between them. "I apologize for what you had to witness. That man's got him a mean on like a boil. You folks got here without any trouble?"

"We did," she responded, then gushed out her true feelings, "and I'm so glad you're here."

It became Preacher's turn to be embarrassed. "Aw, that's kind of you to say, but I ain't nothin' special."

Crimson glowed in Amelia's cheeks. "I think you are," she gushed out.

She reached out a hand, and to her surprised relief, Preacher took it. Without another word, the lean, powerful mountain man led her away into the woods behind the trading post.

"I'm cold."

Terry looked at his sister, seated across the small fire from him. "So am I."

"It will be winter soon," Vickie added meaningfully.

"I know that. We've just got to find Preacher."

Vickie offered an unwelcome suggestion. "We could always go back?"

"No, we can't. We stole and lied to those folks. It wouldn't be fittin'."

"They'd understand, Terry. I'm cold and hungry and so tired. Why haven't we found Preacher yet?"

Frustration at his failure goaded Terry. "I don't know. Leave it alone, will you?" He thought it over awhile, forced himself past pride and stubbornness. "I tell you what. We'll wait it out two more days, keep going north. If we don't find Preacher by then, we . . . we can start back."

"But I want to go back now. I'm scared out here, Terry."

Terry sighed off a heavy burden for a twelve-year-old. "All right. I'll take you back. At least until we're in sight of the house. Then I'm headed for the tradin' post."

Over the next day, some ten long-legged, rangy men clustered in the trading post compound. Well accustomed to the rigors of the High Lonesome, they had heard the call for aid for a fellow and dropped what they worked upon and headed to the small settlement. To Preacher's surprised relief, that swelled their number to thirty-five. Now, if only the Arapaho came in, they stood a chance, he reasoned. Amelia Witherspoon provided him pleasant distraction from the preparations for war.

They sat under a huge juniper, redolent with the scent

of resin and ripe berries. There had not yet been a sharp frost, so the small, round balls, which served as the base flavor in what the English called geneva, had not turned their characteristic dark blue. Amelia had brought a picnic basket, and they lunched on cold fried chicken and boiled turnips. When the last crumbs of a pie had been devoured, she got to the heart of her purpose in being there.

"I know that those people are simply awful, sinful and terribly vicious. But isn't it up to our army to do something about them?"

Preacher snorted. "I ain't seen a soldier-boy in nigh onto a year an' more. They keeps to their little block-house forts and ride the Santa Fe Trail to protect what folks back east call commerce. Now that Santa Fe, an' all New Mexico, is American, business is boomin'. That's what the politicians will want the soldiers to guard. I hear there's even talk of openin' a stagecoach line. *Civilization,*" he spat. "It gums up ever'thin' wherever it goes."

Amelia smiled and patted him on the arm. "I'm not so sure. People are . . . so much more tranquil in the East."

"Controlled, you mean. I've been there. It's like one great big prison. A feller can't carry a shootin' iron down the street without being gawked at, or even arrested in some places. Folks that live like that ain't free."

"But they are safe, and protected."

Preacher looked long and hard at her. "Miss Amelia, I don't mean to pry, or to offend, but that makes me wonder. If that be the case, then why in tarnation did you folk come out here?"

Amelia tried to find the right tone of answer and failed. Instead, she laughed and leaned a shoulder against Preacher. "You have me there, Preacher. I could say it was our calling. Or that adventure beckoned. Truth to tell, I suppose it was to be away from the strictures of society." She frowned and returned to her original theme. "Though, when I think of the price to be paid, the terrible things that happened to Deacon Abercrombie and the others, all the blood spilled—and more to come. It makes me question the purpose behind fighting those sick people out there."

Preacher's voice took on an edge. "Because we're the only ones to do it, Miss Amelia. An' it dang-sure needs doing." He bent in the silence that followed to help her pick up the picnic leavings.

Back at the trading post, Karl Kreuger nursed his bruises and aches and avoided eye contact with Preacher. He would go along, he allowed. "Because I giff my vord."

The next day, three more mountain men straggled into the gathering. That called for another whooping, foot-stomping, powerful drinking welcome. The assorted company had hardly settled down when a lone Arapaho warrior appeared at the gate to the compound. Preacher went out to greet him.

"Yellow Hawk, it is good to see you."

Yellow Hawk returned Preacher's sign of greeting and made the one for peace. "It is good to see you, Ghost Wolf. We have come. There are six hands of warriors from the village of Bold Pony and four hands from the village of the people who lost their braves to the Ro-mans."

Fifty warriors, Preacher tallied. Better than he had hoped for. He nodded his acceptance. "We number nearly as many. More will be picked up on the trail. An' maybe some of my Cheyenne friends would like to get in on this."

Yellow Hawk made a face. All was not love and roses between the Arapaho and the Cheyenne. Yet, they had fought together before and perhaps would again. He signed acceptance. Preacher read the thoughts of Yellow Hawk on his stern visage. No matter. They would get along or not. The Cheyenne could always fight alongside the mountain men.

"Bring 'em on in. You can make camp outside the stockade. We leave tomorrow at first light."

A bit after mid-afternoon the next day, Preacher came upon a complication that left his jaw sagging a moment before he let go a low, controlled roar. "What in hell are you doin' here, boy?"

Saucy as ever, Terry Tucker stood at the side of the road, face beaming, while he waved at the man he so admired. "I want to go with you, Preacher."

Preacher's eyes narrowed. "We've been over this before. Where's your sister?"

"I took her back, then come to find you."

'Back? That mean the both of you runned off?"

"Yes, sir. We tried to find you north of here. Saw a lot of fellers dressed like you, but you didn't come along. Vickie got scared and tired and so I took her back. I can come along, can't I?"

"No. Not only no, but hell no."

Terry looked as though he might cry. "I want to join the fight. I can do it, you know that. I—I'm grateful to you for helping Vickie an' me escape a life of crime, and I want to make amends. I can do odd jobs around the camp, care for the horses, that sort of thing."

What a quandary. Preacher removed his old, slouch hat and scratched the crown of his head with a thick fingernail. "I swear I don't know what to do with you. It's more than dangerous where we're going. I've been there onecst an' it ain't no pony ride. Still . . ." he faded off, considering the alternatives. "I can't spare a man to return you. Nor can I trust you to go on your own, given your stubborn outlook. So, I reckon you'll have to come along."

Terry's face came alive, and he gave a little jump of joy. "Really? Oh, Preacher, thank you."

Preacher bent toward the boy. "You'll not be thankin'

me five days from now when we run into them Romans.
Now, you cain't walk all the way. We got to scare up a
horse for you."

With the same coy expression, an impish light in his
clear, blue eyes, Terry asked the identical question he had
put to Preacher before. "Why can't I ride with you?"

Laughing, Preacher reached for the boy. "I suppose we
can make an exception this one time. At least until I can
scare up another mount." He swung the boy aboard Cougar, noting that the improved victuals had added to Terry's
weight.

Messengers arrived at the palace from the watch towers
on a regular schedule. The one that was just shown in to
Marcus Quintus brought worrisome news.

"Reporting from Watch Tower Three, First Citizen. We
have observed increased movement by the red savages to
the east. All appear to be men, heavily armed and moving
to the south."

Quintus scowled. That did not sound good at all. "Do
you have a count of them?"

"Yes, sir. They number approximately thirty-six."

"Not an exact figure?" Quintus goaded.

Independent service in an isolated command had loos-
ened the reins of discipline for the messenger. "We weren't
about to send someone out to parlay with them and count
heads, sir."

Anger flared for a moment in Quintus; then he regained
control. "No. Of course not. Standing orders remain not to
provoke the savages. I wonder where they are heading?"

Chapter 21

Some ten miles out into the Great Divide Basin, Preacher's small army came upon the advance scouts of the Cheyenne party seeking them. Some grumbling ran through the Arapaho warriors at this, though the two war party leaders, Yellow Hawk and Blind Beaver, kept their men in check. Crow Killer, leader of the Cheyenne, had been a small boy when Preacher first met him. That had been over twenty years ago. He still had the sunny disposition and good sense of humor of his childhood, and greeted Preacher warmly.

"I thought you to be with the Great Spirit by now, Preacher."

"You ain't no spring chicken yourself," Preacher growled good-naturedly.

Crow Killer made a face. "Have you grown as mean as you have old?"

"Dang right. An' fit to wrassel a griz." Preacher let go a big guffaw. "How'er ya doin', Crow Killer?"

"I have a wife now, and three children."

Preacher blinked and cocked his head to one side. "Is that a fact? You had no more than thirteen summers the last time I saw you."

"It has been a long time, Ghost Walker. I have twice that number of summers now."

"An' three youngins. You got started early."

Crow Killer cracked a white smile. "I went on the war trail first time the summer after you hunted buffalo with our village. I took a wife five summers later."

Grinning, Preacher shook his head knowingly. "Ah, but it is the winters that count in catchin' babies, right?"

Grinning, the Cheyenne motioned his men into the column. "We scout for you, Preacher?"

"Yes, that would be good."

Crow Killer's next words surprised Preacher. "We saw these people you go to fight."

"Did you now? When was this?"

"Three suns ago. We rode past their valley of shining lodges. They make ready to take the war trail. Aha! We have known of it for some time. We did not know how evil these men are, so we left them alone. I will grow much honor fighting at your side."

"The honor is mine," Preacher responded modestly. "What can you tell me from what you saw?"

Crow Killer considered it. "They have built some platforms, like burial racks, put up on the ridge around their basin."

"Watch towers. Reckon they saw you?"

"Oh, yes. We did not try to hide."

Preacher chuckled at that. "That must have given ol' Marcus Quintus a tizzy."

"Who? I do not know that name."

"The he-coon that runs that strange place. Injuns make him nervous."

Crow Killer scanned the ranks of Arapaho and his own Cheyenne. "Then he will soon be very nervous."

Laughing together, they rode on. An hour before sundown, the column pulled into a circle, the Arapaho and Cheyenne on the outer two rings, and settled in for the night. Two of the Cheyenne scouts had taken a small elk, and the savory odor of roasting meat filled the air inside the campsite. Most of the mountain men had brought along ample supplies of stoneware jugs full of whiskey, and the mood became festive. Not so for Preacher and the more experienced among them, nor for the Indian leaders.

"We can't let any of them Arapaho or Cheyenne get a hand on that likker. We'd have us one hell of a war on our hands if they did. Keep a good watch," Preacher advised the war leaders, Philadelphia, and Frenchie Dupres.

Early the next morning, Terry Tucker rode beside Preacher. Blind Beaver noted this and rode over. "You have a son now, also, Preacher?"

Preacher looked surprised, then embarrassed. "No. Not likely. It—it's just something that growed to me." For all his denial, Preacher gave Terry a wink.

Blind Beaver beamed. "I have two. One is five summers, the other one. The other is a girl. And she is beautiful."

"I'm sure she is." Preacher gave Blind Beaver a hard, direct look. "When we make camp tonight, we will hold council. I want to paint a word picture of how we will attack these bad men."

Grunting in agreement, Blind Beaver made his thoughts known. "It is good. Are they truly Moon Children?"

Preacher considered it. "I don't think so. Ol' Marcus Quintus might be a lot tetched, but he's sane enough to know right from wrong. So do the others. I figger it this way. They're just lettin' themselves go. The pleasures evil can offer can be mighty temptin'."

"Most true, *mon ami*," Frenchie Dupres agreed from the other side.

"Tell me about this boy," Blind Beaver urged Preacher.

Preacher reached out and ruffled Terry's white hair. "He's a stray. Attached himself to me a while back an' I found a home for him and his sister. Now he's run off to help me in this fight."

"You are young for your first war party," Blind Beaver told Terry in Arapaho, with Preacher translating.

"I'm twelve," Terry responded sharply, with only a hint of his usual defiance.

"When I had twelve summers, I still used a boy's bow and hunted rabbits."

"It was meant as a compliment," Preacher added to his translation.

Terry surprised Preacher yet again with his depth of diplomacy. "I'd really rather be."

"You are brave. You will do well," Blind Beaver told the boy. Then, to Preacher he added, "I will go forward, see what has been found."

What the Cheyenne scouts had found would astonish all of them.

Only the day before, one century of Varras' cavalry (actually only fifty-seven men, not one hundred) had at last discovered the tracks left by the fleeing missionaries. They followed it to the southeast now, hungering for contact. Shouted jests as to what they would do to the survivors flew through the air, flung from their mouths by a quick canter. Their concentration so centered on the anticipated targets, they failed to take note of an eagle feather that seemed to flutter incongruously from the center of a large sage bush.

A close study of that out-of-place object would have informed them that the tip had been dyed red. So had the white goose fletchings on the arrows the watcher carried, the shafts of which bore two red and one yellow band of paint. The watcher's cousins, the Sioux, called them *Sahiela*—which translates loosely into English as "they-come-red"—and the white men called them Cheyenne.

Red Hand had been scouting ahead for hours, and had only swung directly back onto the trail a short while ago. He lived, as did all his brothers, by "Indian time" which took no notice of seconds, minutes, or hours, only of day and night, before high sun and after, of suns (days) and moons (months). So he had no exact idea how long he had ridden forward before his keen hearing picked up the rumble of many mounted men. Alerted, he guided his pony off the trail and dismounted.

His experience quickly led him to the large clump of sage, and he concealed himself there. A hundred heartbeats later, these strange men rode into view. Were they contraries? What odd clothing. That bright red cloth could be seen for miles. And only four hands of them carried bows. What sort of warriors were they? He waited until they had ridden far beyond his hiding place. Then he came out of the brush, gathered dry sticks, and clumps of green grass.

Quickly Red Hand built a small fire. When it went well, he weighted two corners of a blanket with stones, threw the greenery on the blaze and covered it with the square of cloth. He counted heartbeats, then quickly raised the blanket. A large ball of smoke formed and drifted lazily upward. He waited, fed the fire, then repeated the process twice. Crow Killer would soon know.

Crow Killer returned to the mixed column of mountain men and Indians at a gallop. His pony snorted and stamped hooves in excitement at the run when the Cheyenne war leader reined in. He had plenty to tell.

"You weren't gone long," Preacher dryly observed.

"You saw the smokes?"

Preacher nodded.

"There are many. I watched them. Two of my scouts are behind them, to give warning if more come."

Preacher nodded again and spat a blade of grass from his mouth. "That is wise. I'd as leave have half our men behind them, catch 'em in a box. How many?"

"Five two-hands and a hand more and two."

Pursing his lips, Preacher thought on that. "Sure it's the Romans?"

"Yes. All on ponies."

Preacher planned quickly. "Chances are one or two will get away from the fight that's sure to come. Wouldn't do for them to know us boys was out here. I hate to turn down a battle with those devils first off, but it's best if they think it's only Injuns. Bold Pony has some good men with the rifle. How about you?"

"I have three hands who are good at it."

"Fine, fifteen more rifles will sure help. I'll get the Arapaho ready, and you set up your warriors. Have 'em try to pot the leaders first off. This ain't for honor, it's for revenge."

Crow Killer's face indicated he didn't think much of that, though he readily agreed. "That is how it will be done."

"Good. Remember, no individual challenges or fights until the leaders are knocked out of the saddle."

After explaining his plan to Bold Pony, Preacher set about convincing the throng of mountain men. "I know this won't sit well with a lot of you. But we've got to keep our intentions hidden from any of the Romans who get away."

Karl Kreuger seized on that. "Vhat are you talking about?"

"There's about fifty-five, sixty Roman cavalry on their way. The Injuns are gonna take them on. Chances are some will get away. They can't take it back to New Rome that we have this large a force. Plain an' simple. We hide over that ridge behind us until the thing is done. No exceptions."

"Who appointed you general?" Kreuger growled.

"I did," Preacher answered simply. "Now, we'd best be moving. Them boys in the red capotes is not far away."

* * *

Preacher watched the Roman cavalry approach through his long, brass spyglass. First to appear over the ridge that masked off the swale they had so recently occupied came the horsehair-plumed helmets and tossing heads of the mounts. The men showed next. They rode at a canter, up hill. *Stupid,* Preacher thought.

When the Romans reached the bottom of the reverse slope, the centurion in charge raised his hand in the univer sal signal to halt. Changing his field of view, Preacher saw the reason why. A dozen Cheyenne warriors had risen out of the tall grass, as though sprang new from the earth itself. They held drawn bows, the arrowheads angled high, to reach for the enemy. *Clever,* Preacher thought.

Sounding like nothing more than the cry of a shrike, the centurion issued his command, echoed by the sergeants. Swords hissed out of scabbards and made pillars of brightness in the sunlight. Another birdlike command and the sergeants separated their squads from the square formation they had traveled in so far. It also identified all of the leaders to the patient Cheyenne. *Idiotic,* Preacher thought.

From hidden locations on the flanks, puffs of smoke rose from the grass. There followed a fraction of a second, and the four sergeants went off their horses, dead before they struck the ground. The crack of discharging rifles followed the Preacher's ears. The centurion wavered in his saddle, shot through the breastplate. *Brilliant,* Preacher thought.

Left in confusion, the soldiers milled about, their horses made fractious by the smell of blood. Then they were given something to concentrate upon. The meadow came alive with Cheyenne and Arapaho warriors. Their horses snorted as they rolled upright and came to their hooves. Another volley sounded from the hidden marksmen. Arrows flew from the twelve on foot. Swiftly the Indians mounted their ponies. Before the cavalry soldiers realized it, they found themselves the target of a whooping, hooting, lance-waving Indian charge. *Magnificent,* Preacher thought.

Since the advent of the horse, standard tactics for most plains tribes consisted of swift, powerful charges to ring the wagons of white settlers, or an enemy village, then close the diameter with a gradual inward spiral. Or of individual challenges and man-to-man, vicious hand-to-hand combat. Indians, Preacher had ample reason to know, rarely fought in organized, disciplined ranks. Almost anything could end the fighting: victory, or a perception of bad medicine, or omens like an owl flying in daylight, to a sudden chill wind. Pity the poor pilgrims coming after him, Preacher thought, if this fight today changed all that.

It didn't appear that it would, Preacher acknowledged as he watched, telescope at his side now, while the cavalry formation disintegrated through attrition and the Arapaho and Cheyenne braves picked out individuals to challenge. One by one, the kilted fighting men of New Rome met death at the hands of the Indians. Only seven of them managed to keep their wits long enough to make an escape. One of those lost his chance to a long-range rifle shot. Their commander fared even worse.

Frightfully wounded, he much preferred the peace of the grave to the torture and torment that capture meant. He had heard the stories, of course, and chose the only sensible alternative. He removed his cuirass, reversed his *gladius* and pressed the pommel to the ground, then fell on his sword.

Blind Beaver appeared at Preacher's side. "In the end, he was a woman," he stated scornfully of the centurion. Preacher thought that made a good sum-up of the entire battle, which had not lasted fifteen minutes by his big Hambleton turnip watch.

During the next two days, seventeen more denizens of the High Lonesome wandered in. The word had spread far and wide. Duke Morrison was among them. As was Bunny Tilitson and Haymaker Norris. The Duke approached Preacher during the nooning rest.

"Are you serious about these—"

Preacher cut him off. "Yeah, yeah, them Romans is real enough. D'ya check the trophies our Arapaho an' Cheyenne allies collected off the cavalry?"

"No, but I'll have me a look."

Eyeing the younger mountain man, Preacher reached a conclusion. "Duke, yu'rt purty nigh expert at slippin' an' slidin' around after dark, ain'tcha?"

Modesty commanded that Duke eye the ground beyond Preacher's shoulder. "I've done my share of dark-time stalkin'. You don't intend on *sneakin'* up on these Romans, do you?"

"Yep. On some of 'em at least. Now that you're here, it comes to mind that we ought to do somethin' about these outposts I hear the Romans done put up. Best done at night."

Duke nodded. "You're right on that, Preacher. When do we have a go at it?"

"Reckon you an' me, an' a couple of Bold Pony's boys ought to pull out early tomorrow, get a day or so ahead of the rest. Then we can have a look around and see what can be done."

A broad grin spread the full lips of the big man. "I say that shines. Count me in."

Shortly before nightfall, two days later, Preacher and Duke Morrison crested the notch that separated them from the New Rome basin by but another valley and ridge. Careful to remain behind a screen of trees, they made a detailed study of the saw-tooth line across the way. After a seemingly long two minutes, Preacher lowered his spyglass.

He pointed at a shadowy object partially obscured by tree limbs.

"A watch tower, right enough. I reckon they'll be spread around so's to overlap a slight bit of the view from one to another. I counted six men. Most likely there's some snoozin', an' a couple who act as messengers."

"I saw another tower," Duke revealed. "It looked to have the arms of one of those whatchamacallits—you know, a signal thing."

"A heliograph, or something like it, eh?"

"Yeah. That's it."

"That way they don't waste time sendin' a message, at least in daytime. The thing for us to do tonight is hit enough of these things to make bein' here plain uncomfortable. We want to get these boys all bollixed up. Seein' things that ain't there, firing off reports and alarms to call out the soldiers at all hours."

Duke clucked his tongue. "That won't make the troops very happy."

"Nope. An' it will make them careless. You 'member from bein' a kid the story about the boy who cried wolf? Well, by the time our outfit gets here, that's what the regular soldiers will be thinkin' about these fellers on the ridge. Then maybe we pop up . . ." Preacher went on to outline his plan.

They picked a spot on the far side and settled in among the pines to rest until the best time of night. Preacher and Duke gnawed on strips of jerky and cold biscuits to fill the empty space in their bellies, then caught a few hours of sleep.

Elijah Morton had quickly become bored with this duty. They could hang a Roman name on him, make him learn Latin, but he knew who he was, or at least who he'd once been. Elijah Morton had been a small-time highwayman who preyed on isolated trading posts along the North Platte. At least until the urge to move farther west, brought on by an increased presence of mounted federal troops, had brought him into the Ferris Range some two years ago. He had been captured and quickly volunteered to join a legion.

Often after that, he had regretted his decision. Not nearly so much as he would this night.

Elijah did not see the dark figures ghosting through the trees toward the watch tower. He had watch and had grown bored with staring into black nothing. Opposite him, Graccus peered toward the distant platform where two others did the same dull task. He sensed at the same time as Elijah the vibration of a footfall on the ladder leading upward. Could it be their relief?

Not likely, Graccus discovered a split-second before bright lights exploded inside his head, to bring excruciating pain for a brief moment, when Duke buried his war hawk in the top of his head. Preacher swarmed over Elijah at the same moment. His forearm pressed tightly against the throat of his victim, which effectively cut off any sound. Preacher leaned close, smelled garlic, onions and rancid, unwashed body, and whispered in one ear.

"You want to live, keep quiet and do as you are told."

The head nodded feebly. Preacher went on. "How many are there up here?"

"Two," Elijah mouthed. Sudden pain erupted under his left ear, and he felt the prick of a knife point.

"Don't lie to me. I counted six men earlier." Preacher eased the pressure to allow for a reply.

"Four are sleeping. There's the messenger down below. Didn't you . . . ?"

"He's tied up," Preacher answered with part of the truth.

Preacher and Duke had closed on the unsuspecting messenger, to find out he was a mere boy, hardly older than fourteen or fifteen. Preacher clapped a big hand over the lad's mouth and yanked him off his feet. They had quickly tied him up, carted him away from the tower and strung him up, head down, in a tree. He prodded again.

"What time is your relief?"

"I don't know. In another hour, maybe."

"What's you name?"

"Elijah Morton."

"You don't have a Roman name, Elijah?"

"Yeah. It's Virgo. I hate it."

"All right, Elijah, if you want to live, you'll answer everything, and then you'll be tied up and gagged. We won't kill you."

"I'll do what I can."

"Good. What's going on in New Rome?"

Elijah talked freely about the preparations for war. He detailed the training exercises of the legions and spoke of the firearms. That came as a nasty surprise to Preacher. They would have to hit at night, spike those cannon and move right into the city. Somehow the idea did not sit well with him.

"Anything else?"

"Oh, sure. The watch towers were built, and we've been in them ever since. Once a week we are supposed to be rotated back to our legion. So far that hasn't happened, and we're gettin' fed up with it."

"Now, that's right interestin'. Well, we're gonna leave those other boys to snooze, lock 'em in that room over there and wait to see what comes of that. I'm gonna turn you loose now. Don't fight me, turn around and put your hands behind your back."

"I hate this place. Can't I come with you?"

"Nope. We've got more of this kinda thing to do. But if you want to ride away from it when you get loose, head due south. When you come to some folks, ask for Philadelphia Braddock."

"I knew some Braddocks back home."

"Where's that?"

"Philadelphia," Elijah answered simply.

Preacher considered that a moment. "Now ain't that interestin'? Turn around."

Elijah complied in silence. After trussing him up, Preacher lowered Elijah to the platform floor. Then he and Duke eased over to the shelter that housed the slumbering sentries. Preacher located a loose piece of wood and used it to wedge the door tightly shut. With that accomplished, they stole off into the night to visit yet another tower.

They completed their jaunt uneasily close to first light. A soft, silver-gray glow hung along the eastern ridge when they rejoined the Cheyennes. Both of them had big grins and six fresh scalps tied to their belts.

"That ain't gonna do them Romans any good when they think about spendin' time out here. Might be we can raise a little more ruckus tomorrow night."

Chapter 22

Considerable uproar followed Preacher's excursion. The fourteen deaths were attributed to the red savages, and any who had been spared by Preacher and Duke kept their own counsel. It worked so well, Preacher decided, that they would try it on two or three of the other towers the next night. In order to avoid the patrols that had been sent out at first light to search for the perpetrators, he, Duke and the Cheyenne had withdrawn beyond the second ridge out of the city.

"Heck of a thing," Preacher announced when they returned after nightfall. "Looks like our funnin' with them has backfired on us." He referred to the neat rows of cook fires that spread around the meadow outside the walled city.

"What's that?" Duke Morrison asked.

Preacher gave a short, sharp grunt. "That's the legions. They've taken to the field. Changes our plans somewhat. But that can wait until the rest git here. Now's the time to shake them up a bit more."

Things had changed on the final rim also. Two sentries guarded the base of the first tower Preacher and Duke approached. It took them only slightly greater stealth to close on the alert guards than it had the unsuspecting messengers of the previous night. From the moment he had learned that the towers operated independently, Preacher had been working on fateful decisions for those who occupied the ones they would visit tonight.

No more sparing of lives. To create the maximum of fear and terror, all would die. It didn't make a problem for the Cheyennes, albeit he and Duke went to it grimly, taking no pleasure from the task. The two guards died swiftly and without a sound. The slumbering messenger awakened in time to see the blade of a war hawk descending toward his head. His scream died along with himself. The moccasins of the two mountain men made only the softest of whispers as they ascended the ladder to the platform.

One of the watchmen, more attentive than his partner, sensed more than heard the silent approach. He turned, his hand going to the haft of his *gladius*. Preacher bounded up onto the boards of the platform and turned off the source of such commands with his tomahawk. The blade sank to the hilt in the soldier's forehead. Before he could wrench it free, Duke joined him and finished off the other sentry.

Preacher spoke softly. "There's two more in there, most likely."

Duke nodded, and they moved cat-footed to the door. Duke pointed to his chest and then the closed portal, indicating he would go through first. Preacher dipped his chin a fraction of an inch and yanked open the crudely made panel. Duke went through with Preacher at his heels. The scuffing motions of their moccasins awakened a light sleeper. Duke's big Hudson's Bay Company knife sank into the unfortunate legionnaire's chest and trashed his heart.

He died with a soft sigh. Preacher swung to split the skull of the dead man's companion only to find his wrist in a grasp like iron. The big man grunted, but did not cry out. The coppery tang of blood in the air told him there would be no one to hear. He tried to rear up, but Preacher's weight bore down on him and pinned him to the straw mattress. Preacher used his free hand to draw his Green River knife and plunge it into soft tissue below the rib cage. He was aware of the amazing rubbery tension of skin for a brief moment, before the tip sank into muscle and angled upward.

The soldier convulsed as the blade pierced his diaphragm and sped on to his heart. His tremors became more violent, and then he went rigid and lay still. Preacher took a deep breath.

"Time to get movin'," he told Duke.

Cassius Varo stared into the night. Had he seen slight movement in Tower Seven? If so, it could only be the men on watch, he told himself. Bored by long, fruitless hours of this static activity, he paced the two sides of the plank square for which he was responsible. Time went by so slowly. Varo's eyelids had started to droop when a sudden, very wet *thok!* came from below.

Suddenly alert, he touched his partner on one shoulder, then leaned over the railing to call softly to the guards on the ground. "Titus, Vindix, what's going on?"

His answer came in the form of a broad-head arrow that drove into his forehead. His single, violent convulsion sent him crashing over the rail. By then, Preacher had ascended the ladder and had only to swing smoothly to smash the brains from the other sentry with his war hawk.

Duke quickly joined him, and they finished off the sleeping pair without even a stir. Outside, Preacher nodded to the tall, black bulk of another tower, standing out against the starlight. "Two down, one more to go."

At mid-morning the next day, the mountain-man-and-Indian army arrived beyond the third ridge from New

Rome. Preacher and Duke greeted them and called for a parlay of all leaders. Bold Pony, Blind Beaver and Philadelphia attended. Terry Tucker hovered at Preacher's elbow. Most of the former fur trappers stood around in a loose circle. Their long lives of independence gave them license to eavesdrop, or so they believed. Having done it enough times himself, Preacher made no further notice of them.

He got right down to business. "Things have changed. We shook 'em up a little an' they put their legions out in the field. They's camped all around the city. So we'll not be scalin' any walls right off. Put your men to makin' ladders fer it, anyway. We'll need 'em after we deal with the soldiers, I reckon."

"How do we do that?" Philadelphia inquired.

Preacher gave him a smile. "I thought you'd never ask. First thing is we've got to draw them out. I see you brought along a couple dozen more than we had at our last camp together. That's good."

"We're more than a hunderd an' fifty strong now, Preacher," Philadelphia announced. "An' that could git bigger by tomorrow."

"Even better. Cold camp tonight. We don't want our Roman friends knowin' we're here. I know it'll be hard not gettin' in some drummin' an' singin', Bold Pony, Blind Beaver, but you've both done some war trail sneaks before, I'm sure. We can all dance up a storm oncest this is over." The war leaders nodded solemnly. "Now here's how we get them to come to us. First off we have to get rid of all those watch towers they've built. Then, the morning after that's done, we show up in a double line on the last ridge. That'll make us ringtailers and the Cheyenne."

"Vhat about the Arapaho?" Karl Kreuger asked nastily from the sidelines. "You goin' soft on dem vor a purpose."

"Nope. Not at all. Matter of fact, they've got the hardest part of all. Before we show ourselves to the Romans, they've got to sneak down into that valley durin' the night

. . ." Preacher went on to describe where the Arapaho warriors would go and what they would be doing.

"Sounds complicated," Philadelphia Braddock observed.

"It ain't. Not if ever'one does what he's supposed to. If all of us keeps our place and not act on our own, we can have this over before nightfall."

"You said they had cannons," a voice came from a mountain man Preacher did not know.

"Those we take care of the same time we empty the watch towers. Which reminds me. Duke an' me learned a whole lot about how they are run. After the soldiers are tooken care of, we leave two men in each tower to make the morning signal. Then those boys can join the rest of us. As far as the cannons go, I found these little things in one of the towers we hit last night. Must be used for holdin' somethin' together. Thing is, they'll serve our purpose." Preacher unwound from his squat on the ground and went to his saddlebags.

From them he took a buckskin bag about six inches long. From it, he removed three dull, grayish objects. They had been flattened on one end, and the opposite one tapered to a fine point. He raised his arm to show them around.

"While the towers are being silenced, Duke an' me and a couple others will slip in among the Romans and spike the touch holes of those big guns."

That didn't sound too good to Philadelphia. "Won't they hear you doin' that?"

Preacher gave him a confident smile. "Not if we use padded wooden mallets. A couple of pops on each, then break them off. Those tired soldier-boys will think it's just horses stompin' in the night."

"If you say so," Philadelphia relented, still unconvinced.

"I want to go with you, Preacher," Terry pleaded.

"No. You'll stay on the ridge with them towers. An' that's final."

"When do we get all this started?" another mountain man asked.

Preacher swept his arm in an inclusive gesture. "We'll git us a little rest now. Then, when it is good and dark tonight, it all begins. Them Romans will never know what hit them."

Prudence, as much as good luck, guarded Preacher and the five mountain men with him as they glided across the tall grass of the central meadow. For some reason, he had noted, the cannons had been left outside the temporary palisades of the nightly encampments of each cohort. He had no way of knowing that the cause was ignorance and laziness—twelve-pound Napoleons weighed over a ton, and were hard to move around.

The generals had decided where they would fight the enemy when he came, and so the long guns had been laid to provide the maximum effect. There they would stay. Coincidentally, that put three cannon on each flank of the supposed Roman main line of resistance. Well and good, Preacher figured. Shortly before sundown, Haymaker Norris, who claimed to have put his trapping aside for two years to serve in the Mexican War as an artilleryman, instructed the sabotage party in the proper way to spike a cannon. Along with the mountain men who were to take out the watch towers, they set out on foot at midnight.

Leaving a cold camp, their night vision was not effected in the least. Those who used tobacco chewed on sweetened leaf or, like Preacher, chomped on the butt of an unlighted cigar. They moved with astonishing speed and silence. No one spoke; not a loose item of equipment or clothing clattered or rattled. Not even a clink came from the Roman plumb bobs—for that's what the lead spikes were identified as by Four-Eyes Finney, who had been an apprentice carpenter before he ran away to the Big Empty. It seemed no time until they had crested the first of three ridges that separated them from New Rome. Preacher called a short halt there to catch their wind. Funny, neither he nor any of them had needed to do that in the past, even packing around some respectable wounds.

He eased over to each of the men with him and repeated whispered advice.

"We'd best be givin' some time for those boys up ahead to do their dirty work."

"Another ridge to cross," Four-Eyes Finney reminded him.

"Then we'd best be gettin' there," Preacher declared as he set off along the trail. The others followed at once without having to be told.

When Preacher and his companions reached the watch tower beside the main southern trail, not a living person remained there. The other force of mountain men had done their work well and vanished into the night to their next objective. Preacher again ordered they take a breather. They had made it this far without another stop, which pleased him. Now the hard part would begin.

"We'll take the cannons on the right flank first. That's our left," he added for the benefit of Blue Nose Herkimer.

"I know that," Blue Nose whispered back in mock irritation.

"You do *now*," Preacher responded through a low chuckle.

They began their descent five minutes later. Avoiding the roadway in order not to be seen, the mountain men angled across the basin, through the tall grass nearly invisible even to one another. Preacher's long, meticulous survey of the valley paid off. He had a fairly accurate map of the terrain in his head. It took not the least effort to direct the spiking party to a wide, deep ravine that cut diagonally across to the Roman right flank.

At five minutes after three in the morning they arrived at their objective. The perfect hour, when the circadian rhythm of human life ebbed lowest. It was the time of deepest sleep, when dreams formed and the body became sodden with relaxation. Working two to each gun, the mountain men placed the spikes, then rapped on them with padded mallets. The soft thuds that accompanied each blow did indeed sound like the stomp of a hoof. Preacher had insisted that they not strike together or too rapidly.

His precaution paid unexpected dividends. When the last spike had been broken off, they entered a small gully on hands and knees. Preacher's keen hearing picked up soft voices speaking in English from the main gate to the camp as they passed it.

"Lazy cavalry. Picketed their horses outside the camp," came a scornful remark.

"All right with me," the other sentry answered. "I don't like the smell of horse crap at breakfast."

A soft chuckle rose for a moment. "Considering what they feed us, how can you tell the difference?"

Like soldiers anywhere, Preacher thought as he crawled away.

They reached the second trio of cannon without incident. Preacher squared off on the flattened top of a lead plumb bob and gave it a whack. Ice shot down his spine a second later when an inquiring voice came from behind the palisade.

"What'cha doin' out there with horses?"

Preacher thought fast. He'd have to make some response. Fortunately the question had been in English. "Early patrol. The generals are getting nervous." He could speak as correctly as any man when he chose to do so.

"You horse soldiers have it made," came an envious response.

"Don't we though?" Preacher hoped the man would shut up with that. He did not like the idea of chatting away with the enemy when there were so many so close.

"Good luck," served as words of dismissal. Preacher let go a soft sigh of relief.

Plop! came from another cannon touch hole. Then again. Then it was Preacher's turn. He took a swat, then glanced nervously at the stockade. Two more followed his. He suddenly realized he was sweating bullets. Much of this could take years off a feller's life. He tugged at the spike to check its set, then hit it on the shaft. It bent but did not break off. Damn. He did not dare risk another. Preacher raised his hand to signal the others, and they stole off into the darkness, their task completed.

Preacher's small party, and those who had attacked the watch towers around the rim, waited out the rest of the night on the intermediate ridge. Their horses would be brought up to them. Elated, and relieved that they had encountered no difficulties in the night's activities, Preacher chose to spend his wait on a good snooze. He reckoned as how he would need every bit of alertness and stamina he could recover during the day to come. An hour before dawn, the main force arrived. Preacher roused himself to speak with the leaders.

"Yellow Hawk, I want you and your warriors to take your place where I told you about now. Have 'em keep low and be danged quiet. They must stay complete out of sight until I give the signal."

Preacher had brought along six fat, greasy, paper-wrapped sticks of blasting powder from the trading post. He had caps and fuse for them in his saddlebag. Some would be used to distract and confuse the enemy, or to blow down the gates to the city. The first one would be to signal the Arapaho to attack.

"Have them take plenty water gourds, too. Wouldn't do for 'em to get too thirsty to fight proper."

Yellow Hawk nodded his understanding. "You have fought many more battles than I, Ghost Wolf. It is good to have wise counsel. Only one thing worries me. That we are not to fight in the open, pick our enemy and count coup before we slay him and go for another. We have never fought this way before."

"Let's hope you never have to again," Preacher said fervently, recalling his earlier thoughts on the subject. "But this time it is important. The way the Romans fight makes it so. Now, if you please, go on and put the braves in the right places."

Preacher turned his attention to the others. "Philadelphia, you'll lead our boys in this fracas. I'll be quarterin' the field between you an' the Cheyenne. It's gonna be pure hell to keep them dog soldiers from breakin' ranks and countin' coup before we can spring the trap. So I'll mostly be with them."

"Think they'll listen to you?" Philadelphia asked with an eye on the patient Indians who remained with their mountain men allies.

"They'd better, if they want to stay alive. In the right hands, them javelins have might near the range of a Cheyenne arrow. They ain't like a head-heavy flint lance point. Timin'. Everything in this counts on timin'. We're outnumbered, sure's hell. But if we do this right, there won't be enough Roman soldiers left to form one of those . . . what do you call them ten-man outfits?"

"*Contaburnium,*" Buck Sears supplied.

"Yeah. That's the one."

Buck scratched his head. "You seem so sure of this, Preacher. Did you learn it from some army feller?"

"I'll tell you about it later, Buck. Right now, I want to go convince Blind Beaver to keep a lid on his men." Before he could do that, he had one more task to complete. He squatted before Terry and put a big, hard hand on one slim shoulder.

"You do right like I said. Stay here on this ridge tomorrow. Don't move a muscle."

Shortly after the sun rose two fingers over the eastern rim of the valley, the mountain-man-and-Indian army crested the ridge to the south. Not a signal went out to announce their arrival. Below, in the camps of the legions, the soldiers went about their morning fatigue duties of taking down the stockade and tents. The approaching host had ridden halfway down the reverse slope when someone first noticed them.

Brassy blasts on the long, straight, valveless trumpets sent the men hastily to their weapons. Tent mates helped one another into their breastplates and greaves. Bawling NCOs brought order to the ranks, which formed in the traditional Roman squares. By then, the bandsmen had been assembled.

While the invaders walked their horses onto the floor of the meadow, the *buccinae* hooted and the *clarinae* tooted, while the *timpanii* throbbed and rumbled in fine martial style. Lastly, the legates of the legions appeared, dashing on their powerful chargers, the cavalry legion of Varras swinging into the traditional position in the order of battle. They took their reports from their adjutants and began to exhort the legionnaires to do their utmost in battle. The enemy rode inexorably closer.

At about two thousand yards, their double line began to change shape. The flanks, two ranks deep, curved inward, while the middle, consisting of three ranks, hung back slightly. When they had molded in a bison-horn formation, they halted. All of this brisk human activity had frightened the small animals and birds to flight or silence. When the invaders halted, an eerie silence enveloped both sides. Curious eyes studied the "barbarians."

Equally curious eyes took in the boxlike formations of the legions from the other side. Squinty Williams nudged Philadelphia in the ribs. "What they all bunched up like that for? They're just askin' for a shower of Cheyenne arras."

"We'll find out soon enough, I reckon, Squinty," Braddock replied. "Accordin' to Preacher, the old-timey Romans were real mean fighters. Whupped ever'body they went against."

"Wull, they didn't never come against *us* fellers, I bet."

Philadelphia stifled the laugh that rose in his chest. "No, Squinty, they didn't."

Abruptly the drums opposite them began to throb. Bull-roar voices bellowed orders. In full regalia, complete with cavalry and band, the Roman legions began to march forward like a single man, rather than nearly nine hundred.

Marcus Quintus Americus gazed over the ranks of his brave legions. Pride swelled his heart. They were ready. They surely were honed as fine as any soldiers could be. They had about a thousand *stadia* to cover, and then the cannons would open up. The legions had heard them fired enough not to falter when they blasted away. And then the cohorts would pick up the pace to a trot, pilae slanted forward at eye-level to these unprotected barbarians.

Riflemen would open up at the same time. This should be over soon enough that he could be back in the palace for a soothing bath and a light lunch. How tedious these matters could be. It would blood the legions, which they would need. Knowledge of New Rome had undoubtedly become wide-spread outside the valley. Secrecy could not be maintained forever, he knew. Yet, he had hoped to keep the true enemy ignorant of his power and intentions for a while longer. A sudden shout came from ahead of him at the left-hand battery. It was repeated by stentorians until he could make meaning of the sounds.

"The cannon have been spiked! The cannon are useless!"

Those fateful words chilled Quintus. Everything hinged on the artillery. He looked about him in serious despair. He had to act. He must do something, and it had to be right.

Chapter 23

It wouldn't do to start off with all this fanfare and then retreat in the face of a determined, if small, hostile force. There could not be more than a hundred and fifty of them, Marcus Quintus made a quick, inaccurate tally. *Be decisive.* The words mocked him. Yet, he must do something. Marcus Quintus turned to the trumpeter beside him.

"Sound for the legates," he commanded.

With a nod, the signalman put the mouthpiece of his instrument, one which had been coiled to compact it, to his lips and blew. It produced a mellower note than the straight trumpets. At once, Glaubiae, Bruno and Varras turned the heads of their mounts and cantered to the center. They saluted formally.

Quintus spoke brusquely, not meeting their eyes. "I am sure you heard the disastrous news. Somehow those barbarians had the wit to infiltrate our encampment and spike the cannons. That places the burden of victory more directly upon your soldiers. We will advance within range of our archers and pilae. The cavalry is to divide and take positions to sweep those thin flanks back on the main body."

"First Citizen," Varras spoke urgently. "I recommend against splitting my force."

"Why not?" Now Quintus glared directly into the black

eyes of Varras. "Given a good shower of arrows and javelins, these unarmored louts will break ranks and flee. You
will be able to slaughter them at your leisure."

"Need I remind you that they all have guns. Even most
of the red savages."

Quintus found that a subject for contempt. "Savages
cannot hit what they shoot at. See that it is done as I have
said. I will take the center in my chariot."

He dismounted and climbed to the platform of the gold-
chased chariot. There he drew a silver inlay *gladius* and held
it at the ready. Disgruntled, yet keeping their tongues silent,
the legates of the three legions of New Rome rode back to
their commands. There they conveyed the orders of their
supreme commander, and the cavalry departed for the
flanks of the mountain man formation.

When they reached the desired location, Quintus raised
his sword and ordered his troops forward. The band began
again, and the soldiers stepped out with a steady, measured
tread. They came right on until a distance of only fifty
yards separated them from the invaders. Not unlike an
exercise on the drill field, the commands barked from centurions to sergeants to the men. Javelins hissed through the
air while arrows arched above and moaned their eerie
song.

"Now ain't that obligin' of them to come in so close?"
Philadelphia Braddock drawled.

Preacher agreed with him. "Sure enough is. Steady on,
boys," he added as the Romans halted, their formation still
perfect.

Then came the commands to fire. The projectiles
seethed through the air. Unlike the static squares of the
Roman soldiers, the mountain men and Cheyenne allies
were free to move at will. Which they did by jumping their
horses forward enough to be missed by the missiles. A split

second after recovering from the movement, they fired a ragged volley.

Bullets punched right through bull-hide shields. Even the brass ornaments on them yielded to .56 caliber lead balls. Preacher had taken aim at a fancy dude in a glittery uniform who seemed to be in command. His slug shattered the breastbone of Yancy Taggart and ended the career of General Gaius Septimus Glaubiae. The gaudy uniform became a heap of lifeless clothing at the feet of the *primus pilus* of the Thirteenth Legion. At such short range, not a one of the mountain men and Indians could miss. One hundred fifty-seven Roman soldiers went down in that first volley.

Marcus Quintus Americus stared on in horror as he saw his senior general slain with casual indifference. Another flight of arrows and javelins answered the fire, only to be avoided while men rapidly reloaded. The air turned blue with powder smoke once again.

Preacher made quick note that the discipline of the troops they faced had begun to falter. With a little luck, he might not even need to use the Arapahos. He drew a .44 Walker Colt, and the mountain men around him went to pistols also. The more rapid fire had a withering effect on the legions.

It had even more on the fancy-dressed fellow in the two-wheeled cart, Preacher realized as that one—it must be that Marcus Quintus—shouted an order. Another shower of arrows and then the Romans began to withdraw, marching backward, long rows of leveled javelins pointed at the men whom they left in command of the field.

"Well, if that don't just beat all," Preacher declared wonderingly. "Don't know what to make of that."

"Me neither," Philadelphia remarked. "A feller gets himself all worked up for a fight like they did, it usual lasts a spell. They sure's the devil had us outnumbered."

"They may be back. Best pull back a ways and stand fast. I mark that Quintus feller to be a tricky bastard."

While the archers let fly another deadly flock and the soldiers hurled their slender javelins, Marcus Quintus Americus looked around him in confusion. Another ragged volley came from fifty yards off. Why weren't his own riflemen firing? For a moment, it plagued him; then he recalled that he had assigned them to cover the cavalry, which as yet had not engaged the enemy. Another thought struck him.

He would have to get a replacement for Gaius Septimus. His first spear had all the imagination and initiative of a stone post. Who could it be? Rufus Longinus of the Second? Yes. He had almost as much knowledge of military matters as Glaubiae had possessed. Bruno could get himself a new *primus pilus*. But this was hardly the place to hand out promotions. He turned to right and left, bawling out the most bitter order ever given by a commander.

"Fall back on the camp. Make it in good order and keep an eye on the enemy."

Trumpets sounding, the order was relayed by the adjutants of each legion, one in temporary command of his. Slowly the tramp of thick-soled military sandals sounded, and the century squares became a retrograde movement. Dust began to rise in thick clouds. Not enough, though, to mask, let alone protect, potential targets.

Although puzzled by the retreat, the mountain men and Indians kept up a steady fire into the dwindling ranks of the legions until they maneuvered out of range. Quintus ordered his chariot to turn and get around the formations of troops. He wanted to be calmed and refreshed when he met with his generals to promote one man and offer advice. Tomorrow would be a far better day, he convinced himself.

Besides, the omens had not been all that promising at the morning sacrifice.

Four-Eyes Finney seemed mightily pleased with himself. "He who hits and runs away . . . ," he quoted.

"Is a yellow-bellied cur," Jack Lonesome added his own version to the end.

"Naw, that ain't it, Lonesome," Four-Eyes corrected. "It's about livin' to fight another day."

"Why'd they run? Why didn't we just finish them here an' now?" the grizzled mountain man pressed his point.

"Tell you what, Jack," Preacher began diplomatically. "We got 'em whittled down some, and it's for certain sure those cannons don't work. But there's at least five of them for each one of us. What say we pull back to the base of the ridge and settle in. They'll do somethin' 'fore long."

Preacher turned out to be right on that. An hour later, three officers, one with a white flag, rode out from the Roman camp. With them came a number of soldiers and a line of wagons. The one with the truce flag advanced to where the mountain men lolled on the ground, eating and sharing some scarce whiskey.

"Which one of you is the general in charge?"

Preacher came to his boots and tucked the stick of jerky he had been gnawing on in a shirt pocket. "I reckon that would be me. But I ain't no gen'ral."

"What do you call yourself?"

"Folks around these parts call me Preacher."

"By Jupiter and all the gods," the young Varras blurted. "Gaius told us you were the one we saw fight in the arena." His tone turned rueful, and his expression became wry. "No one but you could have made good on that escape." He saw that his flattery had no effect on Preacher. That decided him to come to the point.

"We came to ask permission to recover our dead and wounded."

"He'p yourselves. We've got no quarrel with them."

"But you do with us?"

"Somethin' like that. There's those among us who don't take kindly to having our friends made into slaves and forced to fight to the death.

The trio of officers exchanged glances. The one in the middle, with the flag of truce, looked back at Preacher. "What's wrong with that? It's a good way for a barbarian to make a living." They all laughed.

Preacher instantly developed a thunderous expression. "You keep that up an' you'll be joinin' those you came to get."

Varras' protest came at once. "Bu-but we're under a flag of truce."

Preacher reached up and yanked the white flag from the astonished general's hands. "Funny, I don't see a damn thing."

Youngest and the most nervous of the junior officers, the one on his left spoke in a soft, quiet voice. "Legate Varras, I think he's serious."

"At least *you've* got it right, Sonny," Preacher snapped.

Touching a lightly trembling finger to his lips, the youthful general pushed his point. "Let's—uh—get on with it, shouldn't we?"

To their stiff backs, Preacher said, "You can come back for this rag when you're done." To the others he spoke in a low tone. "We're gonna have to do somethin' about that rudeness."

By the time the dead and wounded had been retrieved from the field, darkness hovered on the ridge to the east. Westward, magenta and gold washed over the pale blue of the sky. Preacher had men busy making objects from the thorns taken from the underbrush and rawhide strips. While they worked, he went among them, explaining what would happen.

"When it gits good and dark, we're gonna take these things out and scatter them in front of those little movable forts of theirs. Really sew the ground with them. Then some of us is gonna pay a visit to the big city."

"How do ve get past dose soldiers?" Bloody Hand Kreuger asked in a surly tone.

"Ve' don't. You'll be with the others spreading these here caltrops. Horses don't like 'em much and men don't either. Messes up their walkin' right smart. I'll pick those goin', and everyone eat a good meal. We'll start out at midnight."

True to his word, Preacher led an expedition out from their camp at midnight. He and eleven others would penetrate into the city and cause what havoc they could contrive. Another party, under charge of Philadelphia Braddock, set off to scatter the deadly four-point caltrops in the tall grass outside the Roman camps. Preacher's picks had smeared soot and grease on their faces, and all wore dark clothing.

They had a variety of flopped hats and animal-skin caps to break up the regularity of the shape of their heads. All carried pistols and knives, a few tomahawks. Rifles would only hamper them. At Preacher's direction, fire pit trestles had been heated and one end of each bent into a hook. Ropes had been attached and knots tied along their length. Preacher had remained secretive about the purpose of these.

When they reached the walls, the fires burned low behind the palisades and everything lay in silence. Preacher wrapped his hook in cloth and shook out a length of rope. He gave it a steady swing, moving his hand and arm faster with each circle. At last he let it go and it sailed upward. It struck a foot short with a soft thump. When it dropped back, Preacher tried again. Once more he failed.

"This one'll do 'er," he assured the others in a whisper. It didn't.

At last, on the fifth toss, the hook sailed over the wall and stuck fast when Preacher pulled on the rope. Quickly the others with hooks began to throw them at the battlement. When the sixth one caught, Preacher leaned back and went up his hand-over-hand, feet braced against the outside of the rampart. More men quickly followed until all twelve had scaled the barrier.

"We're here, now what?" Squinty Williams asked.

"I'd say a visit to the baths," Preacher offered.

"Me?" Squinty squeaked out. "I've done took my summer bath."

"I was thinking of breaking a few things in there and flooding the streets," Preacher responded. "You won't even have to take off those ripe-smellin' moccasins, Squinty."

"Don't you be doin' that to me, Preacher. I'll have to swim for it if you break that place apart."

"Not if you run fast enough. Now, let's go."

The twelve-man party made it to the baths without the *vigilii* spotting them. Inside, they subdued the night watchman and spread out through the series of pool rooms. Buck Sears led the way to the confluence of the underground waterways. There they plied crowbars and mauls to break the plaster away and penetrate the brick walls.

In no time after that, they were walking ankle deep in swift-flowing water. It spread through the baths and headed for the front door. Enough done here, Preacher thought. He directed them to split up into pairs and go do mischief.

"Keep a sharp eye for those watchmen," he cautioned. He and Squinty headed for the central square, the forum.

"What are we going to do there?"

Preacher chuckled as he explained. "We're gonna wake up some ladies and scare them out of their nightshirts."

Squinty cocked his head, then shook it. "You actual thinkin' about dallyin' with some wimmin in a place as dangerous as this?"

"Nooo. Just scare the Vestal Virgins a mite. Stir up some hullabaloo."

Portia Andromeda awakened to something that she had not believed possible. A man in the cloisters of the Temple of Vesta! Not only a man, but a brute-ugly one at that. He had a hairy face, gaps in his teeth, which were too dark to be healthy, eyes too close together and squinched up. The shock of it robbed her of immediate speech.

"What are you gawkin' at, you ugly old prune?" a raspy voice asked her.

By the gods, are those animal skins he is wearing? Portia asked herself. In all of her years in service to Vesta, she had never seen such a creature. As senior priestess, she must maintain her composure, her brain reminded her.

"Get out of this cell," she demanded coldly, finding her voice at last.

A shriek came from another cell down the hallway. Had the barbarian army defeated the legions and entered the city? No. That was too preposterous to believe.

"How about a little kiss first, Sister?"

And then, Portia herself screamed. It seemed to come up from her toes to ululate through wide-stretched lips that trembled from more than the force of her wail. When she again opened her eyes, the man had disappeared.

"Where we headed now?" Squinty asked Preacher after they left the cloisters in shrieking feminine confusion.

"To the gladiator school," Preacher told him simply.

"You joshin' me, ain'tcha?"

"Nope. I told Buck and the others to meet us there."

"What do you want to go there for?"

"Simple, Squinty. There's bound to be about fifty highly trained fighting men locked up in there. We're gonna let them out. If they wants to join us, they'll be welcome."

"I can see that. We need more on our side, right enough. Only, what if they want to stay right there and are willing to fight to do it?"

"We can leave those locked up. Down that street there, the Via Julius."

Fires had drawn all of the watch away from seeking those who had started them. The twelve mountain men reached the gladiator school within five minutes of one another. Preacher advised speed.

"We've got to do this quick-like. Go in, free the ones want to come with us, and get out. Then it's for the walls."

Two guards at the entrance to the cells died swiftly, downed by .44 bullets from one of Preacher's Walker Colts. A quick twist of key in lock and the men beyond began to yell in confusion and some in rekindled hope. Preacher and his band moved rapidly along the corridor, snapping back the wooden bolts that held the cell doors. Forty-seven wanted to join in the fight against New Rome.

"There's all sorts of firearms in a storage room I'll show you in the house of Bulbus." They cheered him loudly as Preacher and Buck set out to lead the way.

All of the noise in the streets had awakened Bulbus. He looked wistfully at the trim posterior of the young slave girl in his bed, gave the bare buttocks a pat and climbed from his bedclothes. Once fully dressed, he headed for the atrium. He got there at the same time the mountain men swarmed into the central courtyard garden.

Swords and javelins proved no hindrance to the blazing pistols of the wild and wooly men of the High Lonesome. They brought down the five guards in as many seconds and surged toward the stores. Suddenly angry beyond any vestige of fear, Bulbus went for them with a *gladius* flashing in his pudgy hand. Preacher turned in time to see the blade poised to strike his head from his shoulders.

Having practiced long ago to speedily unlimber a six-gun, he filled his hand in a blur of controlled movement. The hammer came back and he squeezed the trigger. The small brass cap went off flawlessly, and the powder charge instantly followed. The .44 ball smacked into the thick middle of the master of games. A second ball went higher, through his heart, and flattened against his spine. Bulbus dropped the sword and staggered toward the fountain.

With a mighty cry, which sounded of regret more than pain, he pitched over the lip of the basin and splashed face-first into the water. Preacher watched Bulbus' right foot jerk spasmodically for a second and then turned to the men.

"Right through there. Pick the best, there's plenty of it. An' bring along all the powder, shot and caps you can haul. We have to beat these Roman mongrels to the wall."

Preacher soon found that they had lost the race to the parapets. Helmeted soldiers lined the southern and western ones. He veered his much larger band into a darkened street and plunged along it toward the east wall.

Only a dozen men topped that bastion Preacher discovered when they reached it. Easy as anything. He picked out five of the ex-gladiators who had taken helmets from the fallen guards and sent them up the stone steps.

"Tell 'em you've been drafted to help defend the city," he instructed.

Halfway up the stairway, the "relief" force had attracted the attention of all but one of the soldiers. That was when thirty shots cracked in sharp echoes off the walls of buildings and the stone barrier. Thirty balls sieved the defenders, who pitched headfirst off the parapet or lay where they had fallen. Preacher led the way up after the decoys.

At the top he found a determined sergeant holding the two former gladiators at bay with a *gladius*. Preacher looked at the other man for a second, then clucked his tongue as he fired a fatal shot to the forehead of the sergeant. Then he studied their surroundings.

"Too bad we didn't get back to our ropes. We'll have to go back down and get out through that little bitty gate."

Several looked at Preacher as though he were mad. "We can't make it," one protested.

"I say we can. Now, git movin'."

With trusted mountain men to serve as rear guard, Preacher started the freed gladiators through the low, narrow gate toward the outside. He cautioned them to remain quiet and stay close to the base of the wall. They might not know about the movable forts of the Romans. Nearly half of the escapees had disappeared into the tunnellike passage through the thick base of the stone rampart when others discovered their presence.

Some sixteen of the *vigilü* rounded the corner nearest the portal and stopped abruptly. These watchmen carried javelins in addition to their swords, Preacher noted at once. Made edgy by the sudden uproar within their city, and so far unable to account for it, the men of the watch reacted quickly. They all rocked back, and each hurled a *pilum*.

One whistled past the left ear of Preacher, even as he drew his left-hand Walker Colt. He eared back the hammer the moment the weapon came clear of the holster and quickly aligned the sights. The big .44 bucked in his hand, and one of the watchmen cried out in pain. Other pistols fired a moment later. Eight of the watchmen had gone down in the first exchange. Preacher aimed at another and fired again.

In such an unfair contest, there could be no doubt of the outcome. The remaining eight died in a hail of bullets. Unfortunately, it served to announce the presence of the invaders to those on the walls. Hard sandal soles scuffed on the stones of the parapet as other sentries called to one another and closed in on the knot of men at the gate below.

"The main gate! Open the gate! Barbarians in the city," one leather-lunged soldier bellowed.

While legionnaires poured in through the slowly opening portals, Preacher urged all speed and left New Rome at last. Behind him, the sky glowed orange from the fires in the buildings and gardens of New Rome. Alarmed shouts rose to the stars. Women and children were trampled by panicked citizens and the confused legions who hunted for a phantom enemy. Now all they need do was get past the legion camps and safely back to the ridge. Yeah, that was all.

Chapter 24

Once again, daylight found the legions drawn up outside the bastions of New Rome. With blaring brass and throbbing drums, they formed their battle squares and began a slow, stately advance toward the distant collection of what Marcus Quintus Americus referred to as rabble and gutter-born barbarians. Like before, those he held in such disdain spread out in a long, double line and came forward. Following their strategy of the previous day, they deployed into a bison-horn formation. Only this time they were nearly fifty stronger. That had caused some dispute, and not a little discontent, among the generals.

All was not well in New Rome, they maintained. The turmoil of the past night had left deep marks on many. The senior Vestal Virgin and the Chief Priests of Jupiter and Mars had argued against resuming the battle so soon. The dawn auguries had foretold misfortune, they explained. One of the doves had been missing a heart, and the sheep had a large tumor on its liver. Furious at the insult handed him by the barbarians within his own walls, Marcus Quintus Americus scoffed at the omens for the first time since he had begun his childhood sacrifices at age ten.

Since then, he had completely forgotten his identity as Alexander Reardon. Like his son, he had been fascinated by blood as a child, and had taken an exhilarating, sensual pleasure in tormenting, killing, and examining the entrails of small animals. Now, enraged by the humiliation he felt, he turned his back on that and ordered the legions forward. Although still deprived of his cannons, the process of clearing the touch holes long and tedious, and requiring precision, he went forth with high expectations. The forces of New Rome still outnumbered the enemy by better than five to one. He sent the infantry against the center of the enemy line, now three ranks deep.

Riflemen opened fire first. He had included a number of them with the infantry this time. Poorly trained at best, they had little effect beyond causing a few of the scruffily dressed barbarians to duck with exaggerated motions, which elicited raucous laughter from their fellows. The steady tramp-tramp of sandals made a hypnotic rhythm as the infantry continued to advance. This would be easy! The legions would roll over this ragtag collection like a giant wave, Quintus thought to himself. He had instructed his generals to have the men take as many prisoners as possible. The games that would follow would be quite amusing.

"When they git to a hundred yards, open up on them," Preacher ordered in a calm voice.

Obediently, the mountain men raised their rifles and took aim. The pretty boys in the band would get the worst of it, Preacher considered, pleased that there were noticeably less of them today. When the heads of the musicians rested in the buckhorn rear sights of the long guns of the mountain men, a ragged volley erupted along the line. The first rank knelt to reload while the second immediately fired over their heads.

Down went a third of the band and one centurion behind them. The range had closed to seventy-five yards. Another crash of weapons from the third rank. By then the first rank had reloaded and discharged their rifles from the kneeling position. With each man who dropped in the front rank of the advancing cohorts, another took his place from behind. At fifty yards, there was no longer a band, and the last volley barked from the rifles. From here on it would take too long to reload.

At fifty yards, the first flight of arrows hissed from the Roman squares. Three men among the ex-gladiators went down with slight wounds. Two in the front file, intent on readying their pistols, died for their incaution, transfixed by Roman arrows. The flat reports of handguns filled the air. The Roman enemy kept coming.

With all ranks firing and the flanking "horns" of the formation engaged also, the legions began to falter and slow. Preacher bellowed loudly to his army.

"Hold fast. Just a little longer now. An' watch out for them spears."

A flight of javelins seethed through the blue morning to rattle and quiver when they struck only grassy turf. Another flock of deadly, feathered shafts took flight. To be answered by the roar of a hundred pistols. Cheyenne shafts answered them. More javelins arched in the sky and moaned through their descent. The shield wall of the Romans had closed to within twenty feet. Spear tips darted like the tongue of a rattler, probed all before them. Another bark of pistols brought down thirty soldiers.

Preacher emptied one Colt six-gun and drew the other. Soon now. He eased up the stick of blasting powder from behind his belt and made sure it would come free easily. Three legionnaires brought down as many among the ex-gladiators. They launched a final cluster of spears and drew their swords.

Suddenly the Cheyenne wavered and began to give ground. Soon the entire middle did the same. Menaced by the darting blades of the legionnaires, they appeared to have entirely lost their nerve.

* * *

Marcus Quintus saw it at once. He pointed out the faltering lines to Rufus Longinus at his side. "See? The savages flee in disorder from my magnificent legionnaires," he smugly brayed. "They won't last long now."

Inexorably the Roman center was drawn deeper inside the tips of the "horns," something which held not the least significance for Marcus Quintus. His chest swelled with pride as he saw for the first time a litter of barbarian and Indian bodies on the ground, rather than only his soldiers. Aware now that the one commanding his enemies was the living legend, Preacher, Marcus Quintus took extreme pleasure from watching the destruction of the invaders. He turned to Longinus again.

"Send a messenger to Varras. Have his cavalry sweep the field obliquely. They are to try to get around behind the enemy and prevent any escapes."

"As you wish, First Citizen." Privately, Rufus did not like this the least bit. The evolution of the battle plan had a hauntingly all too familiar appearance. Something they had studied at West Point, he recalled, back in another lifetime, but not the name of the engagement or its outcome.

Stubbornly, the three ranks, minus the Indians, continued to hold, though now bowed in slightly. Then the cavalry began their charge. They had ridden only a few lengths, enough to be within the limits of the "horns," when the buckskin-clad Preacher raised his arm and arched his body sharply. He hurled an object with all his strength.

It exploded a foot off the ground and disintegrated four legionnaires. A dozen more received injuries. Then, before the horrified eyes of Varras, the Arapaho, who had been hidden in a deep ravine to the left rear of the battle formations, rose up and fell upon the horsemen and the backs of the advancing cohorts.

Preacher timed the throw perfectly. With scant seconds left of fuse, he hurled the blasting powder with all his might. "Let 'er rip!" he shouted to those around him.

With the roar of the explosion fresh in their ears, the mountain men steadied their line, and as the Arapaho seemed to materialize out of the very ground, the Cheyenne turned back to face the enemy. They laughed and hooted to show their complete lack of intimidation. It had disastrous effect on the Romans. So did another stick of blasting powder that landed in the midst of a battle square.

Bodies flew through the air, and parts sailed higher. Dust cloaked everything, and the screams of men dying to their rear demoralized the front ranks. The tight, disciplined Roman formations dissolved into swirling masses of men, desperately engaged in hand-to-hand fighting.

A terrible slaughter began. On a low hill near by, young Terry Tucker danced from foot to foot in anxiety. The night before, he had won his contest with Preacher to be allowed closer to the battle. He had not seen *anything* from the tower on the ridge. Even here, the dust had grown so thick he could no longer distinguish Preacher from the other fighters.

The conflict lasted for hours as the Arapaho and Cheyenne took revenge for their murdered brothers. Reduced to tomahawks and big, wide-bladed fighting knives, the mountain men hewed through the struggling legionnaires with deadly accuracy. The scent of blood thickened the air in a cloying, coppery miasma. Unremittingly, the numbers diminished for the Romans. Preacher's men were able to fall back and take time to reload pistols. Their addition to the fray took a brutal toll.

At last, the bedraggled survivors among the legions

broke off and fled the field for the imagined safety of New Rome. Preacher called out to halt pursuit.

"Hold back now! We gotta get organized. Then we go after them. I want a tally of how many we have fit to fight."

Subordinate leaders, appointed by Preacher, and the war chiefs of Arapaho and Cheyenne made quick head counts. It turned out that only forty had been killed—less than the number who had joined from the gladiator school. Another sixty had been wounded, ranging from serious to cuts and scrapes. It left Preacher mightily pleased.

Blue Nose Herkimer swaggered up to Preacher, who was cleaning his revolvers and Hawkin rifle with little Terry Tucker standing proudly at his side. Herkimer had a big smile plastered on his face. He clapped Preacher on one shoulder. "That was sure something, I declare. Never seed the like. How come those fellers was so dumb as to fall for it?"

Preacher thought on that a moment. "They failed to scout the battlefield. And, I reckon they never had much use for old fights fought a long ways off."

"How's that?" Herkimer asked. "An' more to the point, how'd *you* know what to do an' that it would work?"

An enigmatic smile bloomed on Preacher's face. "A little reading I did a while back," Preacher informed him. "About a feller named Hannibal and the Battle of Cannae."

With his forces rallied now, Preacher went about laying siege to Nova Roma. The palisades of pointed-tip lodge-pole pine saplings came down first, then the gaudy tents of the officers and plain ones of the enlisted men. From the bastions, the defeated Roman legions looked on in numb disbelief. How had it happened? How *could* it happen?

More than one asked that of his comrades. Meanwhile, given the distance between the camps and the city, they could retaliate against their primitive enemy only by hurling a few stones and large darts from ballistae and arbalests. Preacher had even considered it safe enough to allow Terry Tucker to join him. With night coming on, the destruction was completed. Fires were kindled and the invaders enjoyed sumptuous hot meals from the supplies of the officers of the legions. At least, the demoralized legionnaires consoled themselves, there would be no more fighting this day.

Early the next morning, their respite ended. Under cover of the most expert marksmen among the mountain men, Preacher rode to the large southern gates and buried the last four sticks of blasting powder under one pivotal corner. He tamped it down firmly, and wedged a big, flat piece of limestone between the ground and the wooden portal. Then he lighted the fuse and swung atop Cougar to race away without a scratch.

Moments later, the explosion shook the ground and threw gouts of dirt higher than the walls. When the smoke and dust cleared, the gate panel hung drunkenly on its upper hinge, canted sharply inward. The scaling ladders would not be needed. A superstitious mutter rose among the Indians. A couple of mountain men made the sign of the cross.

"Awesome," Squinty Williams breathed softly.

Preacher was not done yet. "Let's go!" he shouted, waving a Walker Colt in the sign for an attack.

With a roaring shout, mingled with war whoops, the small army rushed the gate. Boiling water poured down on the assault force until sharpshooters picked off the soldiers who dumped it. Rocks rained down, along with a shower of arrows and javelins. Men fell screaming, yet nothing slowed them.

Mountain men swarmed through the opening and spread out in the streets. They left the legionnaires behind them for the Arapaho and Cheyenne to deal with. Those able warriors did so with grim efficiency. Far better trained, since childhood, they kept three arrows in the air to each one fired by the Romans. Those arrows hit their targets, tumbling legionnaires from the walls in a continuous spill. Shouts and the screams of the dying became a constant bedlam.

In a swirl, the battle turned into house-to-house fighting as the legionnaires abandoned the exposed positions on the wall and rallied in small numbers to resist the invaders. Leading a dozen stalwarts, Preacher made for the half-finished Imperial Palace. From the forum he had seen the distinctive figure of Marcus Quintus Americus disappear in that direction.

Twenty well-armed soldiers held them at bay half a block from the front of the marble structure. Their rifles cracked in irregular volleys. Preacher and the others spread out and returned fire. Two of the guards died. Another one screamed hideously when he discharged an inadvertently triple-loaded rifle. Three times the normal powder load ripped the breech plug from its threads and drove it into his mouth. It mushed his lips, shattered teeth, and embedded itself in the back of his head.

His scream changed to a gurgle that ended as he died. That broke the nerve of two others, who rose from behind the low wall and ran toward the building. Three quick shots dropped them. A deeply appreciated lull followed.

"I'm goin' around back. I got a feelin' that feller Quintus has got a lot of rabbit in him."

Preacher had the right of it about Marcus Quintus Americus. While the legionnaires fought and died outside to buy him time, the First Citizen of New Rome hastily stuffed large panniers full of gold bars and shouted for servants to hurry in packing his clothes. His wife, Titiana Pulcra, stood in one corner of the treasure room and dithered.

"Why are you doing this, Marcus?"

"Shut up, woman, and help me."

Shocked at his tone, Pulcra gathered her past store of grievances and responded hotly. "Alexander Reardon, don't you dare speak to me like that."

Shocked at that, Quintus paused with one ingot in each hand. His voice held an artificially calm tone. "I don't believe this, Pulcra. You have always obeyed me. Please do so now."

Pulcra began to weep. "It's all coming apart, isn't it? We are destroyed, I feel it in my heart." With a soul-wrenching sob she ran from the room.

Taken aback, Quintus stared after her, then recovered. "Faustus, come in here," he yelled. "Quintus Faustus, come to your father."

Woefully lacking in training, the two guards at the rear of the palace fired at the same time. It had been easy for Preacher to trick them into doing so. He had simply jumped into sight at the edge of a marble column, shouted and popped a round into the air. At once they brought up the rifles they carried and cut loose. By that time, Preacher had disappeared behind the pillar. Not even his great experience as a fighting man could prevent him from wincing when the fat balls smacked into the opposite side of the stone plinth. Then he came out with a .44 Colt blazing.

Down went one soldier, who had bent over his weapon to reload. The other died a second later. Preacher advanced when a voice came from behind him.

"Want some company?"

Buck Sears and Philadelphia Braddock grinned broadly as they approached. They found trouble the moment they entered the column-supported hallway. More *gladius*-waving soldiers waited them. With hoarse shouts, the fighting men of New Rome came at the invaders.

"Dang," Preacher quipped. "What is it with these fellers who don't bring the right tools to a gunfight?"

He shot one in the chest, cocked his Walker Colt, and put his second .44 ball through the hand holding another *gladius*. The iron blade rang noisily when it hit the stone floor. Time to change. His second Colt brought down a third who moaned and rolled on the floor, clutching his belly.

Beside Preacher, Philadelphia took aim at a sergeant who lunged at him with a *pilum*. The javelin went wild as the mountain man discharged both barrels of his pistol at once. Slammed backward, the sergeant grew a shocked expression, his eyes wide, mouth round, while he clattered against a wall in numb shock and darkness settled over him.

Wisely, those remaining fled. Preacher sent a shot after them and hastily reloaded his pistols. That accomplished, they started toward the central core of the building.

A trembling messenger stood before Marcus Quintus Americus. Helmet tucked in the crook of his left arm, his face smeared with blood, dirt, and sweat, he panted out his litany of doom. "General Varras and what was left of the cavalry have been surrounded and destroyed by the red savages. General—er—Legate Longinus has fallen in street fighting near the forum. You already know about Legate Glaubiae."

Trembling from the effort to restrain himself, Quintus spoke with heavy sarcasm. "Is there any good news to tell me?"

"N-no, First Citizen. I mean, we continue to fight, and the enemy is taking losses . . ." his voice trailed off.

Bitterness colored the words of Quintus. "Only not so many as we, eh?" In a moment of clarity and sanity, he added in a tone of sorrow, "I am afraid the only advice I have is for you to find your way out of the palace and get as far from Nova Roma as you can."

Relieved not to have been summarily executed as the bearer of bad news, the young centurion nodded his agreement, saluted, then turned to make his departure. That was when Preacher, Philadelphia and Buck stormed into the room.

Preacher let out a roar when he recognized Marcus Quintus. His first shot went wild, but sent the centurion with the First Citizen to the floor in an ungainly sprawl. To his regret, the young officer had already learned that a *gladius* had little use against firearms. He hugged the marble floor, feigning death, until a boot toe dug painfully into his ribs. He grunted in discomfort and rolled over, intending to hack at a leg with his sword, only to find himself staring down the barrel of the oddest weapon he had ever seen.

It had a round part with holes in it that revolved when its owner pulled back on the spur at the rear. Beyond the extended hand and arm, a powder-begrimed face grinned at him.

"The Mezkins has got a sayin', feller," Preacher told him. "It's addyose."

And the centurion learned one final fascinating fact about the strange weapon. Flame spat from its mouth a moment before excruciating agony and utter blackness washed over him and the back of his head flew off. He never heard the bang. Preacher checked on his companions and found them otherwise occupied, each engaging four guards who had rushed into the treasury room at the sound of the Walker Colt. Grinning now, Preacher turned to Marcus Quintus.

"Looks like you're mine," he declared. "Reckon that's sort of fittin', you bein' the bull elk of this place."

"Quite fitting indeed. You really are Preacher, aren't you?"

"Yep. That's what folks call me."

"Then prepare to die like a man."

To the utter surprise of Quintus, Preacher threw back his head and laughed. "I don't allow as how it's gonna be me does the dyin'," he brayed.

Quintus snatched up his *gladius* from the table where he had laid it and charged Preacher. The mountain man held his ground until the distance between them closed to ten feet. Then he raised his arm and squeezed the trigger of his .44 Colt.

Nothing happened. Only a loud click. In the heat and speed of battle, Preacher had forgotten to count the number of rounds he had fired since last reloading. He jumped aside as Quintus made a mighty swing with his sword, and drew his second Colt. The heft of it in his hand told him that it, too, had been fired dry. Quintus came on, and Preacher nimbly jumped over a table, putting it between himself and the Roman tyrant.

"That will not do you any good," Quintus spoke in precise English.

It gave Preacher time to draw his tomahawk. Over the years, the old war hawk had stood him well. He hoped it would again. Quintus lunged over the small table. Preacher batted the leaf-shaped blade of the *gladius* away with the iron head of his war axe. Quintus developed an expression of surprised appreciation. A truly worthy opponent. He maneuvered to get past the barrier that kept him at a disadvantage.

Preacher countered it. A sharp scream punctuated by a gurgling gasp told of another legionnaire on his way to his Maker. Preacher did not break his concentration as Quintus reached a low commode beside a desk. His left hand darted out and snatched up the bowl of pine nuts resting there. With a bellow intended to freeze his opponent, he hurled the confection at Preacher. Quintus followed it.

A spray of roasted pine nuts hit Preacher in the face. The momentary distraction gave Quintus time enough to leap onto the tabletop and execute a horizontal slash with his *gladius* that cut through the buckskin shirt and opened a fairly deep line across Preacher's pectoral muscles. Blood flowed in a curtain. Quintus had little time to savor his brief victory.

Ignoring the pain and accompanying weakness, Preacher swung his tomahawk, and the keen edge bit into flesh in Quintus' left shoulder. The Roman grunted and staggered precariously close to the edge of the table. In the last moments, he righted himself and leaped to the larger counter where the gold reserves had rested earlier. Fire throbbed in his deltoid muscle as the blade of the war hawk tore free. Quintus made another pass at Preacher as he gained the storage shelf.

Preacher batted the *gladius* aside with the flat of the 'hawk and did a fast, two-step shuffle forward. When Quintus brought his arm up for an overhand stroke, Preacher aimed for the Roman's exposed knee. The tomahawk bit deeply, with a loud *plock!* that turned heads in other parts of the room. Face squinched in overwhelming pain and mouth open in a soundless howl, Quintus dropped to his good knee. With a kneecap split, his *gladius* became as useless as his other leg.

He abandoned it for the double-edged dagger on the belt at his waist as Preacher came at him again. Bright steel flashed in the air, and Quintus made a fortunate cut on the right forearm of his opponent. Preacher was forced to drop his tomahawk as blood streamed from a severed vein. Only then did Quintus remember the small .50 caliber coach pistol he had concealed in the folds of his battle cloak. He reached for it eagerly.

"Preacher, here," Philadelphia Braddock shouted when the deadly little pistol appeared in Quintus' hand.

Preacher caught the double-barreled pistol Philadelphia had tossed left-handed and fired it the same way.

"No!" Quintus shouted in useless denial as first one, then a second .60 caliber ball smashed into his body. His eyes went wide as they sought to capture some of the fading light in the room. His body would no longer obey his commands. Slowly he sagged down, his death rattle loud in the silence.

A sudden disturbance at one entranceway drew the attention of the mountain men from the dying man. *"Father!"* young Quintus Faustus shrieked as he dashed through the archway, a dagger held high.

He hurled himself at Preacher, intent on burying the slim blade in the man's heart. Seemingly from nowhere, little Terry Tucker darted into the room at an oblique angle to Preacher and flung himself between the man and the Roman boy.

His exposed chest took the full brunt of the blow aimed by Faustus, though not before he triggered a round from a small pistol he held. The ball blew the brains out of Quintus Faustus before Terry collapsed into the arms of the man he admired above all others.

"I—I got him, didn't I?" Terry gasped. Then, at Preacher's wooden nod, he slumped into unconsciousness.

Blood dripped from his fingertips as Preacher gently brushed the hair from Terry's face as he cradled the lad in his arm. "Awh, Terry, Terry-boy, didn't I tell you to stay clear of the fightin'? But you saved my life, certain sure. Today . . ." the words would not come. Preacher swallowed hard. "Today you became a real man. One I'd be proud to call friend. Go with God, Terry Tucker."

Terry must have heard him, for a small smile froze on his peaceful face as he quietly died.

Preacher took a deep breath and allowed himself no

further time to grieve for the boy who had saved him. He brushed a knuckle at the moisture that stole stealthily from his eyes, cleared his throat, and came to his boots.

"What now, Preacher?" asked Philadelphia, reluctant to intrude on the mountain man's sorrow.

"I'd be obliged if you would bind this arm and my chest, Philadelphia. An' you, Buck, round up the rest. Tell them to clean up this abomination, pull down the buildings, and burn everything. Free any slaves, and any who want can he'p them down to Bent's Fort and a chance to return to a normal life."

"What about you, Preacher?" Philadelphia and Buck asked together.

"Me? Why, I'm off for my winter home. Got myself a nice, blond bed warmer a-waitin'."

"What?" a startled Philadelphia demanded. "You mean that frisky young gal what took up arms and fought her way out of the arena with us?"

Preacher sighed through a spreading grin. "Yeah, that's right. The once-upon-a-time Bible-thumper."

Please turn the page for a preview of
William W. Johnstone's stunning blockbuster
HUNTED.

"He is somewhere in this area," the men were told, their eyes on the map, on the spot touched with a pointer.

"He really exists, then?"

"Yes. For years I've thought it was nothing more than rumor and myth. I couldn't get people into Romania to dig around until the Ceausescu regime was overthrown and the country opened up. But he is real. He is alive and well and has been so for nearly seven centuries. He's about five—ten, well built, muscular, with dark brown hair and very pale gray eyes. He speaks a dozen or more languages and he is a very dangerous man. The ultimate, consummate, eternal warrior—always bear that in mind. The man has fought in every major war since the thirteenth century. He's been a teacher, a priest, a writer, a singer, an actor. He was a gunfighter in the wild west here in America. He's worked as a mechanic, a bookkeeper, a salesman. He can do practically anything. I've recently discovered that while working in Colorado during the gold rush, he found a very nice vein, staked it out, dug it up, and with the help of a San Francisco law firm, invested the money. That investment has grown over the years. He does not have to work. He's changed his name, again, and got a new social security number. Then he dropped out of sight. Questions?"

"He has to be taken alive?"

The man who was paying the bounty hunters' salaries gave the questioner a pitying look. "I just told you, he can't die. He cannot be killed. At least not by any method that I am aware of. If he has an Achilles heel, it has never been found. I want him for study. The man holds the key to eternal life. I want to be the one who unlocks that secret."

Robert Roche looked at each of the twelve men standing around him. "You gentlemen come highly recommended. You are supposed to be the finest mercenaries in all the world. You're being paid well, certainly more than you have ever received for any job. Now prove your worth."

A dark complexed man with hard obsidian eyes spoke up. "What have you not told us about this man?"

"What do you mean?" Roche questioned.

"There is more that you do not tell us. Why?"

Roche hesitated for a second, then said, "Because it is unsubstantiated rumor, that's why."

"What is the rumor?" the hard-eyed man pressed.

Roche sighed. "The man you are searching for is rumored to have the ability to change into animal form."

"Shape-shifter," the questioner whispered. "What animal?"

Again, Roche hesitated. With a sigh, he said, "A wolf."

The Indian's eyes narrowed. "He is a brother to the most intelligent, dangerous and cunning predator to walk the face of the earth. You will never have this man. You are wasting your money."

"Then you refuse to take the job?" Roche snapped out the question.

George Eagle Dancer smiled. "I did not say that. I will take your money, and I will do the best I can. And I alone will survive the hunt . . . along with the shape-shifter. The rest will fail."

"If there are no more questions? You know your assignment. Find this man and bring him to me," Robert Roche said. "Everything you asked for in the way of equipment has been purchased and is at your disposal. I don't expect to see you again until this is over. Good day."

Darry Ranson sighed and cased his binoculars. He lay for a time with his forehead on the cool ground. He was so tired of running. Centuries of running. An endless roll of years, unable to establish any sort of permanent home or relationship. And it just got worse as technology advanced. It hadn't been so bad before the telegraph and telephone and the industrial revolution; life was slower and easier and it had been much simpler to lose one's self. It was getting more difficult each year.

He raised his head and gazed down into the valley. Two more men had joined the others, and Darry felt sure there would be still more. The men had gathered in a small circle and were squatting down. One was pointing toward the west. That was all right, for Darry's cabin lay to the south of the valley. But they'd get around to it, sooner or later.

He wondered just how good these men were. That question was answered a heartbeat later when a voice said, "Mike? You copy this?"

Ranson tensed, not moving a muscle. He didn't even blink. How in the hell could a man get this close to him without his knowing it?

"Yeah, Mike. You can see for several miles up here. There are no cabins in this valley. No signs of human life at all. None."

How close was the man? Not more than three or four yards at the most, Darry guessed, for the voice was clear.

"Yeah, OK," the man radioed. "I see Doolin and Blake. They're comin' out of the timber to the north of you. OK. Right. I'll start workin' my way down to the valley floor. Jennings has already started down. Sure. Let's give Mister Roche his money's worth. Webb out."

Darry listened as the man turned to leave. He moved

well, his boots making only the tiniest of whispers. If the rest of the man-hunters were as good as this one, Darry was in for a time of it.

Six teams of two each. At least twelve men were hunting him. Damn! And the reporter and her camera-person. He'd have to run. He'd have to pack up what he could, put his dogs in the bed of the truck and leave. He had no choice in the matter. None at all that he could see.

Or did he?

Darry lay on the ridge and thought it out. His cover was as good as it had ever been. His driver's license was valid. It would take some organization like the FBI to discover that his past was non-existent—at least on paper—and it would take them several days to do it.

These men hunting him were not government hunters. He was sure of that. Someone named Roche was paying them. But why? He could not remember anyone named Roche in his past.

Roche Industries? the words popped into his consciousness. Robert Roche, he had read somewhere, was the richest man in the world. Worth billions and billions of dollars. He owned all sorts of factories and construction companies and real estate and . . . hell, Darry couldn't remember all of the article. But Robert Roche's holdings were vast. Worldwide.

Could that be the Mister Roche the man-hunter was referring to?

Probably.

But why?

Darry made up his mind. He was not going to run. Not just yet. He was weary of running. He'd stick around as long as possible. Maybe he could bluff his way through. He'd done it before.

But the man-hunters didn't worry him nearly as much as the TV reporter. He could not allow his face to be shown nationwide. Somebody in his past would recognize him. Then there would be hell to pay.

Darry stood up and checked the valley below. The hunters had moved on; tiny dots in the distance, slowly working their way west.

He looked up at the sun. High noon. What was it that Afrikaner had told him during the Boer War? Yes. It was always high noon in Africa. The same could be said for Darry's situation.

Then Darry remembered something about the hunters. They all had a short, tube-like object carried on a strap. What the hell was that? What was inside that tube? Some sort of weapon? He'd better find out. He decided to pace the man-hunters. They had to camp somewhere. And when they did, he'd be there.

Darry, as his Other, covered the distance very quickly, loping along on silent paws. He encountered no other wolves, for the other packs had heeded his earlier warning about the danger of man and were laying low, staying close to the den and hunting only small game.

Darry smelled blood and angled off, coming to the spot where the man had been killed. His body had been removed, but the blood smell was still strong. Not more than several hundred yards away, he could smell men and hear the murmur of their voices. He edged closer and listened.

"I am not moving from this spot," he heard one say. "I'll be goddamned if I'll be a part in the killing of innocent people. I won't do it."

"Same here," another agent said. "I'm staying put, eating these lousy field rations, and keeping my ass out of trouble. This whole thing stinks to high heaven."

"Look, we're under orders to . . ."

"Fuck orders!" another agent blurted. "I was up north of

here on Ruby R'dge a few years back when we attacked the people in that cabin. It was a goddamn federally-sanctioned assassination and that's all it was. You can call it whatever you like, but it was an assassination of family members whose views went against what some asshole liberal bureaucrat in Washington think they should be. Shoot a kid in the back and then blow his mother's face off while she's holding a baby in her arms. Goddamn! That was a set-up, bait and hook, just like this is."

Darry moved on, silently leaving the camp behind him. He visited other camps that night, listening to the federal agents, men and women, talk and grumble and bitch about this assignment He quickly reached the conclusion that about ninety percent of them believed this operation to be a cover-up for the bureau's mistakes. But that still left about a hundred hard-core agents who had to kill those civilians involved or face dismissal and/or prosecution.

Darry headed for his cabin.

William W. Johnstone
The *Mountain Man* Series